The Edge of the Storm

A NOVEL

THE TEXAS PAN-AMERICAN SERIES

The Texas Pan-American Series is published with the assistance of a revolving publication fund established by the Pan-American Sulphur Company and other friends of Latin America in Texas. Publication of this book was also assisted by a grant from the Rockefeller Foundation through the Latin American translation program of the Association of American University Presses.

AGUSTÍN YÁÑEZ:

The Edge of the Storm

(*AL FILO DEL AGUA*)

A NOVEL. Translated by ETHEL BRINTON

ILLUSTRATED BY JULIO PRIETO

Austin   University of Texas Press

Second Printing 1964

The Spanish title of this book, *Al Filo del Agua*, is a farmer's phrase for the beginning of the rainy season and is often used figuratively to mean the imminence or beginning of an event.

Those who wish to do so may call the book *In a Village of the Archdiocese, The Old Order,* or something of the sort. Its pages tell no preconceived story; it deals with lives—"marbles," one of the characters calls them—which roll round, which are allowed to roll round in a narrow stretch of time and space, in a village, any village, of the Archdiocese of Guadalajara.

A. Y.

CONTENTS

The Edge of the Storm

A NOVEL

OVERTURE

The village -- seen from without as a stranger or visitor would see it.

enlutadas — in mourning

ILLAGE OF BLACK-ROBED WOMEN.
At night, at the first stir of dawn, throughout the long course of the morning, in the heat of the noonday sun, in the evening light, they may be seen—strong, radiant, colorless, long-suffering —old women, matrons, maidens in the bloom of youth, young girls; they may be seen on the church steps, in the deserted steets, inside the shops, and glimpsed through a few, the very few, furtively open doors.

women

People and streets absorbed in their own thoughts. The smooth, straight walls present a blank surface, broken only by doors and windows. Doors and windows, set in plain stonework, and fastened with heavy beams of good seasoned timber; there is no varnish or glass and all have the appearance of having been fashioned by the same craftsman, primitive and exact. Time, the sun, the rain, the daily touch of hands have given a patina to the panels of the doors,

introspection

4

to the lintels and thresholds. From these houses no sounds of voices, no laughter, no shouts, no cries escape; but above them hovers the fragrance of fine wood, burned in ovens and kitchens, wrapped like a gift from heaven in clouds of blue smoke.

Inside and out, the same secrecy. In the houses on the banks of the river, on the slopes of the hills, on the outskirts of the village, the noble stonework gives a certain dignity to the adobe walls.

And the lowliest house has its cross on top, and there are wreaths of colored paper flowers at the corners and on the walls stretching endlessly into the distance; crosses made of stone, of stone and mortar, of wood, of straw . . . wide, tall, small, and fragile crosses, some crudely fashioned, others perfect in form.

There are no fiestas in the village; only the daily dance of myriads of sunbeams; the only music is the sound of the bells that toll the passing of the dead, or the tuneless, plaintive melodies of religious chants that express the latent sense of oppression. Never any parties. Dancing is held in horror . . . Not even to be thought of . . . never, never. Families visit each other only at times of bereavement or illness, or possibly to welcome home a long-absent member.

It is a barren village; there are no trees or orchards; no trees even at the entrance or in the Cemetery. In the Square, only watered plants. For most of the year the river is dry; river of large, smooth stones, shining in the sunlight. A landscape of barren ridges stretching tier behind tier to the horizon . . . barren ridge on barren ridge.

There is no "alameda" in the village. The streets lie parched under the blazing sun. Worn pillars of stone and mortar stand in the squares and at the corners of the houses. Village of black-robed women, hermetic and solemn.

Only the general cleanliness of everything reveals the hidden life. The streets are well swept, the houses whitewashed. Not a single one, not even among those by the river, is unkempt. The men are clean-shaven; old men with lean faces, young men with ruddy cheeks, pale adolescents, all wearing clean shirts, clean trousers. Cleanliness pervades the village: clean young men, clean horsemen, clean white trousers worn by the workers in the fields. Clean are the pale-faced, black-robed women, the pale women clad in black, who are the life of the church precincts, the sunswept streets, the furtively open doors. Well-swept streets bring a note of freshness at noonday, at eventide, and in the long hours of the night. Black-robed women, rising early, sprinkle cleanliness from secret wells.

Each house has its well, hidden from the curious gaze of the out-sider, like the pots of flowering plants in the hidden patios and inner passageways, smelling of freshness and peace.

The center of family life is the kitchen; there meals are cooked and eaten; there are the women, black-robed and bare-headed, their hair combed smoothly back from their faces.

Then, the bedrooms. Pictures everywhere. Lamps, a small locked chest, an occasional wardrobe. Clothes hang on hooks, like the ghosts of hanged men. Baskets of grain and a few chairs are pushed up against the wall. The beds are in the corners, with baskets of white clothes underneath them. And in the middle of the rooms, large, empty spaces.

The parlors are distinguished by their many chairs and the pres-ence of a sofa. There is even a bed, the master's bed. On the shelves of the corner cupboards are photographs of special events in the life of the family and the village, artificial flowers, colored glass balls and china jars, a Hand of Providence, a statue of Christ, a Miraculous Cross, which had appeared at some remote time to some legendary ancestor.

From the houses emanates a certain mysterious air of reserve which darkens the streets and the village. The bells ring from the towers at definite times, tolling, pealing, issuing the orders which rule the life of the village.

It is a monastic village. The disgraceful taverns lie out of sight in their shameful district of rocks and brambles, where the ground slopes down to the dry river bed. There are no billiard rooms, no gramophones, no pianos, only black-robed women.

Desire, the very breath of desire, is hidden deep in the heart of the village. To hear even the flutter of its wings, one must pause for a moment and listen outside the barred doors, follow in the wake of the black-robed women, of the solemn men, of the rosy-cheeked boys or the pale children. One hears it in the prayers and hymns in which it takes refuge: a deep, pulsing vibration, feverish breathing, controlled only with great effort. Sometimes the streets echo with the shouts of children. They are not old enough to hide their natural feelings. But do the women sing? Never, except in church, the old hymns handed down from generation to generation.

When the village priest and his curates pass along the streets in their cassocks, the men remove their hats; the men, the black-robed women, and the children kiss the consecrated hands. When, clad in

6

vestments, they carry the Holy Sacrament, an acolyte, wearing a surplice, rings the bell and the people kneel in the streets, in the village Square. When the church bell announces the Elevation of the Host and the Blessing, the people kneel, in street and Square. At the ringing of the bells at midday, at three o'clock, and in the evening, the men take off their hats. In the early dawn when the slow, heavy tones of the church bell summon the faithful to first mass, there is the sound of coughing in dark rooms—the coughs of old men and of those who smoke too much; feeble coughs, virile coughs, long prayers, fervent prayers, sonorous chords whose vibrations are muted. Wrinkled old men and women, early-rising farmers, kneel beside dark beds, dress by the light of hastily struck matches, yawning sometimes in the midst of their prayers, while the clanging bell rings in the dawn, with slow, solemn tones.

Weddings take place at first mass, while it is still dark, or when the first uncertain light streaks across the sky, as though there were something shameful about them, something mysterious. Weddings never have the solemnity of funerals, when all the bells pour their long lament out into the air, like smoke rising from a chimney; when the three priests and four acolytes, clad in rich black robes, pass through the Atrium, through the streets to the Cemetery, lighted by a hundred candles, accompanied by chants and the sound of the tolling.

When a villager draws near to death, the peal for the dying is rung, to ask the prayers of all the people. The villagers say the prayer of the Holy Shroud and join in the petition: "Depart, O Christian Soul, from this world."

When life is extinct, the bells change their rhythm and neighbors know that a soul is standing before the Judgment Seat. All share the feeling of awe which runs through streets, shops, and houses. Those who have gone to help the dying neighbor, return home; others, closer friends of the family, remain to help dress the body, waiting respectfully while Judgment is being given, but beginning their task before the body grows cold.

The bells ring out on Sundays, Thursdays, and feast days. They are cheerful only when they ring while the sun is shining. The sun is the joy of the village, an almost unconscious joy, a secret joy, like love, desires, instincts. Like love, desires, and instincts, fears appear and wave their invisible ghostly hands at windows, behind tightly closed doors; they can be seen in the eyes of the black-robed women, sensed in their hurried steps through the streets and in their tightly compressed lips, in the serious mien of the men and the silence of the children.

Desire, pale, consuming desires, and fear, constricting fears, lurk in the keyholes, in the squeaking hinges of the windows; and there is a peculiar, unmistakable odor, sweaty and salty, in the corners of the Confessionals, the dark Chapels, the Baptismal Font, and in the stoups of Holy Water. In the evenings, in the deep stillness of midday, in the streets, throughout the whole village, this damp, salty tang, earthy and penetrating, pervades the atmosphere, and like an unseen presence, without ever coming into the open, or committing an overt act of destruction, oppresses the stranger while it may perhaps bring pleasure to the natives, a kind of penitential pleasure.

On moonlight nights, the spirits of desire and fear escape in a mad race; one can hear their turbulent flight, along the street, over the walls, above the rooftops. Strait jackets fling about in the air, fists are clenched, fingers twist skirts; they beat against the silence of the houses, blindly, like big black birds in flight: birds with the wings of vampires, owls, or hawks; of doves, too, stupid doves, who, having just escaped, will soon come back submissively to the cage. On moonlight nights, it is the spirits of desire which always lead; the fears run behind, threatening, urging them to wait, screaming harsh imprecations, borne along, with shrill, incomprehensible cries, on the wings of the wind. The spirits of desire dart to and fro, from light to shadow, from shadow to light. In vain, the fears try to follow their course. The age-old dance goes on till past midnight. And, in the early hours of the morning, when the bells ring in the dawn but the moon is still in the sky, the stormy struggle of fears and desires begins again. Morning brings victory to the fears, and, all day long, they will be the first to roam round the church precincts, the streets, the Square, while the desires lie concealed in lines etched on faces and brows, hidden under lowered lashes, in compressed lips and tensed hands, as the struggle continues in dark bedrooms and sweat permeates the air of the village.

On moonlight nights, in houses on the outskirts of the village, sometimes in its very center, hands pluck the muted strings of a guitar, a guitar surcharged with haunting sadness, voicing secret longings. On moonlight nights, lusty songs are heard in the disgraceful taverns, songs of the spirits of fear galloping along astride the horses of desire.

Moonlight nights bring a haunting sadness to the lifeless pillars of the Square; the very stones reverberate with the melancholy of never having known the all-embracing love of the Nazarene, or the compassion of the Samaritan. Not even on moonlight nights have these columns ever overheard the whispered exchanges of lovers, only loneliness and unfulfilled desires are confided to them; never has a loving couple sought their shadow to clasp hands feverishly. Gleaming columns, worn smooth by time and weather.

When the evening sky is heavy with rain, when torrential downpours sweep the streets, when the rain brings out the smell of newly washed walls, of wooden doors, of pavements; when an approaching storm charges the air with electricity; on cloudy mornings, on days when the rain falls steadily in a monotonous drizzle, when the oppressive heat of dog days overwhelms the village, when the intense cold of winter brings a crystal clearness to the air, then, too, the spirits of desire emerge, and one can hear them moving in a dancing rhythm, in the plaintive chords of a popular song, invisible demons that give a drunken, fantastic twist to the crosses on the houses, on the walls, on the corners of the sentry boxes, even to the huge cross over the gate of the Cemetery. The spirits of fear, officers of the Law, warders of the madhouse, must subdue them in strait jackets, and secure them with chains of iron, at the bidding of the bells, in the shadow of priestly robes.

The whole existence of the village is a never-ending Lent. Penitential ashes temper the beauties of spring and summer. Constant reminders of the Day of Judgment are poured like Holy Oil into all ears, the Holy Water of repentance is sprinkled on all foreheads; the Miserere becomes a constant scourge upon all backs; the precept "Remember, O man" is kept constantly before all eyes; in all minds lies the thought of the Requiem Aeternam. The Four Horsemen of the Apocalypse, like municipal police, ceaselessly patrol street, house, and conscience. "De Profundis" is on every tongue, signs of strict fasting on every brow and cheek.

The chief concern is with the next world. Streets are merely bridges, to lead the people to church, viaducts of the bare necessities of life. Black-robed women, carrying rosary and missal in their hands, traverse them with swift, rhythmical pace. Sometimes their burden is a shopping basket. Their faces are withdrawn, the greetings demanded by courtesy are brief and terse. They may pause for a moment in front of the church, to whisper timidly, as though afraid. (But, if you watch closely and long, you will see how sometimes they reach their doors reluctantly, as though unwilling to open them, and they enter like prisoners, leaving all hope on the pavement outside. If you listen very carefully, you may hear a sigh as the door shuts behind them.)

author and reader are outsiders

Yes, of course, there are men standing on the street corners, in front of the shops, sitting on benches in the Square; they are few and they say very little; they seem to be meditating, and in their eyes there is no gleam of the curiosity that reveals an enjoyment of the street for its own sake. At night one can hear purposeful steps and glimpse muffled shadows under the flickering light of the street lamps; and at midnight, or in the early hours of the morning, one may hear the murmur of voices outside the doors or through the cracks of shutters. The great mystery of life triumphs over the Four Horsemen, and breaks down all barriers, but in the shadowy darkness, with ancient discretion, as the customs of the village require and permit . . . while the bells sleep.

The written proposal is better, however; more advisable, more honorable. Shops keep carefully hidden—as though these were shameful merchandise—written messages which can be made to suit all circumstances, and there are also men and women who can compose special letters for difficult or complicated cases. But these one must seek out privately.

writing

Unseen, but none the less felt, are the blows the Four Horsemen rain down upon the legions of instincts as darkness falls, and in the late hours of the night. Bones creak; tongues are dry and thirsty.

Sometimes, too, late at night, mysterious horsemen of flesh and blood ride along the paths on the outskirts of the village and make love to a village girl. In the morning, there is consternation in the village, as though a coyote or wolf had left bloody tracks on the sidewalks, the walls, the doors, and windows; as if neighbors had connived at a rape. Vengeance and death, as well as new lives, are the offspring of such a union. There is no suffering in the village to be compared with that caused by a stain on family honor; any anguish is preferable, any degree of poverty or misery. The situation is accepted with great reluctance. A father's heart has been wounded, and although the marriage is seen as the lesser evil, yet the future grandchildren will always be bitter fruit, the offspring

honor stained

of force. And even this degree of resignation is by no means frequent; more usual is vengeance without mercy, unyielding rejection of the erring daughter and the accursed son-in-law; no one wishing to keep the friendship of the offended family dares mention the "foreign" grandchildren.

Even a formal proposal, when the girl's hand is sought with all due respect for convention, when the suitor conforms to all the traditional customs, when he makes his proposal through the parish priest and has influential neighbors to speak for him, even then it falls like a live coal on a father's heart, plunges his household into mourning, and sows discord between brothers and sisters. The young man is cold-shouldered by all, however good a husband he may make, however much the match has been hoped for; the girl is a shaking reed, ill-treated by everyone. How happy her family would be if only she would repent and refuse to go through with it! When she persists, how pale she is as she arrives at the church door at the early hour decreed for weddings, not daring even to look at the man who is giving her the marriage coins and putting the ring on her finger. How ashamed she is in the first days after her wedding! She is unwilling to go out with her husband, even to church. How great is her embarrassment when she realizes that she is pregnant and finds all eyes staring at her and all tongues gossiping about her! What a martyrdom marriage is in the face of this traditional hostility and collective disapproval! The men, too, in the first months of their marriage, feel a certain isolation; they are conscious of invisible fingers pointing at them, feel eyes watching them furtively; a wall of reserve surrounds them and, with a sense of guilt, they avoid all mention of their happiness, their difficulties, their wives. Young girls blush when they see them coming because they have heard snatches of frightening conversation, vague remarks which arouse dread and fear, although underneath the fear and terror well up eager, formless longings, like those of the young men who would like to talk to the bridegrooms but are held back by a sense of embarrassment.

Village of muted voices. No discordant note affronts ear or eye except on Sunday mornings, and then a spreading tide of life, of sounds and colors, floods the roads and streets, and its bubbling warmth invades the precincts of the Parish Church and the Square. It floods the inn, taverns, and shops . . . a rosy tide whose waters neither mingle with the gray pond nor tint its waters. High Mass being over and supplies for the week bought, stalwart, loud-voiced men and women in bright-colored skirts, orange, pink, puce, and purple, stiff with starch, make their way back to their farms; the noise of squeaking boots, fretting infants, stamping beasts, recedes into the distance and the village regains its evening calm, is again a village of black-robed women, ruled by the monotonous ringing of church bells. Diligently, quickly, the inhabitants sweep away the trail of rubbish left by the visitors. And all week long the inn and taverns yawn in idleness.

The inn and taverns are usually empty. The village is off the beaten track. Occasionally, a commercial traveller, a tax collector, will arrive, or someone bringing a message or doing an errand for an important villager will spend the night. There are no comfortable lodgings or hotels. The idea of comfort is foreign to the village. Life is not for enjoyment.

Food is simple. Generally, beef soup, rice or macaroni, stew, and beans at midday; in the morning and evening, chocolate, bread, and milk. The bread is very good; the smell of freshly baked loaves scents the evening air.

The people make their living farming. Much Indian corn is grown, only one crop a year, for the region is without reservoirs and irrigation. Constant worry about bad seasons leaves its mark on the spirit. Bakers, carpenters, a few blacksmiths and tanners, several stone cutters, four shoemakers, an overseer, three saddlers, two tailors, many herb doctors, a few scribes, and five barbers complete the picture of the village economy. But the moneylenders must not be forgotten. They are legion and veritable whited sepulchers.

The poorest villagers manage fairly well, although they have their bad times. No one in the region has ever died of hunger. The rich, stoical and tight-fisted, and the stoical poor, lead the same hum-drum lives. Resignation is the greatest strength of these people, who, usually, have no higher ambition than to go on living until the time comes for a Holy Death. For them, existence is merely a bridge to be crossed and they are glad when they reach the end. This attitude and the dryness of the soil give the village, the houses, and the people an appearance of age. An air of disillusionment, a subtle corroding atmosphere, floats like a part of the landscape over the plain stonework, over the guarded speech. Landscape and people are alike. A luminous haze, as of perpetual twilight, as of smoldering embers, is seen in eyes, mouths, stonework, the wood of doors and

12

windows, and is spread over hard brown earth. It seems to smolder in glances and gestures. The people are slow in their decisions, movements, business dealings, speech . . . slow, but sure.

"I've been thinking about it all night . . ."

"We'll talk about it tomorrow, at leisure . . ."

"Next year . . ."

"After the rainy season . . ."

"In the rainy season, God willing, . . ."

"If we aren't dead by then . . ."

Barren village, without trees or gardens, not even vegetable patches; so parched that weeping produces no tears. There are no mendicants or whining beggars. The poor man speaks to the rich man with such dignity and self-respect that his attitude falls little short of hauteur. The Four Horsemen are no respecters of persons. Each man orders his life as he thinks best, each man feels free, not dependent on anyone or under any obligation.

"So-and-so doesn't want to be my partner; I'll get someone else."

"Juan turned down my offer. That's all right with me."

"Let him keep his money, and I'll keep my independence!"

"Peace of mind is better than money."

It is a barren village, but on the great festivals—Maundy Thursday, Corpus Christi Day, the whole month of May, the Feast of the Assumption, Good Shepherd Sunday, December 8, and December 12—flowers emerge from their hiding places in the patios and come out into the streets on their way to church; flowers of high and low degree: magnolias, tuberoses, Madonna lilies, geraniums, calla lilies, daisies, mallows, carnations, violets, secretly tended, and sprinkled with water from the deep wells. On no other days will they appear in public, these hidden household treasures, jewels on which such care and tenderness are secretly lavished. Reserve, and austerity too, melt, in moments of great human suffering. In times of illness, death, sorrow, trouble, hands and arms are moved by compassion, eyes are damp and tongues loosened, houses are thrown open and people visit one another. But once the occasion has passed, hands and feelings are once more withdrawn, in impassive reserve.

The pious activities of old and young, of men and women, find expression in many societies. But the two most important are the Association of the Good Death and the Daughters of Mary. The Daughters of Mary, to a great extent, in fact almost exclusively, shape the character of the village, exercising a rigid discipline over the dress, movements, speech, thoughts, and feelings of the young girls, bringing them up in a conventual existence that turns the village itself into a kind of convent. Any girl reaching the age of fifteen without belonging to the Association of the black dress and blue ribbon with its silver medal, the black dress with high neck and long sleeves, its skirt reaching to the ankles, is regarded with grave disapproval. In this Association, all vie with one another in jealous vigilance, and expulsion from it constitutes a scandalous blot on the reputation that follows one through life.

There is strict segregation of the sexes. In church, the Gospel side is reserved for men, and the devout female sex occupies the Epistle side. It is not considered proper for men and women, even when related, to stand chatting in the street or doorway, not even for a moment. When a meeting occurs, brief greetings are exchanged, all the briefer if the man or woman is alone; but this rarely happens, especially if the woman is unmarried, since then she is always accompanied by another woman.

It is a village of ascetic faces and abstemious hands. The women use no paint or powder; their lips are tightly compressed, their skin pale. But the men are brown, burned by the sun. The women's hands, hands that draw water from the wells, are rough; rough, too, are the hands of the men who till the soil, tend the cattle, sheave the fodder, thresh the corn, quarry stone for the walls, ride the horses, tame the young steers, milk the cows, make bricks, and carry water, fodder, and corn.

Among black-robed women they spend their lives. Death comes . . . or love . . . love, which is the strangest, the most extreme form of death; the most dangerous and dreaded form of living death.

4 characters

THAT NIGHT

The 4 insomnias

I

FTER Don Timoteo Limón had his customary supper that night, neither more nor less than usual, he was already back in his room and telling his beads at the first stroke of curfew. He made his intercession for the most neglected soul in Purgatory or the one that stood most in need of prayer. On reaching the third mystery he was almost distracted by the howls of Orión, the dog he had had for so long, but, with an effort, he controlled his wandering thoughts, managed to ignore the ominous note in the barking, and kept on with his pious exercise.

It seemed strange to him not to yawn in the Litany and to reach the Blessing without finding his eyelids dropping with sleep as they usually did.

There was no moon, and not a single breath of wind. To make sure, he opened the door onto the patio. No noise in the house or

in the village. The barking had ceased; but now he remembered
that the pitiful howls had lasted right through the rosary and
through his personal devotions to the Holy Shroud, to the Most
Sacred Trinity, to the Five Wounds, to the Holy Joseph of Arima-
thea and Nicodemus, to St. Joseph, by whose aid he hoped to
achieve a holy death, to the Archangel St. Michael, to Our Lady of
Carmen, to St. George, who defends us against creatures of poison-
ous fangs, to St. Pascual Bailon, who informs his devotees of the
hour of their death, to the farmer St. Isidore, to St. Jerome, and to
his Guardian Angel. There was an unearthly note in the howls; they
had sounded like those with which the sire of old Orión used to an-
nounce impending tragedy. Learned priests have warned Don
Timoteo to overcome these superstitions lest he break God's first
commandment. Hallucinations or coincidences, that's all they are!
But flesh is weak and the heart fearful. Terror stirs in it and goose-
flesh covers our bodies, however much we call upon our intelligence
and faith and hold fast to the commandments, and mask our trembling in words and laughter. Wasn't it through fear that he forgot
his prayers to St. Judas Thaddaeus, to St. Rita of Casia, to St.
Peter's spirit, a moment ago? He cannot even remember whether,
before the Litany, he said the prayer "By these Sacred Mysteries,
let the soul remember" in which Gentiles and heretics, sinners,
wayfarers, shipwrecked sailors, the dying . . . are commended to
God. But he distinctly remembers that while he was praying there
kept appearing before his eyes—who knows how or whence (since
he does not believe that he let his thoughts wander)—visions of
past events, even of things that had never happened: there, in between his words of devotion, floated the face of Anacleto, that
dreadful face which, for twenty-five years, has never given him a
day's, a moment's peace, pursuing him even in his dreams; no, the
dead man has never actually appeared to him, but he has not been
able to get the face out of his mind. He thought at first that he
could forget, and therefore gave himself up to the authorities,
voluntarily; they declared him innocent, judging his action to have
been in self-defense; and ever since, he has gone out of his way to
help the dead man's family; every year, he has a mass said for the
repose of the dead man's soul; but the shrunken face, covered with
blood, the frothing mouth with its black teeth, the stiffened hands,
the dishevelled hair, and the wide-open staring eyes, have left him
no peace. No amount of repentance can free him from the sense of

guilt. Orión's sire had been with him on that fateful night of August 7, 1884, and had foretold the tragedy with prophetic howls, just as, some fifteen years ago, he foretold the death of Don Timoteo's fourteen-year-old daughter Rosalía. It would be better not to go to the Fair at Aguascalientes, as he had decided, unless . . . His cattle deal with Don Cesáreo Islas is already signed and sealed; maybe an epidemic is threatening the region; but this is not the kind of misfortune foretold by Orión's howls. Perhaps something has happened to Damián! It is getting on towards three months since there was news of him. It takes time for letters to come from so far away, of course. Still, something may have happened . . .

Thoughts of Damián came into his mind just as he was about to pray "By these Sacred Mysteries," and the blind panic that assailed him drove the prayer right out of his head.

Now that he was in bed and had put out the lamp, he kept worrying about dangers that might surround Damián . . . Damián, his oldest, who had lacked for nothing at home, Damián, in whose strong arm lay his father's hope for the improvement of the farm and his dreams of a happy old age . . . such a handsome lad— sensible, energetic, free of vices, wholly absorbed in the hard work of the fields. But Damián had succumbed to the temptation to go North, and off he had gone with other farmers, to seek his fortune, when he already had it at home. There is no truth in the local rumor that his father is the wealthiest man in the district, of course, but, thanks be to God, beans, tortillas, even milk, are never scarce in the house; still, young men get crazy ideas about wanting to work far away from their parents. And now, for five years, the poor fellow has been wandering around, from one place to another, from one job to another, in difficulties and dangers; God alone knows among what kind of people, with what kind of friends, in what perils of soul and body. God grant above all that he keep his faith, and that the Shadow of St. Peter and the Cloak of the Blessed Virgin may keep him safe from evil companions and bad women. God keep him from being caught in an electric wire, crushed by a machine, drawn into a fight with a gringo, or having trouble with the authorities, who are terrible up there, they say. God deliver him from the many dangers which may beset him in a strange land. Please God, let him be neither hungry nor ill nor in trouble. It's so easy to get into trouble in all innocence! How many have never come back from the accursed North! How many have come home ill, without even a penny to their name! Doña Eufrosia's son was sent to the electric chair because he would take no abuse and insults from a gringo. Román López has been in prison for fifteen years and is sentenced to ninety! Ninety years! What a sense of humor these gringos have! And those who have died, beaten to death or shot, those who have been poisoned in hospitals, those who have fallen from high scaffoldings, and all those who have just disappeared, leaving no trace. With Damián determined to stay until he has made his fortune. Something must have happened to him, just now when Orión was howling. What a price to pay for the death of old Anacleto! The failure of the harvest for four successive years . . . The death of Rosalía . . . The paralysis of his wife, a helpless invalid now, for ten years . . . Damián's absence, which has been a daily torture . . . and all God's will. God's punishment! Damián would have been married by now, he would have had a family, he would be settled down at work. The girl they say he was courting is married, not a bad young thing, either; she would have made a good daughter-in-law, clean, God-fearing, hardworking, quiet, fond of the house; and it's not easy these days to find good women who will look after a man's things and not gossip . . .

But Damián was probably all right. He was worrying needlessly. Orión often howled and nothing happened. He must get to sleep. Tomorrow would be a hard day. After the first mass, God willing, he must go out to the farm and see if Lorenzo could pay what he owed him. He had no wish to press him, but his "Next month" and "When I sell the corn" were dragging on and he needed the money for seed when the time came; he would foreclose. Lorenzo had had time, too much time for his own good. Even at the moderate rate permitted by Holy Mother Church the interest had mounted up to a considerable sum, because of delays. He'd take the house and Lorenzo would be better off at that; he'd have no more trouble with other creditors or the rent collector. He might lose money, but something was better than nothing and there were times when you took what you could get. He was a good fellow and probably wouldn't give any trouble. Anything was possible, though, with this plaguy young law clerk from the Canyons putting ideas in people's heads. What was the world coming to! A few years ago the law clerks had nothing to do here. Affairs were settled properly, after the conscience. Those were the good days! Men kept their word and feared God. Things were different now, heaven help us! It was time the Deputy brought this injustice to an end and put the troublemaker in his place; he was worse than the others; they'd have to get rid of him. He'd speak to the Deputy tomorrow. But he must get some sleep. Oh! Tomorrow, he must go to the Ravine and find laborers to sow the Gavilanes fields. He didn't want the rains to catch him unprepared.

He wouldn't be able to go to the Retreat this year. Not that he cared more about this world than the next, but he had no one to depend on, and Lent was late. The middle of March already and next Sunday only the Fourth Sunday in Lent. Easter not till April 11. He'd make his confession before then all right, but the Retreat . . . He'd have to explain and hope Father Martínez would understand. How could he leave his poor wife, with her pain worse in this cold weather! He thought she was going to die. Perhaps that's what Orión was trying to tell him. The poor thing was very weak. That doctor he'd had at Candlemas . . . what a fee he charged! . . . told him her heart was failing and they must be prepared. Poor soul, she asked only to see Damián once more. All that money spent on doctors and medicines and no use! Three trips to the capital these last ten years, and no hope. She just got worse and worse. Poor soul!

Don Timoteo turned over in bed. Once, then again and again, with increasing desperation. He pulled the sheet up over his head. He crossed himself seven times. Again the Enemy stood there, lifting the glowing steel-tipped darts, playing the bull with red capes. How horrible! Wonderful, maybe? How frightful! He wanted Don Timoteo to wish his wife dead. Ten years is a long time to suffer! Then he could marry a bouncing girl. The Devil wanted . . . murderous thought! Yes, it was the Devil who placed those figures before his eyes, a hundred desirable women: María, Ursula, Teresa, Paula, Domitila, Rosa, Epifanía, Trinidad, Ventura, Felícitas, Agueda, Cecilia, chubby-cheeked young Cecilia, Martina with her eyes like cherries and her plaits shining like silk, Remigia, Victoria, Eusebia, Marta, full of life, Marta for love of whom two peasants on the farm had killed each other, and Lucía with her white skin and blue eyes, and Consolación, and Marina, and Rosario, and Gertrudis, and Margarita . . . Twinkling eyes, undulating hips, a river of smooth arms, a harvest of cheeks swim before his eyes. There is a roaring in his blood, and his hardened arteries groan. Holy Mary, Mother of God! When his wife had been buried six months . . . Did not Don Eustacio marry for the fourth time two months after Doña Engracita died? . . . After ten years, no one could blame him! . . . And suppose Damián should be disgusted and the family object? Perhaps Damián was dead too . . .

Don Timoteo jumped out of bed and felt for the bottle of Holy Water; he sprinkled the counterpane, the sheets, the pillow, the room, crossed himself again three times; threw himself on the floor. What a sinner he was, O Lord, that these thoughts should come to him! To wish his old wife and the boy dead! Tomorrow he'd make his confession. If he could, he'd get up now and look for the Parish Priest or one of the curates. Anacleto's lips and teeth kept coming back before his eyes with their mocking laughter. If it were only time for first mass! He'd get up. He'd get up as soon as he heard the first bell. Once when he was passing along by the stream at Las Trancas, Gertrudis and Margarita were bathing. What beautiful bodies, and he had watched them without anyone's seeing him or disturbing him! "Miserere mei . . . As a punishment I won't go to the Fair at San Marcos, when it comes at Easter this year. They say the bullfighters are going to be very good and it's one of the few things left to me and there're so few bullfights round here; only once a year or so can I go to Nochistlán, Teocaltiche, Aguascalientes; there's no harm in that . . . no cards, no wine, no women, and not because I don't like them . . . real temptations they are at the Fairs; the singing girls, and the innkeepers' and tavern owners' wives don't need much asking . . ." His blood began to sing again and the Devil returned with impure images.

No, Don Timoteo would not go to the Fair at San Marcos. He would go to the Retreat. As soon as the bells rang for early mass, he would get up and go to confession. His soul was in a state of mortal sin, with the ugliest of all sins! And at his age! Hell was yawning before him . . .

Hell, Death, Judgment, Heaven, his wife, Damián, dead Anacleto, *The night thoughts* the figures of attractive girls, the clerk from Juchipila, his debtors, the spring sowing, the rain, droughts, the barking of Orión, all went whirling round in his brain; his head was going round and round, desperately, all night long, and his body twisting and turning from side to side; do what he would he couldn't get to sleep; he longed to hear the crowing of the cocks, he listened in vain for any signs of life, prophetic barking, neighing, mooing, steps, bells. One would think he'd drunk coffee or smoked more than four cigarettes, but he hadn't. He couldn't sleep; he felt light-headed, no, his head felt heavy and ached with whirling, evil thoughts that were doing him actual physical harm, and throughout the endless hours of the night the effort to drive the thoughts away and get to sleep was more exhausting than a fever. The sin of superstition was to blame for it all; if it hadn't been for his superstitious shudder at Orión's barking, the Enemy would never have come with so many temptations. He was just getting quietly off to sleep when a start brought all the spokes of the wheel circling back on his head again. "Damián must be dead. Suppose my wife were to die. They'll rob me of all I have. We'll have a long drought . . . the singing girls at the Fair . . . I'm going to die . . ." Pointed spokes of the implacable wheel, more grotesque, more insolent, more sinful all the time, as his resistance grew weaker in the never-ending night.

II

That day Leonardo Tovar had had to go to Río Verde for some oxen and got back late at night, very tired. As soon as he'd had a little to eat, he fell into bed; no sooner was he in bed than he fell asleep; he had barely closed his eyes when he was wakened by the groans of his wife. Leonardo was a heavy sleeper and was sleeping particularly soundly that night after walking twenty-five miles with hardly a pause for breath; but his wife's moaning waked him, and he got up drowsy and ill-humored. She waked little Pedrito too and he started to cry. Another night without sleep, after so many since Christmas Eve! They were expecting a child about Candlemas; his wife had had many upsets, and on Christmas Eve . . . What a time she'd had! . . . a discharge like a bunch of grapes . . . Some said it was a tumor, others said a miscarriage; but it did no good to blame it on the eclipse or on enemies who had cast an evil spell on her. From then on, not one good day had she had; headaches, vomiting, hemorrhages, no appetite, weakness; then this pain in her stomach, a burning pain, getting worse and lasting longer every time, a pain which was worse whenever she moved and which had kept them awake so many nights. Leonardo had taken her to all the midwives in the whole neighborhood, even to the witch doctors. Medicines, cure-alls, charms, nothing did any good. Finally, last week, he made a tremendous effort and took her to Teocaltiche, to see the doctor, only to lose their last hope. She had to have an operation right away, there was nothing else for it; but it was three hundred pesos in advance. And where on earth could Leonardo get three hundred pesos! She would just have to die, if God so willed. Even if he sold his corn at a good price for three years in a row he could never get together three hundred pesos, and no one would lend him that amount on his land, which was already mortgaged to Don Timoteo Limón for eighty pesos. It was hopeless!

His wife's cries pierced the night, cutting him to the quick. Neighbors came to try and ease her pain. Some applied mustard plasters. Others bled her and rubbed her with grease. Some recited the Prayer to the Just Judge, while still others burned coyote hair for her to smell. She lay writhing in agony, eyes staring, hands clenched. The movement of people coming and going, the bustling activity of some, the religious resignation of others, the whispering, the prayers uttered aloud, frightened little Pedrito, who lay wide-eyed on the bed, and he began to cry again. Leonardo wandered to and fro, helplessly; he went out into the patio, the verdict of the doctor of Teocaltiche ringing in his ears; he felt a surge of bitter rebellion choking him. His head was bursting. Don Jesusito Gómez came out and offered him a sip of brandy:

"You'd better fetch the Padre, Leonardo. Concha will take the little one home and put him to bed."

They carried Pedrito away, howling loudly. His mother shrieked like a lioness whose whelp was being taken from her:

"Please leave him with me. Can't you see I'm dying anyhow? Let me have my one bit of comfort!"

Leonardo's eyes filled with tears and the women were weeping openly.

"Go for the Padre!"

"Go get Don Refugio; the apothecary cured my aunt when she was at her last gasp!"

"Go get Doña Remigia, she knows all the prayers for the dying!"

"Don Refugio isn't likely to come at this hour!"

And above everything else, above the whispering and prayers, above the barking of the dogs and the crowing of the cocks, could be heard the unceasing cry:

"I'm dying! I'm dying!"

. . . .

"How long Leonardo has been gone! He won't get back in time!"

"The Padre has to put on his clothes and go to the church for the Holy Oil."

"Someone else should have gone."

The street is full of shadows, of footsteps . . . the neighbors are waiting for Death to arrive.

"Here's the Padre!"

Leonardo's eyes ask the question his lips dare not form.

"She's still alive, but that's about all."

The ceremonies that accompany the administering of the Reserved Sacrament and the Sacrament of Holy Unction are impressive. When the Priest takes his departure, the dogs bark all along the road. Some of the people go home; others fall asleep. Martinita seems to be quieter after the Sacraments; she wouldn't be the first to recover after being anointed with Holy Oil.

Leonardo goes out into the patio again and looks despairingly at the sky. When will it be light? What a long night! And his mind goes back to the night Pedrito was born. How different that was! Then, too, he was wakened by the cries of his wife; then, too, the neighbors had come, and Doña Genoveva, whose help had been asked for earlier. But how different those cries were! They had almost filled him with joy. They were as loud as these, but there was hope then; they worried him very little; on the contrary they filled him with secret delight; they wouldn't last, and once they were over, his happiness would be complete, as indeed it was, when he heard the child cry. Never had Leonardo felt so thankful; and a new tenderness towards life, towards the land, towards the work in the fields, welled up in his heart. But these groans tonight held no promise, no hope; they were sterile; they held no expectation. Yes, they did. They were filled with expectation of the worst, of death. A miracle? His eyelids were dropping with weariness, and he hadn't the strength to hope for miracles, not even strength to say "Our Father . . ." The dark shadow of an unknown, painful mystery engulfed him. When would it be light? And then, again, in all its force, the heart-rending cry: "I'm dying! I'm dying! Leonardo . . . Pedrito . . . I'm dying!"

The cocks are crowing now. The bell of the Parish Church is ringing. It is beginning to get light.

. . . And the Angel of the Lord announced to Mary . . .

III

Mercedes Toledo, Leader of the Catechism Class, and new member of the Daughters of Mary, didn't know how the letter had come into her hands. When she realized what it was about, she started to tear it up, but as steps sounded in the next room and the call to dinner was peremptory, there was barely time to thrust it inside her blouse. She promised herself that as soon as dinner was over she'd go out to the privy and tear it into tiny shreds, and make certain that no one would ever come across a scrap of it, or be able to keep it or read it. Holy Mary! If her mother or one of her sisters had happened to find it, as she did, lying discreetly on the floor beside her bed, when she came back from the Rosary! Or, good heavens, her father or her brothers! What would have happened? She dared not even think of it! What if her brother Chema had found it? And he so jealous and bad-tempered. Holy Mary! Who in the world put it there? One of the maids—which one? —must have been in on the plot, for it wouldn't have been lying so neatly if it had been thrown in from the street, and she couldn't think that Julián would be rash enough to compromise her in this way . . . Julián . . . the very name set her head and her body on fire. The letter, inside her dress, burned like a live coal. Surely they would notice it! Hot and cold shivers ran over her body, and dinner seemed endless. She tried to hide her emotion, and talked of the plans for decorating the Altar of the Sacrament on Maundy Thursday; but her voice trembled, she trembled all over, as though Julián were there before her, looking at her with those strange, burning glances which, for weeks, had followed her wherever she went, boring into her like red-hot pokers, and she had given him no encouragement at all. The first time she had been aware of his eyes fixed upon her, such a peculiar feeling came over her that she almost fainted. She felt as though she'd been caught naked, as if she'd been undressed by force; what loathing, what indignation she had felt, what a desire to accuse him, to tell the Parish Priest, to tell the whole village, and see if that would make him stop looking at her! But she was held back by a horror of the scandal it would cause. What efforts she had made to go out as little as possible, only when it was absolutely necessary! The worst of it was, she could confide in no one, ask no one for help . . . her only support was in her own virtue and her anger against the daring suitor. That he should have dared to write to her and succeeded in getting the letter into her hands, inside her dress! She had given him no reason whatsoever for such impudence . . .

"Your face is very flushed; you look feverish . . ."

Her secret was discovered. She would have to explain. An instinctive impulse of self-protection, almost without her volition, brought out the words:

"I may have been in a draft, Mama. I felt cold coming away from the Rosary."

"How many times must I tell you to cool off before leaving church! Go to bed. In a little while, I'll bring you a cup of good hot cinnamon tea to make you sweat, and we'll see how you are in the morning."

First she would go to the backhouse and tear the letter into shreds; that cursed letter, some of whose searing words were etched on her brain in letters of fire: "love" . . . "sadness" . . . "desire" . . . "opportunity to talk" . . . "mutual understanding" . . . "all our lives" . . . Certainly they were the words of the Devil. She was consecrated to God and His Holy Mother. Temptations! But how absurd! If only all temptations were like this! The Devil would see, straightway, with what rage and determination she would destroy the letter. Tomorrow she'd treat Julián with the utmost indifference and scorn. That would stop him! If his glances had upset her and his very name was enough to send the color to her face, it was only because she was angry at his boldness; but now it was time to show how immune she was to temptation, how unshakably faithful to the Immaculate Virgin . . .

To show, indeed, how firm she was, and to learn to what lengths men will go in daring and wickedness, she would read the letter again before tearing it up. It would be an exercise in will power. After this test she would be stronger to resist new trials. It was no sin to find herself assaulted by temptations if she withstood them. She would read . . . she read, the letter. She shivered . . . with indignation, she thought. What effrontery! She tore it up. She hesitated before throwing it in the filth, where it belonged. Wasn't it her duty to hand it over to the Padre in charge of the Daughters of Mary the Immaculate, so that he might understand the wiles with which the Devil besets his charges? It would be better to memorize some of the words and tell him in confession. She read the scraps again, crumpled them up in her hand, and threw them in the filth, their proper place.

She went to bed. Her mother brought her a cup of hot cinnamon tea and a couple of pills. She was feeling better now. But as they talked, she grew thoroughly wretched. How dared the man look at her and write to her? She had given him no encouragement. She wanted to fling herself into her mother's arms and cry. She would have liked her to stay with her all night. She asked her for her blessing as though she were going to die. They prayed together.

"You're very restless."

"It must be the medicine."

When her mother had gone, Mercedes sprinkled the room with Holy Water, crossed herself three times, got into bed, but couldn't bring herself to put out the light. For an hour she tossed and turned in anguish. Her mother's voice came from the next room:

"Why haven't you put out the light? Do you feel all right?"

"I'm praying."

"Put out the light and go to sleep. Make sure you're well covered up; if you get cold while you're sweating, you'll catch pneumonia."

She put out the light. She was certainly perspiring, but she couldn't get to sleep. She seemed to hear a furtive, persistent step on the sidewalk outside; a breathless panting near her window; low whistles in the street, whistles with a note of desperate pleading.

"It must be nerves," she thought. And the words of the letter came back into her mind: "I have suffered a great deal from this pride of yours, and will not put up with unjust treatment any longer, for my intentions have always been honorable and I do not deserve your contempt."

"Lies! He's not suffering! But suppose desperation really did make him do something dreadful! I won't be responsible! How could I be?"

"*You will be responsible, and you alone, because, after all, my proposal is a natural one . . .*"

"Natural, no! I belong to the Daughters of Mary the Immaculate!"

"*And have you thought of what he means when he says he will not go on suffering?*"

"What has that to do with me?"

"*He may mean that he will grow ill, that he will expose himself to dangers, that he will die perhaps, and the blame will be on your shoulders . . .*"

"His own folly and boldness will be to blame!"

". . . But he may also mean that he will not be responsible for his actions . . . that, driven desperate by your scorn, they will escape his control, like the river in flood, which, respecting nothing, descends in its fury on houses, trees, and orchards, drags off cattle, drowns human beings, leaving desolation in its wake."

"I don't understand."

"Like runaway horses that throw their rider, kill him, and destroy everything in their path."

"What do you mean?"

"You know well enough."

"All right, then, let his madness burst all bounds, and let him reap the reward of scoundrels."

"He may be killed, that's what you mean, and you are wishing the death of your neighbor, which is not a Christian thing to do; if he is destroyed, he may destroy you first. What then?"

"I won't let him!"

"There's a certain wavering in your determination . . . as if you were enjoying the danger . . ."

"Maybe."

"Yes, there's a certain pleasure in fighting against the Devil, and you are trying to make a devil of this man."

"He is the Tempter, for me . . ."

"Then I am this man, and I am in your heart, fighting inside you and gaining ground in your heart while you think of me . . ."

"You're only a passing thought, evoked by anger, kept alive in my mind by the medicine which won't let me sleep."

"I am the reason for your sleeplessness. My letter, my whistle, my breathing, close outside your window. What a flimsy rampart separates me from your bed and from your restlessness: a slender barricade of worm-eaten wood, and a feigned resistance of your mind to the impulses of your blood, which will finally triumph because they are the stronger! Of course I'll reach you, for I have managed to get my letter close to your heart! I'll come to you today, or tomorrow, sooner or later, and you yourself will desire—don't you already desire?—my coming! You'll want to keep me with you always! My absence, separation from me, will be your greatest torture! Your blood, pulsing throughout your whole body, demands it, and all the resistance of the poor, weak, timid notions that you try to defend yourself with is useless! Do you hear my steps? They are *drawing closer to your bed, like invaders who are joyfully awaited and who count on the support of innocent prisoners, your woman's desires . . ."*

The furtive creak of a door, cautious steps, here, inside the house, close by, stealthy. The girl started up in bed with an inarticulate cry of terror.

"Try to rest, my child. I've been listening to you tossing and turning all night. Do you still feel miserable? I'll go to the kitchen and get you another drink of hot cinnamon, and, as soon as it's light, we'll see what the druggist can send us."

A violent fit of fresh, uncontrollable shivering comes over the girl. She really does feel ill now, after such a fright! A malignant fever. And, maybe, in her heart of hearts, there lurks a secret feeling of disappointment, disguised as shame, for having let her thoughts wander so far as to frighten her with fear of an impossible danger, so that she mistook the loving steps of her mother, and, in a few seconds, lived through years of tremulous sensations in which horror and delight were mingled, and plumbing the depths of existence, dying, being born again, she experienced in the swift passing of a moment, all the longings, pleasures, and pains of a lifetime, of many lifetimes. At first her sensations resembled those she had felt once, at Teocaltiche, when she had tried the electric shocks which were the great novelty and surprise of the Fair; a tickly feeling inside and a fluttering of the nerves; then a sudden faintness, as when one dreams of falling into a bottomless pit; then a weariness as of great weakness, a peaceful lassitude; renewed trembling. Now her guilty conscience, convicted of sin, condemns her . . . for the transgression of a minute . . . to the pains of Hell. ("Suppose I were to die, now . . .")

"I must make my confession at once! Mama, for pity's sake!"

"You're feverish, my child; don't fret so."

"For God's sake, Mama, a priest!"

"I'll get the boys up. What sort of pain do you feel? Where is it? They'll go get the Priest and Don Refugio."

"No, don't wake up the boys. Wait till it gets light. I'll try to sleep. Stay here with me. No, don't wake them! Let's say the rosary and see if I can't fall asleep."

Lying beside her mother, she was quieter for the rest of the night, although she did not fall asleep; she was miserable with the thought that she was liable to eternal damnation and too weak to withstand further attacks of the Devil. "If only we could move away!" she thought. And, like an echo of distant thunder, the intrusive voice replied:

Away? Where can you get away from me, since I am yourself, your woman's nature?

"I won't read another novel, that's where these thoughts come from . . ." but the thoughts persisted. Tomorrow, when she comes out of church, Julián's eyes will be fixed on her again, and she will be unable to avoid the dreaded meeting.

If only she could sleep for a few moments, just the few moments left before dawn! Is she the only wretched and shipwrecked traveller in the ocean of the night? Lucky those who can sleep! All the neighbors must be asleep, with a clear conscience! "What about Julián?" Again the odious memory! "God help me! Suppose he is still awake! Take this bitter cup from me, O Lord! . . ."

Are you sure it is bitter? . . .

"This bitter, unbearably bitter cup! . . ."

Could you not watch with me one night? . . .

"Never shall I be able to watch with you."

Today you have been with me, and you know well that it will not be the last time . . .

"Daughter, did you get to sleep?"

When she realized that her mother was awake, the girl pretended to be asleep. And once again she envied her neighbors, thinking that they would all be peacefully sleeping the sleep of the just.

Her frantic longing to sleep kept her awake. She, alone, was suffering this punishment for her sins. The dreadful sins of thought, of feeling, of consent. To have lived in one minute, to have experienced in a moment of voluptuous consent, a whole sinful existence! How could she go out into the street, take part in the religious rites of the Association, teach the children? The whole village would read the disgrace written in her eyes, on her brow; old people and children would see it with sorrow, young men with smiles; the pious would pity her, her fellow members of the Daughters of Mary would look at her with disapproval; and what would *he* think? . . .

He would never see her again; whatever sacrifice was necessary, she would make it. Her conscience felt relieved at the memory of saints who had conquered the Devil; she would follow their example, she would dress as a beggar, cut off her hair and disfigure her face; if necessary, she would pluck out her eyes, follow the advice of St. Paul literally. A life of strictest penitence would cleanse her eyes and brow of the stigma of what she had read, of the guilty minute in which the thought of being embraced by an impious intruder had filled her with ecstasy. How ashamed she felt!

"Dear God! But, starting tomorrow, or rather, this very day—it will soon be light now—I will renounce the world, and soon, in a convent, my soul will be free from these torments, serene, strong against the temptations of the world, the flesh, and the Devil."

Overcome by weariness, she did not hear the bells ring at dawn. Sleep brought relief, at last.

The flesh surrendered to sleep at the first light of dawn.

IV

The peace of the night was shattered by the sound of horses' hoofs and muffled voices. They entered the village, coming down the hill by the tannery, through the lower section in the center and up Fresno Street to San Antonio, disturbing the sleep and rousing the curiosity of villagers, who were tempted to open their shutters to see who the late arrivals were.

It was the Rodríguez family coming back from Mexico City and Guadalajara. They had been delayed and had chosen to arrive late rather than spend another night away from home.

The household had long given up expecting them. They had to knock and knock before they could get the door opened, for Juanita and the servants had all gone to bed.

"We waited up for you till eleven o'clock. We decided you must have stopped for the night in Jarrilla or San Ignacio."

"Good heavens! It's nearly one o'clock," said Don Inocencio, looking at the watch he had taken out of his pocket while the servant was pulling off his riding boots.

The servants were moving about the patio with lanterns in their hands, turning it into a sea of flickering light and shade.

"Bring out some chairs," ordered the master. "We don't want to go inside like this."

"I'm dead tired and sleepy, Papa; my head is still aching terribly, so I'm going straight to bed."

"What a girl! If I'd known you were going to behave like this, I wouldn't have taken you with us."

"What's the matter?" her Aunt Juanita asked, and without waiting for an answer, went on:

"Are you going to bed without anything to eat? The chocolate'll be ready in a minute and we've got a delicious chicken and better enchiladas than any you tasted in Mexico City, I'm sure."

Micaela began to cry.

"What a girl! What a girl!"

"Not even a glass of milk."

"I don't know what we're going to do with her," said Doña Lola. "You're old enough now to know the risks you're running, Micaela. You'll get a chill or even pneumonia."

"All right, you stubborn child, go to bed then. If I'd known you were going to behave like this, I'd never have taken you with us," said Don Inocencio for the second time that evening.

Juanita went to turn down Micaela's bed and started to help the weeping girl undress.

"I'm going to sleep in my clothes," she snapped.

"What on earth's the matter with you?"

"Isn't it matter enough to come back to this wretched village?"

"Saints preserve us!"

"To have to come back and live in this graveyard!"

"Holy Mary, Mother of God!"

"Just as I was beginning to know what it's like to be alive!"

"But, my dear child . . ."

"And now my clothes will get faded and my parasols moth-eaten, just because they say it wouldn't look nice for me to dress like people in other places, and they won't let me powder my face, or wear a corset, or put on bright dresses, or thin stockings, or even a few drops of perfume, because the men and women of the village will criticize me. What a life of hypocrisy! I can't stand it. I won't do it! They can't force me to! Help me, Aunt Juanita. Get them to send me to a boarding school, even in Guadalajara . . . ," and she burst into bitter sobs.

Juanita was horrified. Seizing the first excuse that came into her head, she left the bedroom and went to join her brother and his wife in the dining room.

"What on earth's the matter with Micaela? Has she gone crazy?"

"You can see what a state she's in."

"She's been in tears ever since we left Guadalajara."

"We don't know what to do with her."

"We felt like slapping her."

"We wept over her."

"We offered to take her back soon."

"Nothing has done any good."

"She even wanted to go back alone."

"As we were coming into the village, she grew almost hysterical, and if I hadn't been firm . . ."

The stable boys were bringing the horses through the patio before unsaddling them, moving to and fro with steady, unhurried gait.

Doña Lola went up to see if her daughter was in any better mood, if she needed anything, if she'd like a cup of camomile tea. The room was in darkness. The moment her foot touched the threshold, Micaela sobbed, "Leave me alone. I want to sleep."

"Just drink this tea; it will help your headache."

"Please leave me alone. I don't want anything."

"Did you say your prayers before going to bed?"

"Mama, for heaven's sake, how you fuss!"

"You seem to have taken leave of your senses! Aren't you afraid of God? Think, Micaela."

Don Inocencio coughed, and Doña Lola went out to join him.

"It's better to leave her alone; she'll have to get over her foolishness, and she'll do it quicker if she's left alone."

He pulled out his watch. "Good gracious! It's half-past two! Let's go to bed."

"How're we going to get any sleep?"

"And you haven't even told me if you got what I asked you for from the Virgin of Guadalupe, and brought me Holy Water from the Well," said Juanita.

"We clean forgot to tell you. It went right out of my head! We'll show you tomorrow what we've brought. It's a surprise."

"And the rosaries?"

"We've got them, too, and they've all touched the Blessed Ayate of the Virgin of Guadalupe. You'll see it all, tomorrow, Juanita. I want to ask you about everything here, too. But I've been so worried about Micaela!"

"Go on to bed, then. The beds are ready. Good night."

"Just tell me if Crescencio brought the money, and how much you gave the farm hands at Pastores."

"In spite of all the messages I sent, Crescencio didn't come; he sent excuses and kept putting me off. I'll show you the accounts tomorrow."

Don Inocencio sucked his teeth in irritation.

"Good night."

"Good night."

So they went to sleep. Sleep? Juanita kept thinking of the scandalous example that Micaela's ideas would set in the village, principally among the young girls, particularly if she took it into her head to wear the clothes she had brought back. What finally drove every vestige of sleep away was the suspicion that by thought, word, or deed . . . (and here the theatres and moving-picture houses, dances, trains and carriages, the many dangers of big cities swam in diabolical confusion before her eyes) her niece might have endangered her immortal soul. "I can't see what my brother was thinking of, to expose his daughter to such risks; city customs, the way those people treat each other, with no fear of God in their hearts, the fashions . . ."

Doña Lola was amazed at her daughter and couldn't get over her bewilderment; she could imagine what people would say and think of this four-week trip, and the memory of various scenes began to pass before her mind's eye in the darkened room. First, Micaela's wide-eyed amazement and the rapturous enthusiasm with which she enjoyed the novelties of that new world: the first time they went downtown and walked along, looking in the shop windows; when they went into the French shop; when they visited the famous "Salón Rojo" of Mexico; when the well-bred young man who took them through the museum, offered to take them to Chapultepec, to Xochimilco, to the Desierto de los Leones, and had come to see them off at the station with bunches of violets and a box of expensive chocolates. The wild expression in Micaela's eyes frightened her. The girl was miserable when she realized the time had come to go back to the village, and there was no way of reconciling her to their return. At this very minute she was probably crying bitterly, unable to sleep. Doña Lola got out of bed, with the idea of going to her daughter's room, then stopped . . . "No, it'll only make matters worse, much worse."

Don Inocencio had not approved of the attentions of young Estrada, especially on the day they went to the Desierto de los Leones. Doña Lola had been ashamed of his rudeness to the young man, but David either did not notice it or hid his feelings politely. How different from the young boys around here, with no manners, no future, no refinement! For Micaela's sake, Doña Lola would like to live in Mexico City, although she wouldn't dare breathe this to anyone. Micaela, obviously, had no vocation to be a nun, and her impulsive nature would expose her to many dangers before she married. She must marry—Doña Lola dared to put the thought into words for the first time that night—she must marry! But, who could she marry in the village? That was the problem. And what a problem!

Don Inocencio was thinking the same thing, tossing and turning in bed. She's a problem! And her mother spoils her so! His own firmness, his anger, his advice, don't do much good. As soon as he issues an order, they find reasons for disobeying it and do the opposite behind his back, permitting what he has forbidden and undermining his paternal authority. He'd have to pull in his belt and take radical measures. God! What a problem! Particularly, when, as in this case, there was only one child, and that a girl, brought up to have everything she wanted, so that you couldn't even scold her without putting the whole house in an uproar. They'd all lose their appetites and be upset for days. The whole trip was a disaster! What a stupid waste of money! Father Martínez was right when he warned him but he'd paid no attention; he'd thought it was just the usual prejudices. He didn't know where it was going to end. But, whatever it cost, even if he had to shut her up in a convent, he was going to get the upper hand and put an end, right now, to this pampering, to these ideas of hers, and these tears. He'd very nearly taken the whip to her as they came into the village; it grieved him, and it still grieved him, but he wasn't going to change his methods, and if harshness was the only solution, he'd remember his early days when he had a reputation for taming colts. His meditations ended . . . Loss of sleep was adding fuel to Don Inocencio's anger. Would it melt away quickly, as it always did whenever he decided to take Micaela in hand?

Micaela felt as though she were buried alive. Was it likely that David Estrada would remember her when he was surrounded by so many pretty, well-dressed, and intelligent young girls? Micaela would even be sorry to see him keep his promise and come to this gloomy village, so lacking in amenities and amusements; it was worse than a convent, it was a graveyard. What hope had she of ever going back, even in her dreams, of ever again enjoying his conversation, wandering through the forest of Chapultepec, strolling through the Alameda, walking down San Francisco Street! When

Ruperto Ledesma found out she was back, he'd give her no peace, by day or night! How could she ever have encouraged him? Such an uncouth, spoiled boy. She pitied him. What a disappointment he was in for! And the Daughters of Mary? For some time now Juanita had been suggesting that Micaela should wear the blue ribbon. The old maids would be furious when they saw her dressed in the latest style, with powder on her face, eye shadow under her eyes, and tight-fitting dresses; when they heard her tell what she saw and heard, what she did and felt, what she would invent to scandalize them and rouse their envy. They'd avoid her, they'd isolate her and allow no one near her. All the better! Then life would become impossible for her and her parents, and they'd take her away from the village all the sooner. What if she should make up to the most attractive boys in the village and steal them out from under the noses of the prudes? That would be amusing, only it was a pity the creatures were so slow and dull-witted! However, it was the best she could think of, and, besides, it would be the surest way to make herself even more hated and criticized, so that her father would have to let her out of this prison.

Kept awake by these bitter reflections, she felt like getting up and running away; she wished it would never grow light so she wouldn't have to see the people's faces and know for certain that her return was no nightmare. Did she really go to Mexico City and meet David Estrada, or was it only a dream, dreamed in her prison house? The man in the Post Office would make fun of her when he looked through the General Delivery without finding the letters Micaela would be expecting! But David wouldn't disappoint her. It was wicked to try to keep her shut up in this tomb, with no freedom even to dream, let alone to see things, to talk and go out. What a shock they were going to get if they thought she was the same naïve child as ever, concerned about what the neighbors would say, submitting to the pettiness that ruled in the village! Wait till they saw her tomorrow! But better . . . let tomorrow never come, even if she must endure forever the torture of tossing and turning between the sheets.

Inexorably the church bells announced the dawn. Inexorably life stirred in the village. Inexorably the routine of a new day summoned the villagers to their accustomed tasks.

RETREAT HOUSE

I

ONG BEFORE DAYBREAK, before four o'clock, often at three, even as early as two, the parish priest, Don Dionisio María Martínez is awake, his sleep routed by thronging visions of his parishioners. His waking thoughts embrace them all: the fall-en, struggling on the threshold of sleep, their eyes full of burning sand; those, living in sin, and dead to remorse, who sleep the sleep of the foolish virgins; those whose dreams are of lust; those who will wake to their old anxieties, temptations, and problems; those over whose heads, over whose souls, hangs the sword of Damocles; chronic invalids, victims of ac-cidents, and those who have no one to look after them; those who have just died, and souls no longer remembered in anyone's prayers; men who walk about with guns and evil hearts; the unforgiving, keeping fresh the memories of old wrongs; the unhappily married; widows, old maids, young girls, children; this one, that one; young

men scheming to cheat the watchful eyes on the riverbanks, and old men obsessed with carnal thoughts; hardened sinners; the strong who resist the wiles of the Devil and the weak who this very day will succumb; the rich man who will commit injustice; the poor who will be ill-treated; the debtor who will be hounded into paying his debts; those who will set bad examples and those who will follow them; those starting out on long journeys or beginning dangerous tasks; those condemned to suffer; half-hearted believers, the troublesome, the wayward.

They all claim his first thoughts, his first drowsy, wordy prayers. "Hail, Mary, Refuge of Sinners, conceived without sin. In the name of the Father, the Son, and the Holy Ghost." With arms outstretched, he enfolds them all in the gesture with which he crosses himself, and kneels down and kisses the floor. "I have sinned, O Lord, have mercy upon me. I repent of my sin and desire to make amends." He brings the discipline down across his shoulders, suffering for his own sins and for the sins of his people. Humble, kneeling, he sings the hymn "Come, Holy Ghost," then repeats "We plead before Thee, O Lord," and the penitential psalms, continuing the flagellation till the last word is uttered. Pedro, Juan, Francisco . . . each one of his parishioners, each of their needs, passes through his mind, and his thoughts move outward to embrace the four corners of the world: impious journalists, anti-Catholic rulers, atheistic teachers, infidels . . . the sinners of Messina whose awful punishment astounded mankind, blasphemers who insult the Holy Virgin and fill Guadalajara and the whole Archdiocese with indignation . . . growing license in manners, increasing ungodliness throughout the universe, complete destruction looming over the heads of the poor defenseless flock entrusted to him.

When the time comes to dress, he begins the rosary of the fifteen mysteries. Round his waist, next to his flesh, he girds the discipline. He lights the lamp, puts on his clothes, cassock last, and walks along to the Sacristy, where, on his knees, he finishes the rosary, makes his meditation, and says Matins.

He always celebrates the first mass himself. It comes at five o'clock, summer and winter. Between the first and second bell he sits in the Confessional. On the last stroke he rises.

The celebration is scrupulously slow; he robes slowly, consecrates the elements, and swallows them even more slowly. He bends over the prayer desk in prolonged thanksgiving, head bowed on hands.

Mass over, he says Lauds and returns to the Confessional for one, two, three hours. Thus, from dawn till breakfast time, he talks to no one; no one dares disturb his meditations.

Sometimes, before breakfast, he bears Communion or Holy Unction to the sick, but he dislikes visiting homes even for this purpose. When he does so, and this is only when his ministrations are urgently needed, his manner is even sterner than usual, especially if the parishioner is wealthy or is a woman. He has never accepted invitations or gifts. After twenty years in the village, he is on intimate terms with no one, has no close friend, although his manner is pleasant to everyone. He prefers to conduct all business in the Presbytery, which is open to all his flock, without fear or favor, at any hour, in all its strict simplicity. He never receives women alone.

He is daunted by no obstacles or difficulties, for he is conscientious, modest but strong-minded, and exceedingly jealous of his authority and responsibility as a priest. He eats sparingly, fasts twice a week, every day in Lent, and on all fast days. His clothes are simple and neat, his words few and effective; he dislikes parties and gossip, is interested in nothing outside his parochial duties. He is a tall man, gaunt, with big hands, bushy eyebrows, thin graying hair, and a manner so stern it barely stops short of harshness except on rare occasions. Only in his physiognomy does he reveal his unbending character and the steely strength of his virtues, the greatest among which is charity. As his nature is reserved, he exercises this charity, grown into compassion, secretly, and, if there is any danger that his real feelings may show, he deliberately assumes a forbidding look.

He was born in Arandas in 1850, studied at the Seminary in Guadalajara, and was ordained in 1876, on St. Lawrence's day. His first appointment was to San Cristóbal de la Barranca as mission priest, and three years later he was made curate of Apozol, which he left to take charge of the parish of Moyahua, where he served nine years. The hot climate aged him, but his blue eyes retain the brightness and his cheeks the glowing color typical of the hill-dweller. He still enjoys riding and can stand days of nine or ten hours in the saddle to hear confessions in remote corners of his parish.

The Confessional is the center of his activities, and from it he directs the life—the lives—of the region. Tender-hearted penitents or hardened sinners, faithful daily communicants or recalcitrant evil-doers, to each he gives special attention and he treats none lightly; twenty years of dealing with similar problems, thirty years of pastoral work, have not made him mechanical in the office of hearing confessions; even on days when the church is crowded, when he spends eight or more hours without getting up from the Confessional, he refuses to give in to hurry or to weariness. His is not the Confessional of ready-made formulas for like cases, and it is this that gives him his compelling force. In the Confessional he puts off his habitual diffidence and is transfigured and speaks with authority, although he can share the troubles of his penitents, weep with them and preach confidence in the Infinite Mercy of God.

Stern and solemn, he preaches his straightforward sermons with no sign of pulpit oratory . . . his is the solemnity of the man who believes himself a minister of the Eternal Word. Stern and solemn, excited and angry at times, sometimes tender and tearful, always moving. There is nothing routine about his sermons; they reveal thoughts and feelings long meditated upon and the sure eloquence of the man who lives what he is saying, down to the least-important detail.

Stern and solemn when he takes a Retreat. Inexorable when he preaches his Advent meditations on Sin, Death, Hell, and Judgment, he puts his whole being into his message. Then, his voice roars, his hands are clenched, his eyes almost pop out of his head with fear, his body trembles and imparts terror to all. He never repeats the same thoughts, illustrations, details, for this might weaken the effect from year to year.

When he arrived in the village his first undertaking was the construction of a large building to serve as both the Hospital and Retreat House. At Moyahua he had attempted a similar project. In more suitable surroundings, here, three months after taking charge of the parish, he laid the cornerstone, and calling all the people together, men, women, and children, and rousing their enthusiasm, he succeeded in getting the foundation laid by the end of Lent, 1890. The next year, even before the building was completed, the first Retreat was held in it, and, on the Second Sunday after Easter, Good Shepherd Sunday, the first patient was admitted to the Hospital.

Retreat House was completely finished in just three years. The plans and general supervision were the personal work of Father Martínez. It is a sturdy, spacious, and imposing building, and it expresses the character of both the village and the priest; there on the top of the hill at the southern end of the village, it faces the Cemetery on the northern hill. Each of its four walls is nine hundred feet long, twenty-five feet high, and three feet thick; there are no windows looking out on the street; the cornice, corners, buttresses, and doorways are of stone; so is the Chapel of the Holy Spirit, shaped like a Greek cross, which forms the center-half of the building. On the left is the Hospital door and on the right, the door of Retreat House; both are wide and adorned with big crosses. The Hospital has two patios and Retreat House another two. In the center of each patio is a well, encircled by a curbstone. At the far end of the left wing is the nuns' section, a little oratory, and a kitchen. The rooms of the Hospital are well lighted, but those of Retreat House are gloomy and connected by narrow echoing corridors whose walls are covered with texts reminding one at each step of death and judgment. At the end of the right wing is the Refectory for those in retreat, spacious and dominated by a huge crucifix and pulpit, with a skylight in the center. The floors are tiled, and in the rooms destined to be dormitories, they are marked out as in a cemetery, with crosses the size of the human beings who will lie there.

The door of Retreat House is open only the evening Retreat begins and the morning it ends. On their arrival, the retreatants find a coffin in the entrance hall with four wax candles at the corners, and above it are a black cross and a yellowed skull. When they are ready to leave, this is replaced by the Altar of the Good Shepherd, covered with flowers and crowned with a crucifix on which Christ lies with arms outstretched.

Retreat lasts for seven days, from Sunday to Saturday, except the one for young men, which begins on Ash Wednesday and ends the next Sunday, the first Sunday in Lent. This afternoon the Daughters of Mary begin theirs; next week there is one for women, then one for unmarried men over sixteen, and, lastly, one for married men, which ends on the eve of Passion Sunday.

The retreatants may bring their own mats, sheets, blankets, and pillows; only in exceptional cases, never out of consideration for official or social position, is it permitted to bring a mattress or special food or to hold any communication with another or with the outside world. Strictest silence is the first rule, silence which is broken only at breakfast time on the morning Retreat ends and the food which each family sends is allowed in. Many, rich and poor, prefer to sleep for the six nights on the bare floor, on the black crosses. Many, truly repentant, decline to speak at the last breakfast, and offer others the good things they have received from home.

Apart from Lent, there are three or four series of Retreats for different Brotherhoods or pious groups that ask for them. Hundreds of retreatants come from the villages round about; some years there are such crowds that it is impossible to accommodate all who wish to take part and there have to be new series in the following weeks.

The ceremony that ends the Retreat for grown men is the Temperance Oath, in which those present promise, their right hand on the Bible, not to take a single glass of wine for at least a year.

II

At noon, on this twenty-first of March, the parish priest, the Reverend Father Martínez, is very happy. It has taken him the whole week to bring round various recalcitrants who were making excuses for not going to the Retreat beginning today. Don Antonio Pérez had no one to leave in charge of his shop; Don Inocencio Rodríguez had just got home and his business affairs required his undivided attention; Pancho López was worried about his daughters, who were being courted by young men he couldn't bear the sight of, yet he was afraid to let them out of his sight for fear they might take advantage of a careless moment to deceive the innocent . . . *et sic de ceteris.* But these victories are not the main cause of his joy; these men, though they may be lukewarm and wrapped up in their worldly affairs, are still sheep of the flock, they are not wholly evil. No! The wonderful achievement is to have succeeded in getting—it still seems unbelievable—Don Román Capistrán, the Government Deputy; Don Refugio Díaz, the local pharmacist; and Don Pascual de Pérez y León, the law clerk, all three reputed to be liberals—heretics, according to some, cursed as Masons by others; the first, a murderer, the second, a witch doctor, the third a thief, according to popular report.

"Blessed be God!" This is all Father Martínez can think. He was talking to one of his curates, Abundio Reyes: "I don't share your doubts, Father, and I'm not one to be overconfident."

Reyes replied, "Well, I usually am guilty of overconfidence, but, in this case, like St. Thomas, I'll believe it when I see it."

"You're forgetting the ways of God and His divine mercy."

"No, I merely distrust these tricky gentlemen. I know them like the palm of my hand. What a time it's taken me to find some way of influencing them! There've been complaints to the Bishop about my associating with them! Every day the fearful run around with a bit of new gossip: they've heard me 'enjoy their tales and stories'; I 'encourage their licentiousness and don't try to restrain their wickedness.' "

"Your labors have brought forth fruit."

"God grant they have! But they're hard birds to pluck! Especially Don Pascual. And when has Don Román ever shown any respect for human beings?"

"Well, you'll see. Of course, the arrangement is for them to arrive at nightfall, in time for the first address. Naturally I don't like this much, and I agreed to it reluctantly, but you have to smooth the path for straying sheep. It'll be up to you to deal with any difficulties that might come up at the last minute. You'll have to use your wits."

"I won't let them out of my sight. The others are coming only if Don Román makes up his mind to come; so I'll have dinner at Don Román's. He'll send for the other two; our three tricky customers will invent new excuses but Doña Cenobia will be on my side."

"God be with you, Father; and don't forget that faith moves mountains."

"I hope to move these particular mountains to Retreat today."

III

Eight years before, the ecclesiastical authorities had sent Father Reyes to this village of ghosts and he felt a special sense of devotion to it and its stern Parish Priest. In the Seminary, Abundio had been considered a problem. He was original, quick-witted, and always up to some mischief or other. No one was better than he at organizing festivities, "gaudeamuses," excursions, concerts; he improvised speeches for any and every occasion, he recited, sang, took the lead in any conversation. Without him his companions could do nothing: wish the Rector a happy birthday, ask their superiors for special favors, carry out practical jokes, get hold of cigarettes or delicacies, invent excuses in time of need, compose humorous verses, prepare for their examinations, soften stern wills, or bring good humor into the routine of Seminary life. Wherever his superiors perceived Reyes' hand at work, they proceeded with caution, afraid of failing through overharshness or excessive indulgence. He was subjected to severe tests before receiving Orders, and his ordination was postponed for a year for fear he would fall victim to liberal ideas and unpriestly dissipations; on the other hand, his gift for handling people and his organizing ability gave rise to flattering hopes. The authorities would have liked to see him more pious, more thoughtful, less restless, less prone to playing jokes.

Zapotlán el Grande was his first post after ordination. In this small town with its busy social life, its easy-going manners, industrious and comfortable people, within easy reach of Guadalajara, the energetic young priest saw an excellent opportunity for carrying out his dreams of great organization and apostolic enterprises: dynamically-taught catechism classes for men and boys, classes from which routine and boredom would be banished; schools based on the most modern methods; the circulation of good newspapers; active groups of young people of both sexes, ladies' guilds, joint meetings of labor and capital, Catholic societies like those that flourished in some European countries. He soon made the acquaintance of the most distinguished families, and inspired confidence in the men dubbed "Liberals." This aroused suspicion, particularly in the mind of the Parish Priest, to whom the plans proposed by the new curate appeared "modernistic" and dangerous; he would tolerate no innovations in the life of his parish, nor any illusions created by doing things foreign to the traditional religious pattern of the Archdiocese. To put teeth into his refusal to allow the inexperienced and naïve young fellow to fall victim to the dangers of social life in a town with a worldly atmosphere, the Parish Priest kept him away from the people of the town, gave him jobs to do in rural areas, and deprived him of the opportunity to put even the least of his plans into practice, that for improving teaching methods. In the end, the full weight of the Parish Priest's admitted prejudices fell upon Father Reyes' head, with the result that, before the year was up, he found himself almost penniless, and transferred to an unknown village, which he reached by bridle paths that were barely usable at the rainy season, when the news of his transfer came. As he passed through Guadalajara, in a state of depression which filled those who knew him with foreboding, the reputation of the new Parish Priest under whose orders he was to work put the finishing touch to his despair: narrow-minded, strong-willed, exacting, maybe even already set against a curate who came partly in punishment to a village so humble its strange name went unrecorded on the maps of the Republic.

Riding across rough country with simple pack-drivers, travelling donkeyback in all kinds of weather, stopping at wretched inns, pass-

ing through lonely regions and desolate settlements, he ended his
journey at nightfall of the fourth day. How dark the village was!
He was aware of a peculiar atmosphere, of strange smells seeping
through closed doors, of shadows flitting to and fro. A dark, silent
village, depressing to the newcomer. The monotonous clanging of
bells pounded against his temples; his head ached; he was ready to
burst into tears. A pack-driver offered to house his things until the
Parish Priest could provide something else. The refuge was a
murky, one-story hovel where a ragged woman and whining children shared the thick and filthy air with grunting pigs and sleepy,
cackling hens. A storm was approaching. They might not even
reach the Presbytery before it broke. Drops of rain began to fall
slowly, then faster and faster. Steady flashes of lightning streaked
across the sky. The wind howled. The storm would be bad. But
they reached the dark Presbytery.

In the presence of Father Martínez, Father Reyes shook off his depression; he determined to make every effort to gain the confidence
of the older man, in whose blue eyes he glimpsed a secret gleam of
cordiality. The reception was unexpected. The Parish Priest made
no attempt to conceal the unfavorable report he had received of
Father Reyes, but with simple, fatherly eloquence, succeeded in
putting him at ease and restoring his self-confidence and zeal. He
urged him to stay there until he found lodgings to his liking, sent
for his luggage, and ordered an early evening meal. Throughout this,
Father Martínez treated his guest with every courtesy, and if he cut
short their conversation it was to let the tired fellow get to bed as
soon as possible. In his rather brusque manner there was no suggestion of hypocrisy; he revealed the understanding sympathy of a
man who has suffered like bitterness and learned through the years
not to attach importance to it.

Never, in the following days, months, years, did Father Martínez
show any lack of trust in his curate, though he watched him closely,
especially during the first days. Frankness and tact, with a certain
measure of comradeship, guarded and shy, set the pattern of their
relation. Father Reyes, for his part, remained faithful to his resolve
to take no initiative and to study the character of Father Martínez
with the minute care of a man checking a piece of machinery which
has brought him to grief; he learned his likes and dislikes, the kindly
nature under the show of harshness, the things that moved him pas-

sionately, the strength of his virtues. His own recent defeat helped him to understand the Parish Priest's complex nature and to achieve and maintain a *modus vivendi* with him.

The passiveness he forced himself to maintain, so foreign to his temperament, the mechanical nature of his tasks, an overwhelming spiritual dryness within and without, but above all, the atmosphere of the village and the dreariness of the landscape, drove Father Reyes to the brink of despair during his first months. There were moments when he feared he would go mad or, at least, turn misanthrope. This danger rose from his recent experience and was aggravated by the enigmatic life of the village, the circuit of close-sealed eyes and hearts. He had no wish to enter into friendly relations with these families whose members displayed very little affection in public even to one another, yet he was irked by his inability to do so. It was a world completely foreign to his cheerful nature, one in which nobody understood him and nobody felt the least desire to do so.

Time, the demands of his work and, above all, his own character, gradually undermined Father Reyes' intention to keep aloof. The Parish Priest helped, too; he noted his curate's gifts, the unmistakable skill with people that he himself lacked. First, he gave him an opportunity to organize catechism classes for the children, then he enlisted him in helping with Retreats. The results of both tasks were surprising and Father Martínez' confidence increased and the curate's returning enthusiasm found greater scope. It was his persuasive, appealing voice which touched the souls of the backsliders. The young people liked his frankness and he grew daily more popular, as popular as possible, considering the nature of the village. His sermons roused new feelings of devotion; he preached challenging sermons on current events, a contrast to the Parish Priest's powerful solemnity. His influence spread over areas which the older man could not reach. The village, in its turn, exercised an influence upon him. It did not occur to him to organize literary evenings, concerts, plays, bazaars, picnics, things he had enjoyed so much in the Seminary, and which had brought upon him the disapproval of the Parish Priest and many serious-minded parishioners in Zapotlán.

By now he was limiting his activities to forming a choir of men and boys, for church services only; he had as few dealings with women as possible; when he visited houses or offices, he went with a specific purpose, following the practice of Father Martínez; and if he appeared to enjoy a chat—which did not escape criticism, especially when he talked with people like the Deputy, the pharmacist, the law clerk, and others whose orthodoxy and moral purity were suspect in the general opinion—the fact is that some tasks required indirect methods, and persuasion is sometimes better than force.

Father Reyes has been in the village for eight years; only twice has he gone to the State Capital, the center of the Archdiocese, and then on business; it was useless for friends in Zapotlán to invite him to visit them, he always refused. Three years ago, he received the order for a transfer to Lagos; with his consent, the Parish Priest and local men went to Guadalajara and managed to get the order rescinded.

"Whatever spell have they put on you in that God-forsaken hole?" asked his friends, who wanted to get him away to a better position. He recently had had word that they were trying to secure him a chaplaincy in the State Capital, and he wrote to stop them.

Sometimes, when he was alone, lines came into his mind from a poem learned long ago:

> The nightingale prefers a simple nest
> Of straw and feathers in the wood, and sings,
> However plaintively, how much more blest
> The hidden tranquil ways are than the things
> With which the prince rewards a flattering guest
> In a cage of gold, mourning its captive wings.

IV

When Don Timoteo Limón realized that—for how long, he couldn't tell—he'd been standing next to—almost shoulder to shoulder with—his archenemy, the man he hated most, the unprincipled scoundrel who had caused him so much trouble and worry; when he realized—and, yes, there could be no doubt about it, the first glance from the corner of his eye had not deceived him—that the man beside him was the dreaded law clerk, he trembled. But his agitation was nothing compared to that of Porfirio Llamas, who, hearing footsteps behind him, turned to find himself looking straight into the eyes of Don Román Capistrán. Apparently with deliberate intent Don Refugio Díaz, the village pharmacist, had come to stand beside Melesio Islas, who blamed Don Refugio for the death of his son.

All through the sermon, Porfirio had the feeling that Don Román was holding a gun in his ribs. ("That's just what he would do," he thought. "Dear God! Don't let him recognize me.") Don Timoteo and Melesio, like Porfirio, felt their hearts sinking into their boots. The boots felt tight. Then their blood began to seethe and they wanted to hurl themselves upon the enemies so unexpectedly within reach. Once again Melesio could hear his dying son's heavy breathing, see his staring eyes, his desperate convulsions, hear him shouting, "Mama! Papa!" begging for help. All the details of that agony, for which the druggist's cure-all had been useless, crowded into his memory; he would have given Don Refugio his life to save his son. He remembered how the boy had fought against death even after he had lost the power of speech, and clung to his father and mother with his eyes horribly glazed with terror . . . and here was Don Refugio right next to him, now as then, unconcerned. Murderer! Robber! Robber who had taken away his happiness forever.

In spite of the sermon and the compulsory silence, the news spread like a cloud of dust, disturbing the whole assembly, making it impossible for the men to devote their thoughts to the beginning and end of man. After evening prayers, in the interval before supper, the general uneasiness and air of conspiracy and revolt were evident. All were asking themselves how they could sit beside "those men," at the same table. How could the same roof shelter them all? Like lightning flashes, the memories of past wrongs came blazing into the minds of the men. Nearly all those present had good reason to hate the three:

"My mares he made off with!"

"My little piece of land he sold at auction!"

"The bank draft he swindled me out of!"

"The twenty pesos he got out of me and didn't give me any treatment!"

"The day he sent for me, shouting that he'd arrest me and send me to jail!"

"The hour I spent with his gun stuck in my ribs!"

"His wooden face when he told me there was no cure for croup, and stood there, watching my child choke and making no effort to save her . . ."

"Perhaps they've just come for the sermon . . ."

"God grant they've gone . . ."

"Let's hope they're not really going to stay . . ."

"God help us!"

But in the Refectory, it was quite clear that the three had come to stay. The objections of many to sitting next to the Deputy, the druggist, or the law clerk were quite evident; but Father Reyes' tact soon solved everything. Don Román Capistrán went to sit with friends, Don Timoteo Limón on his left, Don Ceferino Toledo on his right, Don Rómulo Varela in front. Don Refugio Díaz was given a seat between two men noted for their excellent health, and Don Pascual de Pérez y León was seated between villagers so poor that they had never needed legal advice nor were likely to need it.

The retreatants, a hundred and four in number, eat in silence. Their feelings—still violent—grow calmer in the stillness. Their glances find mutual reassurance, founded on the common desire for salvation. After dinner, in silence, a strange silence, they return to the Chapel, gliding, like ghosts, along dark corridors, and, half an hour later, look for the place where they are to sleep. How many, as they cross the patio, glance up at the sky, at the stars, and think of their families, their business, the problems left behind!

"Forget your wife, your children, your cattle, the sowing of your fields, your debts . . ." The Priest's tone was sharp. "The Devil is full of wiles to take your attention away from the principal matter for which God in his mercy has brought you here; in these first hours, the first night especially, he will give you no rest with his attempts to disturb the peace of this holy house with unworthy images, with feelings of hatred, with worldly cares. Imagine you are dead and stop worrying about what you have left behind. Those living today will be the dead of tomorrow. The assaults of the Devil will be even more terrible than they are now. Lie down as in your tomb. This first night . . ." The Parish seemed to sense the spiritual turmoil, in the silence and darkness of the echoing house, where one was transported to another far-distant, timeless world from which there is no return.

V

A few yards below Retreat House—so shrouded in silence that not even the barking of the dogs could be heard, probably not even the ringing of the bells, still less the faint sounds of the village—in kitchens, in dim-lit passages and courtyards, in parlors and bedrooms, the souls of the women are filled with sadness or fear, with fear and sadness.

"Why are you worried, when you know he's serving God, carrying out his most important obligations?" Mothers-in-law try to reassure their young daughters-in-law, sisters-in-law speak comfort, and sisters and friends support newly married women, alone for the first time since their marriage. But even the old women, who have celebrated their silver and their golden wedding anniversaries, women with many children, also feel the emptiness of their houses. Knowing that their husbands and sons, fathers and brothers . . . sweethearts, are serving God, brings no term to their sadness or relief to the undefined desire they feel. It must be a temptation of the Devil; it is so strong in many of them, so frantic, that they feel like rushing out into the street and shouting, or plunging, weeping, into the darkness. Tonight, during these seven nights and days, they will realize the strength and mystery in a companionship they try to forget during the rest of the year and are ashamed to admit in public.

In private and in public, their only topic of conversation now is Pedro, Juan, or Francisco; their joint sufferings and joys, their joint hopes.

And in private, but to their hearts' content, now that Pedro, Juan, and Francisco, absorbed in meditation, are not supposed to be thinking about worldly matters, girls who have exchanged glances, letters, or actual promises, may indulge in memories and hopes, permissible now, since they concern men who are engaged in pious exercise. (Of course, the Devil tries to turn even this to his advantage. For instance, he puts it into the head of Mercedes Toledo that Julián may be sleeping on the very cross where she was lying a fortnight ago.) If the young men feel the same towards the girls when they come out of Retreat, this will be a sign that God approves, and the girls may accept their proposals, although first they will pray for seven Sundays to the most chaste St. Joseph, asking him to tell them the right thing to do. (All week a few are afraid in their secret hearts that after strict examination of his intentions in solitude, so-and-so will come out of Retreat with a change of heart.)

The young girls envy the familiarity with which the married women speak openly of their absent ones, in the street, on their way out of church, as they go about their business, morning, afternoon, and night. To give one another mutual companionship and help, in these days, as in times of grief and need, there is a lot of visiting. Conversations turn always on the same topic: Pedro and Pablo, Andrés, Jaime, Tomás, Santiago, Felipe, Bartholomé, Mateo, Simón and Tadeo; Lino, Cleto, Clemente, Sixto, Cornelio, Cipriano,

Lorenzo, Crisógono, Juan and Pablo, Cosme and Damián. (The young unmarried girls feel that the names of the boys they are interested in may only be breathed in their inmost secret thoughts; these unuttered names will never be spoken, never reach any other ears, never be borne along by the wind in the deserted street; these names are guarded in the deepest hidden core of modesty, while the married women talk of their husbands in endless conversations.)

"Jesús is so good he didn't want to go to Retreat, with Martinita so ill—we wonder, every day, whether this one will be her last. A tumor in her stomach! Cancer! Think of it, Paulita. A dreadful pain that gives her no rest. The poor woman's skin is like wax . . ."

"And Pancho! He wouldn't leave us alone for the world! He can't have an easy moment, shut in up there, wondering how we're getting along . . . !"

"If I'd known that that man was going to Retreat—but how on earth could it have occurred to anyone!—I wouldn't have insisted so on Porfirio's going. I was so worried last night I couldn't sleep! You know how he keeps after him, having him arrested on one charge or another; only a year ago he tried to shoot him on the Teocaltiche road, claiming he thought he was a rebel, and now he says he's a follower of Reyes . . . Porfirio, who wouldn't hurt a fly, who's as good and peaceful as St. Francis . . . !"

"Well, Doña Nicolasita, how did you get Don Refugio to go?"

"The poor man didn't want to. There are so many people sick. You know how much faith they have in him, they come looking for him even from Juchipila, though some ungrateful creatures say nasty things about him, as if a man, like God, could cure any sickness. The truth is, Father Reyes kept on at him about it, and so did I. When Don Román and Lawyer Pérez agreed, Refugio decided to go too. Blessed be God! He isn't a wicked man, that's only what his enemies say; just the opposite. He likes to do good, but he doesn't want anyone to know it. The calls he makes for nothing are far more than those he gets paid for. And he goes to confession every year. The man who admits he's never been to confession is Don Pascual!"

"Saints preserve us! And how did they manage to get Don Román to go?"

"Well, I think . . . I think . . . But I'd better mind my own business . . ."

"Those women must have gone by now. Do you remember the year we drove them out?"

"I heard the last one went last night. Some farmhands who brought in some straw were talking about it. Let's hope they stay away, this time! One of these fine days, their evil lives will bring down punishment from Heaven upon our own heads! The village will be destroyed because of their wickedness and not one stone will be left upon another."

"They'll be back again, when we least expect them! Maybe Don Román won't let them come back after Lent this year, even if he has winked at their being here in past years."

"Timoteo is so good, so thoughtful; he's been like a father to me, and me so old and useless, especially since I've been paralyzed. He's a real saint, my man . . . and so kind to everyone! No one comes to him in vain—he gives something to each one: money, advice, corn. They say he sometimes goes over there with those women. Lies! He's a God-fearing man! But people's tongues are always wagging."

"How I miss Melesio! It seems as though he's been gone forever! He's so reliable! No one has a sense of duty like he has!"

The newly-weds don't say much; but their sighing grows stronger and stronger, as though it would drive the days before it in swifter flight.

VI

All day Monday, they meditated on Sin; Tuesday, on Death; Wednesday, on Judgment; Thursday, on Hell; Friday, on Our Lord's Passion and the parable of the Prodigal Son, which was the subject of the last address for the night.

They rise at half-past five, go to Chapel at a quarter to six for meditation, followed by Mass; silence until the breakfast bell at seven, continuing, after breakfast, until half-past eight, when it is time for the first part of the Rosary and the first address of the day, given by the Parish Priest. Silence again, until ten o'clock, time for the Stations of the Cross, followed by an address by Father Reyes and self-examination. Dinner at midday. At two, the sorrowful mysteries of the Rosary and subjects for meditation; at four, devotional reading and a sermon; at six the last part of the Rosary, a talk on morals, a sermon, and flagellation. After dinner, they come together to examine their consciences in light of the day just passed, and they finish with the Miserere; by nine o'clock, all should be in bed.

The periods for silent meditation between the sessions in Chapel are to give the retreatants time to ponder the themes of the sermons; to get their ideas in order, repent, amend their lives, ask for grace and perseverance. They may walk through the patios and corridors, remain in the Chapel or dormitories, but in strict silence, each man alone, under penalty of expulsion, a penalty it has been rarely necessary to apply.

The walls—wherever the eyes happen to turn, in the Chapel, the corridors, the cloisters, the Refectory, the dormitories—are covered with vivid pictures and texts which induce further meditations. Well-known texts and familiar lines, easy to remember, alternate with pictures of awe-inspiring realism. Huge Stations of the Cross adorn the walls of the Chapel, and over the Altar are sculptured dramatic figures of the Crucifixion, against a terrifying background of big black heavy clouds, flashes of lightning streaking a desolate countryside, and a cluster of dark-red houses representing hapless Jerusalem. The walls of the cloisters, too, are plastered with pictures and texts, creating an atmosphere of gloomy unrest: allegories of the last four things—here, the death of a sinner, there the separate hells of the lustful, the miserly, the proud; robbers, murderers; farther along, a body in a state of decomposition, where the painter has delighted in the presence of the worms, making them look alive as they busy themselves at their gruesome task. On the central dividing wall, facing the Chapel door, is a picture of the Day of Judgment, fearful even to those who have often contemplated it. The torment of Dives and the wretchedness of the Prodigal Son, who would fain have eaten the food of the pigs in his charge, are the themes of the two huge canvases in the Refectory . . . Overwrought souls emerge from the Chapel with solemn words ringing in their ears: Death, Judgment, Heaven, Hell . . . , to confront the fearsome paintings and the dread texts inscribed in huge letters. They find no rest in their struggle against desire and sin, not even in sleep, for there too, impressions of the evening float before their eyes, like disembodied ghosts.

All must observe the same rules of fasting throughout the week. The sick, those unable to fast or those excused from fasting, will have special Retreats at another time, so that no exceptions need be made at mealtime.

Before hearing confessions, the Parish Priest and his curates, as St. Ignatius counsels, move about among the retreatants, "not wanting to question or know individual thoughts or sins," but trying to learn "the various perplexities and worries, so that they may prescribe suitable spiritual exercises for the greater good of all." During the periods between the addresses, they draw parishioners aside one by one and talk with them quietly, reinforcing individually the common labor, which rises steadily towards its culmination.

The first night there was no appointed time for flagellation; but on the second day the retreatants were reminded in the afternoon to bring to the next service the instrument their piety had suggested to them. After the anathema against sin, with the exclamations of horror still echoing in their ears, when those present had been stirred up to the scourging of the body, of the flesh which had led the soul into sin, the lights were put out, the hymn "Pardon, my God! Pardon and indulgence . . ." began, and a dull sound was heard, heavy, rhythmical, terrifying; some, in the darkness, took off their shirts, to whip themselves with greater harshness. A quarter of an hour, an endless quarter of an hour, for some too short. The flagellation came to an end at the command of the Parish Priest, the lights were lit again, slowly, to give time, in silence, a silence broken by choking sobs, for faces to regain composure.

That night, before going to bed, the retreatants heard the Priest suggest the main points for their meditation on death, and when they were asleep, at twelve, at one o'clock, they were startled out of their sleep by a coffin borne along through the dormitories, followed by lamentations and the singing of the Requiem Aeternam. In other years there had been processions of ghostly-looking, skeleton-like figures, bearing flaring alcohol lamps which lit up skulls dangling from the ceiling, while groans came in through the windows.

When he had recovered from his first shock, Don Román Capistrán, now wide awake, decided that he had had enough. A firm hand, the hand of Father Reyes, placed on his shoulder at the right moment checked his first movement and gave him time to reflect. It should be said that Don Román came to Retreat to curry favor with the people. He has spent six years in the village, hoping in vain that his friend, Governor Ahumada, would have him transferred to a more important position. Not always honestly, he has gradually acquired more and more land, cattle, houses; he has grown accustomed to the local way of living; to the patient, good, hard-working, economical people; to the land which rewards their efforts with its produce, to the simple customs. On the other hand, his political future is not improving as time passes; he thinks it would be better to forget about political preferment and consider settling here definitely, paying more attention to his finances, setting up some kind of business, maybe organizing some industry.

He is aware of the dislike, often deserved, reflected in the faces of his neighbors; he knows that when he ceases to be in authority, the feigned respect which is the product of fear will turn to indifference; he may even find some of his neighbors trying to pay off old scores. His friendship with Father Reyes was a step forward and the invitation to Retreat, resisted half sincerely, half out of shrewd calculation, affords him a means of winning confidence. He had been about to refuse, postponing action. Even inside Retreat House, he decided to leave several times: first, in the Refectory, when he realized that he was the center of general amazement; and later when he had awkward encounters: with the Macías brothers, outlaws for the past two years on account of several murders in La Cañada for which they had been responsible; then with Porfirio and so many men suspected of cattle stealing, so many lawbreakers, so many guilty of acts of disrespect towards authority. It is obvious they are suspicious of his motives; his presence is disconcerting and they avoid him. The food and atmosphere of Retreat House irritate him. He has never been an unbeliever, but the desire to obtain good posts in the government has increased his indifference. When he arrived in the village as deputy he made irreverent remarks which caused him to be disliked; when he realized that his reputation of being a Jacobin set people against him rather than otherwise, he changed his attitude; he began to go to mass on Sundays; last Corpus Christi he was one of the bearers in the procession and turned a blind eye to the outdoor religious ceremonies. He allowed Father Reyes to remove the portrait of Juárez from the village hall. In Retreat, after the disrespect and the discomfort of the first hours, he felt a compelling influence working upon his soul which forced him to meditate upon the eternal verities, and he finally capitulated, completely, the third day.

However, no power on earth could make Don Pascual stay after the shock of the macabre procession. Early next morning he crept out of Retreat House and out of the village, for good.

"And Don Refugio . . . ?" "Don Refugio," was the answer, "opened one eye, looked at the coffin, and went back to sleep, lulled by the groans and chants of the Requiem." "Maybe," said the gossips, "in his dreams he thought they were carrying out one of his victims to his grave, and slept more soundly." "What about Don Inocencio? The fright must have been enough to make him dirty his pants!" "And he wasn't the only one."

"Death, how bitter is thy sting!" This Tuesday is full of painful memories for those who bear on their consciences the heavy burden of the lives they have cut short; the earth-filled mouth, the stiffened hands of Anacleto; the last twitching movements of the rioters killed during the Fiesta at La Cañada, nearly two years ago now; the open eyes that no amount of pressing managed to keep shut, and the vainly threatening fists of Pedro Ibarra.

The fifth commandment was the subject of the address and self-examination that day. (Who? What? Where? To whom? How many times? Why? How? When?)

"It was a Sunday," remembered Francisco Legaspi, examining his conscience, "it must have been about three o'clock, time to go back to the ranch, when we met Pedro Ruiz, the pack-driver, on his way from San Antonio and he told us we'd better go around by the upper road, because, farther along, at the corner by the village hall, Gumersindo was waving a pistol and threatening to shoot anybody who tried to pass. More out of curiosity than anything else, I paid no attention to Pedro and went straight on. I soon heard the singing and raucous shouts of the drunken man. Standing on the corner, in some of the doorways and looking out of the windows, were a few curious men and women, calling on God for help—but they didn't have to be there. I kept on, for why should I turn back because of a drunk who wasn't bothering me, somebody I'd never done any harm to? If I turned back now, it would only be worse; he'd become more violent, everybody would laugh at me and nothing could keep me from being called a coward. If I proved too tame to fight now, the boys would never leave me alone, they'd keep taunting me to see how much I'd stand, how much it would take to make me lose my temper. Gumersindo was sitting on the edge of the pavement, with a bottle beside him, so drunk he couldn't keep his feet, singing and cursing. When he saw me, he offered me a drink. I took no notice of him, and kept on.

" 'Can't you hear me, you son of a bitch? No one's going to get by me. I say so, and my word is law here, you son of a bitch,' he shouted at me. No one said a word. I kept steadily on, watching him carefully all the time; he shot at me, almost hit my head. I took cover in the Loeras' doorway, and looked back to see if the shot had sobered him up any. He was rushing towards me, furious, yelling threats and curses; he was a good shot even when drunk; I shouted to him to stay where he was but he kept on. No one dared try to stop him.

" 'Take one more step and I'll shoot,' I yelled. His only answer was to fire another shot, and then . . ."

This commandment is also broken by quarreling, insulting one's neighbor, bearing malice, ill-will, sinning in thought, word, or deed. What? Against whom? How many times? Why? How? When?

At the words of the Priest there came into the minds of his listeners thousands of memories, each one with all the details, hidden for many years, which the consciences noted with scrupulous care: "There was a beautiful moon, that night . . ."

"It was back in the days when drinking wasn't considered a vice, and that evening I'd had a couple; I wasn't in full possession of my senses . . ."

"Every time I've seen him, two or three times a day, for the past thirty years, I've wanted to hit him and send him to the Devil . . ."

"I must have struck her with the dagger four or five times; what I remember was how she squealed just like a pig in the slaughter-house . . ."

"The day I beat her to death near the river, she was wearing a navy-blue dress, with black trimming, and her cheeks were painted. She looked disgusting! Poor thing!"

Signs of blood were more abundant that night, when the lights were again lighted in the Chapel after the scourging; the atmosphere was thick with disinfectant, sprinkled over everything so that the senses should come to meditate upon Death with greater clarity.

The terrors of the Last Judgment depicted in awe-inspiring words by the Parish Priest, the stentorian cries of "Depart from me, ye cursed of my Father, into eternal fire!" uttered at the end of the sermon on Wednesday night, and repeated at the time of the scourging by a voice which seemed to be of another world, amid the clanging of sheets of tin, the strident sound of a trumpet and other terrifying noises, broke down the resistance of Don Román Capistrán; his tears began to flow and that night, he was one of those who took off their shirts for the flagellation.

The address and self-examination on the sixth commandment coincided with the meditation on Hell. Here, a whole underground world of evil thoughts, desires, and deeds, of hidden crimes and secret shames, began to weave its invisible nets about the retreatants, stripped of the semblance of pleasure, so that "the eye of the mind might see the great fires and the souls walking about amid the flames; the ear might hear the lamentations, shrieks, shouts, blasphemies against Christ, Our Lord, and against all his saints; the nostrils be filled with smoke, sulphur, and the decaying stench of the sink of iniquity; the mouth taste the bitterness of life, with tears and sadness, and feel the gnawing pangs of conscience; the flesh feel the flames touch and envelop the soul." From the evening before, the aim of the preliminary addresses had been to make the men see "the length, the breadth, and the depth of Hell with the eye of the imagination." The Parish Priest's specialty is the condemnation of the vice of lust, and he paints it in all its horror; he is compelling, again, when he preaches on the torments of Hell, using real sulphur and pitch to create his effects, filling the Chapel, this night, with acrid smoke. This night, when it is time for the scourging—and this is usually the most severe, the most bloody—his choir boys drag chains through the choir and the singers utter frightful shrieks. (This time, Don Refugio was the one moved by grace; he took off his shirt to flagellate himself, determined never again to return to the brothels.)

On the stroke of midnight, the bell summoned all to the Chapel to make their meditation on the Battle between Good and Evil, followed by the Litanies on the Passion to which the Friday sessions were dedicated. The windows were covered with black; on their knees they crawled to the Stations of the Cross and on their knees made the Procession of the Three Falls; many, refusing to taste food at midday, preferred to remain on their knees, in memory of the three hours Our Lord spent on the Holy Cross. How fitting, at the end of the Sorrowful Journey, was the sermon on the Prodigal Son, preached eloquently by Father Reyes. The sermon was interrupted by a dramatic scene re-enacted every year. On hearing the words: "I will arise and go to my father," one of the retreatants, the worst sinner (this year it was Donato, fallen again into the vice of drunkenness) rose from the door of the Chapel, where all had seen him on their way in, lying under oak branches, among acorns, dressed in rags and wearing a torn hat; he advanced slowly, went up to the Priest, and when the orator, moved, reached the passage, "But when he was yet a great way off, his father saw him, and had compassion, and ran, and fell on his neck, and kissed him," the sacristan moved the hinged arms of the figure of Jesus of Nazareth, which, dressed in a big cloak, stood beside the Altar, and let them fall upon the shoulders of the sinner, while the musicians began to play, and those present started to sob. The lights were put out, and the scourging began, the music and sobbing continuing.

Father Martínez, Father Reyes, and the other five priests of the parish had spent the night hearing confessions; nearly all the retreatants had been moved to make a general confession. (What? Why? How? When? How many times?) There lay the underground forces which could explode in violence if Retreat did not keep them in check.

The steady recital of sins, one after another, all more or less alike, usually brought no surprise to the experienced confessors. But that night, the ears of the priests heard strange, alarming things: "I'm guilty of accepting and passing along papers which speak evil of God, Our Lord, of the Virgin, the Holy Father, and the clergy; also love stories which I lent to my cousin . . ." The Padre who heard this referred the case to the Parish Priest. Another confessed to having brought a collection of pornographic photographs to the village and having shown them to some friends. Another said that the last time he was in Guadalajara he had attended a Masonic meeting, had brought home some books on Masonry, and had mentioned his doubts on religion and weakened the faith of many. From different penitents, nearly all the confessors learned to their surprise of a Spiritist meeting which a travelling agent had held in the village a few weeks before. The Liberal and Socialist infection was also evident; one man had taken part in a strike in the North; two or three had confessed their hatred of the rich; one confessed working with people from Teocaltiche to found a Juarist Club, and another declared that he was involved in a conspiracy to revolt and attack the rich "if Don Porfirio was re-elected."

The threat of such great dangers, stirring below the surface, worried the Parish Priest to such an extent that he became ill weeks later. The glow of pleasure which usually accompanied the end of Retreat was absent from his eyes and brow on this occasion, and he made an excuse not to attend the final breakfast, when the seal of silence was broken and the Refectory was filled with voices. There was a tinge of bitterness in his voice as he took leave of the retreatants, and he put into the fervor of the Gloria, the Plenary Indulgence, and the Temperance Oath, a tone both stern and unusual at this time. "The village is surrounded by perils, it is in a state of siege, and the agents of the Enemy are within our gates. Woe unto him through whom comes disaster! Better for him that a millstone were tied around his neck and he were cast into the depths of the sea . . ." His sermons on Death, Judgment, and Hell contained a new note. He even discouraged the playing of the usual cheerful music at the gate of Retreat House when the retreatants emerged, nor would he allow firecrackers. "Sad days are in store for us, days of calamity, and nothing can bring us joy," he explained.

VII

The doors of the houses are open and adorned to receive the retreatants, with altars in the entry ways, in the halls, or in the parlors. Places are set for visiting relatives. People are talking again in their normal voices, in the streets and doorways. "What's been going on in the village these past days?" With what shyness, with what secret pleasure, the newly-weds meet again! It is a day of deep rejoicing, when doors and hearts are opened. The eyes of the youths are bright. Taking advantage of the general confusion, they slip into the houses and manage to gaze into the eyes of the beloved a long moment, a long, happy moment. There is even time to entwine fingers and slide the confidential slip of paper into the sweetheart's hand. Who will notice blushing cheeks, perturbed glances, when neighbors who have been the bitterest of enemies are to be seen embracing each other? One man publicly begs his family to forgive him, another restores a sum of money; no one wishes to lag behind in furnishing proofs of spiritual reform. The retreatants have returned from a far country, whose bounds are death, and all of them hope to profit by the experience. The warmth of things loved, the gentle rhythm of life regained, fills them with joy. Some timorous souls are afraid to face the din of the world, their daily world; the light dazzles them and they cannot bear even to hear the voices of the women. Back sweep the old worries, the old gossip. (Was anyone raped during these days? Did anyone die? Did anything special happen in this house?) There is one piece of news: Don Román Capistrán invited Porfirio Llamas to dinner, and he made no move to arrest the Macías brothers.

With the doors shut again, shortly after midday, silence is restored. This is the afternoon on which the sacristans cover the altars and statues with purple veils, a solemn event recurring every year in the life of the village. The great days begin, shadowy twilights, with echoes of joy and anguish. The men have come home. They have come back.

Who will be conceived this night? March 27. Abel or Cain? A priest or an outlaw, the savior of his people, or their shame and scourge, their glory or opprobrium? Perhaps merely useless lives. Not even on this night does the Parish Priest give in to weariness; after dinner, he returns to the Confessional, finishes hearing confessions, says the last part of the service and the Rosary, comes into his room, and bending low before God, scourges himself (today with pressing anxiety that the success of Retreat has done nothing to mitigate) and prays for the whole world, especially for his parishioners, especially for Pedro, Pablo, and Francisco, for those who are in the way of temptation and those who are falling into sin of thought, word, or deed; for women, adolescents, and children, for his clergy, that they may be kept pure and full of zeal: for Father Reyes (in danger because of his youth and his temperament), for Father Islas (with his narrow-mindedness), for Father Vidriales (with his quick temper), for Father Meza (with his love of routine), for Father Rosas (with his laziness), and for Father Ortega (with his timidity). His own helplessness and lack of ability are the final subjects of his meditations and supplications.

Tonight, he has decided not to take his customary stroll through the village. It is past eleven when he puts out his light and tries to sleep, but he finds himself beset by worries about the dangers facing his flock: liberalism, laxity in manners, Masonry, Spiritism, Socialism, impious books, revolution! "We'll have to do this, that, and the other . . . Don Inocencio's daughter had the audacity to come to Rosary in a low-necked dress, and by paying no attention to the service, caused the thoughts of others to stray . . . Where, God in Heaven, could the Spiritist meeting have been held? I've started a hunt for those novels, today; but tomorrow we'll have to . . . That boy of Alfredo's isn't at all well, not at all well . . . the mail, Father Reyes can look into . . . the novels, Father Islas . . . Will I be able to ward off the attacks of the Devil? I don't like the way the law clerk fled . . . The schemes of those from Teocaltiche, this growing hatred (partly justified) of the rich . . . Lucas González' widow is treading a dangerous path. The shamelessness of some of the young girls is alarming; but worst of all is the infiltration of these ideas, these ideas . . . More good newspapers, more subscriptions to *La Chispa* . . . tomorrow—but it must be tomorrow already . . .

Who had been conceived that night? Who would be conceived in the early hours of the morning? It is already Passion Sunday. Memorable days are at hand.

MARTA AND MARÍA

I

ARDLY MORE THAN BABIES, Marta and María came to live with Father Martínez in Moyahua when their father died. Their mother was his sister. But she survived only briefly the climate and the shock of her loss, and the two little girls were left in the care of their grandmother. The grandmother, too, died, soon after her daughter, a victim to her years and to her asthma, for which the air of the village was bad. It was a blow to Father Martínez to lose his mother; he had depended on her . . . and his sense of bereavement was heightened by the problem of little girls not only unable to make a home for him but needing special care themselves, and guidance and tenderness. God alone knows how he managed, what efforts he made to be understanding yet just, to keep a balance between kindness and severity, to be circumspect yet helpful in all matters.

Marta is now twenty-seven and María twenty-one. Marta's soul is veiled in shadow, María's radiant, unclouded by the general inhibitions. Marta is pale and thin, with an oval face, deep-set eyes, bushy brows, and long lashes; she is flat-chested, with a thin, colorless mouth and a sharp nose; her step is quiet and her voice low. María, on the other hand, is dark, with a round, rosy face, a full mouth with a faint mustache on the upper lip, and big darting gray eyes; the tones of her voice are deep and playful. Both are strong-willed, the elder serene, the younger impatient. They have never been away from the village, but María's secret ambition, hidden deeper and deeper in her innermost being as she finds it seeming more and more impossible of realization, is to travel, at least as far as Teocaltiche. When she was younger, she used to enjoy (and even now, when she is absolutely alone and no one can know or guess she delights in it) imagining what a city is like: León, Aguascalientes, Guadalajara, Los Angeles (where her father lived), San Francisco (where he died), Madrid, Barcelona, Paris, Naples, Rome, Constantinople. She loves reading; she knows, almost by heart, the "Itinerary of the Holy Land" and the novel *Staurofila*. Since she knows how much her uncle dislikes this habit of hers, and he has often scolded her severely for it, she reads furtively. She used to be passionately fond of geography books but Don Dionisio finally took them away from her and forbade her to read them, for she would become excited, and ply him with questions, begging him to take her on one of the pilgrimages. When letters, advertisements, and newspapers arrived for her uncle, her eyes would devour the postmarks: Guadalajara, Mexico, Barcelona, Paris. In the Year Books where there were advertisements for sacramental wines, candles, religious supplies and the like, she never wearied of reading the addresses: Madrid, such-and-such a street, number so-and-so; and the newspapers . . . it's probably her fault that her uncle no longer takes any magazines except religious ones and *La Chispa;* he dropped his subscription to *El País,* which had pretty pictures and interesting bits of news in it. Father Reyes still gets it, and occasionally lends Father Martínez a few copies, which María reads in secret. Lately she has been reading *The Three Musketeers,* but she is no longer allowed to go and visit Micaela Rodríguez, who brought the book back from Mexico City. Micaela was her best friend; they had always got along well, ever since they were children; now that she is back from Mexico City, María can't even manage to see her and ask her about all she's seen. She admires her, and envies her, too. What dresses! She has

come home quite changed. Self-assured, and inclined to put on airs, but one can forgive her a great deal for having been to all these wonderful places and seen so many wonderful things: the motion pictures, theatres, restaurants, the train, streetcars; but Father Martínez didn't approve of Micaela's conversation and still less of her dresses, which he said were indecent, and he forbade her even to speak to María, and threatened to send her home if she ever set foot in the Presbytery again. It seems to Marta and María their uncle really doesn't like them to be friendly with anyone; he's more withdrawn from them every day, speaks only when it's necessary, conveys his meaning by glances, gestures; anyone would say that he had no affection for them, if he didn't give himself away by certain eloquent signs. Last year, for instance, when María had a severe intestinal infection, Father Martínez looked even more distraught than if he'd been her father.

María and Marta are, indeed, his one vulnerable spot; the effort he makes to hide his fondness for them is the best proof of the depth of his love. In his heart of hearts, his favorite is María, who came into his care when she was a wee thing, only a few months old, and whom he taught to pray (with what tender emotion he remembers!); maybe he even prefers her because of her waywardness, which gives him so much anxiety. Marta is a niece to depend upon; she keeps the accounts of the household and the parish, looks after the money and hands it out; she is the homemaker. What would he do, humanly speaking, if it were not for these girls, his own flesh and blood, almost his own children, what would the old man do without them?

II

It looks as though Leonardo Tovar's poor wife will not live the day out. They say her stomach and breasts are riddled with cancer and it's now showing in her face. God in his charity knows it's better for her to die and end the cruel agony that nothing can relieve. Two months of unceasing pain, getting no better, no nearer the end. She hasn't been able to speak or recognize anyone since yesterday. They summoned Father Martínez urgently, knowing she was dying. He hurried off there, leaving copies of *El País* in the dining room. María crept into a corner and began to read them furtively. The first one she opened was the issue of March 27 and there, in big headlines, was the following: ANOTHER WOMAN-SLAYER

Sentenced to Death. . . . The couple involved were mere children, the girl fifteen, the boy not quite twenty. They met and fell in love, experiencing the false and fleeting happiness that causes so many tragedies in this world. They had had no experience of life; they had not been trained in religious and moral principles nor had they learned to control their human passions; filled with misleading modern ideas, they were lost in their dreams, the awakening from which cost the life of one, and the destruction of the other. *Ephemeral and tragic* . . . Such was the love of Antonio López and María Luisa Boyer. The girl, young and pretty, soon tired of the love she had inspired in López, in whose heart, love, converted into caprice and desire, was too deeply rooted for him to let her leave him, as he would have done, no matter how painful, if there had been any religious feeling in his heart. Unfortunately, there was none, and Antonio López, who had known the pleasures of her love, refused to accept his dismissal. Their relations were brief, and, if they reached an understanding quickly and began to live together, they separated with equal speed. *After the orgy* . . . María Luisa Boyer fled from the house of Antonio López and went in search of other adventures and orgies, which we will forbear to relate. The Boyer girl's excuse for her conduct is obviously false, since the way of living she had entered upon showed an inborn wickedness. *The mad insistence of her lover* . . . As often happens in these cases, Antonio López didn't have sufficient will power to forget her, nor did she have any idea when she left him of the fatal consequences her action was to have within a short time. Antonio López hunted for her with the persistence of a madman, and, when he discovered where she was, went there and tried to rescue her from the house of ill fame. *I was afraid of him* . . . He managed to see her, though she tried to avoid him, because she was afraid of him and suspected that he was in a desperate mood. During their meeting, he begged her to return to him and she agreed, but apparently only through fear. They arranged to go to Toluca together the next day, but she didn't keep her word. He was furious and from that moment, swore to take a bloody vengeance . . . He came to the house where she was living; she ran and hid, but he persisted in his entreaties and she refused outright to go with him. Crazed with disappointment, he went off in search of a gun and returned with one in a short time. He found her, and without a word shot her twice, then turned the gun on himself, pointing it at his mouth. A bystander wrested the gun from him and the bullet went wide . . . The Boyer girl died a few days later and López was taken to Belén Prison, charged with homicide and rape . . .

The tolling of the bell reached María's hiding place, but, immersed in her reading, she paid no attention; she recalled the secret conjectures of a few months before, when the body of a woman was found in the stream at Cahuixtle, with seventeen dagger wounds in it. People said that a man had killed her, but the murderer had never been discovered.

Another newspaper, dated March 30, had a striking headline: GENERAL ACCUSED OF HOMICIDE BEFORE PEOPLE'S JURY, and as she read, her attention was caught by the following details: In the absence of Señor and Señora Olivares, General Maass had attempted to seduce their sister, but they discovered this in time to take strong measures to protect the family honor. In spite of having given his word that he would not attempt to molest Felisa, the General kept in touch with her by letter, and managed to talk to her through the window and make plans without the family's knowing it. María looked eagerly for the next issue: Señora Virginia de la Piedra, now the widow of Olivares, was present at the trial. This is the second General sentenced to death for murder. General Maass was sentenced to pay the funeral expenses and to provide a pension for the children of the victim. The convicted man entered Belén Prison.

The passing-bell, ringing the agony of the dying, changed to the tolling for the dead. Instinctively María started to pray. Her hiding place had been growing darker and darker. She was seized with a feeling of depression, sadness, a sense of shock. She often felt like this. The thought that her uncle would be back, wanting the newspapers, troubled her not at all. Still leafing through the other numbers, she found more headlines that caught her attention: SENSATIONAL DIVORCE IN GERMANY. WEDDING ENDS IN BELÉN. HORRIBLE TORTURES INFLICTED BY HUSBAND. And below, on the same page, with the subtitle "The Height of Immorality," an item from Tonayón, Veracruz. If her uncle reads this, he will ask Father Reyes to stop taking *El País,* for he cannot understand how a Catholic newspaper can print such scandals, even in the effort to prevent them; she can imagine what he will say:

"Did you read this? ('. . . in this town, prostitutes have taken a house and opened a canteen not far from the center . . . and in one of the most respectable homes, several young people . . . began drinking, went on and on, for the greater part of the night . . . suddenly they took it into their heads to go out into the streets naked, the girls as well as the boys . . . paraded through the streets, arm in arm, in this fashion . . .') Just suppose this were to fall into the hands of some boy or girl who had never even imagined such indecent behavior? You must not only cancel your subscription, but write a strong letter of protest to Sánchez Santos as well."

María wished she hadn't read the papers. She hastily put them back where she got them; but then she saw the announcement of the Diocesan Pilgrimage to the Shrine of the Virgin of Guadalupe; the newspaper printed a copy of the Archbishop's circular to "Parish Priests and Others," exhorting them to go, with as many of their faithful parishioners as possible, to Mexico City. The sale of tickets would begin on Easter Monday . . . "the pilgrims will have twenty days in which to make the journey in all comfort . . . the committee recommends to the priests the Hotel Colón in the street of San José del Real, and the London, situated in the street of the Third Order of St. Agustín . . . priests who head a group of pilgrims will have a free round-trip ticket . . ." Oh dear! Uncle will keep the circular to himself this year as in other years! Once Father Reyes had wanted to organize a pilgrimage and they almost quarreled. "This is where we'll celebrate our festival in honor of our Most Holy Mother, as the circular recommends to those who cannot go," is Don Dionisio's invariable answer to those who want to go. "The journey is full of dangers to body and soul; there are many inconveniences," he adds, and, to those who like their comforts, he describes the poor meals and the old beds in the hotels. He dissuades the miserly with an account of the expenses; and for the timid he has a full account of the evil customs and bad examples of the Capital. He interrupts María's pleadings with a "Well, we'll see," which he has no intention of fulfilling, and shows the same irritation as when she asks him to let her go away for a holiday.

"So Martinita is dead; the poor soul has gone to her rest at last." The voice of her sister brought María suddenly back to the darkness of the night and the narrow confines of the village.

III

At the dinner table Marta voices her pity—three or four times—for Martinita's little boy. "What will happen to him, such a wee little mite?" Then, a few moments later, "They say the poor soul's greatest worry was not knowing what would become of her little one." A third time, "Who's going to look after him? Neither Martinita nor Leonardo has any near relative, any woman who could take care of the child." When her expressions of pity broke out again, Father Martínez raised his eyes and looked at her steadily, with a mixture of concern, surprise, and disapproval, while María, coming out of her musings, remarked in a tone bordering on sarcasm: "It sounds as if you'd like to have him to look after yourself." Her uncle frowned sternly at this impertinence and she dropped her eyes. Marta, recovering rapidly, said, "No, but I would like to help find someone to take care of him; he's big enough now to start learning about God. I feel sorry for him, poor baby, losing his mother just when he needs her most." Turning to her uncle, she added, "Wouldn't it be possible for the Sisters in the Hospital to take him in?" Don Dionisio was silent for some time; finally he answered, "It isn't easy. We'll see what we can do. Let's see what Leonardo thinks."

"Why couldn't I take him and look after him?" is Marta's unvoiced thought, all her maternal instincts, human and fallible, to the fore. Marta still looks after her dolls, makes clothes for them, still, in great secrecy, and with a vague sense of shame, enjoys being with them. When María catches her at this, she teases her: "You ought to have children of your own. Your vocation is to be a mother." At other times she says, "If you don't get married, you ought to be a nun, one of those who look after children in orphanages." Marta blushes. She does love children. They are part of her dreams. Hasn't she been a mother to María? It was her job to take her in her arms, look after, spoil her, from the time she was a tiny baby. But she cannot deny that she has thought about having children of her own. In her innocence, she does not fully comprehend the mystery of motherhood; but she suspects that there is a mystery about it that it is forbidden even to ask. "Married people can and do have children; I know that some women also have them without getting married, but then, they're treated like lepers. Perhaps . . . but I'd better not worry about things that don't concern me."

All the same, her heart beats faster with confused emotions. There is nothing Marta likes better than to stroke the faces of children . . . to teach them the catechism. Marta looks after the little ones who come to the catechism classes; she has never wanted to change, and the tenderness with which she speaks to them, the sadness with which she bids them goodbye, are both very moving.

In spite of being a Daughter of Mary, it is the figures of the Virgin with the Christ Child that fill her with greatest devotion, just as in the Litany it is to Our Lady, Mother of the Divine Grace, Most Pure Mother, Mother Most Admired . . . that she addresses her most fervent prayers.

Over her bed hangs a picture of Mary, Our Lady of Succor, in her arms a beautiful child with a charming face. There are two other pictures in her bedroom, also in color. One portrays the Nativity: the Virgin is holding the New-born Child in her arms . . . it is Marta's greatest pleasure at Christmas, every year, to arrange the Parish Crib and a smaller one which fills the living room at the Presbytery . . . The other picture shows a guardian angel watching over the steps of a fair child.

Faithful Marta, loyal Marta, devoted Marta, mystic Marta, Marta the helper of those in need, Marta of the good advice, Marta troubled by thoughts and feelings she does not wholly understand.

HOLY DAYS

I

HE HOLY WEEK FESTIVAL really begins on the Friday of Dolores, the Friday before Palm Sunday. To the villagers the word "festival" signifies a certain easing of isolation and severity in their daily lives; work stops, special dishes are prepared, people spend the whole day in church or taking part in processions, visitors come from other villages, stalls are set up in front of the church and on street corners. In some homes, usually those on the outskirts, there are *incendios* with lighted candles that provide an excuse for relatives, close friends, and near neighbors to gather as at a wake; chairs are placed by the doorways, in the halls, in the patios, in the parlors; but instead of coffee, traditional cool drinks are served, and the cooing of the doves placed on the Altar of the Mother of Sorrows replaces the sound of sobbing. In the center of the village, homes with incendios keep their doors and windows shut, but not these on

the outskirts, which offer the people, each year, an opportunity to make a nocturnal pilgrimage, some to pay their respects, others just to see the altars, flaming with wax tapers and candles, whence the name "incendios."

What a pity the Toledos don't open their windows and doors to everyone! They have a big, beautifully fashioned, life-size Calvary, and, for this day, they build a mount and on it put trees brought from the hills, potted palms, cultivated flowers, pots with stalks of young barley growing in them, oranges on sticks and little gold flags, large glass balls of different colors; there are also doves, finches, canaries, and nightingales; lastly, tall candlesticks of burnished bronze which hold dozens of candles . . . an incendio that causes much talk and speculation every year, a legitimate source of village pride! Rivaling the incendio of the Toledos are those of the Delgadillos and Luis Gonzaga Pérez. The Delgadillo sisters have a proper Oratory with the privilege of holding public worship in it; the Patron Saint is the Virgin of Solitude, and they say that the grandfather of the present Delgadillos brought a beautiful image of Her from Guatemala more than seventy years ago; for the Friday of Dolores, they dress Her in a full skirt and cloak of rich black velvet embroidered with gold thread, they place in Her hands a lawn handkerchief with the Cross and Nails worked on it. "Can there be a more beautiful Virgin of Solitude anywhere in the world, such an expressive face that you can almost hear Her weep?" the Delgadillos ask proudly, and the whole village replies in unison, "No, there's no Virgin of Solitude in the world like this one." (In 1879 the Reverend Crescenciano Gálvez, Chaplain of the Oratory, published a thick book on the "History and Miracles of the Venerated Statue of Our Lady of Solitude, Worshiped in the Oratory of the Delgadillo Family in This Village"; whatever the authenticity of the facts related in this book, now very rare, the sense of the miraculous in popular fancy has been adding exaggerated versions of them and passing them from mouth to mouth: one Good Friday the statue sweated blood; one Fifteenth of September they heard Her weeping and groaning; when Maximilian was shot, the handkerchief She was holding in Her hands was soaked with tears. Ex-votos cover the walls of the Oratory: small gold and silver hearts, arms, legs, plaques, marble tablets with inscriptions . . . here, several dead men said to have been miraculously restored to life; there, paintings of accidents, quarrels, brawls; a shooting where the victim escaped with his life; ten or twelve etchings of diligences attacked, of robbers lying in ambush half-way up a mountain, of armed bands with guns in their hands surrounding a village. The people can visit the incendio at the Oratory. It is simple yet impressive. Behind the statue, a curtain of black velvet fringed with gold covers the Altar; against this, the whiteness of the face and hands of the Virgin, the trimming on Her robe, and the masses of Madonna lilies show up in vivid contrast. Around the reputedly solid-silver base on which the statue stands are seven rows of blood-red lamps; six large candlesticks—also of solid silver, they say—hold thick wax candles. ("It was mighty nice in the days of Don Fortunato, about twenty years ago; he used to bring musicians and a choir from Guadalajara for the Stabat Mater on the Friday of Dolores and he'd give money to the poor that night.")

Luis Gonzaga Pérez used to be a Seminary student and now his peculiarities have made him the talk and laughingstock of the village. He is the only son of Don Alfredo Pérez and Doña Carmen Esparza Garagarza, and very spoiled. The allegorical fascinates him; his incendio is always full of conceits and every year Father Reyes has to intervene to keep the boy's imagination from getting out of hand; his incendio contains a world of figures, from Adam to Porfirio Díaz, including Maximilian and Juárez; they are painted life-size on pieces of cardboard, then cut out and stuck on wooden frames by Luis himself. A couple of years ago, below the level of Calvary, he had portrayed the scenes of Abraham's Bosom and Hell; there he had put Juárez, Luther, Henry VIII, Nero, Pilate, and so on, with Don Porfirio, Maximilian, Hidalgo, Hernán Cortés, Charles V, and Godfrey fighting on either side of Golgotha, against Jews and Roman soldiers. Every Friday of Dolores there is great speculation as to what Luis will have thought up this year.

If Father Martínez had his way, there would be no incendios, which are "an excuse for worldly show"; he tolerates them but has succeeded in removing the greatest elements of dissipation. Naturally no one has prevailed upon him to visit the incendios in the homes, and it is only with great difficulty that Marta and María get permission to visit the Toledos' house for a little while. Marta is a close friend of Mercedes; they have no secrets from each other; it is at Mercedes' earnest request that Don Dionisio permits Marta and María to go out. ("What strangers will come to sow seeds of disturbance this year during the Holy Days?" This is the question troubling the Parish Priest, especially as he remembers the work, the long months, it has taken in other years to prune away the growths of a few days.)

Mercedes and Marta find some excuse to get off by themselves. "Have you heard the latest about Micaela? They say she's after Julián now. Did you know that?"

"That's just gossip, Mercedes," replies the gentle Marta, "Julián's a reliable boy. He's been courting you, hasn't he?"

"Oh, Marta! I can't stand it! I had to see you and talk to you. Ever since I've realized what Micaela is up to, and how bold she is, I haven't been so convinced that I shouldn't even think about Julián. It's been a terrible struggle, but I've actually come to feel sorry for the way I've treated him. I don't feel ashamed of his advances the way I used to, and I don't think it's a sin to think about him, either. To tell the truth, Marta, I never did really mind his wanting me. You're the only one I can talk to like this. Now that he acts so cold towards me, I feel as I never dreamed I could feel. What do you think I ought to do? I used to stay awake all night, trying to think up ways to avoid him, but now I do just the opposite. And the worst of it is, I'm not sorry about it. And me a Daughter of Mary! This very minute, I'll bet, she's trailing after him or he after her; they're probably at the Pérez' house, or in the Oratory, or they might even be pretending to visit the incendios down by the river. You're lucky not to be going through anything like this, it's just horrible! No matter how hard I try, I can't stop feeling this way, jealous, ready to cry, to fight, to die, full of hate—almost ready to be like Micaela. No, not like her, God forbid! Marta, why do you suppose there are women like her?"

Marta's black, deep-set eyes are full of sympathy. Two years ago, inspired by Marta's eyes and face, Luis Pérez conceived the idea of making his incendio with live people. In a state of exaltation, he went around exclaiming, "What a wonderful Dolorosa!" Don Dionisio has rarely been so angry as the day Pérez asked permission to carry out his project.

Marta, with gentle wisdom, takes Mercedes' hand in hers. "You've got to keep yourself under control. I think your feelings are perfectly natural, but don't let anyone suspect how you feel, least of all Julián. You've got to keep your dignity and remember your pride."

"Father and my brothers are constantly talking about the goings-on of Micaela and Julián and criticizing them. They pretend they think I can't hear them. I know they hope this will make me hate Julián, but it does just the opposite."

Marta listens, with deep understanding, to Mercedes' troubles; sometimes she interrupts her: "You must be prudent . . . Don't let anyone guess what you're going through or what you long for . . . I don't think it's wrong to want something when it's not contrary to God's law . . ."

(Marta of the good advice, where have you learned the wisdom of life? In what school did you learn prudence, wise Marta, Marta intuitively wise?)

They talk, too, about Leonardo's child, left with no one to look after him. "I'd gladly take him," says Marta. The prudent young girl breaks off this topic, so very close to her heart, to suggest that they'd better return to the living room in case someone is looking for them. "Hold your head up, Mercedes, and trust God. Whatever you do, don't let yourself get depressed, that's the Devil's work," is her final word of advice to her friend. (And you, Marta? Why are your eyes sad and your face clouded, mother undefiled?)

The house smells of the hillside, of pines, brought down in huge logs. "They cut them early this morning and it took ten strong mules, walking all morning, about twenty-eight miles, to bring them from Balcones."

"How well Sarita's barley did this year!"

"It just wasn't possible to get any more clover. Juan Díaz has some on his farm, but he promised it to the Parish Church and the Sanctuary for Maundy Thursday."

"And those lovely colored glass balls, how long have you had them?"

María couldn't wait. When Father Reyes arrived, as soon as the formal greetings were over and everybody had praised the incendios, she asked innocently, "When is the Pilgrimage to the Basilica of Guadalupe going to be this year if the twelfth comes at the beginning of Holy Week?"

"It's been postponed till April 21."

"Then why don't you persuade my uncle to let some pilgrims go from here? You're the only one able to get round him."

"María, you just can't get over your yearning for novelty, can you? You'll get your fingers burned again."

"You aren't going to start disapproving of travelling now, are you?"

"Look, before you go to bed, read what I've written down here. The first part of it was written by a Frenchman who knew a lot about this world, I think. Be sure to read it, now."

Here Sarita enters with some glasses of barley water and jamaica.

"Padre, did you go to the Pérezes' incendio? What ideas did Luis have this year?"

"He had the scene of the Last Supper. St. Peter had the face of Maximilian. At first he was going to make Judas look like Don Porfirio, but his father and I persuaded him not to. You remember last year he wanted to put him in Hell."

"He'll probably end up an anarchist."

"Judas has the face of Juárez."

"Were there many people there?" asked Mercedes, trying to mask her anxiety under apparent casualness.

"Well, you know Doña Carmen doesn't like many people."

"Who did you see, Padre?"

"Don Refugio, the druggist, was there . . ."

"Very changed since the Retreat, isn't he?" said Sarita.

"Thanks be to God! Don Timoteo was there, too; his trip to the Fair at Aguascalientes didn't come off because he got a letter from Damián; he's on his way home."

"Don Timoteo has headaches in store for him! And the village, too!" said Don Anselmo, "Heaven save us from the Northerners!"

"You can't even get into the Oratory."

"Just like every year."

"Do you believe all the miracles they attribute to that statue, Padre?"

"You'd have to examine each case." (Don Anselmo would have liked to insist on an answer, but Father Reyes rapidly changes the subject, turning to Mercedes and Marta.)

"I hope the Altar decorations for Corpus Christi this year will be good."

"Ask God to help us."

"What about the incendios on the outskirts?" asked Sarita. "Has there been any commotion? Are they crowded?"

On the corner outside "El Pabellón," in the shadows beyond the moonlight, near the Loeras' house, hidden from those going to the incendios of the Barrio Alto, some young men were talking in muted tones:

". . . I saw her going into the Oratory."

"So did I; she brushed against me as if by accident, in the doorway."

"What happened then?"

"First, accidentally, then . . . well, I'm a man."

"Did you enjoy it?"

"I'm a man."

"She kept looking at me as I went past."

"Then, I went on pushing against her, on purpose."

"You took hold of her?"

"I'm a man, after all."

"And she didn't make a fuss?"

"She didn't say a word. She was kind of laughing."

"That's the way she is at any gathering, they say."

"Did you follow her?"

"She went off with Don Alfredo."

"And was making eyes at Julián at the same time."

"I'd go after her if I were you."

"She acts like a streetwalker."

"All the better!"

"Tight-fitting dresses!"

"Enough to tempt anyone!"

"She's after Luis, too."

"And me, I tell you."

"She walks along with her mother and her aunt as if they weren't there."

"That Micaela Rodríquez! . . ."

(The conversation continued, interrupted by sudden explosions of hidden violence and sensuality, barely kept under control. The moon was full.)

María did not find Micaela. When she got home, more from perversity than interest, she read the passage Father Reyes had given her: "Some people become corrupted through much travelling and lose the little religion they once had; they see new cults, different customs, different ceremonies, every day." (La Bruyère.) She didn't want to read any further, and Marta picked up the sheet of paper: "To remain where one is, as one is, to avoid all change which threatens to destroy a perfect equilibrium, this is the desire of the classical age. The curiosity that stirs a troubled soul is dangerous—" (Marta read the words aloud. María interrupted her: "Don't you ever get tired of sermons!" Marta continued without a word.) "dangerous and foolish, since the traveller who runs to the ends of the earth never finds anything but what he takes with him: his human nature. And even if he should find something else, he would still have been living in distractions. Rather let him concentrate his whole soul on eternal values, which will not vanish into thin air. Seneca has said, 'The first indication of an ordered spirit is the ability to stand still and hold communion with oneself'; and Pascal has revealed that all man's unhappiness stems from the same source, the inability to remain quietly in one room. *This, too, comes from a lay author.*"

"Who's the author?"

"It doesn't say."

"It has all the earmarks of having been written by our uncle or his spiritual director." Without waiting for Marta to reply, María went on, "To change the subject, the bereaved husband, father of your little orphan, certainly won't be out visiting the incendios."

"Why do you say that?"

"Oh, just because . . ."

"María! You make me more and more afraid. Sometimes you seem to be downright wicked!"

"Marta!"

"Let's say our prayers. Forgive me."

(That night María had more nightmares, in which what she had read in the paper got mixed up with the events of the day. She and Micaela were walking along the street, laughing, when some boys came after them, tried to take them by the arm, to strip off their clothes, to take them down by the river, but policemen arrived and carried Marta and Leonardo away. General Maass shot at Uncle Dionisio, the Belén Prison was horrible, the man who got married that morning was there and lent her *The Three Musketeers*. They shot Micaela. Who shot her? The Parish Priest . . .)

"María! María! Wake up! Surely you couldn't have crossed yourself reverently!"

II

"I wonder how many boys dreamed about me last night?" thought Micaela, when she woke on Saturday morning. "What a pity Ruperto Ledesma won't leave his farm! David ought to take advantage of the Holy Days to come down; he's suggested it in

80

his last two letters. But Ruperto is sure to come in at just this time, too, and he's so touchy. Heaven help me! How these village boys act when they see a woman! Last night they were ready to devour me. And the girls? They were sizzling with rage. The boys were almost beside themselves. It was funny! Poor innocents! How they're going to suffer when David comes! That will teach them what a fashionable young man is like. And that goody-goody Julián who's already swallowed my line! Supposed to be in love with the saintly Mercedes! That conceited creature was getting under my skin . . ."

"What's the matter, Micaela? Aren't you going to get up and go to confession? The first bell for eight o'clock mass has already rung. Don't leave your confession till the last minute when there're so many people. On Tuesday or Wednesday it will be impossible. Just lying there awake gives the Devil a chance to put evil thoughts into your mind."

"Oh, Aunt, please leave me alone. I know my duty. You and Mama never get tired of lecturing me."

III

When he returned from the Seminary, Luis Gonzaga made out a timetable for using his time to better advantage and getting on with all the projects he had in mind. Get up at six-thirty, wash face and hands. Go straight to church. Meditate in a quiet spot. Seven o'clock, hear mass. Meditate on the way home. Breakfast at eight. Free time till nine. From nine to ten, study philosophy; from ten to eleven, Latin and Spanish, reading of the classics, and literary exercises (the thoughts of selected poets). Rest. Eleven-fifteen, one day drawing, another music. Twelve o'clock, alternate days, study geography and history. At one, dinner and free time, to be used exchanging ideas with some worthy and learned priest, concerning his studies, inner life, and other activities; three o'clock, a brief siesta; four o'clock, study mathematics, alternating with physics, cosmology, and astronomy; at five, academic and artistic activities; half-past six, tea and free time; half-past seven, reading of *The Christian Year* and other books of devotion; at eight, meditate on the Holy Rosary; half-past eight, supper and free time; nine-fifteen, silent meditation, customary devotions, self-examination, writing in diary, and straight to bed. He decided to take his meals in silence and live apart from his family, as far as possible; to visit no one except the priests; to choose a Spiritual Director. (He

wavered between Father Reyes and Father Islas, and finally decided on the latter.) He resolved to eschew firmly the sight of all
women; to make a list of his sins and particular faults in order to
overcome them, one by one, over a period of weeks or months. He
would try hard to keep his resolutions. On Thursdays and Sundays
he would go for a walk in the country, absolutely alone . . .

Alas! Every hour, every day, every week, the edifying schedule
was broken. By December, the December after he left the Seminary, he should have known "The Criterion" by heart and the two
books on the Philosophy of Balmes. Four years have passed and he
still hasn't finished the first book. He was absorbed in literature (he
read all the novels of Fernán Caballero, Father Coloma, and Pe-
reda); then drawing and painting became his main interests; then
music; later, architecture, designs for churches and altars; he began
to write a "Treatise against the Reform Laws" and a play attacking
lay schools and the impious press; recently, he has been sending articles against Liberalism, commentaries on Church Doctrine, and some
mystical poems to La Chispa and El Regional of Guadalajara, which
up to the present they have not done him the honor of publishing.
He wrote some "mysteries" which were sung by the Daughters
of Mary on the eighth of last December, and he is now compos-
ing a Solemn Mass. He wants to set up a branch of the Congregation of Mary in the parish. No one will ever manage to convince him
that the best men have not been self-taught; for this reason he left
his studies in the Seminary and every day he makes resolutions—he
has been doing this for four years—to stick rigorously to his plan of
study. Who has a better knowledge than he of world history, of
national history, or such an original point of view? When this Holy
Week is over, he intends to start writing a new "Theory of the Cos-
mos" that he has been pondering for some months now; when he
goes to Guadalajara in June, it will be to publish a book of his
poetry, and to get Don Amando de Alba to correct his "Ode on the
Centenary," which he means to send to El País next year, after pol-
ishing it with meticulous care. With this, he hopes to achieve undy-
ing fame. Then he will start on his great work: "My Judgment of National History and Suggestions for the Salvation and Prosperity of
the Country."

Yesterday, Palm Sunday, he composed a poem inspired by the
Procession of the Palms; he was quite satisfied with it, so that today he got up with great spiritual energy, ready to hold himself

strictly to his timetable. The morning was sunny; he seemed to enjoy the water on his face and arms more than ever before; he dipped his head seven times in the brimming basin. And in church, it was easy to lose himself in meditation on the Gospel for the day: Jesus in Bethany at the house of Lazarus; the description of the place was so perfect that he thought of making a painting of it that very day. Of course, disturbing thoughts came into his mind during the meditation: that forward Micaela who came to his house last Friday and tried to distract him was really disturbing. Was the Magdalene like that when she was a sinner? He wondered. The Gospel also mentioned Marta . . . Marta, the Parish Priest's niece . . . But he resolutely thrust away such thoughts and his soul grew light with the joy of this certainty: "Today is Monday in Holy Week and tomorrow must be the day on which Jesus visited Lazarus in Bethany." Ever since he was in the Seminary, perhaps even before, the coming of Holy Week has brought him a joy difficult to describe: he would like to compose great harmonies, paint great murals, write a poem, long or short, which would be one of the jewels of world literature. He is a different person, light-hearted, happy; gone is the excessive nicety of everyday, the fears, the failures, the pride, the frustration.

"Today is Monday in Holy Week. Tuesday and Wednesday of profound hope. Then ineffable Thursday, with its morning full of church bells, its afternoon solemn, and its night mysterious: Thursday which should never be over, but stay arrested, like Joshua's sun."

Luis Gonzaga, in his happiness, returns home and—curious metamorphosis, common to the mad—greets the passers-by affably. "Today is Monday in Holy Week," he says to them.

"And tomorrow is Tuesday," jokes Don Refugio.

"And then Wednesday and Thursday, Maundy Thursday," exclaims Pérez, ascending on clouds of joy.

IV

Early-rising Marta. At four o'clock the Parish Priest, after hearing so many confessions, came to lie down for a moment. Marta was already up, ready to see to the last-minute tasks of this great day (on which, as the Rodríguez Calendar informs us, every year "the Immaculate Spouse of the Lamb repeats the touching story of the Beloved Disciple: 'Jesus, knowing that the hour had come when He should return to the Father, having loved His own which were in the world, loved them unto the end' "). It was twelve o'clock last night when Marta got to bed, after they finished decorating the Altar. (It's going to be a surprise! All who see it today will say, "They really did a wonderful job.") She has been up late all week, making things for it; some nights Mercedes Toledo stayed with her, discussing the events of the day, both of them nodding, hardly able to keep awake.

But who doesn't work hard in the village on Monday, Tuesday, and Wednesday in Holy Week? They work doggedly, anxious to leave nothing undone, for no one will start work again before Easter Monday; if by midnight on Wednesday the tailor hasn't finished the suit, if the dressmakers haven't finished their work, if the shoemaker hasn't finished the shoes, there won't be new things to wear until later. Even the poor, the day laborers, the sick in the hospital, have something new for Maundy Thursday: a shirt, pants, sandals, and, ascending the social scale, shoes, dresses, shawls, ties, caps, derby hats. When daylight dies and the slow bells ring out, work is suspended—Monday, Tuesday, and Wednesday—so that all may go to the Mission: Rosary, the triduum of Our Lord of the *aposentillo*, public discipline, and procession of the Stations of the Cross; the figure of Jesus of Nazareth carrying His cross. When they come out, about nine o'clock, they have their evening meal, and work continues. The confessors do not stop to eat, the penitents teach the catecumens; the two tailors, the four village shoemakers, and in addition those from Cuquío, from Mexticacán, from Yahualica, from Nochistlán; and the seamstresses in each house hurry with their stitching; housewives in the kitchens hurry to do the cooking. ("Back in the old days," the women say to one another, "when customs were really Christian and the fear of God was in all hearts, no fire was lit in the homes from Wednesday to Saturday, and people spent all their time in church.") Some families still keep up the custom of not even preparing meals during these days lest the mind be distracted; they have the leftovers from Wednesday, fruit, bread, and boiled milk; but this excessive zeal is rare; it has become the fashion to eat sandwiches, and good fast-day meals on Maundy Thursday, which forms a kind of bridge between Holy Week and Good Friday. And now Maundy Thursday is here, eagerly awaited by all: the black-robed women, the children, the sick, the sad, the poor, the old; hot-blooded boys from the country in their Sunday best, and men who wear derbies . . . all look forward eagerly to this day, just as the children in other places—but not here—look forward to the Feast of the Three Kings.

Marta, like many others, is looking forward to nothing definite; but the general rejoicing and the prospect of the day ahead get her up before four o'clock. She is restless, but no one would notice it. She feels a vague and pleasurable anticipation, sad and joyful at the same time. Can it be a holy feeling? A profane feeling? Unable to keep still, she goes up into the tower to watch the day appear, to see the holy day dawn. The sun rises at 5:42 today, according to the Rodríguez Calendar. It is still night in the village, a moonlit night, but the morning star marks where the sun will rise. There is complete silence. Not even the dogs bark. The day about to be born is a day of music and light. The mysterious darkness and utter silence are fit prelude to its coming. Is that moonlight in the east, or is it the first glow of the dawn? Brightness slowly prevails, gently dispersing darkness. The silvery moon pales before it, the sky turns blue, yellow, green, then a soft pink; the clouds take on a rosy tint, and the slow-moving mystery bursts into a dazzling display, purple rapidly changing to bright-red, stately pavilions of a colossal Altar dedicated to the sun, which rises heralded by flaming gold. Thrilled by this starry liturgy, Marta tries to capture each second, each thousandth part of a second, to hold the infinitesimal changes of shadow and light which pass swiftly before her eyes, each more wonderful, more fleeting, than the one before. Now has the sun risen on Maundy Thursday. The morning of the Holy Mysteries is here. The sky a heavenly canopy. Marta hears invisible music, breathes a fragrance not of this world. Her ecstasy is heightened by the silence in the village, an extraordinary silence in this early-rising village, which occurs on only one, at most, two days in the year, an expectant silence, as early-waking ears are strained to catch the new note in the bells, for on this day the bells seem to ring out with a new yet age-old sound ("a perpetual memorial of the sufferings of His Passion and a sure token of eternal glory," says the Rodríguez Calendar), a sound as old as the ages yet new as though never heard before. Their peals ring out in the sacred silence, re-echoing in the splendor of the morning, shouts, songs, proclamations; such sounds are heard only on this day, no mournful note, no ordinary rhythm, different from any other Feast day, even Corpus Christi, the Assumption, or Christmas. At half-past seven, the first peal of bells rings out in the morning air, the summons to the Celebration of the day. What a word this is . . . Celebration . . . full of mystery, used only on holy days, grave and solemn, a compendium of the Greater Liturgy, to be spoken, as the villagers say it today, gravely, solemnly, with archaic reverence.

People come out in their new clothes in full view of all, and fill the streets and the Parish Church. On this day, too, cherished garments are taken out, garments worn only on this and other very special days. Today the women may wear colored dresses without exciting comment; no one laughs at the frock coats, gloves, and derbies of the men who carry the poles of the Canopy and the silver candlesticks, or at the boys in their caps and ties, or at the bizarre costumes of the country visitors.

All seems new because it is unusual, new and full of a bright, not mournful, solemnity: the Altar, the Chancel below, the Cross, the crosses, covered with white veils. How happily, yet how wistfully, in the radiant serenity of the deserted village, of the deserted treeless countryside, its sky adorned with shining clouds, the bells ring out their final Gloria, their swan song (for now they will ring no more), the final Gloria rung by the bells bidding farewell, their voices so rarely gay that when they start to ring on this morning of the Sacred Mysteries they fall silent; they will not sound the same on Holy Saturday or on Easter Sunday. The mass continues in plain song; the *matraca* sounds its rattle for the Sanctus and for the Elevation: the special wooden rattle with which the Liturgy speaks with a different note, beloved because seldom heard: soft tones of advice, inspiring renewed devotion: a catholic note, ecumenical note of the broken liturgy, an echo of the past, a past of tradition and fervor; a great unmistakable voice, heard only on the greatest days in the year: Maundy Thursday and Good Friday. (Would that the bells might never sound again their routine note, so that the spell of the past evoked in these Holy Days might always hold us fast.)

The congregation—villagers and people from the surrounding farms—begins to assemble as the time for the main procession draws near. A chaotic medley of banners waves above the crowd, banners of every variety, richly decorated and elegant, homemade and gaudy, painted and embroidered, beautiful and plain, some belonging to unknown and now extinct guilds, some from remote and deserted hamlets. Special scapularies, cords, and ribbons appear on all breasts; the woman who is not a Daughter of Mary is a Christian Mother; the man who does not belong to the Company of the Apostles belongs to the Order of St. Vincent; and all, young, old, men, and women, belong to the Order of the Good Death. On some breasts hang four, seven, or more medallions. Groups and rows are formed as candles are passed from hand to hand. The sacristan and his helpers light the candles round the Monstrance, behind the curtain which conceals it . . . a misty twinkling . . . and the outstanding villagers, in their medallions, ties, frock coats, gloves, polished boots, and solemn dignity, more dignified than princes of the blood, remain near the Canopy, among them Luis Gonzaga Pérez.

A messenger comes to Luis, sent by the Parish Priest: "Father Martínez says for you not to try to take part in carrying the Canopy, because he won't let you do it, and he'd rather not embarrass you in public . . ."

"What? But why?"

"Go ask him if you like. I'm just giving you his message."

Livid with rage, Luis Gonzaga rushes up to Father Reyes.

"Do you need to ask why? You went to the Spiritists' meeting, didn't you? And you'd better not make any objections . . . you know Father Martínez."

Luis Gonzaga's eyes are blazing. He would like the earth to open and swallow him up, or better, swallow the Parish Priest, his assistants, the faithful, the religious old women, the gossips: "Stupid village! Humiliating me, shaming me! Ignorant, fanatical, intolerant Parish Priest! Setting himself up against me! I'll complain to the Bishop. To insult me like this—me, the only intellectual in the village, the only cultured person! An artist like me embroiled with a parish priest like that! It's impossible. He'll pay for this! With his little culture anything is possible! He hasn't a grain of breeding! He shall pay for it! This is the last straw . . . I'll denounce him! I'll publish a pamphlet, several scorching pamphlets, pour ridicule on him, expose him, with all his prejudices, his narrow-mindedness, his blind fanaticism, his fierce attacks on everything progressive. I could avenge myself, too—yes, I could—with one of his nieces. That's what I'll do! Just see if I don't! And I'll stir up the people against him. Down with clerical tyranny! Down with the rule of ignorance! I'll become an Apostle of Light; I'll encourage reading; I'll organize a club for free discussion; I'll end the isolation of families with little parties, picnics, plays. Micaela has already suggested this, and no one shall stop us now. And scandal. A scandal every day, until the village gets used to it and overcomes its prejudices . . . What if I did go to the Spiritists' meeting? Why shouldn't I be interested in everything that concerns mankind? If people are being deceived or misled, I can fight the evil if I know about it. If Father Martínez had his way, nobody would read anything, no one would bother about learning or culture. How he infuriates me! I'll forget prudence! He'll find out what kind of enemy he has to deal with now!"

Breathing fire, Luis Gonzaga rushes out of the Parish Church into the country. The empty streets and fields are shining in the sunshine on this morning sacred to the Holy Eucharist; no people in the streets, no bells, merely the soft spring breeze and the slow-moving, silvery, feathery clouds. The freshness, the intense, exciting freshness of the morning.

The rhythm of church worship continues faithfully. When the Tabernacle returns in procession from the Atrium, to the accompaniment of the beat of the matraca, deep sighs, the hum of many prayers, and the *Pange Lingua,* sung with grave solemnity by Father Reyes' choir, the veil covering the High Altar is drawn aside and the wonderful "Monument" can be seen, an allegory of the Feast of the Tabernacles, the latter like huts made of flowering branches, and in the center, the great Tabernacle of the New and Everlasting Testament. A whispered buzz of admiration goes round, "What an original interpretation! What good taste! How appropriate!" say the villagers, well-versed in these matters. The comment is repeated, in tones of surprise, by those who have forgotten or who have never heard of the Jewish Prophetic Festival.

"What wouldn't Luis Pérez, with his love of allegories, have given to have this brilliant idea . . ."

"Luis? He was here, all ready to help carry the Canopy, when he suddenly rushed out like one possessed by the Devil, muttering to himself."

"He's losing this Thursday."

"I think he's lost the whole week and it's not his fault. Do you want to bet that the Parish Priest had something to do with the way he rushed out?"

"Very likely."

"I'd like to know why, and I'll soon find out, just as I managed to learn about the message he sent to the Rodríguez family."

"You didn't tell me that. What did he say?"

"That if Micaela came to church in her fashionable dresses, he'd order her out in front of everybody."

"I didn't see her."

"She must not have come. Let's see if she comes to the Ceremony of the Tabernacles, to the Washing of the Feet, or to the Arrest."

A pause for breakfast and the worship continues. People come and go, like a fine column of black ants. The most devout visit all the churches: black-robed women, austere old men, young farm lads, wide-eyed children. Meanwhile, diligent hands are filling the kitchens with all kinds of savory smells, trying to get just the right taste, for this is the only day in the year when it is permitted to enjoy one's food, and also, on this day alone, double pleasure, is it permitted to break through the customary isolation and send from house to house, different tidbits, *empanaditas,* all kinds of cakes, *capirotada y turco, chongos,* salads, fruit, jams; the whole village, old and young alike, enjoy themselves, big and small look forward to the Feast of Maundy Thursday, special day of joint family rejoicing. (*Where is the room where I shall celebrate the Passover with my disciples? And he will show you a big room, carpeted, and there you will prepare the supper. . . . With great desire have I desired to eat this Passover with you before my Passion, since I shall not anymore eat thereof . . . Love one another. . . . By this they shall know that ye are my disciples.*)

Then, at the beginning of the silent, luminous evening, as the people are finishing their dessert, the rhythm of worship pervades the patios and sidewalks; the sound of the matraca is heard by all, sounds like those of creaking carts, or, to those who know the sea, like the roaring of the waves.

"It's time for the service of the Washing of the Feet."

"They're summoning us to the Ceremony of the Washing of the Feet."

"It's time for the Washing of the Feet. Hurry up."

"Hurry up so we can get a seat."

"There'll be a crowd."

"The Apostles are coming out."

The Apostles are coming out, watched by the curious, standing around the open doorway of the Tiscareños' where the Supper for the twelve was held. (Twelve poor men, just out of the hospital.) Embarrassed by the stares, they walk with their heads down, dressed in white cassocks tied with brown girdles. (Marta wanted them to choose young boys from the catechism class for the Apostles, as they had done in other years, silent young boys, eager to learn, lads from the poorest families.) The matraca sounds its second call. (Marta would have made their garments, given them their meal, and performed the ceremony of washing their feet.) When the matraca sounds its last call, there is no more room in the Parish Church. The devout throng around the benches of the Apostles. The Parish Priest (*as He had loved His own which were in the world, He loved them unto the end*), after washing and kissing their feet, the towel still girt over his alb, goes up into the pulpit and preaches on the text: "Et vos mundi estis, sed non omnes. Sciebat enim quisnam esset qui traderet eum: propterea dixit: Non estis mundi omnes."

The people began to realize with surprise that Father Martínez had been preaching on Judas' act of betrayal ever since Passion Sunday; but this sermon at the Washing of the Feet left them in no doubt as to the local application of the theme; it was a violent sermon, like those on the "Four Last Things," and the allusions were so clear that people began to try to name the Judas, or the Judases, of the Parish.

"Can it be Luis Gonzaga Pérez?"

"It sounds more like a woman. It might be Micaela Rodríguez."

"I think he means the law clerk."

"It's more likely the Deputy."

"I bet he's referring to the Spiritists."

"But are there really Spiritists here? I can't believe it."

"Of course there are! Just as there are Liberals and even Masons. They say some people ate meat today and killed a pig so they can have cracklings tomorrow."

"Heaven help us!"

"Who? Oh, just rumor; I wouldn't dare put a name to them."

"Fire and brimstone will rain down upon this village."

"And all the plagues of Egypt."

"Even Masons here! I'd like to know their names so I could at least cut off one of their ears."

(Are there none, among those so shocked, who had better keep quiet, being in no position to cast the first stone?)

It is a lovely clear evening. The countryside is deserted, but the streets are swarming with people. (María thinks of the people visiting the Tabernacles now, at this moment, in the streets of Guadalajara, Mexico, Puebla, Madrid, and Paris.) The peaceful glow of the evening, the changed appearance of the people in their new clothes, the opportunities to chat between station and station banish gloomy thoughts. People walk with a new step, their faces are different; new steps, new faces, full of life. Groups go through the streets, praying; glances meet and sparks fly as from a glowing brazier when the wind blows.

There are new faces in the village; the one that arouses the greatest curiosity is that of a lady . . . "How elegant her hair looks! What an unusual face! But how beautiful she is! And her eyes! They must be painted. How pretty her shoes are, so shiny. That must be what actresses look like. Yes, she might be an opera singer, they're the most elegant. But they say opera singers don't speak our language. That's true, they're Italian or French, I'm not sure which. She certainly can't be a teacher, with such fashionable clothes. Of course not. And have you been close to her? I happened to be right beside her during the visit to the Oratory. What perfume! She smells nicer than any flower. Like Micaela Rodríguez' perfume? Good gracious! There's no comparison. Even her clothes are quite different from Micaela's! As different as night is from day! And she walks like a queen. She must be a 'society' woman, as they say in Guadalajara. But bad women can dress like rich ones. Do you think that if she was that kind of woman the Pérez family would have invited her? Of course not. That's just a manner of speaking. I don't think we've ever seen such a really fashionable woman in the village."

"Well, I don't think much of these fashions. These so-called 'fashionable' women look ridiculous . . . it's only natural when they come from Guadalajara for the boys to make fun of them."

"Even if it weren't for her clothes, you must admit that her face, her eyes, her whole appearance, her way of looking at things, of moving her hands, her walk, is very distinguished, very 'aristocratic,' as they say in Guadalajara; a lady who's staying with the Pérez family and is being showered with attentions by Doña Carmen . . . They say she arrived late last night, after they'd given up expecting her . . . Her name is Victoria . . . I don't remember her surname, it's a very strange one."

At the time of the services, scarcely anyone noticed her in the crowd, since she was wearing a shawl over a simple dress; but now, at the Washing of the Feet and the visits to the Seven Altars, they all seem to be staring at her, fascinated, men, women, even the children.

"Some cousins of the Rubalcavas were there, too. They're from Ixtlahuacán. They say the oldest is married and lives in Guadalajara."

"The youngest, over there with Mercedes Toledo, looks full of life."

"The one with her face pitted from smallpox?"

"That's right. Don't you think so?"

The Loeras have a family from Aguascalientes staying with them. The Cornejos from Mexticacán, who come every year, are staying with Don Cornelio Ruiz. There are people from Cuquío, from Juchipila, from Moyahua, from Yahualica, from Nochistlán, from Teocaltiche. The houses are full of guests, and the inns are overflowing. Tonight and early tomorrow morning, there will be still more new faces. Among the strangers from the farms there are some pretty girls, twelve, fourteen years old, scarcely more than children, but with blushing cheeks already, and shy, troubled eyes.

There are students, too, home for the holidays; and villagers who have moved to nearby settlements.

"What a fine, sturdy lad Esteban turned out to be! He was such a puny little boy."

"Eulalio Rubio has grown sons already."

"Matilde Gómez' two daughters are young ladies now."

"Pedrito Robles has his whole family with him. I hardly recognized my godson."

"Time just stands still for Luis Cordero; he hasn't aged a day since he went to live in Guadalajara."

"But Ponciano Plasencia, now, looks so old you'd hardly know him. All that trouble he had certainly left its mark. One of his sons was a Mason and I heard the Masons killed him because he wanted to leave the Masonic Lodge."

"That's true. He died without confession, too."

"They poisoned him."

"Stabbed, I heard."

"No one knows what really happened."

There are some students from Guadalajara over there, who came with Darío, Don Pánfilo's son. Stuck-up creatures, with their scornful glances, big words, and tight-fitting clothes!

There're some outsiders too, unknown to anyone in the village, who have come just out of curiosity to see what's going on. They are staying at the inn and wander about like dogs in a strange house.

Micaela Rodríguez is still waiting, a little disappointed. Time is passing and David has not arrived. He wrote her from Guadalajara on Sunday that he was on his way. What can have happened to him! Couldn't he find anyone to bring him? That's what comes of living at the end of the world, in a village with no means of communication.

Micaela visits the Altars with her parents, attracting hardly any comments, indifferent to the interest aroused by the elegance of the lady staying with the Pérez family, indifferent to the remarks of the youths from Guadalajara, indifferent to the attentions of Julián. and to the presence of Ruperto Ledesma, who looks at her with tears in his eyes.

Steps, voices, glances, like birds just set at liberty, like children when the teacher leaves the room, weave nets, pierce walls, chase shadows over the golden ground, over the velvety patches of golden ground: the vast countryside, its evening curtains gilded by the sun, the sun, heart of all things, forge of the world. Merciful sun, good Father of all, good Shepherd who leads the flock along mysterious paths, making faces and garments shine, and quickening desires.

"Didn't you go to the Sanctuary? It's beautiful."

"We've just come from St. Anthony's. Father Vidriales has done a wonderful job with his Monument."

"We're going there now. Don't miss St. Michael's."

("It's pagan sensuality that seeks to adorn altars," the Parish Priest says reproachfully.)

Many, for pleasure rather than from devotion, visit the Altars several times. They go from the Parish Church to the Calvary, from the Calvary to St. Anthony's, from St. Anthony's to the Church of the Sacred Heart, from Sacred Heart to the Oratory, then to the little chapel of the Magdalene and the Sanctuary of St. Michael out on the edge of the village.

First as a joke, then piercing the crowd like a dagger, the rumor spreads that Government troops are coming to keep them from having the processions and to see that the Reform Laws are kept.

"Unfortunately, the rumor seems to be true. News has just arrived that the troops had their siesta in Potrerillo, sixteen miles away. The Liberals in Teocaltiche started this, incited by Don Pascual Pérez, God forgive him! And how many here are in league with him? [Unanimous protests.] I had news of this last week, but I didn't want to believe it, nor spread it. I hoped that God would change the minds of the wicked. Now we can only put ourselves in His hands and resign ourselves to His holy will . . . Put up your swords and do not expose the village to harm . . . No, no, I assure you that Don Román had absolutely nothing to do with it and is as sorry about it as I am. Don't bother him. That would complicate the situation and it would be unjust. Leave him in peace. Father Reyes is going out to meet the troops and those who wish, may go with him; but let them be few and level-headed . . . The rest of you, try to calm the people down. Let's carry on the strictly religious program just as if we had nothing to fear. The public ceremonies? Well, we'll see, depending on the circumstances. As a personal favor to your Parish Priest, I beg you, don't harm anyone. I trust you. Let's leave the punishment of the wicked to God."

With the removal of all doubt, general apprehension increases. A number of villagers, among them some of the least expected, make excuses, but finally four are chosen from the volunteers to go with Father Reyes.

With the coming of evening a shadow of apprehension spreads over the village. In vain does Don Dionisio rush out into the street, overcoming his habitual reserve, to enhearten and calm the people. Many of the visitors have gone. Windows and doors are shut again as though it were not the Thursday of the Blessed Sacrament. Churches and chapels are again left in solitude. A few men gather in the Atrium and make grim plans. Only Marta has eyes for the gentle twilight, a twilight the color of forget-me-nots, splashed with streaks of flame.

In the Parish Church, Don Dionisio preaches the sermon on the Institution of the Blessed Sacrament to a reduced congregation. He continues to use texts which refer to the traitor: "Truly the Son of Man must go, as it is written, but woe unto that man by whom He is betrayed: it were better for him never to have been born." The people regain courage and, as the moon comes up, when the matraca sounds and the mournful fluting of the *chirimías* is heard through the streets, the people with great resolution, as though they had reached a common agreement, parents overcoming their own fears for the sake of their children, husbands for the sake of their wives, flock in a body to the ceremony, procession, and sermons of the Betrayal, which are pathetic as never before, on this night of vigil, when each one feels himself the ordained victim of the enemies of Christ.

"They say that they'll take the whole village prisoner, without respect to women or children; not one stone will remain on another. It will be another Jerusalem."

"Let them do what they will. After all, it's for Our Lord and our holy religion."

"We'll suffer gladly, like the martyrs."

"Nothing will stop our confession of the Faith."

Fervor increases, producing hallucinations. Suddenly, with no warning, the silence of the night is rent by the words of the Miserere, uttered with one voice, in the streets, in the Atrium, in the Parish Church.

Over the Nochistlán road, the moon is rising, a blood-stained moon whose steady glow turns the night darker and the singing and the hidden emotions more fearful, and brings a lump to the throat. One man hears the soldiers approaching. Another can hear their shouts, can detect the lust to sack and pillage in them. Yet another can see the shadows of riders approaching the village from all sides. It needs only the bells to sound the tragic alarm.

"No sight or sign of Father Reyes. What do you suppose has happened to him? Nothing good, that's sure."

"How worried his sister must be and the wives of those who went with him!"

"This is a moon of ill omen. No one can convince me otherwise. My hunches are never wrong."

"Moon of Judgment Day. The end of the world has come."

Now the cohorts and the servants of the Chief Priests and Pharisees are at hand to take Jesus of Nazareth prisoner; they carry lanterns, axes, and weapons; men of the Brotherhood of the Garden of Gethsemane, dressed like Roman soldiers and Jews as their tradition is, have charge of the scene; no one wants the role of Judas, because of its nature, and the bad luck it brings, so they draw lots; this year, whether he likes it or not, it has fallen to the lot of a tenant farmer of Don Inocencio Rodríguez' whose name is Emilio Iñiguez and he is trembling as though he were about to be put to death.

The crowd waits at the corner of the Square as the sermon on the Agony in the Garden comes to an end. (The pulpit and the Altar of Our Lord have been set up in front of the church, and Our Lord, surrounded by the twelve Apostles, who pretend to be asleep, is prostrate before an angel who offers Him a chalice by the light of the moon and eight thick wax tapers.)

The people, in high, mournful voices, chant the Act of Contrition. The sermon on the Betrayal begins. The crowd, headed by Judas, advances. The hinges on the statue of Jesus of Nazareth move.

The Parish Priest: "Sleep on now and take your rest. It is enough. The hour is at hand, the time now is when the Son of Man will be handed over into the hands of sinners. Rise, let us go hence, for he who will betray Me is at hand."

"Whom seek ye?"

"Jesus of Nazareth."

"I am He."

The crowd moves back and falls on its knees. The voice of the Parish Priest continues:

"Whom seek ye?"

"Jesus of Nazareth."

"I have already told you that I am He; if ye seek Me, leave these alone."

Judas moves forward and, in a trembling voice, barely audible to those standing nearest, says, "Greetings, Master," and kisses the cheek of the carved figure.

"Friend, wherefore art thou come? Judas, betrayest thou the Son of Man with a kiss?"

The Jews lower the statue from the altar, tie the hands, the people weep, the flutes play again, the Procession of Our Captive Lord starts on its way . . .

"Yes, yes, through the streets, as always!" shouts the crowd. And with tears and prayers, they go around the Square, take the street to the right, pass in front of the Oratory, return to the Parish Church, and the Divine Captive is placed in the little room off the Baptistry.

But the people, anxiously waiting for the arrival of the enemies of true religion, have no wish to return home, especially since Father Reyes and those who went with him have not yet returned.

In hushed tones, they tell of things they remember, legends, terrors, horrors.

Remember what happened to Riestra some years ago? This Riestra was a tax collector who insisted that the innkeeper's wife give him meat and pork on Maundy Thursday and Good Friday; nothing would induce anyone to slaughter on those days to satisfy his whims; then, gun in hand, he tried to make the innkeeper's wife prepare tripe and sausages for him; the people turned on him and if it hadn't been for the Parish Priest, Riestra wouldn't have been alive to tell the tale; the villagers had to be content with burning a Judas resembling him. Furious, he ordered the people to apologize; troops were sent, many of the villagers were taken prisoner and carried off to Guadalajara, some even taken to Mexico City, where their relatives had to buy substitutes for them in the Army before they were allowed to return. They were nearly sent to San Juan de Ulúa. The late Gregorio López went mad as a result of this business . . .

"There was a moon like this the year cholera broke out . . ."

"They tell you you can go, and when you think you're free and turn around, bang, bang, they shoot you where you stand. That's their *ley fuga.*"

"Look at García de la Cadena who was betrayed into their hands . . . and Ramón Corona that Don Porfirio had assassinated because he wanted him out of his way . . . and all those shot in Veracruz, with the famous order, 'Strike while the iron's hot!' "

"I think they've taken them for the Army. The Liberals don't respect even priests. Look how many they've shot, cassock and all!"

"Just like in the days of Rojas and the '*chinacos*'; my father used to tell me that when they passed through a village, their favorite pastime was to throw children up in the air and catch them on their lances."

In this atmosphere of strain, María, Father Martínez' niece, silently accepts the idea of a violent irruption of strange men. She takes pleasure in imagining it. She may not be the only one.

But sleep gradually steals over the village. Only the Apostles, who take turns watching with the Lord all night, Don Dionisio, Father Reyes' sister, and the wives of those who went with him, resist weariness and go on praying with dogged persistence for a miracle.

V

Good Friday. On getting up Luis Gonzaga knelt down five times in memory of the Five Wounds. He had just done this when he heard from his mother a version of the "miracle" which had so moved the village.

"Give thanks to God, my son. Haven't you heard yet? No, of course, you couldn't have. Father Abundio and those who went with him have returned safe and sound. The soldiers retreated. It was a pure miracle. Just fancy! With no apparent reason, the stream at Ocotillos rose as it does in the rainy season and stopped the soldiers; some who attempted to cross, at the command of their leader and urged on by the wretched law clerk, were swept away and drowned. The others were so frightened they went back to Teocaltiche. The villagers who went and Father Reyes himself saw the stream still very swollen and can't explain how it happened; they learned also from the people around what the soldiers intended to do and how fast they made their way back. Do you think that in the face of such a plain miracle they will tempt God again?"

"They may."

"I just pray God that this season will pass peacefully."

"So that we can have a good time again."

"What a boy you are, Luis! No, but so our worship won't be interrupted."

"Indian mummery! I don't see how the Parish Priest, with all his zeal, still allows it to go on."

"Good gracious! You really do dislike Father Martínez. And I don't say . . ."

"No, don't say anything, Mother mine. Don't even lie to me."

"But you mentioned him first. I'm telling you that no good will come of your reading the Holy Bible as you please, like a Protestant."

"Are you going to start on that now?"

"No, let's change the subject. What do you think of the miracle?"

"Oh . . . It was raining in the mountains . . . it was just a tale that the federal troops were coming . . ."

"You have a mania for criticizing everything. Sometimes you sound like a heretic. People saw them coming and the people of Ocotillo heard them say they were going to take Father Martínez prisoner."

"That would have been a great idea!"

"Be quiet, for heaven's sake. Victoria may hear you. What would she say? She's up now. And, by the way, Luis, I wish you'd be a little more attentive to her. Yesterday you refused to visit the Monuments with her. Won't you at least go to the processions? They're what made her decide to come. The Rubalcavas have invited us to use their roof. You can hear the sermon of the Meeting so well up there, and at night the one on the Sacred Burial."

"It's no use keeping on. I've already told you that nothing will induce me to go to these tableaux, this Indian mummery. Of course strangers come to look at us, as if we were a Punch and Judy show. The village ought to be ashamed of allowing these primitive customs to continue."

"But Victoria was telling me that in Germany . . ."

"Germany or no Germany, I'm not going and that's that. I'm going out into the country as I do every Good Friday. No, I won't even go to the services."

"I hope God won't see fit to punish you."

The worst of the storm unleashed by yesterday's rage was passing off in Luis' shallow, changeable soul. He will not always be an apostate; but he will never speak to Father Martínez again, and he will do his best to have him removed from the village. The thunder still rumbles in this capricious genius, only child, spoiled and worshiped by his parents; no one, not even those parents, can contradict him, and when they make bold to offer even a timid remonstrance, they act like subordinates dealing with a superior.

He would have liked to go to the services, but he wasn't willing to risk a public rebuff. He contented himself with reading the Mass of the Catechumens. *Flectamus genua.* This was the Mass he wanted to celebrate more than any other when he aspired to the priesthood, perhaps because of its special ritual. *Levate.* He still thought about it. The yellow candles extinguished, the altar bare. *Flectamus genua. Levate.* Priest and servers bowing low. *Levate.* In the funereal silence, a muffled chant, unnamed, with no responses. *Flectamus genua. Levate.* And the dialogue of priests and choir: *Passio Domini Nostri Iesu Christi secundum Ioannem.* Imitating the voices, Luis chanted: *Quem quaeritis? Responderunt ei. Iesum Nazarenum . . .*

Ecce Rex vester.

Illi autem clamabant: Tolle, tolle, crucifige Eum . . .

Erat autem scriptum: Iesus Nazarenus, Rex Iudaeorum . . .

Quod scripsi, scripsi . . .

Et inclinato capite tradidit spiritum.

The slightly ironical laugh of their guest Victoria interrupted him: "There you are at last, Luis. Will you come with me?"

The young man's eyes flashed fire, but he controlled himself and didn't even turn around.

"You look like a full-fledged priest."

He went on chanting the prayers. *Flectamus genua. Levate.*

"When you're ordained, I'll come and make my confession to you, you're so serious." He shot a furious look at the impertinent intruder.

"You're just like your Parish Priest."

Speechless with rage, he shut his missal. He wanted to give vent to his feelings in furious words. The woman had gone. He felt ridiculous and proud, boorish and shy, uneducated and cowardly at the same time. He took his copy of *The Names of Christ*, and, making his way along the deserted streets, went out into the country.

Flectamus genua. The roads and even the paths were deserted. The sight of the vast horizon filled Luis' soul with the spirit of the day, and the sight of the huge Mission Cross which dominates the village moved him to make up for the services he was missing. He began to chant: *Ecce lignum Crucis, in quo salus mundi pependit*, and, kneeling down, continued, *Venite, adoremus.* As he climbed the mountain, he kept repeating: *Ecce lignum Crucis* . . . and, bowing low, with his face to the ground: *Venite, adoremus.*

The verses of Jesus' Lament re-echoed in his memory: "O my people, what have I done to you or how have I afflicted you? Answer Me. Because I brought you out of the land of Egypt, you prepared this Cross for your Saviour. *Agios O Theos. Sanctus Deus. Agios ischyros. Sanctus fortis. Agios athanatos, eleison imas. Sanctus immortalis, miserere nobis.* What more could I have done? I planted you, My most beautiful vine, and you have rewarded Me with bitter fruit; you quenched My thirst with vinegar and with a spear you pierced the Saviour's side . . ."

The landscape . . . earthy, chalky, treeless . . . is a fitting background for the day.

"For you I smote Egypt in her firstborn; and you have handed Me over to be scourged. O my people . . ."

Good Friday landscape. No refreshing shade, no fountains, no greenery.

"I opened a path for you through the sea, and you have opened My side with a spear. O my people . . ."

Yellow, parched lands, like the dried bed of an ocean. The sun glitters in the sky as in a sea of bronze.

"I went before you in a column of smoke; and you brought Me before Pilate's tribunal. O my people . . ."

The distant lines of walls and furrows mark out the landscape in asymmetrical patterns. The heat of the sun burnishes the brown earth and the deep ocher takes on a blood-red hue.

"I sustained you in the desert with manna from on high; and you wounded Me with buffetings and lashes. O my people . . ."

The village is as though turned to stone, its bells silent as death.

"I gave you refreshing water from the rock to drink; and you gave Me vinegar and gall."

Village, proud of its resemblance to Jerusalem, to which, because of its desolate landscape, because of its air of lamentation, a missionary from the Holy Land was assigned. Village of Crosses.

"For you I smote the kings of the Canaanites; and you smote My head with a reed . . . I gave you a royal scepter; and you placed on My head a crown of thorns . . . I lifted you up to a position of great power; and you lifted Me onto a felon's cross . . . What have I done to you, My people? How have I afflicted you? Answer Me."

He reaches the Cross. *Venite, adoremus.*

From the Cross he has a panoramic view of the village facing it; streets, yards, patios, rooftops, all turned like an opening flower towards the Cross on the mountain. Along the streets, first one, then another, then more and more, women in deep black make their way towards the church. *Flectamus genua.*

The Atrium is packed with people, the shirts of the farm laborers make white patches among the black robes of the women and the mourning of the fashionable. What woman dares to go out today with her head uncovered? No one would dream of such a thing. Deep grief from early morning till late at night. *Levate.*

Beside the Cross, Luis Gonzaga kneels. *Flectamus genua.* From the Cross he sees the village with its houses. *Levate.* The arches of the empty arcades surround the deserted Square, their pillars of worn stone gleaming in the sunshine. Only the names of the shops can be seen . . . shops with their windows and doors tight shut. The patios are empty. *Flectamus genua.* Everyone is in church, except the women who have come from other places to sell food to the visitors; they stand waiting near the market with saucepans, clean plates, glasses, cups, and tablecloths, placed on makeshift tables. *Levate.* In the farmyards lambs and sheep, tame deer and pigs are

all left together; the silent cocks parade, their hens and chicks around them. The only sign of motion is the graceful fluttering of the doves from roof to roof; but the thick black path of the swallows cuts across the flash of white in a childish game, unbefitting the solemnity of the occasion. *Flectamus genua.* The panorama distracts Luis, brings back sights, memories; he fixes his glance on one spot after another and his memory flits around in white-and-black flights, like doves and swallows, like butterflies and bats. *Levate.*

"My village, bitter and uncomprehending, ungrateful, indifferent. I love you, and you reject me. I thirst for your glory, and you humiliate me. I fight for your greatness, and you resist me. I strive for your reputation, and you scorn me. I lie awake long hours planning for your prosperity, and you make a jest of my aspirations. My sacrifice is a source of mockery unto you. My sufferings raise your laughter. You jeer at my travail, and there is no undertaking of mine that is not subject to your ridicule. Rightly indeed have they compared you to Jerusalem. The day will come when your hardness will turn to amazement, your indifference to tenderness. When you hear my name proclaimed on trumpets, you will repent of the insults showered upon me, you will reach out to draw me into your now unwelcoming arms. O hermetic village."

Not a cloud in the sky, not the slightest breath of wind, a burning Good Friday morning.

"You will try to remember what I looked like, it will be your delight to recall my gestures, my steps, the things I liked. All will claim to have been present at my birth, to have cradled me in their arms, taught me my first words, discovered signs of talent. You will throng my favorite places. You will set apart the places where I lived on earth and where there are legends of me. You will ask the people who knew me, and you will be surprised not to have felt my presence, foretold my future, heard my voice."

The sun is directly overhead; not even the shadow of a cloud. Time seems to stand still.

"From this place, I can read your history and your secrets; I am moved by your pettiness and wretchedness. To me, as I stand up here, free from you, you look like a Punch and Judy show, and I can move the puppets according to my fancy: first those in that box where the dead repose, good and bad, all mixed together, their graves forgotten with the passing of the years. Where is the tomb of Benito Zamora, the terror of the region in the sixties, a Liberal hero, shot down behind the Parish Church, when he was caught red-handed, one morning, boldly trying to recapture the village Square? They buried him next to many of his victims, perhaps beside my grandfather, whom he killed and dragged to the Cemetery to the sound of music and firecrackers because, in two hours, he collected only four of the five thousand pesos demanded as a forced loan. My grandfather liked music and had founded the village band? Well, he would have all the music he wanted up to the Cemetery, where they buried him without a coffin. I wish they would all come alive, in whatever garb they please. Would the men and women, united within the walls of the Cemetery, separate again? There, mounted on one of his famous horses, comes my conquering great-grandfather, the Don Juan of the district, famous for his affairs with women; he rides towards the house, looking for Victoria; it is useless for my uncle, the priest, to follow him, useless for my jealous great-grandmother to shout after him, useless for his legitimate offspring to try to stop him.

"Now the scene changes. It is the village without pianos where my mother weeps throughout her honeymoon, losing the wonderful voice which moved Guadalajara, crossing the deserted streets as a stranger. I see her walking through the Square on her way to church, a pretty girl of eighteen. How the black-robed women and the narrow environment have changed her! In this very Square, over there under the first arch, in front of Don Refugio's shop, Don Cipriano Valdés fell dead, at the hand of Father Soto. What an unforgettable scene! It was a Holy Saturday, and no one dared accost the murderer, who was wearing a cassock and carrying a gun in his hand. No one ever knew where he disappeared to. My village, with all its crimes and sorrows! Under that roof, I was born; my father under that one over there; that's where my grandfather died, and we carried him along that street to his funeral: that is the first thing I can remember. Weeping, near this wall, my mother bade me good-bye the morning I left for the Seminary. Today, all is deserted. No boys are playing, no men looking towards the river. Up there, Retreat House is shut and gloomy, as lonely as the Cemetery opposite it. My village, village of stone and dry wood. Victoria, why do you pursue me? Why did you interrupt me when I was praying for virgins and widows, especially for widows? I will conquer your obstinacy, my village, I will conquer the obstinacy of your Parish Priest and your blindness. I was born to save you, and your jeering exalts me. Victoria, your eyes are full of seduction, and you are a widow; but I am high up on the hill now, and from here I no longer see your charm. I shall come back the morning you go away . . . may it be soon! . . . and take with you Micaela, María, Mercedes, Marta, Gertrudis, and Isabel. Why am I thinking about you today?"

Down below, the black and white specks can be seen moving in the Atrium. It must be the Procession. Then, the voices of the Choir can be heard distinctly, singing:

> Vexilla Regis prodeunt:
> Fulget Crucis mysterium . . .

Hysterically, in one of the fits of exaltation that often seize him, moved by the solemn hymn, Luis Gonzaga climbs the steps leading to the Cross, and, kneeling, embraces the wood, crying out, "Deliver me from my thoughts!"

THE CHOIR: Qua vita mortem pertulit, Et morte vitam protulit . . .

LUIS: Deliver me from the assaults of the Evil One.

THE CHOIR: Beata, cujus brachiis Pretium pependit saeculi . . .

LUIS: Deliver me from all evil, present, past, and future.

THE CHOIR: Ut nos lavaret sordibus, Manavit unda et sanguine . . .

LUIS: Deliver me from sin this day.

LUIS AND THE CHOIR: O Crux, ave, spes unica . . .

In this state of exaltation, Luis resolved to go down to the village, make a public act of penitence, apologize to the Parish Priest, kiss his feet, and then retire to a monastery and seek admission as a simple lay brother. With the eager desire for monastic life, there came into his mind another hymn that he probably learned in the Seminary, and he sang it aloud:

> Crux fidelis, inter omnes
> Arbor una nobilis . . .

Suddenly the thought came to him, "If anyone down below should see me so transported, I might appear boastful and presumptuous."

He leaped up and began to run in the opposite direction from the village. From time to time, with the phrase *Flectamus genua* ringing in his ears, he would turn towards the Cross, fling himself on the ground, and burst forth: "We adore Thee, O Christ, Who didst, through Thy Holy Cross, redeem the world and me, a sinner. Amen." *Levate.*

With these words on his lips, his soul filled with lofty resolutions, he hurried on. *Flectamus genua.* Beside a cliff he sat down in the bright sunshine, opened *The Names of Christ,* and began to read the page beginning with "Mountain." *Levate.* The prose fascinated him and he remembered Father Reyes' words: "Luis, you are a Catholic like Chateaubriand; you like the externals of religion and the aspects which appeal to the senses. You aspired to the priesthood in order to deck yourself in its robes, so that people might kiss your hand. You were right to give it up." No, no, Abundio is wrong. To seek literary quality in spiritual readings is to kill two birds with one stone. (Today, this expression is irreverent.) Of course, people are often won by literary excellence.

"But the proof that I am not attracted by the showy side of religion is that I come to this lonely spot to avoid the tableaux that attract so many curious onlookers from other places and at which all the villagers without exception are present. This pagan Indian custom shocks me. I have told Father Martínez so. 'How can you permit such customs?' I asked him. And I described what happened last Good Friday during the procession of the Christs brought in from the country districts. The people from Zapotillo with their small Christ were blocking the way of those from Jarrilla, who usually head the procession with their huge Christ. The steward from Jarrilla shouted to the others, 'Get your measly little stick out of our way!' The others replied, 'Listen to that! It's done more miracles than your big log . . .' and they almost came to blows over it. The throng of men from the farms will now be joining the Procession, dressed as scribes, Pharisees, and Roman soldiers; there are Pilates; any peasant from Manalisco, from Huentitán or from Las Huertas may appear as Simon of Cyrene, the Centurion, Barrabas, Gestas, Dysmas, the Holy Apostles . . . Pah! And the people gazing in wide-eyed admiration! It's just as well that Our Lord and the Virgin are only images. And such swarms of people you can't even hear the sermons from the middle of the Square; and the Passion represented in all its stages by common people; and Victoria, who prides herself on her fastidiousness, enjoying herself . . . No! I won't think about it anymore. Let them enjoy themselves on this sacred day. As an act of contrition—*Flectamus genua*—I will do penance."

And he crawled on his knees over the stones, kissing the ground at intervals.

"Contemplate, my soul, the place where they laid on the bruised shoulders of Our Beloved Jesus the weight of the Cross . . ."

A snake suddenly darted out beside the penitent and his first impulse was to kill it. A whole world of superstitions crowded into his mind, superstitions concerning Holy Week, especially Good Friday . . . what happens to anyone who kills a snake on this day, to anyone who bathes in a river, who eats an herb called Iscariot. He can see Mina Hill, where idols were found buried, and they say that on Maundy Thursday morning and Good Friday night you can hear a silver bell ringing; he remembers all the tales he's heard since he was two years old, miraculous and impressive: the pilgrims who were turned into stone because their attention wandered during the Via Crucis at the sight of some swallows; the Wandering Jew who arrived in the village many years ago and brought an eclipse of the sun; children born on this day who turned out to be freaks.

"They're probably talking about these and many other silly tales, at this very minute in the village. It makes me ashamed to think that they believe such things! But why didn't I kill the snake a few minutes ago? It got away from me while I was thinking this nonsense."

He tried to go back to *The Names of Christ;* but the fear of falling into folly made him prefer meditating on—*Flectamus genua*—the path to Calvary, trod under this same sun at this same burning hour, eighteen hundred and seventy-six years ago that very day.

At his chronological exactness, the demon of irony drew near, planting seeds of criticism and doubt.

"I believe! I believe! I believe!" cried the ex-Seminarist, feeling himself about to fall into temptation. "*Et ne nos inducas in tentationem . . . ,*" he implored. "*Dignare die isto sine peccato nos custodire . . . ,*" he added, exhausted, turning his eyes towards the already distant Cross of the Mission.

"I won't fall into critical subtleties today. I believe. '. . . suffered under Pontius Pilate, was crucified, dead, and buried.'"

The sun was reaching its zenith. The horizon was shimmering with waves of heat. Sky and earth, with no sheltering shadow, were alike implacable. Heat beat down from above, heat rose up from the center of the earth, heat pervaded the atmosphere in solemn silence.

"This is the moment when they should be reaching Calvary, yes, when they should be taking off His garments, this is the moment when under the burning sun they gave Him gall mixed with vinegar to drink, this is the moment, too, when in the gloomy silence there should be heard from the Hill the first stroke of the hammer, on the hand of God Himself. *Flectamus genua.* Blessed be forever our Great Lord, and His Most Holy Mother, who suffered such great grief.' " *Levate.*

Flectamus genua. "This is the moment when they should lift up the Cross. It must be twelve o'clock. *Flectamus genua.* From now till three, that dreadful hour when the world came to an end with the murder of God, I shall remain motionless in the position of a cross, on my knees. *Flectamus genua.* That is what the Parish Priest should do instead of carrying out pagan mummery. Alas! No. To think thus is a grievous sin of pride . . ."

And he beat his breast, remembering a thousand and one prayers in Latin and in Spanish. "Lord, I have sinned . . . we have sinned, and the burden lies heavy upon us . . . have mercy on us . . ."

The mystical rapture was increasing. Superstition made him contort his face in grotesque grimaces to drive away evil thoughts; he twisted his arms and crossed his fingers; he felt that his abject body was the dwelling place now of God, now of the Devil; he rolled his eyes until only the whites showed, and longed to feel his body rise into the air; he was seized with the most tormenting despair, thinking himself condemned for life. In this confusion, the words on his lips were nothing more than mechanical echoes: "*De parentis protoplasti* . . . Well, then, lady, to look at you, to touch you, to enjoy you, is to be deceived . . . *ars ut artem falleret* . . . Consider, O my soul . . . Through your immaculate conception . . . *terra, pontus, astra, mundus* . . . In this valley of tears . . . *quo lavantur flumine* . . . Our debtors . . . When I contemplate the heavens . . . These, O Fabio . . . *flecte ramos arbor alta* . . . Thou shalt honor . . . Foolish men . . . Sing, heavenly muse . . . *Pange Lingua* . . . On swift feet . . . We owe a hen to Aesculapius . . ."

He struggled with his thoughts; words and phrases flowed dizzily into one another. The sun was hammering his temples and neither mind nor devotion could concentrate on the Seven Words.

108

The weak flesh trembled, the knees bent and almost let the body fall, and he could no longer hold up his arms. With what remained of consciousness, he realized from the length of his shadow that it was not nearly the end of the three hours, only half-past twelve; there was still time, an endless time, before three o'clock.

"I will fight against weakness and try to watch the agony of Our Saviour for two more hours."

The buzzing in his ears grew worse and worse. Long before one o'clock he collapsed.

Down below, the Procession no longer moved along the paths. Those returning early would do so after they had heard the words of the penitent centurion; but most of them would come back in the moonlight after the Holy Burial and the Sermon on the Bereavement.

Everyone keeps strict fast—today there is no fire in the kitchens—lips are white and dry, and heavy garments aggravate the heat. There is scarcely time to rest in the shade. And this sacrifice is only right, when one thinks of the suffering the Saviour endured in such hot sunshine. The houses, the halls, the patios, are empty. Processions and services follow one another with little interruption. Exhausted, sweating people gladly go through the day. The sermon of the Seven Words is over at quarter-past three. At four o'clock the sermon on the Spear Thrust takes place. At six, the meditation on the Taking Down from the Cross; there is no pause . . . Procession of the Holy Burial, the condolence sermon . . . in the Atrium . . . the depositing of the coffin with the figure of the Dead Saviour in the Convent outside the walls, and the Procession, accompanied by weeping, of the Soledad, whose image, together with those of St. John, the Magdalene, and the Holy Apostles, returns to the Parish Church. At nine o'clock, or ten, the people eat a piece of bread, a tortilla sprinkled with salt, drink a little water, and thus bring the day to an end.

OLD LUCAS MACÍAS

I

O, OLD LUCAS isn't the oldest inhabitant—there are many old men in the village—but he has the longest memory and the liveliest wit. He's an animated public inventory of individuals, families, deeds, and events. Something of a soothsayer, "not through witchcraft," he says, "but just from old age," he knows a little law and a little medicine, but would never dream of trying to make money from his knowledge. He can't read, but by sheer persistence manages to inveigle someone into reading to him whatever books, papers, or magazines he can lay hands on. If he had the money, he would pay someone to read to him all day long. In this way he has forged his philosophy, or distilled it out of his experience and reading, so that he never errs in remembering a date, recalling a precedent, prescribing a solution for a problem, suggesting a legal recourse, or predicting the future. They call him, jokingly, "the philosopher of the

wake," because he is always there beside the coffin, pouring out his ideas and advice in full spate.

A faithful chronicler, he has no personal history; all his life he has been merely the observer and recorder of things that have happened to other people; he knows his own age only approximately; he is certainly over eighty, because he remembers clearly when his father went off to the Texas War, and to the Pastry War, too, when they cut off Don Antonio's leg. Antonio's name is always on Lucas Macías' lips, as well as the names of other famous men of the time: Bravo, Pachito García, Don Valentín, Alvarez, Comonfort, Zuloaga, Don Benito, Don Miguel, Don Tomás, Osollo, Maximilian, Carlota, González Ortega, Rojas, Lozada, Escobedo, Vallarta, Don Porfirio. Lucas never met any of them, for he has never been out of the village, but he knows as much about each of them as if he had been an intimate friend; he knows their special characteristics, the way they dressed, their life within the family circle, all details related to him by people close to them. With the same profusion of detail he describes places which he has never seen: streets, squares, villages, and cities which he has never visited—"the room where Don Benito died, looking out on Moneda Street, just a block from the Cathedral as you go towards the Santísima . . ."

"But you've never been to Mexico City, Lucas."

"What difference does that make? I've got imagination, haven't I? Lots of it. I'd rather imagine than see some things; I can see them life-size then, in my mind's eye, I don't have to see them as they are now."

His sense of smell and his keen sight are the mainsprings of his memory. He loves betting with the young men as to who will see things first from farthest away, who will first recognize those coming down from the Cross or along the ridges of the distant hills, who can identify from the Cemetery those going up to the Calvary. And he nearly always wins. The present and the immediate future do not interest him much, except for their resemblance to the past, and as an indication of the future. Lucas seems almost indifferent to the present, but, when the present becomes history, the scenes come rushing back vividly into his mind as he talks.

The main topic of conversation in the village at present is the enigmatic Victoria, but Lucas shows no sign of being aware of her visit. For him, the important happenings of the moment are: the return of Damián Limón—since the shock of his arrival caused the death of his mother, and the news brought such a crowd to her wake; the illness of the Parish Priest; and Luis Gonzaga's seizure. In the past tense, as is his wont, old Lucas Macías comments and prophesies:

"I was a boy when a circus once came to the village; it was a famous circus, but they certainly had a bad time of it and had to leave in a hurry. They didn't even make enough to buy their food, and no amount of pleading could get them credit at any of the shops; to make matters worse, one of the dancers got double pneumonia, so, as they couldn't take her with them and weren't willing to leave her behind, they made one last effort one Sunday and invited all the people to a final performance. For some reason the clown took it into his head to start making remarks about how close-fisted the people were, how mean, saying that the people of Nochistlán knew how to appreciate a good thing, and he set the village in an uproar. Some of the people, raging like firebrands, broke up the show with a few well-aimed stones and swarmed up to the inn to drag out all the performers—to shave their heads, some said, to duck them in the river, according to others.

"It was like the Day of Judgment, and the troublemakers were getting more and more out of hand. They battered at the doors of the inn, which the owner had just managed to get locked. Don Ladislao Anton (may his soul rest in peace!) arrived at this moment, and since he was the village elder, managed to make his way through the crowd. By this time, a lot of people who hadn't even heard the clown, had joined in the fray, and when a tomato hit Don Ladislao right in the face, he got furious, laid about him with no respect for persons, yelled for the police, and if the Parish Priest, who had been visiting the circus people with some of the friendly villagers, hadn't arrived at that very moment, there's no telling how the affair would have ended. They gave the circus three hours to clear out. That was about three in the afternoon, and before five, off they went, more dead than alive, escorted out of town by the Parish Priest himself and two of the clergy, as well as Don Pablo Casillas, Don Aniceto Flores, and Don Crescencio Robles (may God rest their souls!). They stayed with the circus people along the Teocaltiche Road until they passed Mascua . . .

"But what I started out to tell you about is that the dancer, almost dead from pneumonia and shock, was taken in by one of the families in the village. You know the old saying 'Condemn the sin but not the sinner.' Well, to make a long story short, the sick woman got better, and after she was completely well, she said she didn't want to leave the village and would like to repay their kindness by working for the family as a maid; if she couldn't do that, she begged them of their charity to find work for her, as she could sew, do fancywork, and paint on linen. There was a lot of hesitation and some doubt about taking a woman of her class into the family. For all of her modest behavior now and her desire to serve, she had led a wanton life and she was still attractive. But she turned so devout they could hardly get her out of church, and by her persistence she managed to stay on, in spite of the meanness of a lot of people. She embroidered handkerchiefs for one woman for free, painted some cushions for another on the same terms, and did the little lamb, which, as you know, is so life-like it almost talks, on the banner of the Perpetual Veil. She greeted everybody with great humility and people began to like her better. They even came to think of her as a virtuous woman, so much so that the idea of a miraculous conversion spread about. She went about all muffled up in black clothes to keep from looking like the dancer who had scandalized so many when she pirouetted half-naked on the trapeze, turning and twisting like a snake.

"But many of the men couldn't get that sight out of their heads. They kept watching her, trying to get her to 'be nice' to them, though she gave them no occasion to act like that and she seemed harder to approach than any other woman in the village. Nobody could ever be sure (and the truth will probably be known only on Judgment Day) whether she was a crafty hypocrite or whether temptation finally proved too strong for her. But the fact is that one fine day the villagers breakfasted on the news that she'd run away with the oldest boy of the family who'd taken her in, a boy who was studying at the Seminary and who used to come home for the holidays. He'd certainly had his fun with her before. He gave up the Church, and people heard later that they were trying to make some kind of a living on the stage, and that she finally left him, ruined, a gambler, and half-crazy from drink. (They even said that she'd started him drinking when she was in the village, and that she had bewitched him.) The poor fellow ended up in a madhouse, and died a lunatic, though he was so talented, so outstanding in debates and public speaking, and had had such an excellent record that everybody had thought he'd have a brilliant future. You all know that most men who leave the Church end in a madhouse, especially when there's a woman at the bottom of it. I've never seen one get over it."

"But Luis Gonzaga hadn't taken Orders," objected one of his hearers.

Lucas paid no attention to the present, to which the interruption was designed to bring him, but went on enumerating instances of the bad fortune which had overtaken not only priests but even just students who had left the Seminary because of a love affair.

II

"Well, I didn't get to the Fair at San Marcos!" Don Timoteo was obsessed by the idea; for the thousandth time it re-echoed in his brain as he sat quietly without a word at the end of the hall.

"I do hope Father won't make any trouble about giving me my share of Mother's legacy," was the thought in Damián's mind while, at one moment, he spoke of his deep grief and the next he was telling proudly of the wonders of the North compared with this "backward" country.

"What's Damián going to do?" This was the question which tormented Bartolo Jiménez, now the husband of the girl who had been going to marry Damián.

"Perhaps this will soften Don Timoteo's heart, so he'll forget that little debt I owe him," was the hope of at least one of his debtors.

"I'd rather have the father, now that he's a widower, than the son, any day." This feeling stirred in the heart of one anonymous woman, in the secret depths where desire is not yet conscious.

What would Don Timoteo do? Would he marry again? This question was asked by men and women, and most agreed, without putting their thoughts into words, that he was still "hale and hearty."

"He's capable of burying another wife! How the dead woman clung to him!" thinks Doña Dolores, the ironing woman.

"How ugly my aunt looks! I wouldn't go close to her for the world," thinks one of the young girls, distant poor relations, given a home by Doña Anastasia, but really treated as servants in the house. And another, "They say she's asleep, but she isn't breathing, and they won't leave her alone for a minute; but they don't go up to her, either, even Uncle Timoteo and Uncle Damián seem afraid of her, and so does her friend Gabriela, who says she's so fond of her, and Doña Pepa, who used to hang round her like a sheep dog."

"What could Uncle Damián have done to her, for her to die as soon as he got here?" wonders the first girl.

"She certainly won't be scolding Justina and me for everything anymore, or pulling our hair; she was really bad-tempered," thinks the second girl.

"She was so mean; she didn't even like giving to the Church." (Doña Rita, the seamstress, remembered her meanness.)

Don Ponciano Retes was thinking, "Father Reyes had no time to get what she was going to give to the Church. She was already dead when he arrived, and he absolved her only conditionally, sprinkling Holy Oil on her." (The gossip was spreading. How dreadful! They say she didn't have time to make her confession! Damián's sin is all the worse!)

"It was probably her fault that Timoteo was so close-fisted!" This, from Petra, Julio Trujillo's widow.

At her age, poor soul, maybe because of being paralyzed, she was a martyr to jealousy; she wouldn't let any woman even speak to Don Timoteo. These and many other hidden thoughts, memories, hopes, unflattering opinions, grudges of different kinds, were present at Doña Anastasia's wake, circling around, invisible, unexpressed, disguised in polite comments which meant the opposite. Thus the man who thought that the dead woman's soul was in mortal peril because she died without the aid of a priest, said out loud that she was to be envied for always being prepared for the end; those who were remembering her defects vied with one another in praising her virtues: "so pious, so charitable, so home-loving, so patient under the afflictions visited upon her by Our Lord . . ."

Nearly the whole village was there. It was eleven at night. The mourners were beginning to go home. The room where Doña Anastasia was laid out was almost empty; the only ones now left were a few women talking to Doña Remigia, who was always summoned to care for the dying.

"She was already dead when they sent for me. But I shouted the prayers in her ear, anyway. I remember, when Praxedis died suddenly, he heard me and moved his head as though joining in the words I was saying." Then more gossip: The stranger hasn't come, and won't come now. They were bringing Luis Gonzaga, unconscious, along one street, as Damián arrived by another. Out of respect for the family of Doña Tacha, there were no Judases that year. Then she returned to her grievance . . . "When they sent for me, she was already dead . . ."

The patio and the hallway were still full of people. Some were talking about the bulls at Aguascalientes, others of how Luis Gonzaga Pérez was found unconscious. Someone started to laugh; many seemed to have forgotten why they were gathered together. But these were brought back to thoughts of death by those who took the opportunity to suggest another rosary for the departed soul.

At half-past eleven Clementina, Don Timoteo's oldest daughter, and her husband arrived from Jalpa. They'd been expected since nightfall, as a special messenger had been sent off early with the news. Clementina burst into passionate sobbing, and Prudencia, the old maid of the family, upon whose brain for the last twenty-four hours the single thought has been hammering: "Damián killed her! Damián killed her!" began her long-winded account.

"We were all in bed when we heard a knocking at the door; I heard father get up to see who could be there at that hour of the night. But I heard nothing more, and as I was tired after going to all the services and taking part in all the processions, I was about to drop off to sleep again, thinking that Mother hadn't been awakened. But I heard her calling out: 'Aren't you going to see who it is? I believe Damián has come.'

" 'I don't hear any noise,' I said; 'Father's gone back to bed.'

" 'Go see who it is, for heaven's sake,' she begged me.

" 'But, Mother, there isn't a sound.'

" 'Then I'll get up myself, even if it kills me,' she said, getting angry. 'I heard Damián's voice distinctly.'

"To keep her quiet, I began to put on my clothes.

" 'Hurry up,' she kept saying. When I went out I found that she wasn't mistaken. There, in the kitchen, were Father and Damián.

" 'What're you doing up?' Father asked me. When I told them how excited Mother was, they looked more worried than ever.

" 'We must be careful not to give her any kind of a shock,' Father said.

" 'She won't listen to me; you'd better go.' We both went in.

" 'What ideas you get in your head!' I told her, 'Lie down and don't keep thinking about things that are bad for you.'

"She got furious. 'You're both trying to deceive me; I heard

Damián's voice clearly and I want to see him; my heart tells me my boy is here.'

"We spent half an hour trying to quiet her down enough to go to sleep. Father was sure that Damián hadn't spoken since he'd come in, and that she couldn't have heard his voice, for he'd warned him to be silent the minute he saw him, and made them lead his horse slowly to the stable so Mother wouldn't hear it.

"She ordered me to get her clothes so she could get dressed; when Father insisted that she lie still, it only made her angrier. Then he said: 'To please you, I'll go and see if anyone has come from Guadalajara who can give us any idea when Damián will get here.'

" 'If you refused to let him come into your house, bring him here right away, unless you want me to get up and go get him.'

"I stayed to get her ready, so the shock of actually seeing him wouldn't be so great. I made her some orange water and rubbed her with cologne. When they came in, a little after midnight, she tried to get out of bed and was weeping bitterly. When she put her arms round Damián, she had convulsions, and then an attack . . . [Here the sobs of the listeners broke out again.] By this time the girls were up. Father and Damián went to fetch the Parish Priest and Don Refugio. We kept trying everything we could think of: we rubbed her with alcohol, put cold compresses on her; we couldn't bring her back to consciousness; I felt that she was dying and there were still no signs of Father or Damián. We started to pray while we were still trying to bring her round; I sent Justina to the Presbytery to look for Father and Doña Remigia, but she had barely left the room when Mother gave two sighs and it was all over." (Here Clementina's sobbing became louder.)

Then Doña Remigia took up the story: "Neither the priests nor Don Refugio were at home; they had gone to the Pérezes house because some men had come across Luis Gonzaga lying unconscious by the roadside and brought him home. Father Reyes and Don Refugio came with Don Timoteo as soon as he found them, but it was too late then."

Clementina's sobbing again interrupted the account, this time louder than before.

"Then Mother didn't have time to make her confession?"

"Yes. Father Reyes gave her absolution and anointed her with

Holy Oil while she was still warm; and she was always prepared; Father Martínez brought her communion just last Thursday—Maundy Thursday—and she'd asked for it again tomorrow, Sunday. May death find us all as well prepared!" ["No, no." Neither the fearful listeners nor the speaker are ready to die with their sins unconfessed.] "She can't even have had to pass through Purgatory, since Our Lord had already sent her there with her twenty years of suffering. In this and all the other troubles which Our Lord has visited upon her since the death of Rosalía, her resignation has been an example to us."

"Have you let our brother Pancho know?"

"We sent a messenger early this morning and hope Pancho can get here before the funeral; that's why we put it off till ten o'clock . . ."

At midnight they arrived with the coffin. There are no funeral homes in the village; when one's hour comes, Don Manuel or Don Gregorio starts making the coffin, to measure, the same day. Many, in their devout determination to be prepared for death, have their coffins and the wax candles which will be used at their wakes made while they are still alive, and use them as a theme for meditation; some of them keep their coffins and shrouds for fifteen or twenty years, in their bedrooms or even in a more conspicuous place. Don Timoteo was always opposed to the pious desire of his wife to be prepared like this and they had quarreled about it.

The coffins are usually simple, stained with pitch or varnished; they cost from two to five pesos, depending on the wood and the finish, and are ready in two or three hours. Sometimes, though, vanity demands its luxuries, even here: wood of the best quality, lined with cloth or silk, or well-lacquered, with good hinges and brass-headed nails, at a cost of sixty or eighty pesos, which would have been "better spent in masses" in the opinion of the villagers. Damián insisted on having an American style of coffin, and they had to send to Teocaltiche for the glass and metal medallions to put outside, and a nickeled crucifix. They wanted so much extra that Don Gregorio, the best carpenter, would have preferred to turn the job down. It occurred to him, but he kept this to himself, that they were likely to be asking him to make a coffin for Luis Gonzaga Pérez at any moment and he wouldn't have enough wood. As usual the curious invaded the street where Don Gregorio's workshop was, and crowded round, watching the grim task, until the carpenter shouted at the boys: "Go watch Don Manuel, he's making a coffin for Manalisco." Don Manuel had his curious onlookers too, who went to and fro from one workshop to another, but Don Gregorio had the larger audience because of the novelty of the "gringo style" coffin.

"When will the things arrive from Teocaltiche?"

"What time will you finish, Don Goyo?"

"How much are they going to pay you for such a job?"

He had enough of the questions. To his friends and important members of the community he made civil answers, but even though he threatened the youngsters with his handsaw, plane, or hammer, and told them to go pull cats' tails, he couldn't get rid of them. He had to stay up till midnight, and the crowd stayed too. At the house, the arrival of the coffin renewed the commotion.

"How beautiful it looks! . . ." "What luxury to put in the ground!" These comments came from the street.

Loud sobbing broke out again in the house itself. Prudencia and Clementina were almost exhausted. Don Timoteo got to his feet and, in spite of opinions to the contrary (it was the local custom not to put the body into the coffin until just before leaving for the church, unless it had begun to decompose), gave orders to proceed with the painful task.

Clementina begged to be allowed to say just one more rosary for her mother while she was still lying on the bed. This was done. Then the women stood around.

"How tight her eyes are shut!"

"Right away, as soon as I thought that the Judgment was over, before beginning to dress her, I put salt on them and kept my fingers on the eyelids for a long time."

("They're really sunk in her head, like a corpse; I'll dream about them tonight," thought Doña Dolores, the ironing woman.)

"Shall we take off the cloth round her jaws?"

"Better not; they might fall open."

(With her thin mouth and protruding cheek bones, she looks like a skeleton; her bony hands are clasped together, the black dress is starched and well ironed; her head is covered with a shawl, and they have placed medals and scapularies on her breast.) Neither Prudencia (the phrase "Damián killed her!" still echoing in her head) nor Clementina could take their eyes off her, trying to stamp her features into their memories forever.

Suddenly it came to Prudencia that she would no longer have to endure her mother's violent rage. Illness had aggravated this, of course, but it came from her irritable nature just the same. Prudencia turned around guiltily as though she had been a willing accomplice in her mother's death and cried out, "Poor soul, how she suffered!" Like her, the two cousins and Don Timoteo were conscious of the evil thought, "After what we've put up with from her, at last we'll get some rest!" Their sobbing grew louder. The men pushed the women aside and laid the body in the coffin.

"God's will be done."

"She's better off; our turn will come."

"We'll make this bitter cup an offering to God."

The comments came from those present, among whom old Lucas was the most eloquent and talkative; he cited examples of great resignation.

"Remember Cayetano Castañeda when they killed his two sons? And what about Doña Tacha herself when Rosalía died? What an example she gave us of resignation to God's will . . ."

They tried to persuade Don Timoteo to lie down for a while. He took no notice of them, wouldn't even sit down, but kept walking from one end of the hall to the other, all night long. Seeing him still so hearty, Prudencia had another thought even more dreadful than her "Damián killed her!"; she felt a sharp pang, as if a snake had bitten her: "Suppose Father marries again?" She covered her face in horror, racked by a fresh fit of sobbing.

"Why did they sprinkle so much lime and formaldehyde on her before they closed the coffin? It makes our eyes water."

By this time only relatives, tenant farmers, debtors, and those who feel under some obligation to Don Timoteo are left. They will watch all night, although they haven't been offered anything to eat, and the cups of black coffee are passed round sparingly. (This adds to Don Timoteo's reputation for meanness; people will always remember, "When his wife died, he didn't even give us coffee.") Conversations take on a lower tone, become more intimate and confidential. Inner thoughts are revealed.

"She had some nice clothes; maybe I'll get some of them," thinks Doña Dolores.

"When he sees how much Doña Tacha's death has upset me, and how I couldn't leave her all day and won't until she's buried, the master may give me some better land to farm, like the Agua Colorada field, say." This from Ponciano Romo.

"I wonder if he'd get me a new yoke of oxen. But heaven knows what ideas young Damián has come back with; he may be worse." Pablo Peña doesn't voice this thought.

"The coffin is pretty and fits her well," says Clementina.

"What's the good of that when she can't see it?" answers Prudencia, the thoughts "Damián killed her!" and "Suppose he marries again?" buzzing round in her brain.

"Well, it's a comfort, anyhow."

(Why have they sprinkled so much lime and formaldehyde on the body?)

"All day long I could hear Don Gregorio's saw and hammer, so near I thought my head would burst, and I felt each blow in my heart, thinking of your poor mother; she was always good to me, and helped me many a time," said the seamstress as she thought, "Are you going to give me something worth having, or just some shoddy cast-offs, as useless as the dead woman lying there?"

"Didn't the Rodríguezes come?" asked Clementina.

"It would have been better if they hadn't, with that crazy Micaela; she's as bad as a streetwalker. Can you believe it? She was flirting with Julián all the time and nobody could keep them from talking, they were even laughing. I felt like telling her to go home. Such a way to act in the presence of the dead! You could see that everyone was annoyed, but she was quite unconcerned, the little hussy!" said Prudencia, furiously. ("Suppose he marries again? . . . Damián killed her!")

"She really did behave outrageously. It's hard to believe," agreed Doña Rita.

"It's past believing!" added the ironing-woman, vying with the other in expressing her anger.

"Just wait. If she comes here tomorrow or to the Rosaries," threatens Clementina, catching their indignation, "I won't stop at just watching her."

"Just imagine! They even say that crazy girl is trying to provoke a quarrel between Julián and Ruperto," announced the seamstress.

"What's the village coming to . . . ?"

"That Señora Victoria . . ."

Don Timoteo paced up and down, paying no attention to the scraps of conversation which his debtors and tenant farmers directed to him from time to time. Before his eyes, clearer than ever, floated the dead face of Anacleto, with its fixed expression, seeming to cry out for vengeance; when he tried to put it out of mind, it was followed by guilty regret for the Fair he missed. The bulls were supposed to be so good at Aguascalientes, and he kept thinking how insufferable Doña Tacha had been about his going. He couldn't escape from these thoughts! And the greatest of all his worries was the argument he had just had with the Parish Priest. He couldn't think what to do.

"Where is Orión?" asked Clementina.

"They took him to the farm this morning because nobody could stand his barking. He wouldn't move from underneath the bed where Mother was lying; they had to haul him out with a rope. It was pitiful to see him!"

By this time Damián was so drunk that no one could put up with him (his drunkenness was already creating a scandal in the village), and the worst of it was that he was trying to make all the others drink. He paid no attention to his father's stern expression. The most he'd do was to step out the street door when he took a drink.

It was two o'clock in the morning.

"All day long I kept hearing Don Gregorio's saw and hammer, the noise boring into my head . . ."

Don Timoteo couldn't persuade the Parish Priest or any of the other priests to listen to his arguments and he didn't want anyone to know what the trouble was. The problem made his head throb more than any of the thoughts that assailed him.

"Why did they sprinkle so much lime and formaldehyde on her?" (That's why, because of the firm stand taken by the Parish Priest and his assistants.)

Don Timoteo finally lost his temper at Damián's behavior, and finding words useless, took the bottle from him by force, hurled it to the floor, and locked him up. (There hadn't been such unbridled drinking in the village for some time.)

It was dreadful. ("It would be a 'Northerner,' with no fear of God in his heart.") People at the wake were horrified. Even Lucas Macías was silent. The women wept quietly. ("Damián killed her!") Don Timoteo resumed his restless pacing up and down the hall, and his grim silence filled the bystanders with fear.

("What will I do, if he marries again?") Don Timoteo went into the room and snuffed out the candles angrily.

"All day long the whine of Don Gregorio's saw could be heard . . ."

"They didn't even nail down the coffin. It's a comfort that they just shut it gently with a key, like a suitcase. The sound of the hammer would have been agonizing," said Clementina between her sobs. Changing the subject, she added, "What just happened was horrible!"

"With Mother gone, everything will get worse and worse. Even you are far away, living your own life," moaned Prudencia. ("If he marries again . . . Damián killed her!")

"What's bothering Father?"

"I don't know. Look . . ." Prudencia and Clementina got up from the low chairs they had been sitting on and, moving a little away from the others, Prudencia continued:

"Twice today he was talking to Father Reyes; the second time, Father Islas came too, and they were shut up together for an hour; Father looked so upset I could hardly recognize him, and that's saying a lot. You know what he's like. He went out, to the Presbytery, I think . . . they say the Parish Priest has a 105-degree temperature and can't see anyone; Father Vidriales came back with Father and they stood on the corner and talked for ages, and nobody dared to speak to them. I've no idea what it's all about, and I don't want to know. They couldn't toll the passing-bell because it was Easter Eve, but when they rang in the morning, they rang loudly enough. It may be a sin, but the sound of the bells pierced my very soul, and when I looked at Father, he seemed to be feeling the same."

"That must be it."

"No, I think it's something more important, and I'd rather not even wonder what it is."

"She would die on Easter Saturday!"

The two women returned to their chairs, sad at heart. ("Damián killed her!") Only Lucas Macías' voice droned on, tireless, monotonous. Don Timoteo kept pacing, ceaselessly, up and down. ("Why so much lime and formaldehyde?") In the morning air the coughing increased. ("That sound of the saw, all day long.") Unexpectedly, like a bucket of cold water, the bells, ringing the first summons to the Mass of the Resurrection, fell upon the ears of those at the wake. An expression of pained surprise and irritation appeared on their faces. ("How little they care for the griefs of others!" The involuntary thought crossed the minds of all, only to be thrust away at once as sinful.) Their eyes turned towards the coffin, towards the flickering light of the wax tapers and the kerosene lamps. Tears filled the eyes of the women again.

"The Lord is risen!" proclaimed Lucas Macías.

Don Timoteo continued his pacing, a prey to conflicting emotions. Justina woke; she had been dreaming that her Aunt Tacha was boxing her ears and pulling her hair; she glanced towards the coffin. It was half-past three. The mourners braced themselves to hear the second and last bell ring for the Easter Mass.

"All day long we could hear the blows of the hammer in Don Gregorio's workshop."

"The Lord is risen."

III

How does Lucas Macías sense what is going on? He was the only one to suspect the reason for Don Timoteo's agitation. The priests and Don Timoteo had managed to keep their arguments secret so there would be no gossip beforehand; but, in his indirect fashion, Lucas Macías was giving proof that he knew what the trouble was.

". . . and no amount of begging or threatening could do any good. How could it do any good against the express command of Holy Mother Church? They offered the parish priest anything he wanted, because, as they said, how could they bury Don Celestino like a dog, without taking him to church, without saying a mass for his soul? It wasn't as if he'd been a heretic! Don Celestino, who'd been so pious and was charity itself. It would be a stain on the family honor, handed down from generation to generation, and nothing on earth would make them insult the memory of a man whose only fault had been that it pleased God to call him to His kingdom on Christmas Eve. In vain the parish priest tried to explain to them that there was no shame of any kind in postponing the funeral for a day; for centuries the Church had forbidden funeral masses to be held in church on such days as Christmas Eve; there wasn't any question of discrimination, far from it. But the Cornejo family had always been ones to have their own way and they refused to listen to reason. They insisted that there must be a mass, whatever the day; it wasn't their fault, they said, nor Don Celestino's, that he died on this particular day; they would take his body to the church and have a mass said for the repose of his soul, the best mass anyone ever had. It wasn't for nothing, surely, all their money and all their devotion . . ."

(Don Timoteo was reckoning up, and hating himself for doing it, the money his wife's death was going to cost him.)

Lucas' voice continued the tale:

". . . things began to take an ugly turn when Pascual Cornejo, the dead man's son, got drunk, lost his temper, and started threatening. He'd been with the troops of General Márquez and used to boast of having shot several revolutionaries who posed as doctors in the town of Tacubaya. When Juárez came to power, Pascual went into hiding on his farm and no one saw him until the time of Don Sebastián. Well, this Pascual, drunk as he could be, swaggered off to the Presbytery, gun in hand, to frighten the parish priest. The priest at that time was Father Robles, a good old man who was made a Canon soon afterward and died in Guadalajara. He gave me my first communion and was in the village a long time. I remember what a talker he was; he used to do a lot of visiting. Once he went on a pilgrimage to the Holy Land and brought back relics which he distributed among his flock. I had a rosary blessed in the Holy Land; I can't remember when I lost it. Pascual arrived at the Presbytery, brandishing his gun, but here he came up against Father Robles. By this time, some of the villagers had gathered to disarm him and there might have been a killing if it hadn't been for Father Robles' good sense. One thing was sure, there'd be no mass and the Cornejo family had to keep the body another night and, as they hadn't taken any precautionary measures, the corpse began to decompose; nobody could stand the stench. The second night of the wake—I was there—there wasn't much respect— even the relatives were weary from lack of sleep; the coffin was carried out by farmhands who stuffed cloths soaked in alcohol in their mouths, and the church stank so they had to disinfect it; if they'd sprinkled lime and formaldehyde before nailing down the coffin . . ."

(As the women dressed the body and laid it on the bed, as he took her in his arms to lay her in her coffin, Don Timoteo again could see his wife as she had been on their wedding night; he could see her as she was the night Damián was born. These thoughts and images filled him with shame, a shame he would remember to his dying day.)

". . . Father Robles didn't believe that spirits come back to haunt places where they've lived, even if vows have been left unfulfilled or treasure's been buried, much less for just being denied a church service; but I've known many a truthful person who said that the dead had spoken to them; children giving complete descriptions of people they didn't know; men who'd been frightened out of their minds, and women who'd fainted. To tell the truth, I've never seen a ghost myself, and I've lived in houses where they were supposed to frighten people. One night, I remember, I was staying at the house of the late Margarito Pérez and had to go out in the yard. I saw a white form beckoning me; my knees started knocking together, and I couldn't make up my mind whether to run or speak to it.

" 'In God's name, tell me if you're of this world or the next,' I said. 'Devil take it, I'm damned if I'll run away. I'll see what this is, even if my heart is beating like a sledgehammer. I'll speak to it, maybe it's trying to tell me about a buried treasure.' I marched up to it and out flew a hen that had been scratching herself under some clothes hanging on the fence, and her head and wings had appeared to beckon me . . ."

(Don Timoteo was still pacing up and down, muttering disconnected snatches of prayer while in his mind he was thinking of things far removed from the prayers in his mouth.)

". . . Going back to the subject of the Cornejos, the laws of Holy Mother Church certainly couldn't be broken just for their convenience; they had to sit up with their dead another night . . ."

Don Timoteo came over to Lucas Macías with visible signs of irritation:

"You'd better be going to Mass," he said.

Subdued, the old man rose to his feet; in a subdued tone he asked:

"And when is the funeral, so that I know when to come back?"

Don Timoteo glared at him; he pursed up his mouth and grunted:

"I don't know; it depends on what time Francisco arrives."

But he has certainly heard Lucas' story and he could murder him, because the rumor will now spread through the village: "Since it's Easter Day they can't take Doña Tacha to church, they'll have to wait till day after tomorrow. What will Damián, with his quick temper, do when he hears? No matter what he does, they'll have to wait, or take her to the Cemetery today, like a heathen, without even the tolling of the bells . . ."

EASTER

I

UICKENING DAY. How welcome its coming is, the early morning sounds, the sunshine, the bells, after a sleepless night!

"His temperature's gone down and he's calmer," said Marta, and in another part of the village Doña Carmen Esparza Garagarza de Pérez uttered the same words.

"We had a job to keep him from getting up to say mass," said the one.

"He still seems delirious," said the other.

II

"In the morning I would be dead."

He persuaded them to give him the missal and made an attempt to say mass.

"You'll hurt your eyes, reading," said Doña Carmen.

Luis insisted. They gave in to him, as usual.

"*In the morning, when the new fire is lit. . . .*" He remembered Holy Saturday mornings. As an acolyte he used to stand in the doorway of the Parish Church while it was still dark and help to light the new fire with tinder and flint, and he was carried back to the olden times when the world was just beginning, to the days of the prophets. "*I would have been born like the light. My soul would have been lit, like the candles, like the thuribles, with the sacred flame; with new fire, like the three mysterious candles on the reed, lit, one by one, during the procession through the church while the words 'Lumen Christi' resound in new tones, in a new church, in a new world, and the soul, kindled anew, worships as it enters the church, as it reaches the middle of the nave, and as it draws close to the Altar.* Before it is lit, the paschal candle represents Christ in His tomb; lit, it symbolizes the Saviour illuminating the world with the splendor of His Resurrection, like the column of fire which went before the Hebrews."

"Don't read. It's bad for you."

"Leave me alone. Go away."

They had never crossed him.

"*There are five stars in my soul as in the paschal candle* . . . tuba insonet salutaris . . . *like the candle with its five grains of incense* . . . totius orbis se sentiat amisisse caliginem . . . *in a Greek Cross on my breast* . . . sancti luminis claritatem . . . *the stars* . . . haec nox est . . . *like the stigmata of St. Francis* . . . columnae illuminatione purgavit . . . *and the five wounds of our Saviour* . . . o vere beata nox . . . *blessed night on which I should have died in order to shine like a meteor, when the candle is lit from the blessed reed, and the morning star which never sets would find me shining, that star which knows no setting, which returns from Hell, shining serenely upon mankind. Moses* . . . flectamus genua . . . *Isaiah, Ezekiel, Jonah, Daniel, all the holy patriarchs and prophets* . . . Levate . . . *Prophesy.*

"My beloved has planted a vineyard upon a fertile hill and built a winepress in it. *I would have entered upon death in a purple cloak, with a cross and candlestick and candle, and a reed and a thurible* . . . like the panting hart . . . *at the hour when the priest goes to the baptismal font and blesses the water, dividing it in four parts with the sign of the Cross* . . . like the panting hart . . . *as he bids all evil spirits flee hence, and the water is free and blessed by the living,* the true, the holy God, Who, in the beginning, separated the water from the land with a single word and Whose spirit broods over the water . . . God changed its bitterness into sweetness, He struck a rock with His rod and water gushed forth; He turned water into wine, and walked on the face of the waters . . . *I would have died at that hour when the priest breathes three times on the water, and dips the lighted paschal candle three times into it, then sprinkles it over the people, and distributes the Holy Water to be used at the hour of death, and pours chrism and oil into the baptismal font where I was baptized . . . to be born again as a spark, a threefold light, candle, water, on Holy Saturday, to the rhythm of an eternal liturgy, sung in all the worlds of the universe. Jehovah would appear, clad in a cope and wearing a beard, like an ancient High Priest.* Omnes Sancti et Sanctae Dei. *The bells would not have tolled; they would peal with joy as the veil of the flesh was rent, and the choir of angels would sing* 'Alleluya!' "

When Doña Carmen and Victoria entered the room, they found him face down on the floor, chanting the Litany of the Saints in a feeble voice that sometimes changed to discordant cries as he tried to speak louder. "St. Mary Magdalene, St. Inez, St. Cecilia . . . all the holy virgins and widows . . ." When he realized that Victoria had come into the room, he tried to speak, but could only mutter as though unable to get the words out. ". . . virgins and widows . . . Through you I am condemned, I see it clearly, for God would not let me die like a martyr, a monk, a hermit, and ascend to Heaven like new fire on Holy Saturday, like the morning star at the hour when the candle with its grains of incense is lit, and the three mysterious candles on the reed shine in the darkness . . . *Lumen Christi* . . . and the water in the font is blessed. Leave me, Victoria . . . *libera nos, Domine, te rogamus, audi nos, ab omni malo, ab omni peccato, a morte perpetua, in die iudicii, ut nobis parcas, ut nos exaudire digneris . . .*" And he started in again: "St. Michael, St. Gabriel, St. Raphael . . . St. Sylvester (Jehovah is like St. Sylvester . . . I am lost! God did not grant my prayer!) . . . *vere beata nox . . .* Condemned alive! Go away!"

The paroxysm was frightening. Doña Carmen fainted. Poor Don Alfredo—who was always timid and weak—was a pitiful sight, his face dead white. Victoria, too, either from emotion or contagion, was white and trembling; it occurred to her, nevertheless, to suggest that they fetch one of the priests to calm him.

"Yes, yes," said Don Alfredo, in a daze, "but not Father Islas. It's his narrow-mindedness that's to blame. Still less Father Reyes. Luis would only grow worse at sight of him. Nor Father Vidriales . . ." and in the end Don Alfredo did nothing and the discordant cries continued. "It's the stranger's fault that I am lost, her fault and Father Martínez'; God would not grant my prayer, He would not let me flee and die on Saturday in the early hours of the morning, in order to rise again in the blessed Font, in the paschal candle, in the three candles on the reed. I am lost. My hands . . . my head . . . my whole body is afire! Don't touch me!"

III

On Tuesday there was an alarm. A posse of police arrived. The streets were darker than ever. The shops were all shut. It was learned that the detachment had come with the new Deputy. Don Román Capistrán had been relieved of his post! The village would have to begin again with a new Deputy, a man with new ideas, sent, or certainly recommended, by the Liberals of Teocaltiche!

IV

On Thursday, mail day, notwithstanding the arrival of the new Deputy, Father Reyes went to the Post Office to carry out his parochial duty of checking the correspondence coming into the village, especially the arrival of newspapers which might get into the villagers' hands. There was a package of papers addressed to the new authority and Father Reyes determined to watch their distribution. With the exception of those who, in one way or another, depended on the Government for their living, only Damián Limón had ranged himself on the side of the Deputy. Apparently the Deputy liked to drink. Supervision of the mail didn't throw any light on the secret functioning of Liberal and Spiritist centers, but one must remember that donkey-drivers carry a lot of private correspondence and are good at pretending to know nothing. It is difficult to find out what they bring and carry; their travelling around, on the other hand, gives them an excuse to sneak away; they don't go to the Sacraments or Retreats, and make no contribution to the spiritual welfare of the village; they bring in liquor and afford a means of transport for undesirable women (it's rumored that at least two of these have come back to the tavern district, and it's barely Easter Thursday). They bring secret messages and carry out dubious commissions, besides being in contact with dangerous and disturbing elements that threaten the peace of the village. They are, in fact, enemies of the soul, carriers of infection between the village and the world outside.

There was a letter for Micaela, sent General Delivery. ("Some important people from Mexico City asked me to go to Chapala with them and I couldn't very well refuse. So, as it was hard to find any way of getting to your village, I had to give up the pleasure of visiting you. How I wished you were in Chapala with me! It's Paradise compared to other parts of the Republic that I know. We have had some wonderful moonlight nights and twilights that held me spellbound. Much as I hate to, I have to return to Mexico City today, very much against my will . . .")

V

"Will Father marry again?" The question kept coming into the minds of the bereaved Limón girls, especially during the Rosaries for the dead woman; they didn't dare share the thought with each other, but each felt as though she had suddenly been brought face to face with the facts of life again.

On Monday the village was awakened by the sound of the postponed tolling for the dead and this continued all morning, in all the belfreys, as though it were the Pope or the Archbishop who had died. And some, forgetting already the death that had occurred three days before, asked, "Who is it? Who're they tolling for?" There were even some who wondered if it might be the Parish Priest whose last hour had come. A few laughed up their sleeves at so much bell-ringing so long after the event.

When the Deputy arrived next day with the police, they would have liked to toll the bells again, but there wasn't a bell-ringer to be found.

VI

On Saturday the Daughters of Mary had their usual meeting. There was a catechism class, too. The meeting was surprising because there had been no meetings, not even choir practices, all week. The days had been more boring than ever, weary contrast after the busy, lively days of the previous week. A gray Easter. The sound of work was heard again, but its rhythm was slow and reluctant. Even the crowing of the cocks, the lowing of the cattle, and the barking of the dogs came slow, reluctant, drowsy. So did the bells.

The Rodríguez family didn't go to the Rosaries for Doña Tacha. On Saturday they had been insulted. Micaela was furious and discovered in Damián an instrument for her vengeance. Why hadn't she thought of him before? Good material!

It was said the new Deputy's name was Heliodoro Fernández, that he liked to drink, and that he had uttered threats.

THE NORTHERNERS

I

IKE PLAGUE-LADEN WINDS, themselves a plague, worse than the donkey-drivers. (It's hard to say which is worse, their absence or their return . . . To say nothing of the families and fields deserted.)

"It's worse when they come back," most people say.

"And they gain nothing from their experience."

"Even those who come back with money aren't satisfied here any longer."

"Many of them don't want to work anymore; they just strut around, air their opinions, and criticize everything."

"They're a bad example, making fun of religion, the country, the customs."

"They sow doubt, undermine patriotism, and encourage others to leave this 'filthy, poverty-stricken country.'"

"They're the ones who spread ideas of Masonry, Socialism, and Spiritism."

"They've no respect for women."

"Nor sense of obligation at all."

"They're vicious and quarrelsome, always ready to pick a fight."

"They've lost the fear of God, that's the sum of it."

"And there are more and more of them all the time. Nobody gets any peace. They meddle with everything—with the rich for being rich and the poor for being poor. They have no respect for anyone."

"Miserable people! Poor country!"

"They think because they can roll off a few strange words they know more than anybody else and are a cut above other people, but they can't read a bit better than when they went away."

"Just because they have some gold teeth and are always ready for a fight."

"Because they come back with round-toed shoes, felt hats, wide-legged trousers, and shirts with wristbands and shiny cuff-links."

"With their hair bushy in front and shaved behind."

"They don't even have a mustache."

"They're ridiculous."

"They certainly are. When poor old Don Pedro Rubio's son-in-law came back and saw them stirring *atole*, he said he couldn't remember the word for it!"

"But he remembered how to stir up trouble all right."

"They're ridiculous."

"What gets me most is the way they laugh and brag."

"How can anybody forget the language he's been brought up with?"

"They're traitors, that's all there is to it. Whether they know it or not, they're the advance scouts of the gringos, sent to take our land away from us."

"How the women put up with them is more than I can see."

II

"No, Padre, I'm sorry to say so, but when we come back, we realize what the people here have to put up with, the injustice and the living conditions. Why should a man have to sweat all day to earn a few cents? And sometimes not even that. The rich are past masters at juggling accounts, and put the peasants off

with promises they don't mean to keep, stop their mouths with
enough corn and beans that they won't die of hunger, and just say,
'We'll see . . . at harvest time . . . next year . . .' If they struggle for it
they may get a few yards of coarse cotton cloth, and a few more of
cheap percale, but their debts are never paid, they're handed on
from father to son. You never have a house of your own, and if you
do manage to get a little plot of land, you're forced to sell it for less
than you paid for it, tricked out of it. The family lives in a hovel, the
children grow up there, they have nothing to wear when they're
alive and when their time comes, nothing to die in.

"I tell you, Padre, it can't go on like this; sooner or later the worm
will turn, and for better or worse, things will change. To be frank, it
would be better if the gringos did come and teach us their way of
life than for us to stay the way we are now, living no life at all.
Who enjoys it? Tell me. The poor? No. Nor the rich either; they don't
even know how to spend their money. The women work all the
time like slaves, raising families, always wearing black, always
afraid to move. What are we working for? The next life? That's all
right, but I believe we ought to make this one a little better and live
like human beings. Why can't we eat our fill and enjoy it, have a
drink now and then, have some fun for a change, sing, visit, speak
our minds, talk to women, wear decent clothes that fit us, work in
freedom like the gringos? They at least aren't hypocrites. Here life is
always sad, we sigh without knowing why, we don't even dare to
draw a free breath. We take pleasure in making ourselves suffer.

"This is no life, Padre, forgive me. Those of us who have known
what freedom is will never be satisfied with these customs again.
No. The worst sin is exploiting others, and the sin is greater when
it's hand in hand with hypocrisy. Don't tell me that the men here
don't feel like men, or feel their gorge rising, just because, outwardly,
they pretend to be meek. Don't even try to tell me that about the
women. The saint that slips is soon a devil, as the saying goes, begging your pardon. You can do anything if you go about it the right
way, but pretense and the use of force make matters worse; a rope
strained too much will break. Many of the women who have run
away, so many unhappy women, might have had a happier lot if
they'd been allowed to behave according to their feelings and hadn't
been forced to pretend.

"We who have been away are criticized because we see how

things are and speak out. But this state of affairs can't go on. Oh, I agree that nobody here dies of hunger, but don't tell me that most people are doing more than barely living. You know as well as I do how they struggle and worry for half enough to live on. But go to Cuernavaca, Puebla, Chihuahua, where I worked, and you'll really see hell let loose, on the sugar farms, the huge estates. The people live worse than slaves. If anyone so much as opens his mouth, he's stabbed to death or beaten till he's half-dead. I saw tortures worse than the Christian martyrs went through. You don't realize what's going on in other parts of the Republic; when the Revolution starts it will catch us unawares here. Mexico isn't just our region, and you priests, begging your pardon, ought not to pull the wool over the people's eyes.

"I won't deny that life can be hard in the United States; but you can live in comfort and freedom. I'm not denying, either, that in some parts of the United States, especially in Texas and California, there are people who think Mexicans are no more than animals; there're a great many Mexicans there and they have our Mexican faults. But if you go a little farther north, you'll see how different it is; besides, even in Texas and California it depends on the place you make for yourself. I could live there comfortably enough. They say that the money we earn there has wings; the truth is, it's in our blood to spend it as fast as we get it and we can't keep our hands on it; the poorest earns four times as much as he earns here—in ready cash too, not in promises. And when you come back, the minute you reach the border you get a different treatment even from your own fellow countrymen, and you feel let down. That's why so many fellows won't work when they get back but only dream of going away again. Call it whatever you like—Socialism, or Liberalism—but that's the truth. The Church doesn't deny human nature, does it, or want a man to spend all his time praying? Well, then . . . ?"

("Our good postal inquisitor," says Father Vidriales to Father Meza, referring to Father Reyes, "is failing in his efforts to found a religious and social club for the Northerners. There he goes, paying too much attention to them, as usual. They'll let him get everything arranged, but when he draws in his net, they'll slip away. He's trying to carry water in a sieve."

"A waste of time," agrees Father Meza.

"All the same, something has to be done, though that's not the way to do it. And at once, too. Those who aren't converted to Protestantism, the gringo's means of infiltration, come back indifferent to religion. What would you do?"

"I haven't had the strength or energy to think about it. Anyhow, it's not my business now. Leave me to my masses and hearing confessions. My fighting days are over. When I was younger . . ."

"I'd treat them like public sinners and not allow them inside the church. I wouldn't admit them, or their families either, to the Sacrament, unless they were at death's door."

"Since Father Martínez, who's after all more strong-minded than you, hasn't done that, it would probably be very difficult to do. Naturally you'd like to see Reyes fail."

"I can't stand the smug way the younger men go about their jobs. It's as though they were saying to us older ones, 'Look, this is what you should be doing.' "

"To tell you the truth, it doesn't bother me anymore. I want only to be left alone. God leaves each man to his conscience and his strength. I'm grateful that He's never sent me more responsibility. I've never longed for a parish or an independent chaplaincy, and I've never been jealous of a colleague's preferment. Here, at first, Don Dionisio tried to get me to do more; then he gradually left me in peace. I don't understand why they start all these new things nowadays; in my day . . ."

"Ah, Father Meza, I envy your forbearance."

"It comes with age, my son, with age. Don't fret yourself over those Northerners, nor this young inquisitor, nor the good Dionisio with all his demands, nor Father Islas with his neurasthenic circle. Don't let what happened to our holy young Luis Gonzaga happen to you."

"How I'd like to ask for a transfer! And if I were the parish priest, what changes you'd see!"

"First you'd send the Northerners back where they came from And then, what would you do with Father Reyes?"

"You must have your joke, Father Meza!"

"No, I won't joke. Let there be peace and harmony among the leaders. If Reyes fails with the Northerners, do you intend to try your hand?"

"No. I'm only the farmers' confessor; my job is village routine. But you can be quite sure that Father Reyes will fail. I've heard some of the things these impudent fellows say to him . . .")

"No, Padre, I don't know what you'll say, but the only way I can think of for doing what you want is to organize one of those community clubs like they have up in the North, with meetings and parties and even—begging your pardon—dances. What's the harm in it? Up there, after the services, they turn the churches into movie houses, or have a bazaar or a play. If you try to get men to pray all the time or go to confession or meetings like the Daughters of Mary, or have outings for men only, of course they'll balk. Put it to them in a way they can feel. Help them when they're sick, get them jobs, life insurance, and some fun. Have a little orchestra or a choral society to sing cheerful things. Let them act out a play. That's the way to do it, and you'll see, it will succeed. Otherwise—why beat about the bush?—I wouldn't join it myself."

III

Although he hadn't actually seen anything, Bartolo Jiménez, the husband of the girl who'd been going to marry Damián, suspected that Damián was following her about and bothering her. His fears were like buzzards, circling overhead and biding their time. He had the feeling that people were hiding something from him, looking at him with pity or mockery. Never having dared to look into his wife's eyes, through timidity, or rather, modesty—it seemed like looking at her nakedness—he was now incapable of reading in them the confirmation of his unhappiness. Neither of them had mentioned Damián's return and they seemed afraid to acknowledge the unhappy fact.

On Saturday evening, his eyes avoiding Bruna's, Bartolo remarked casually that he had just been to Doña Tacha's wake; Bruna, equally casual, had replied, "May her soul rest in peace." They shied away from mentioning the village gossip about her sudden death, without confession, and the other topics of public interest—among them, doubtless, Bartolo's watchful anxiety and his wife's state of mind. Not even when the whole village was talking about how scandalously Damián had behaved when they couldn't take the body to church on Easter Sunday, and discussing the violent scene between Don Timoteo and his son, and the four-day drinking bout during which Damián said so many outrageous things, and the disgraceful fight over the inheritance; not even when people began to say that Doña Tacha's ghost had been unable to frighten Don Timoteo or his children into any signs of carrying out the wishes of the dead woman—not even then did Bartolo and his wife allude to these matters.

Bartolo was right. On the very day when Doña Tacha lay in her coffin, Bruna realized that Damián was following her; Holy Saturday night she listened, keeping perfectly still, to his drunken mutterings as he walked up and down in front of the house, keeping her in an agony of fright lest Bartolo should arrive and the two men fight. Afterward, on her way out of church, in the Square, as she went about her daily errands, it was obvious that he was following her. However, she managed to keep his glances, which she carefully avoided meeting, from leading to more, and she made sure she was not alone when she went out, or that Bartolo would be home most of the time.

Stories and rumors of infamies committed by the Northerners obsessed Bartolo. Who but one of the Northerners could have killed the poor woman found in the stream at Cahuixtle with seventeen dagger wounds? A scarf like those they bring from up there was stuffed into her mouth, and a gringo dagger had been used, too. Who but the Northerners had been carrying off girls lately? (Bartolo trembled at the thought that he might be the first man whose wife was carried off.) It wasn't for saintliness that Doña Eufrosina's son was sent to the electric chair and Román López given ninety years in prison. No one trusts them. Baudelio Bravo there owes the barber alone over fifty pesos. And when the owners of La Paz went to Florentino Barrios to collect the three hundred pesos he had owed them for years, he out with his gun and threatened them. Their highhanded doings have brought business almost to a standstill. Don Juventino, the tailor, was at his wits' ends in trying to deal with cunning rogues who seem to have gone to the States only to learn fast talk and how to outwit everyone. Why, just this Holy Week, Barrenado talked Don Juventino into letting him have a suit he was making for Julián Soto. He wanted it for just a little while, he said, so that his uncle, Don Arcadio, who was thinking of ordering a similar or even a better one for himself, could have a look at it. Now the poor tailor doesn't know what to say to Julián. The Devil must tell them about other people's business so they can turn it to their own advantage. Why, just two months ago, Juan Méndez came to Don Zacarías Tovar's one morning to say that Don Inocencio Rodríguez had sent him for five hundred pesos, with this-and-that they'd talked of the night before as security. Don Inocencio couldn't come himself because he had to leave in a hurry for the farm, but he'd sent an IOU. That was the last anyone saw of Juan. Did anybody ever see Tereso Vallejo again after he'd tricked Don Cayetano García out of his best horse? Sometimes by fraud, sometimes by threats or by pleading hunger, they get goods from one man, cash from another, beans and corn from a third. They kill or steal cattle. They can steal hens better than a coyote. There's no orchard they haven't stolen fruit from, no trickery they haven't been up to. And their guns are always loaded . . .

Though a peaceable man by nature, Bartolo decided to buy a revolver. He'd never handled a weapon in his life, but now he went out of the village every day for target practice.

"You've been looking worried for days, Bartolo," Salomé Torres said to him one night. Bartolo hesitated, trying to think of a plausible answer. "Debts . . . and not knowing how the year will turn out, if there'll be a drought as the almanac says . . ."

"Well, why don't you ask the Ouija Board that Néstor Plasencia brought from the North? It said that Doña Tacha was going to die, told where the treasure of Saturnina Rueda was buried, and Margarito Lizarde made a fortune out of it. And just think how long that old moneylender has been dead and no one even knew where her grave was! It tells the fate and death of everyone: it told Néstor Plasencia not to ride chestnut horses. It warned me not to go out in a thunderstorm. It told Damián Limón that he'd go to prison on account of a woman. It told Lucas Ruano not to marry the girl he was engaged to. It also told what was going to happen to Don Alfredo's son. It doesn't seem possible, but there's no hidden thought the Ouija Board doesn't read, and no future happening it doesn't predict. Where do you think Néstor got his money from? You know he came back without a penny, and now he has a house and a farm. But there's just one thing: you've got to swear to keep all this secret, for if the priests hear of it, you can imagine what a fuss there'll be. If you don't swear and give your word to keep absolutely quiet about this, you won't learn anything even if you ask Néstor himself."

Bartolo hesitated, afraid of being made a fool of, but it was a wonderful opportunity to learn more about the tricks and fortunes of the Northerners.

"You can even talk with any dead man you want to, and his spirit will answer. You'll see that there can't be any trickery," Salomé went on.

"So these are the 'Spiritists,'" reflected Bruna's husband, his conscience troubling him. As though reading his thoughts, Salomé said, "You've heard about men being found dead, nobody knows why. If you don't want that to happen to you, keep your mouth shut, whether you decide to have a go at the Ouija Board or not. Not even your shadow must know what I've told you. I'm trying to help you. Keep your mouth shut."

Bartolo was forced to protest, "Don't you trust me, hombre?"

"I wouldn't have told you if I didn't; but it won't do any harm to remind you of what could happen if your tongue got to wagging."

Could he talk to his greatuncle, the late Don Baltasar? Nobody knows where he kept all the money he had and he died leaving his family in poverty.

"Look, the other night a lady (I won't mention her name), very fond of reading the *Twelve Peers of France*, talked to Charlemagne's spirit, and he told her things that weren't even in the book, and it's certain that Néstor didn't know anything about it, for he can't even read."

But what Bartolo wants most is to discover his wife's intentions, and Damián's, too. Is she still in love with Don Timoteo's son? Would she like to talk to him again? Salomé's remark that Damián would be put in prison because of a woman seared his brain like hot coals. "Because of a woman!"

"If you give me your word, we'll go see Néstor. He charges five pesos entrance fee for the Club. Then we'll set a time and place. I'll let you know beforehand. If you don't want anybody else there on that day, you'll have to pay another ten pesos." ("No wonder nobody has been able to find the Club!" thought Bartolo.)

After much hesitation, Bartolo finally made up his mind. They went to Néstor, gave him his first five pesos and, in great secrecy, after more oaths and threats, arranged to meet him at ten o'clock the next night at the corner of the Cemetery; from there they'd go to the house where the session was to be held. Bartolo would be led blindfolded to where the Ouija Board was, he must not take a gun, and he would pay the ten pesos in advance. (That explains why it's such a mystery!) He would pay the ten pesos to make sure that he wouldn't run into Damián there. Damián, Damián, always Damián!

The next day, he avoided his wife even more than usual and said nothing. "Suppose it's all a trick of the Northerners? Suppose it's a trick to keep me out of the house so Damián can get into it? Of course! What an idiot I was! Not to think of that! And the five pesos I gave them? I deserve to lose them for being such a fool. But, once bitten, twice shy. What a simpleton! I nearly fell into their trap, worse than Juventino, worse than Cayetano García or Don Zacarías Tovar. Those pestilential Northerners! How can I get my own back? But I may be just imagining this . . . no, nobody's going to get me out of the house today . . ."

And Bartolo began to oil his gun and wait for nightfall. Damián Limón would go to prison "because of a woman . . ."

MARBLES

I

IKE A COMMANDER, the new Deputy came with orders to found a Re-election Club to support Don Ramón Corral, but he preferred to make no public announcement of his mission or his plans before having a frank talk with the Parish Priest, whose curiosity was aroused by the insistence with which the Deputy sought the interview.

Righteous indignation, worry, and fatigue from his Lenten activities had driven Father Martínez to his bed. He was frantic. He was angry with those who affectionately yet firmly prevented him from going back to work. "You won't have to answer for me on the Day of Judgment," he would say; but it was his own bodily weakness rather than the insistence of those around him that kept him from doing as he wished. Twice, three times, determined to say mass and hear confessions, he managed to get dressed, only to have his legs give way under him. Conversation tired him, too, his head would begin to swim, and the doctor that Don Alfredo had brought from Teocaltiche for Luis forbade all talk. "Absolute rest," he ordered, "and avoid all agitation; it's a case of exhaustion complicated by an infection of the liver that might be serious."

But Don Dionisio kept asking what was happening in the village, who had arrived, who had left, who was ill, who was causing trouble, who had stopped coming to Communion. They tried to keep all disturbing news from him, but the old man was constantly worrying about one parishioner or another. Where will the follies of Don Inocencio's daughter lead? And the restlessness of Lucas González' widow? and poor Luis Pérez' idiosyncrasies? Have all the strangers left, especially the woman staying at Don Alfredo's, who has excited the imagination of so many men? He would know what harm she had done if he could hear their confessions. What did God have in store for Marta and María? María, so restless! What will they lead to, the efforts of enemies banded together against the village that God has put in his care? What will be the upshot of so-and-so's quarrel with so-and-so, of so-and-so's inclinations towards so-and-so, of Pedro's debts, of Juan's work, of Francisco's doubts?

The destinies of his parishioners, moving along their appointed paths, made him think of marbles in those games at a Fair where an imperceptible movement sends them shooting down different paths, surprising both players and onlookers. The parish is a huge inclined plane in which hundreds of lives move round, according to individual wills; but, when least expected, the movement is halted at the Decree of Providence. There are times when Don Dionisio would like to know the fate in store for this one or the other, he would like to know in advance the outcome of conflicts and passions that perturb him, the rewards of virtue. He would like to speed up the movement of the marbles. But he immediately rejects this distrust of Providence; his job is only to influence the exercise of the will. Marbles! A painful thought in these hours of helplessness!

On Good Shepherd Sunday, April 25, St. Mark's day (the Fair at Aguascalientes, with all its attendant evils, will now be in full swing), though Marta, María, Father Reyes, and Father Islas opposed it, Father Martínez got up and celebrated mass. But he was not able to carry communion to all the sick in the parish, as he wanted to. He almost fainted at the end of the service, and they had to help him off with his vestments and carry him to the vestry.

But that didn't prevent him from having an interview with the Deputy that same day. The interview was the subject of much speculation.

"No, he just wanted to bring everything out in the open, dot his i's and cross his t's, so there wouldn't be any misunderstanding later. He has strict orders and he's going to try to see that they're carried out voluntarily."

"What? He's giving in, at the very start? And they said he was a priest-hating revolutionary!"

Some even surmised that he had fallen in love with Marta and wanted to get into her uncle's good graces. Others maintained that he had come to ask for money. Some thought that he was ordering Father Martínez to leave the parish, others that he was demanding an explanation for the constant breaking of the Reform Laws or telling him not to stir the people up, now that Don Román Capistrán and Father Reyes were going to be put in prison.

II

While the humble marbles of the parish rolled slowly about, the life of the country was quickening its pace. Two years had passed and people were still talking about the shooting of the workers at Cananea and Río Blanco. It was public knowledge that forces raised by the Flores Magón brothers had attacked several towns on the border. On the second of the month, General Díaz and Don Ramón Corral were proclaimed candidates for the presidency and vice-presidency, respectively. "Don't they say Don Porfirio told an American newspaperman that whether his friends liked it or not he'd retire from the Presidency? Heavens, what a thing politics is! We're in for a fight!" "Fighting! Fighting!"

III

One marble bumps into a second one, and a third rolls away to wait for another, which hasn't yet appeared. Still another rushes off in pursuit of the agate caught at the junction of two crossing wires, the agate all would like to reach.

Damián swallowed the hook Micaela had baited for him. Julián returned to Mercedes, who, finally, set a date to give him his answer. Ruperto was caught between Micaela and Damián. ("I've had enough of her airs and graces. I'll take her by force! I'm sick and

tired of being made a fool of! I'll have her, whatever the consequences!") Damián had the hook firmly in his mouth.

Who is the agate?

Victoria!

The minds of old and young were filled with thoughts of her. Victoria had made such an impression on the men that the very Confessional, where this was revealed, was unable to banish her image, even in the case of the married men. It was an epidemic with different symptoms, usually hidden, so that even Father Rosas, who didn't usually let anything worry him, was filled with alarm; in the women it took the form of sadness, distrust, dislike, anger; there wasn't a single man who hadn't fallen victim to her charms, at least to a mild degree, but there were serious cases of old men, married men, adolescents, who not only couldn't get her out of their heads but actually took pleasure in the malign image. To a man, the curates reflected: "Never has the Lenten effort been so ephemeral, nor the victories gained in these holy days of such short duration. If Father Martínez could see how many a conscience has been upset in so short a time, he'd suffer a relapse from which he might never recover; maybe it's all to the good that he's ill."

Doña Carmen Esparza y Garagarza de Pérez was not exempt from the agitation that disturbed the village, chiefly because she blamed Victoria for Luis Gonzaga's state. "I don't know what to do. I invited her for a month, but this is impossible. I can't think how to get rid of her. I suggested that she go to the Fair at Aguascalientes. I suggested that she go out to the farm for a few days. I exaggerate the inconveniences of the house and the village—how much she must miss the electric lights, streetcars, and theatres. I delay serving meals, taking her clean clothes up to her, doing her room. I can't go beyond this, common decency won't let me, and besides, I'm indebted to her for all her kindness to me when I stayed with her in Guadalajara. Luis is rude to her, but she pities him and takes no offense. People are staring at me. The priests throw out hints. Really, I don't know what to do, and there's no one I can talk to, least of all my husband. It's intolerable. There's nothing to do, it seems, but put up with it, keep quiet, and wait. What was I thinking of when I invited her for such a long visit? But who could have imagined the outcome?"

Even Don Alfredo himself had fallen victim to evil thoughts.

"The flirtatiousness of Micaela," said Father Vidriales to himself, "is a mere child's game compared to the evil that this woman has un-leashed. And without any intention on her part."

Which is the new marble that bumps into the agate?

An obscure marble—Gabriel, the parish bell-ringer, and a mem-ber of the Parish Priest's household.

They are back from the Fair at Aguascalientes. "Just imagine, there were car races at San Luis Potosí; there was also going to be a boxing match, just like in the United States, but this was called off at the last minute." Those back from the Fair fanned the burning cu-riosity of the villagers. Sensational news: the Degollado Theatre in Guadalajara had burned down.

IV

"First of all, Señor Deputy, let me say that I'm very grateful for your kindness in coming to see me, and I assure you that I'm at your service. If I hadn't been ill, I'd have been the one to welcome you. Our tasks should complement, not oppose each other, as the modernists think. That's the assumption I base my opinions on concerning the subject you've come to discuss. Militant politics are outside the scope of my ministry, and nothing could justify my becoming a partisan, much less a fellow organizer of an electoral party. Such an act would reduce my authority in matters that do come within my sphere of influence, and the Church guards these limits jealously. It would be just as unacceptable for the civil gov-ernment to legislate concerning the administration of the sacraments as for a priest to intervene in temporal questions that have nothing to do with faith or conduct. What would you think of me if another political party came on the scene, and I supported it? Or what about my parishioners who hold different opinions? What would they think if I were to get mixed up in a political party? Catholics are at liberty to join any party, provided that party respects the rights of the Church. I want to let you know where I stand at the very beginning. You must realize, too, that our remoteness here, the difficulties of communication, and other circumstances which you will gradually become familiar with, create a special state of mind in the villagers; it makes them apathetic and quite uninterested in political and social matters. I mention this now, lest you fall into the convenient error of attributing to our counselling the lack of en-thusiasm you'll find in the village when elections or similar subjects are mentioned. I admit, though, I've never understood or been in-

terested in these matters. You may be quite sure that neither I nor
any of the priests in the parish will be on one side or the other. If
you want our support for a party working to secure order, national
progress, religious tolerance, and so on, you must convince the authorities from whom we receive our orders . . ."

The Re-election Club for Corral was founded, and was received
with manifest coolness on the part of the villagers.

V

The downfall of Damián Limón caused a change
in Bartolo Jiménez' life.

When he learned that Damián had fallen under Victoria's spell,
and was so enamored that he'd even forgotten his quarrel with his
father over his inheritance, Bartolo had a glimpse of heaven. Then,
when he perceived that Micaela was trying to attract Damián—
she was quite shameless about it—and convinced himself that it was
no idle pastime, that Damián had really fallen victim to her wiles,
he felt even better. However, he said nothing to his wife, nor
could he bring himself to meet her eyes or stop his target practice.

But on the day of Damián's arrest, Bartolo, before learning of it,
came home, trembling with rage and fear, shaken by the terrible
deed, but secretly elated because he had no further need to worry,
and selfishly proud of being able to show his wife what kind of a
man Damián was. As he related the event, in all its details, he
couldn't help watching the expression on her face to see the effect it
was having. He had never before dared, either when they were engaged or after they were married, to look into her eyes. But what
he saw there that day, August 24, 1909, was worse than if Damián
had buried seven bullets in his heart.

VI

María was just finishing the reading of *The
Three Musketeers;* she had read it so furtively that not even Marta
had observed her. (Why don't we live in the days described in the
novel? Maybe, somewhere far away, there is a country like that!)
She'd heard of another book, *The Mysteries of Paris,* which was
wonderful. Of course it was! María was thrilled by the mere title.
(Who could lend it to her? Father Islas is now going around in-
specting books in all the houses. The other day he burned a pile,

among them *Les Miserables, The Wandering Jew, Resurrection, The Count of Monte Cristo.* They say that *The Count* is very good, too.)

VII

"You know," said Lucas Macías, "the stones of the old convent church of Santo Domingo (it used to be where St. Joseph's is now, but it covered many more blocks). Well, the stones were used to build the Degollado Theatre, which used to be called the Alarcón, but they changed its name in honor of Don Santos Degollado, the general who used to mend his own clothes and, every time he was defeated, formed a new army overnight. He was a good man, Don Santos, not a savage. He was charitable, too; he died with less money than I have. Just imagine! Giving away all his money! Well, as I was saying, they used the stones of Santo Domingo to build the Degollado, and from that moment people said that something would happen to it. All the same, I don't think that this is the fulfillment of the prophecy, or rather revelation, granted to a Carmelite nun, though, because according to that it was supposed to collapse when it was full of people, and that wasn't what happened. If I went to Guadalajara, you couldn't pay me to go into that theatre. If I were going to any theatre, I'd choose the Apollo, where they put on pastoral plays, although the Degollado is really the best one. Not even in Mexico City is there anything like it. It has figures painted on the dome like a church; the hall is big enough to hold four altars like the one in the Parish Church, and it's full of velvet curtains and mirrors . . . Well, even if this wasn't the fulfilling of the prophecy, or rather the revelation, it's still a warning from God."

"The world is all topsy turvy," Lucas went on. "The Degollado Theatre in Guadalajara burned down, the Flores in Acapulco, the Juárez (it would be the Juárez!) in Monterrey, and the Houses of Parliament. There're frequent earthquakes in different places, floods, revolutions the way it is in Spain, with convents burned in Barcelona. And here, in this village, I have a strange feeling, as if the end of the world might be coming soon; at night when I think about what's happening now, and forget what happened in the past, which I always liked best, I ask God not to forget and leave me down here. I don't want to be around to see the end of the world! I'm afraid! You may laugh at me, but I think the Antichrist has been born—yes, that must be it. And Reyism? Do you know what Reyism is? Well, it's like strikes. I beg God to take me away from here soon."

"Tell me, Lucas, do you think Don Porfirio is going to die?"

VIII

The leading editorial in *El País* on Thursday, July 1, was headed DUST AND MUD. "We have already explained," said the writer, "that what is incorrectly termed the 'political awakening' of the country is no more than a spurt of exasperation. One of the most deep-rooted and pestilential plagues in our present society is the lack of justice, which is one of the primitive bases, together with authority and law, on which society rests. A society can have no real life without justice. Justice is as important to the social organism as health is to the human organism, and the society without justice is a sick society, threatened with dissolution. There is no justice in Mexico now, from one end of the Republic to the other. Listen to the cry that rises. . . ."

And on Saturday, July 24, under the heading REYISM AND CORRALISM: "Reyism, as far as the people are concerned, is not a political but a social phenomenon. Hundreds of times, in the pages of this newspaper, we have denounced the servile caciquism which has prevailed throughout the Republic almost from its beginning . . . Hundreds of times we have said, *The nation is suffering!* The backs of the people are scarred by the whips of brutal caciques who call themselves Political Leaders. The people are ready to rise against the domination of the Political Bosses, against monopolies, judicial and administrative arbitrariness . . . If, instead of 'General Reyes!' the cry had been raised for any other strong man, capable of leading the suffering people under his banner against the proud tyrant, the name would have been acclaimed. Reyism is essentially impersonal. It expresses a reaction, a longing, a necessity of society . . ."

The next day, July 25, there were serious uprisings in Guadalajara, caused by the visit of the supporters of Corral for re-election. The news was greatly exaggerated by the time it reached the village: street fighting, injuries, deaths . . . a real revolution. The fighting was starting! Either on his own initiative or on instructions received, the Deputy paid another visit to Father Martínez to ask him to intervene on behalf of the feeble Re-election Club. The Parish Priest refused to budge from his position. Then began a period of threats against the recalcitrant, with especial severity toward those suspected of hostility to Corralism and sympathy for Reyism: force, fines, arrests, forced labor, government intervention in judicial matters, lenience for debtors who were loyal to the cause, barefaced suspension of the rights of the rebels, ominous tampering with the census and public records of property ownership. The poor got the worst of it.

The editorials and events, and even more his failure to organize a club for the Northerners, all of them now under the shadow of Damián's crime, inspired Father Reyes with the idea of a ministry more adapted to modern life. He forgot his previous experiences and resolutions. He went to see Father Martínez and laid before him the urgent need for an organization on an economic basis: a bank that would advance money to farmers and artisans; a co-operative society to deal with production and consumption; life insurance. It would be successful because it would attack usury, the worst social evil of the region.

"The number of men who've lost their lands has grown, and so has the number of those who can't till them because they have nothing to work with. Tenant farmers, deceived by the owners who supply their food and get them embroiled in tangled accounts and endless debts, never receive a penny. The difference between the price received by the landowner and the price he pays to the farmer at harvest time is an abuse that arouses them. The people are long-suffering, but their patience is coming to an end."

IX

It was not poverty, nor even the danger threatening their religious ideas, that was undermining the spiritual life of the villagers. It was the growing sensuality, already hardened in some cases, which must be fought without mercy.

Alarmed by the influence Victoria was exerting on men and women, Father Islas decided that it was his duty to report it to Father Martínez, even though the knowledge might be bad for his health.

"Assuming that the woman is not personally to blame for having roused so many desires, in any case it's a symptom of the moral corruption invading the village, and this at the end of Lent, when everybody seemed really repentant . . . Pure hypocrisy! It's the hidden illnesses that are the worst. When have we ever seen the things that are happening now? You have the case of Mercedes Toledo, one of the Daughters of Mary, who might have been an example to the others. Now, she's publicly engaged to Julián and doesn't care who knows it. The next thing you know, they'll be walking in the street together, as they say couples do in the cities. There's no need for going into the follies of Don Inocencio's daughter, the scandalous behavior of the Northerners, the number of pornographic books and pictures that are being passed from hand to hand. Sensuality disguised as love, that's the point of entry for the evil. Let's look at this frankly. You know better than I do how those who sin against the sixth and ninth commandments neglect the Sacraments. The case of Victoria is serious, and I felt it was my duty to bring it to you."

For the first time, Father Martínez could not see at once what measures to take. The failure of his efforts troubled him even more than his physical weakness; Retreats, the Confessional, sermons, were no longer enough to save the sinful soul. Perhaps God no longer required the services of this sinful and aging servant.

The next morning, Tuesday, July 27, no power on earth could have prevented him from getting up early and going to hear confessions.

X

Micaela's plans (Man proposes and God disposes) were to make Damián look small in order to avenge herself on Prudencia and Clementina for the way they had treated her; but she would also avenge herself on the whole village for their wagging tongues and collective disapproval. They should see who would win, she or the stranger who was trying to attract Damián, among others. The defection of David Estrada, and still more that of Julián Ledesma, who had made up with Mercedes Toledo just when Micaela thought he was safe in her clutches, had driven her "out of her mind," as the saying was.

She would get Damián to propose to her, and then, the day before the wedding, when everything had been arranged and paid for, she would walk out on him. The sting of memory led her to conceive even crueler plans: she would flirt with Don Timoteo, arouse his senile passions, lead him on with false hopes, provoke a fight between father and son. It was rumored that Don Timoteo would hardly wait more than six months to marry again.

Alas! Micaela's plans, like those of the milkmaid carrying milk to
market, ended in disaster.

It was an unlucky day, that May 2, when Micaela Rodríguez set
out in earnest to subjugate Damían Limón. A disastrous night!

XI

They were talking about the interview between
Don Porfirio Díaz and the President of the United States. Lucas
Macías, as usual, seemed to change the subject, by talking about the
shootings in Veracruz in 1879. "The famous General Mier y Terán,
who said 'Strike while the iron is hot!' suspected trouble everywhere and everyone accused him of going too far. I think he in-
herited a strain of madness, because, you remember, his father, in a
moment of madness, killed himself on Iturbide's tomb. Well, to go
back to the son, who was Governor of Veracruz: he was a wealthy
Creole and the words 'cristiano, cristianito' were never off his lips
when he was talking to people; Don Porfirio was a grand 'cristiano,'
they were great friends, friends of long standing; so much so that
when Mier was disgraced, because of the shootings in Veracruz
(the truth of the matter is that everyone blamed Don Porfirio, but
no one dared say so to his face), Don Porfirio invited him to Te-
huacán and showered attentions upon him, as much as to say to
everyone: 'Let him alone. Receive him in your homes.' But, since
there is One above Who allots rewards and punishments, Mier went
mad a few years later, and the friendship of no man could save him.
Divine Providence is just, and no one escapes its decrees."

One day the Deputy went to see Father Martínez, carrying a
copy of El País, in which the leading editorial began, "It is now
clear, beyond all doubt, that Reyism in Mexico has been the step
from revolution to anarchy."

"This is printed in a Catholic newspaper, and still you won't make
up your mind to give your support to the Party that is fighting to
preserve order and salvation in the country and, what is the same
thing, in religion, from the most frightful of all dangers, from anarchy? You know what happened in Barcelona, and the revolution
which was threatened because of the shooting of the anarchist Fer-
rer. Anarchy!"

XII

The marbles were rolling towards their final destiny, some slowly, some swiftly. Some of them hesitated at a cross-slot, and then were pushed violently forward. Just like the games at the Fair, played on painted boards, where the paths are marked out by nails. The ball was rolling! Things were on the move!

VICTORIA AND GABRIEL

I

N THE STROKE OF FOUR, or a little earlier from April to September, Gabriel wakes. At four o'clock sharp from April through September and at half-past four throughout the rest of the year, he begins to ring for the first mass. To those tossing sleeplessly, torn between hope and despair, longing for the dawn, the bells are a godsend; to those who must get up although they would like to go on sleeping, to those just fallen asleep, and to those whose pleasant dreams are abruptly cut short, they are a nightmare. All the hopes and fears of the village are summoned to life by the hand of the early-rising bell-ringer, center of the life of the village, especially at this important moment of daily rebirth. Gabriel presides over the days of many men and women, his image, his name, recalling them to ambitions and sufferings, setting the wheels of routine in motion, summoning the village to duty, drudgery, and weariness; and his

hand, which gives the signal to begin the old communal round in its stubborn, set order, also brings it to a halt, with the curfew bell, at nine o'clock in winter and at ten in summer. Gabriel holds sway over joys, torments, and sufferings; his is the common tongue, speaking through the bells, in the tones of this barren community of black-robed women. Gabriel, evangel and pendulum.

Nobody, not even Lucas Macías, knows how and when Gabriel made his first appearance in the Parish Priest's house, a small five-year-old, dark-haired, with dark smooth skin and sad eyes in a sad face, knowing nothing of games or friends, shy, churlish, and uncouth. The bell tower was his place of refuge. When Gabriel was nine, Father Martínez tried to make an acolyte of him. He couldn't learn what to do in his cassock and surplice, after two long months of trial he knew no more than on the first day or at the end of the first week. He would trip and fall, he would burn himself with the incense burner, he couldn't keep the candle straight, he would spill the Holy Water; his clumsiness became even worse in the Chancel, it was like going to the gallows. He felt all eyes fixed upon him, he tried to hide, not to look at the congregation, but he couldn't make the proper movements, find his place in the mass and the rosary, learn what he was supposed to do and when to do it. He could never put the Missal in its proper place, fill the flagons, take the purificator off the chalice, hold the candle for the priest at the time of the celebration, put the candles in the large candlesticks, put incense in the incense burner, or help the priests to robe. One night he broke a lamp with the processional candle, another time he slipped and broke a large china jar. At one early mass he nearly set the altar on fire when he brought the candle for the celebration. It only made him the clumsier for the Parish Priest, the curates, and the sacristan to scold, and for his fellow acolytes, the choirboys, and other youngsters that joined in with them, to laugh at him. Gabriel was their meek victim, and they abused him and struck him with impunity; no one heard him complain, no one saw him cry; he kept everything to himself. Not even in Marta did he confide his misery; but Marta understood and sympathized, and persuaded Father Martínez to leave him in peace. Besides, he performed the humble tasks of sweeping, bringing water, cutting wood, and running errands, most conscientiously.

Gabriel's origin is a mystery. Even Lucas, with all his wiles, hasn't been able to ferret it out. Father Martínez refers to him as his nephew, but not very often and in rather vague terms. Little given to discussing personal matters, Father Martínez changes the subject when the conversation touches on the topic of the boy's parents. Marta and María, when they were small, asked what relation Gabriel was to them; they don't remember what their uncle replied, but he must have given them a satisfactory answer, because they felt they should have a cousinly regard for the new arrival. As the years passed, Father Martínez' efforts to maintain and increase the distance between the boy and the girls without letting them realize it, were redoubled.

The village takes it for granted that Gabriel will marry María; no one questions it, it's not even discussed, since both live in a world of their own, Gabriel in the clouds, with the bells as his brothers, until he feels that his very soul is sonorous bronze, and María in the far-off days of romantic legend, in far-off cities—Paris, Vienna, Constantinople. Those who, by intuitive conviction rather than any process of conscious thought, have paired them off, are quite sure that one day they will discover each other, and be surprised at having lived so close together and yet so far apart. Marta shares this opinion, which is subconscious, not even based on affinities that link María and Gabriel. If the affinities were apparent to the busybodies, the prospective marriage would be on all tongues.

Gabriel is imaginative and fanciful like María, but his flights of fancy are so tenuous and ethereal that they seem to be no part of this world, and to have no abiding place in it. He would like to travel, although he realizes, before setting out, that what he is looking for will not be found on earth. His longings, none the less disturbing for being formless and subconscious, cannot find the gateway to reality. Maybe he is dimly aware of them in a pattern first sensed in the bells, then in the music of a harmonium, in songs, in sound, in silence, in a silence where Gabriel hears, as it were, a melody of eternal bells, cast from the metal of the stars, in the kiln of night, by Thrones and Dominations, for heavenly, not human, ears. This is the melody he seeks to reproduce in the bells entrusted to his care . . . bells whose task is to awaken souls . . . the ringing of temporal bells; and this eager hope makes him feel like the Archangel Gabriel, lord of the air, the mighty archangel, captive in the tower, without wings to follow the music and overtake it, mocked by the resistance, by the obstinate stubbornness of bronze bells whose muted sound will not "rise through the heavens to the highest sphere and hear another kind of everlasting music, the best of all." ("When, freed from this prison, shall I wing through the sky?") But he loves his prison in the tower, and every day, with loving patience, he tries different combinations, searching for the tones that speak to him from the depths of infinity, perhaps from nearer at hand, from no greater depths than those of the Cemetery, from the foundations of Retreat House, from behind the tightly closed doors and windows of the village, through the seams of the crosses, from below the stones in the dried-up river bed, in the dark streets at night, in the tense faces of the villagers, in the black dresses and shawls of the women, from the underground stream whence life's anxieties well up, here and now.

"Wouldn't you like to be a bell-ringer in Rome or Seville?" María once asked him.

"Why? It wouldn't be the same. I couldn't."

He meant, "I would be a stranger in those cities, and couldn't make their bells talk."

The bells of each place are as individual as the speech of a man: one has a deep voice, another a high-pitched one; one man stutters, another rattles along; no one tries or learns how to speak like this; each man's voice is determined by his nature and expresses his way of being, his virtues and weaknesses. Gabriel has learned this by experience. Two years before, Father Martínez, who wanted to test the boy's vocation and if possible to get him into Holy Orders, sent him to study in the Seminary at San Juan de los Lagos. His inclination led him to the tower of the Sanctuary, where he would spend the greater part of the day. One Saturday, the first time he was allowed to ring the bells, for the "Salve María," the Chapterhouse and the neighborhood were filled with consternation. ("Why are the bells tolling?") Because he could ring the bells only as he rang those in his own village, and a hidden impulse, over which his will had no control, guided his hand. It was as if he himself were talking, as if his village were speaking through him, and he was his village; he bore its character deep within him, its unchanging essence. Even later, he was never able to give to the bells of San Juan the same tones the official bell-ringer gave them, nor could he ever express the character of his village with them—the homesickness and longing, which throbbed in his every heartbeat for the village which drew him back with each memory and was never out of his thoughts. He could never copy someone else's way of ringing the bells; when he tried to, he felt ashamed, as if he were telling lies. He never felt the rhythm of the strange town, nor any love for it; he yearned to go back to his own bell tower, dominated by the Cemetery on one side and Retreat House on the other. Nor would the bells of San Juan respond to his touch; they rebelled against the hand of the "foreigner," who could not learn to speak their tongue. If his hearers were displeased, he himself was even more so.

When the contemplation of the changing sky, of the unchanging landscape, and his bells left him time, which was not often, Gabriel liked to read. He was not a voracious reader like María, but read slowly and with concentration. He preferred poetry to fiction, the harmony of verse suggesting the harmony of bells; many lines stayed in his mind, and even though he did not fully understand them, he would recite them to the sky, to the night, to the village, and to the bells. No one knew about this habit of his. Once he was reciting, to himself, as usual, when Marta burst into the tower. Gabriel was afraid that she had heard him and was ready to sink into the ground with mortification. Never had he felt so ashamed. But Marta hadn't discovered his liking for poetry, and after that he took exaggerated precautions against betraying himself. He found novels harder and slower work. He had read but few. *The Finale of Norma* kept him awake for several nights, and he still remembered, with enjoyment, the "Daughter of Heaven" as an ethereal vision. The naturalistic ending displeased him; he would have preferred for Serafín to be left with an unattainable dream, unincarnate into a woman of flesh and blood that he might marry. Now he was reading *Les Miserables*. No one knew how he had managed to get hold of these books.

Neither the lively María nor the silent Gabriel was aware of their affinity; they felt poles apart.

II

On Easter Monday morning, Victoria's amazement, which had been growing ever since the extraordinary ringing of the bells on Maundy Thursday, reached its peak. She was moved to the core of her being. It was as if, in the same concert, triumphant and macabre at the same time, she were lifted to heavenly heights and plunged into abysmal depths, as if she were in purgatory, in hell, in eternity—celestial and tragic eternity. Who was making the humble bronze bells speak with such an unearthly voice? Each stroke, however insignificant or ordinary, had overtones that shook her. Wasn't this the secret of her liking for the village? Joy and torment . . . new sensations, affecting her innermost being. Thrilling paradox: pleasurable pain, painful pleasure, inextricably mixed.

It was on that Easter Monday morning that her whole world came tumbling about her ears. Her elegant arrogance crashed to the ground. She was filled with overwhelming tenderness. It was as if she felt anew all the griefs experienced in this and many former lives, as if in this moment, when her very foundations were shaken, she could feel again the sufferings of even her most remote ancestors. In her veins coursed the pulsing joys and sorrows of countless men and women, buried under the layers of centuries, passing the bounds of death and communicating with her across the centuries. She was so moved that the burden of these reborn emotions was a fearful pleasure. Beyond the bounds of Death. A joy unexampled in her dreams or in her experience of intellectual and physical pleasures. Travel, parties, friendship, family relationships, nothing had ever afforded her such pleasure—or suffering—suffering great enough to cause instant death. A dread of empty space, beyond death, as though, when the bells began to toll, she had begun to fall, and were falling, falling into the dreaded void. Beyond the bounds of Death. Solemn bells, like an unearthly organ, played by the wind, by winds laden with eternity. An organ played by Death himself.

Who was the artist that only yesterday and the day before yesterday, had sung the world's hymn to the Resurrection, and now, minister of Death, was banishing all joy from the world? He must have supernatural strength—and the hands and heart of the archangel that drove Adam and Eve from Paradise, of that other archangel that slew the first-born in Egypt, of the archangels of the Apocalypse. Like the Four Horsemen, he would purify the world before the Day of Judgment. (This Easter Monday morning, with its bells ceaselessly tolling the death knell, was a kind of Judgment Day.)

Never in all Victoria's experience had any emotion shaken her as those harmonies did, yesterday glorious in their hymn to Life, today in their exaltation of Death. Harmonies from the bells of a small village church, wrought by unknown hands. Only the Archangel of Death could make bronze vibrate like this, raise the transitory to the eternal, the regional to the universal, and, strange alchemy, turn horror into delight.

What man could convert a few humble bells into an instrument of such unearthly music? Overwhelmed, Victoria imagined a hieratic, translucent being, without eyes and without feet, hands like a gravedigger's, a woman's pierced hands of crystal, arms crossed above a tongue of fire. A faint aura formed the head. The crossed arms were attached to ceaselessly fluttering wings. She would seek him out as before she had sought out great pianists, celebrated actors, famous people. She would seek him as she never would seek a husband. And if he were Death himself? She would find him!

III

Death! Death that cruelly tears the skeleton of days apart, minute by minute, until only separate seconds are left. Love, they say, does this too. Love is like death. Is it love or death that moves Gabriel's hands? Is it love or death that causes the fever? Is it love or death that has changed the rhythm of the bells? One minute they peal frantically, the next they are faint and weak. They ring out gaily for the evening Angelus, and for early mass they toll wearily.

"Gabriel is playing with the bells," say the people in the privacy of patios and bedrooms.

But this has been going on for days now. It cannot be just a passing phase. Then, as they meet in the street, the people ask, "What has happened to Gabriel?"

The crazy ringing of the bells is growing intolerable.

"Gabriel's making fun of the village," say the people in the Square.

One evening he rang the passing-bell for a meeting of the Daughters of Mary. There was no mistake about it. The village was indignant. "Gabriel's making fun of our traditions."

Another time, instead of ringing the evening Angelus, the bells played Christmas Carols.

"Gabriel's making fun of us."

Either the bells rang so rapidly that the sound of the trebles was lost in the swift evolutions and the noise of the clappers deadened other sounds, or they chimed with the exasperating, slow, tuneless, uneven beat of a clock whose mainspring is broken.

"Has Gabriel gone crazy?"

This went on for eight, for twelve, dreadful days.

"This is impossible!"

With its rhythm upset, the village could not function properly. The pattern of everyday life and thought was awry. There was general restlessness.

"This is unbearable!"

No one could work, let alone pray. No one could bear to be alone. The whole village felt oppressed and confined. The people could hear their own breathing and the beating of their own hearts, and were conscious of sadness, of repressed longings.

"This cannot go on."

After twelve mad days Father Martínez gave way before the general indignation and the evidence of his own senses, and forbade Gabriel to ring the bells.

How ordinary, how dead the bells sounded, rung by other hands! Most people, mindful of sacrilege, and resentful, were relieved to have it so. A few objected, those who preferred the living voice of a madman to dead, mechanical ringing. Victoria found this unendurable; it drove her away from the village before she had planned to go. No one knew the reason for her sudden departure. Only a few were malicious enough to connect it with the sound of the bells.

IV

Victoria and Gabriel met only four brief times. Their words were labored: a few phrases from Victoria, a few monosyllables from Gabriel . . . halting words punctuated by silences, illumined by glances, charged with what words could not utter. Only four times, only a few words.

Four times. Once, Victoria had taken Gabriel by surprise as he was ringing the passing-bell. It was the first hour of the afternoon, the shopkeepers had not yet come back from dinner and the shops were still shut. On Victoria's restlessness the sound fell like sparks on a powder keg; she left the house and made her way through the deserted streets, drawn, but with no conscious purpose, to the church. There her eyes sought the little door that opened upon the circular stone stairway. Instinctively, she looked about her. Did she dare? But the little door invited her to enter; from the tower came convulsive peals of agony. The stone serpent, its gullet polished smooth by those it had engulfed through the years, swallowed her, and step by step she mounted the winding passage. She was alone in the dark labyrinth, terrified by the frenzied ringing. If she met someone in the darkness, on the stairway . . . She would go back.

When she emerged into the light at the top, she looked older; her lips were drained, trembling, and her eyes were bright with fever. The booming of the bells struck on her senses like thunder. The height made her ears buzz.

A thunderbolt falling at his feet could not have startled Gabriel more. How long had she been there? Victoria remained outside the bell chamber, silent, watching the hands that pulled the ropes so rhythmically, like a conductor guiding the unseen strings of an orchestra, with the agile fingers of a harpist; the hands of a celebrant, swift-moving and solemn. She yearned to kiss those hands! His profile, she saw, was a strange one, both gentle and harsh. She could find nothing around which to shape an impression. The features, unformed and contradictory, eluded her; sometimes the lips and nose seemed delicately chiseled, then the mouth would relax in some sensual impulse and look repulsive, only to lose itself in ecstasy again, temples, cheekbones, forehead, and eyebrows tensed in contemplation. His eyes were not visible, but she could guess what they were like, gleaming from black depths. His head, his movements, his expression, gave him an air partly angelic, partly demonic; his features were at once fine and heavy; he was ugly, unkempt, indifferent to his surroundings, yet he had an indefinable charm.

He was sitting astride some beams, leaning against the wall, his shoulders hunched, his legs twisted awkwardly, his hair untidy, dirty. When he began to ring the bells, his indifference suddenly disappeared and his limbs sprang to life, moving in a smooth rhythm, except for the constant tension in his hands, which flashed to and fro with unearthly swiftness. Victoria watched him for a long time, struggling against her repugnance, facing her disappointment. ("He's just an immature youth, and his features still have all the physical and moral unattractiveness of an adolescent.") But she could not bridge the gap between them and understand the mystery of the man in front of her. The bells had ceased to ring in her ears as she stood there, and the force of her emotion must have roused Gabriel from his absorption. The sudden appearance of the most fearsome beast would not have made him spring up in such panic-stricken violence, ready to hurl himself upon the intruder. It was not so much the gesture as his fierce expression that struck her. She was no longer listening to the bells but was conscious only of the man who, by pulling rhythmically on a few ropes, drew her up to heaven, beyond the clouds, above the sun. She was reminded of an officiating priest, a consecrated genius whose hands, illumined by powerful floodlamps, send out their message in the religious darkness of a packed theatre to a spellbound audience. Now they were released from the spell, face to face, after years of waiting.

Gabriel felt as if a wind from far away were beating against his face, penetrating the pores of his skin, filling his nostrils and ears, overwhelming brain and heart, blotting out thoughts and feelings.

He could not recognize her, for he had known nothing of her visit to the village. Before, he had never known what a hallucination was. Now he knew. She couldn't be flesh and blood, or a statue, or a painting—an apparition like this, at this hour, coming on silent wings, in this village of black-robed women and death, couldn't be real. Where had it come from? Why had it come?

"I must be going mad! They say this is the way Luis Gonzaga started seeing visions; but the visions that drove him mad weren't like this one; this one would have made him humble and gentle."

Where could she be from, if not from heaven? Could she be a figment of his imagination? They wouldn't dress like that in heaven. Was she out of a novel? The vision of a disordered brain? Yes, she must be a delusion, maybe a kind of heavenly madness caused by the bells, their sound itself transformed into the vision . . . of a woman! Could it be a temptation like those pictured in the *Christian Year*? In this form, in this place, at this hour, it could only be a temptation: the Devil in the shape of an angel, dressed as a woman. The singer in *The Finale of Norma* must have looked like this! The destroying wind kept changing Gabriel's expression each moment, from fierce to gentle, from gentle to fierce. (Years later, when he saw the "Victory of Samothrace" in the Louvre, he felt no surprise, but recalled the violent emotion of the terrible moment in his life when he saw Victoria moving towards him, a flesh-and-blood Victory, head, magnificent arms, rounded hips, moving forward, in fierce, instinctive modesty.) The force of the wind increased, there was a ringing in his ears, and he thought he would faint. Whence had she come? How? Why? It was impossible to flee from her, to turn his back on the fascinating vision, to let her out of his sight. It was impossible to speak, for he was tongue-tied as always. He was no longer the pale youth of three minutes ago. The blood rushed to his face, he was ready to sweat blood.

Victoria was moved to pity. The loathing she had felt at the sight

of his pimply adolescent face was replaced by bondage to the archangel glimpsed underneath this outward appearance. Her loathing
changed, yes, to bondage, to adoration—it changed, but she felt
pity, too, and a maternal impulse.

"He's innocence incarnate," she thought. "It's overwhelming."

"How mysterious a woman is!" thought Gabriel.

"The bells have spoken to me in his voice."

"She's what I've been seeking, in the sounds I could never wring
from the bells."

"The impossible is happening," said Victoria, sadly.

And Gabriel replied: "This is death, the approach of death."

Victoria (woman, goddess, and statue) and Gabriel (archangel)
stood motionless, each in the center of a whirlwind, joined in a
mood of exaltation, but each, without realizing it, afraid to touch
the other.

When Victoria, imperiously, took a step forward, her gesture triumphant—thighs, breast, arms, and head like those of the statue, the
wings invisible—Gabriel was powerless to move back. He could
only shut his eyes. Then he collapsed. Compassion surged through
her: a fallen archangel, with battered wings and a dirty face, a bird
blown into mud by a storm, its wings useless. A blush of shame red-
dened the earthy color of his face. Victoria could not resist. She bent
down and, her eyes shining through a prism of tears, stretched out a
trembling hand to him and asked, "Are you ill?"

But the wasted wings found strength again; they drew themselves
up and spread. Before she could touch him, the archangel moved
back, waving his mighty wings, while his lips repeated the mono-
syllable, "No! No!"

Wings stronger than those of the Greek goddess carried him back.
He was the archangel of wrath, magnificent in his splendor! Fierce
eyes and clenched fists, inspiring awe. A menacing Gabriel, not the
gentle messenger of the Annunciation, with the Madonna lily in his
hand, a star on his brow, but the angel with the flaming sword at
the gates of Paradise. "No! No!"

His attitude was so fierce that Victoria's compassion turned to
shame, and she crept down the circular staircase in confusion . . .
Eve driven out of Paradise.

The second time Victoria and Gabriel met was a night when Victoria had stayed in church, perhaps deliberately, a long time after
the Rosary was over. Only the lights of the Reserved Sacrament

were still burning. Carrying a lantern in his hand, Gabriel came to lock up. Making out the loitering form, he rattled his keys. Victoria rose and in the darkness followed behind him, overtaking him behind the Chancel. As she was emerging, she turned and said, "Good night."

("I'm such a boor and so rude I didn't even answer her greeting. I didn't even ask how Luis is! But what do I care? What do I care?" thought Gabriel silently, when he recovered from his first emotion.) The thought kept him awake all night, his first sleepless night.

Next morning, the bells were out of tune. The jangling grew worse, like a rising fever, on Thursday, Friday, and Saturday. By Sunday it was sounding in the very heart, the crazed heart, of the village. And there was general consternation.

Wednesday, Thursday, Friday, Saturday, and Sunday, the question gnawed at Gabriel's consciousness, "Why didn't I answer her greeting?" And the senseless, automatic answer was repeated, "What do I care? What do I care?"

Sunday. Sunday afternoon in the village. The Rosary over. Silence in the Square. The farmers gone back to their farms. The shops shut, the people indoors. The bells silent, the streets deserted. Gabriel felt a mounting restlessness. Nowhere to go, nothing to go out for. The sun still high. A bright afternoon and nothing to do. The blood throbbed in his veins till he felt they would burst. The worst time of the week in this place, shut up in this place. Forbidden to work, forbidden to visit people. Nothing to do after the evening service, and still a long time to dinner and bedtime. Boring conversations in the houses . . . yawns. A pity it's such a lovely evening! Occasionally a man's step. Some could read or sleep in their houses, but these were few. Sunday, after the early evening service is over.

So it was that Gabriel and Victoria met for the third time. Gabriel, driven by his restlessness, set out towards the country like a sleepwalker, that Good Shepherd Sunday. Afterward, he could have sworn that he had no intention of entering the street where the Pérez house was. For two days he had been able to keep his desires in check, but this evening, he felt like a criminal. He had left the Presbytery like a man setting out to commit a crime. ("I'll walk along in front of the house, quickly. Why shouldn't I? It's all shut up, anyhow.") At the corner, in front of La Camelia, he met Don Alfredo.

"Well! Where did you come from?" Gabriel trembled like a thief caught red-handed. "You're just the person I want to see. Is it a fact that Father Martínez is with the new Deputy at this very moment? They told me—but why are you trembling so? Is there bad news?"

"No, Don Alfredo, I've been running. Excuse me."

"Wait, tell me about Father Martínez—"

Gabriel rushed off, leaving Don Alfredo muttering, "They're all crazy in this village."

(Gabriel, covered with confusion, was thinking, "He must have read my thoughts. I'll go straight out into the country. And, to prove that I can walk somewhere else, I'll walk around by the inn. Why do I have to walk in front of her house? What do I care?")

He had no idea how he came to be in front of the house a few moments later. He could swear that he had turned off towards the inn. He must have decided that there was no need to change his course. No one was likely to look out of a window, certainly not . . . But he saw a half-open window, and, as if the Devil were taking a hand in this, a shape, a face, appeared, a hand waved to him.

("I didn't know what to do, because I hadn't meant to—but she was coming out—I did want to see her—but I thought nobody would be there, or I wouldn't have come. It must have been the Devil. But even before that, the Devil was inside me, saying, 'Go on. What difference does it make? You won't see her, anyhow. Don't be afraid. You're not a child. You were rude to her the other day, not answering her. And she's so polite.' She's a troublemaker! And when it was too late to go back, there she was, right in front of me. If I could only forget her! I feel ashamed!")

"Excuse me, Gabriel, could you tell me if there's any truth in the rumor that the Deputy has been to see Father Martínez . . . ?"

("I couldn't have moved, even if I'd wanted to; I couldn't turn around and run away. I wasn't even sure how I'd got there, I'd meant to go out into the country.")

". . . please don't think I'm asking out of idle curiosity. I wouldn't bother you, but there's trouble brewing . . ."

("Did she really call me to ask about the Deputy? Why did this woman, who was beginning to sound like a busybody, suddenly set my blood on fire?")

"Never mind. I admire your discretion . . ."

And suddenly, the questions came, falling thickly, like hailstones:

"Haven't you ever been in Guadalajara?"

"Wouldn't you like to study music there?"

"Wouldn't you like to conduct an orchestra?"

"Wouldn't you like to go to Europe?"

("I didn't even understand what she was saying.")

"You have great talent."

("Her eyes were gleaming—she frightened me.")

"I would like to help you."

("Pleasure and the fear that someone might see us were goading her on . . . Her cat's eyes were gleaming . . . What impracticable ideas!")

"Your way of ringing the bells fascinates me!"

"My way . . . ?"

"There's something tremendous about the way you ring them."

"I . . ."

"Forgive me for keeping you."

"I?"

("I didn't hear the rest. But did she really say these things, or did I imagine them? I must have imagined it all, even the cat's eyes! But how would I think up such ideas, let alone put them into words? I didn't even say good-bye to her. But I didn't really see her or talk to her either. I must have imagined it all. Why is it I can't get her out of my head? And those eyes! They say more than her lips.")

On Tuesday and Wednesday, it was impossible to listen to the mad ringing of the bells. The following Sunday, Gabriel was no longer bell-ringer.

On Monday, May 3, the day of the Holy Cross, Victoria and Gabriel met and talked for the fourth and last time.

HOLY CROSS DAY

I

AY OF WRATH, DAY OF ANGER, night of divine
vengeance, when the abomination was conceived
and the Supreme Judge prepared to visit his anger on the village. But nobody noticed the signs
in the heavens. It was Sunday, the second of
May.

At three o'clock in the afternoon it clouded
over and the heat became stifling, without a breath of wind. Thunder rumbled but not a horse neighed, nobody recognized the omens.
Clouds hung over the village like leaden balloons, puffy, not pregnant, barren wombs filled with tumors instead of life. There was no
moisture in the air, no fragrant promise of rain, of damp earth. Between four and five o'clock, the clouds began to take on a purplish
tinge. At six a sinister brightness bathed the crosses and the horizon.
Night fell, a night of evil promise.

"Still no rain!"

"I thought I felt a drop!"

"Isn't it ever going to rain?"

No, it wasn't going to rain. The sky was full of signs, but nobody recognized them. The night was unbearably hot. People wanted to open windows, to go up on roofs, to stand in doorways, to take off their clothes. It was as though an invisible army with flaming brands were passing along the street, and not even the darkness of the night could cool the burning tracks they left.

The suffocating heat sparked Damián's purpose to have an answer from Micaela before the day was over. ("Or is she leading me on, just to make a fool of me? That she won't! Not if I know it! There have been others before her, like those American girls, and no stuck-up village girl is going to treat me this way! She'll give me an answer before the night is over, or—")

Micaela, too, was nearly out of her mind; she couldn't resign herself to being buried in this monotonous existence day after day. Her growing sensuality demanded satisfaction, but she was not a little afraid. ("Can I hold him off? I can't stay shut in like this forever, afraid to say a word to him. It's pretty funny, being afraid of a mere farmer. If I let this one get away, too . . . No, I *will* see him. I'll make him wait, but I'll look—interested. Besides, I am interested —in getting even! And I *will* get even. What's there to be afraid of? I'm not even a Daughter of Mary! I don't mean to spend the rest of my life wondering what it's like to have a man in love with me. And Damián isn't 'just anyone.' He's a lot better than Ruperto Ledesma. I'll show that meddling Victoria! I *do* want to see him! I *do*. I wouldn't even mind if he made love to me. There! That's the truth. How hot it is! I'd like to take off all my clothes and lie down in the grass . . .")

Who could sleep in that heat, in the suffocating bedrooms! Many found an excuse to go out; they had to make arrangements for the next morning. Until nine o'clock that night, there were shadowy figures and voices in the dark streets; lanterns moved to and fro, and snatches of conversation could be heard.

"We'll meet in front of the church before five, and from there we'll go along the path by the river, as we do every year."

"Good, we'll catch up with you."

"We'll leave right after first mass, with Doña Tomasita."

"We're going with the Islas family. They're going straight from the Oratory."

Each comment was followed by the exclamation, "What heat! What unbearable heat!" as though the words were stamped with red-hot irons. The words cracked like a whip against the blackened walls. The second of May, Sunday, Eve of Holy Cross Day.

"We want to be among the first to get there. We want to get back in time for the singing of mass."

"We want to be back before seven."

Darkness and heat shrouded the bare crosses, which would be covered with flowers before sunrise.

Damián hid, lying in wait. Micaela, somehow, managed to discover his hiding place without his seeing her. Malice shone in her eyes. "Let him suffer!" she thought, taking care to keep out of sight while she calmly watched his face and movements. It excited her pleasantly to watch the signs of impatience in his gestures and restless movements! To think that this man, who had been to the North and had the reputation of being a woman tamer, was under her spell! With what intenseness she watched the shadows on his face: it was congested like that of a hanged man, livid, as though he'd been drowned, earthy, like a disinterred corpse! She felt like an executioner gloating over the death throes of his victim, and watching the color of death creep over muscles, alter features, blot out the signs of life, still the pulse.

The frequent striking of matches and the flickering glow of cigarettes that lit up the darkness betrayed his restlessness. He left his hiding place and paced up and down the street with less and less caution; he was coming nearer, she could hear him breathe, grunt, curse. He turned away. "Suppose he goes away for good?" she thought. She almost started after him, the words were on her tongue. But she smothered the impulse. With the calm of a gambler, she moved away and lay down in the darkest corner of the patio. There were no stars in the sky. Hours passed.

Damián was working himself up to violence, growing more and more desperate as time went on. Juanita went out and returned. The Martínez family came and fetched Doña Lola and Juanita away with them. Don Inocencio emerged. No sign of Micaela. Don Inocencio returned. He stood by the door, and finally, shut it noisily. A boy arrived with two horses saddled. Doña Lola and Juanita came back. Damián could hear the key turn in the lock. No sign of Micaela. She was certainly tantalizing him. She was well barricaded in.

"We'll see whether you can make a fool of me, my girl. What do you take me for?" he muttered.

Micaela heard a noise on the roof. "There he is!" She was completely calm and stayed where she was in the darkness. She couldn't see, but she felt someone watching her. A pleasant, prickling sensation. "Now, I'll go," she said, and got up quietly, went to the kitchen, lit a pine torch, opened the door into the yard, and waited, beside the stable, with incredible composure. Damián climbed on the wall.

"It's me, Damián, don't be afraid."

"Why should I be afraid?"

"Listen."

"I will listen to you, but if you jump down, I'll scream."

Her harsh tone checked him. Her voice betrayed no trace of the fear that the panting, threatening note of supplication in his words aroused. She thought he would jump down and strangle her; she could already sense his rough fingers at her throat, ready to tighten; his sweaty smell close to her face, his hot eyes searching hers, with hate and desire. *Desire!* The thought made her tremble. With an effort, she managed to speak.

"What do you want?"

"Why . . . why didn't you . . . answer my letter?" He stuttered with emotion, and she felt a savage joy, followed by disappointment at the ease of her triumph. She no longer cared whether he stayed on the wall or not. She recovered her composure.

"Because I'm nobody's plaything. I won't take someone else's leavings. Did you think I was like the others that you found so easy? You can't catch me that way."

"I swear I'll do anything if you'll only love me. You're the only girl who ever made me feel like this. Please, let me come down."

"If you do, I'll call for help."

"Micaela, Micaelita. *Please.* Tell me you love me."

"And let you go round tomorrow boasting of it!"

"Set me any tests you like. Anything! But don't refuse me, or . . ."

"Keep away from me."

"Micaela, Micaela, for God's sake. You try me too far."

Was there no bolt of lightning to strike one of them down at that moment? Could the earth not open and swallow Damián? Then the murky night would have borne no evil fruit. No such lasting shame would have stained the village. What evil spirit had bound Micaela's eyes and blinded her to the omens? How could even the dogs have slept and given no warning bark? How had it all escaped Lucas Macías' sharp eyes and Father Martínez' watchfulness? They should have come running through the streets sounding an alarm, prophets with tongues of fire. A silence of death filled the dark cavern of the night. Micaela, instrument of vengeance overtaking hidden sins, warning of the growing corruption, opened the gates to the Furies.

"Well, . . . I'll give you a chance to prove yourself. But it will take time."

"What do you want time for? You aren't a Daughter of Mary, are you?"

Damián jumped. Micaela uttered no cry.

II

Holy Cross Day.

In the darkness of the early morning the streets filled with people. There was a scent of flowers, lanterns could be seen moving, brief conversations could be heard. When they reached the dry river bed, where the path to the Mission Cross started, the groups merged and everyone began to make his hundred signs of the cross.

In chorus, each group with its own choir chanted:

In the sign of the Holy Cross . . .

And during the pauses between the chants they prayed aloud, in slow and solemn tones:

> Man shall die as dies the grass
> In the strait and fearsome Pass
> Where the hosts of Satan mass.
> Face them there, cry not, "Alas."
> Cry out, "Retro, Satanás,
> In me thou shalt have no gain but loss,
> Because on the Day of the Holy Cross,
> A hundred Ave Marías I prayed,
> And a hundred signs of the Cross I made."

The tone expressed fervent faith in the prophecy, comforting and nostalgic at the same time.

In the strait and fearful Pass.

They sang the words with a will, as though the slope they were climbing were the Valley of Jehoshaphat itself, and at the challenge of their words the Enemy sallying forth to meet them must retreat, his tail between his legs, put to flight with ridiculous ease, impotent to face them and the fervor with which they chanted:

In me thou shalt have no gain but loss.

They repeated it ten, twenty, thirty, forty, fifty, sixty, seventy, eighty, ninety-nine times, with the same number of Hail Marys and signs of the cross: *In the sign of the Holy Cross, deliver us from our enemies, O Lord* . . . There was no early-morning drowsiness in these voices; they sounded clear and alert with the optimism of souls at war, advancing firmly with steady pulse, against Satan.

Dawn revealed a leaden sky.

On reaching the top of the hill, hardly any of the groups had finished making the sign of the cross a hundred times; they walked along the crest, around the Mission Cross, until they completed the allotted number; then, prostrating themselves, they offered their devotions:

> Blessings on Thee, Holy Cross,
> On which God's only Son,
> Died for us on Calvary,
> Saving all from pain and loss,
> And the snares of the Evil One.

Other prayers followed, long or short, according to the devotion of the leaders. Each group returned to the village in silence so that the prayers of those still ascending the hill might not be interrupted.

Sibilant consonants re-echoed against the rocks and in the hollows, with monotonous repetition: *Pass . . . mass . . . Satanás.* The words *In me thou shalt have no gain but loss* rang out with indomitable vigor. Spirited in the phrase *the sign of the Holy Cross,* the voices turned plaintive on *Hail Mary,* only to return to the confidence, the intoxication, of *Retro, Satanás.*

Upwards they climbed, groups of black-robed women, men with set faces, round-eyed children. As objects became visible, the lanterns were extinguished. Now it was daylight.

Conscientious pilgrims, and there were many, afraid lest they had let their thoughts wander and miscounted, repeated twice, three times, their hundred invocations to make quite sure of victory in the Valley of Jehoshaphat.

Blue smoke rose slowly from the chimneys, the bells rang slowly. Sound and smoke seemed to rise in worship. *In the strait and fearsome Pass.*

The sun was pale and watery. ("What happened last night? Something must have happened last night!") The sky was streaky.

"It's going to be another hot day."

"Yes, the heat will be unbearable!"

"Look at those clouds!"

From the Cross, wreathed in flowers, patches of color could be seen: green, white, purple, blue. Between the crosses, on the smooth walls, there were strips and rosettes of colored crepe paper, green leaves, bougainvillea, daisies, hibiscus, ivy. No cross was unadorned, all of them—those on stone houses, those on adobe houses, those at street corners, those that marked where someone had died —every one had its paper streamers and fringes, bunches of freshly cut flowers, green boughs, placed there early in the morning. Streets and walls were no longer plain and unbedecked. Since midnight, hands had been working in the darkness to set wooden and stone crosses, mortar, and even straw, abloom.

Fleeting smiles appeared and the fingers making the sign of the cross reflected the colored light.

III

Gabriel had never been noted for outward piety, but no one seemed to find this strange. It was tacitly agreed that his place was in the bell tower. There, they left him in peace. He occasionally accompanied Father Martínez when he went to carry Extreme Unction to one of the parishioners, but neither then nor in church did he show any visible signs of devotion. He performed his tasks mechanically, with complete detachment, as though indifferent to the events going on round him. Victoria's hope of meeting him in the Pilgrimage to the Mission Cross was a vain one. When his bells were taken from him, he kept to his room, except in the early morning hours of his household chores. No one imposed a task upon him. He was suffering from a kind of sleeping sickness. He was surprised, at first, that he felt the loss of his bells no more than he did, and his lassitude seemed to increase. Marta and Don Dionisio watched him unobtrusively. His stillness worried them. He had made no protest and seemed not to be angry when he came down as usual to draw water from the well, cut wood, and sprinkle and sweep the Parish Church and porches, the Presbytery, and the street. His appetite was apparently the same as ever. He had never been a big eater. The only outward sign of distress was that he took no notice when people spoke to him; he was absent-minded and went around in a daze as though drugged; there were circles under his eyes from lack of sleep. To avoid all conversation or questions, he finished sweeping the church and street before five o'clock, by six he had finished his chores and retired to the patio or his room, keeping away from even Marta and María. By eight or nine, he could keep awake no longer and would sleep until eleven or twelve. Then he would have his dinner and go back to sleep, but in the evening all desire for sleep left him and he would stay awake till the small hours of the morning.

The sound of the bells began to hurt his ears. Not for the first few days, though. At first, he merely felt as if he were in a distant village, under a remote sky, ruled by hostile bells. (Victoria, Marta and María, Luis Gonzaga in his saner moments, Lucas Macías, and Father Reyes felt the same. This feeling, recognized clearly by some, more vaguely by others, spread through the village.) But when the sound of chanting voices reached the village on the morning of Holy Cross Day, and the bells were ringing for mass, Gabriel felt daggers piercing his heart. Emotion choked him. For the first time, his hands itched to seize the bell ropes and pour out all his pent-up feelings.

The agony, the anguish, the urge were so strong that, without waiting for breakfast, or telling anyone, he fled along deserted streets to get away from the sound. A sudden idea made him stop and turn back: the visiting stranger who looked like a statue, the woman who had been constantly in his mind, she must be among the pilgrims to the Mission Cross ("Why can't I forget her?") and maybe, he might see her or talk to her ("Why can't I forget her?"); perhaps she would be glad to see him, and he would find words to say to her and he would ask her . . .

Gabriel stopped, turned around, and took a few steps back, looked up towards the hill, hesitated, looked down at the ground, undecided whether to go forward or back. Suddenly, a gust of wind brought the sound of the chant to his ears . . . *Life will pass. Life will pass.* He could hear the sound of the big bell. (How dreadful it sounded! As though a dead man were listening to the voice of a woman who had been his wife, speaking to another man. What a horrible thought! How did it come into his head?)

Gabriel quickened his pace and walked until the hill, the village, the chanting, the bells, and all sounds of life were left far behind, but he could not escape from his absurd thoughts. ("I'm getting like Luis Gonzaga Pérez. They say she drove him crazy, but that's not true, because he was crazy before. Why did they take my bells away from me? I didn't think they would do that! Perhaps someone heard what the woman said to me, and that's why. The sooner she goes the better! Conduct an orchestra? How ridiculous! How do people think of such foolishness! When will she go away and leave me in peace? She'll have to go through the Valley of Jehoshaphat. Suppose they gave me a trumpet to play there? I think she'd recognize me and come to my side, but her husband wouldn't let her out of his sight! What could he have been? I wonder why he died? Did she drive him crazy? I'd better make my hundred signs of the cross here to see if I can't drive these thoughts out of my mind. *In the sign* . . . I'd better not go back to the village. *From our enemies* . . . But this isn't getting me anywhere . . . *Deliver us, O Lord. Hail Mary, the Lord be with Thee* . . . Her name is Victoria . . . But I'd better stop praying if I'm going to get everything mixed up like this. In me thou shalt have no gain, but loss, Victoria, because on the day of the Holy Cross . . . I wonder if I'll see her again . . .")

He stopped praying after he had made three signs of the cross, lay down near some rocks, and fell asleep.

IV

That night, the night bridging the second and the third of May—*Dies irae, dies illa*—Father Martínez had a disturbing dream—*Quidquid latet apparebit.* In it, he felt as though the years and his fears had taken their toll and his blood was getting thinner in his veins—*Cor contritum quasi cinis*—he felt older, sadder, weaker, at the end of his tether, like a dead man forced to rise from the grave.

He awoke feeling dazed, in the grip of a formless terror; he tried to pray, to implore God's mercy,

> *Rex tremendae majestatis,*
> *Qui salvandos salvas gratis,*
> *Salva me, fons pietatis.*

As a turn of the screw brings new suffering to the victim on the rack, the memories of his dream returned to torture him, there was a buzzing in his ears. Scattered details re-assembled and took shape before his eyes. Livid shadows of the early morning passed in front of him, as though he were lying in his tomb watching the procession of hours file past, hours lived and burned away by time:

Dies irae, dies illa,
Solvet saeclum in favilla:
Teste David cum Sibylla.

Shadows . . . the Presbytery, in darkness, at nightfall, and a man lying in wait, hidden behind the arch in the hall near the kitchen, where the silhouette of a woman could be seen. Is it Marta? Is it María? The man whispers something to her, she tries to escape, he catches her. "No, no," groans the woman. It is Marta's voice, but the movements are María's. "I've already told you not to come back— please don't, for the love of Holy Mother." The man is silent; breathing heavily, he seizes her. Father Martínez remained rooted to the spot, speechless with rage, his lips and tongue paralyzed. What is Micaela doing in the Presbytery at this hour? Hasn't he forbidden María to see her, much less invite her to this house? Because it *is* Micaela. There is no doubt of it. The voice is hers and the gestures. The man? Who can the man be? She breaks away—María—it's her step and her sobs he hears as she runs to her room. "Wretched girl!" The man, too, is lost to sight, still panting like an animal.

It is pitch dark. Don Dionisio gropes his way along, touching familiar objects: the second pillar, opposite the dining room; the window that looks out on the sacristy; the flower pot with the tuberose in it, the table with the hand basin on it, the filter with the steady sound of water dripping in the darkness. Instinctively he stops to avoid bumping into the door post of his bedroom. A trembling hand pulls at his cassock, and an anguished voice speaks: "I am a miserable sinner, Father. I come to make my confession." Don Dionisio starts to refuse; the words "Not to me" are already on his lips, but he stops. The hand still clutches his cassock. He touches the head of the bed, the chair, the edge of the table, his books. He can recognize the shape of *The Glories of Mary*, which he has been using to prepare his sermons for the month of May. Here he should find the lamp and a box of matches. Where is it? He feels for it, on the table, on the bureau, on the chair. The penitent continues to beseech him, still clutching his cassock. Who can have hidden the lamp and the matches? In the pitch-black darkness he hears a thud as the penitent falls to his knees and begins his confession: "I deserve to be burned alive on earth and then to burn in Hell. I am a miserable wretch. You ought to have killed me, Father; I have abused your hospitality and your paternal affection, I have trampled your gray hair in the dust and mocked all your goodness. Judas was an angel compared to me. Kill me."

Father Martínez feels his strength ebb away; as when, in his youth, his companions insulted and provoked him, his blood is now pounding in his veins. He starts to call out, "Is that you, Gabriel?" but he is stopped by the memory that he is there as Judge, not accuser, however impossible it may be to forget the name of the sinner, and the injury done. He chokes back the anguished cry: "My nieces!" and murmurs, "Continue, my son." Doubly his son, son of his spirit and son of his blood; so the betrayal is double.

With difficulty he manages to control his hands which itch to seize the monster and his voice which would have cried, "Is that you, Gabriel?" and says, "Continue, my son." The cursed voice continues, "And the worst is that it is not María that I love, but Marta; and, loving Marta, I have made love to Micaela, deceiving both Marta and María." The Priest's trembling hand is raised again in anger, but in mid-air the gesture changes to one of blessing. This is not Gabriel's head! No! Then who—who—is it? Could it be Damián? The old man clenches his hands and an unwonted feeling of loathing seizes him. Immediately he grows ashamed; a priest in charge of souls must not give way to likes and dislikes, to vanity and ambition. He must overcome repugnance for a member of his flock and treat him with pastoral compassion. He must listen to evil outpourings.

The voice continues: "It is my sin to desire all the women in the village—Daughters of Mary, married women, it's all the same. And that's not all. The thought of any woman, even a stranger, even far away in time and space, living in Paris, in Germany, a historical figure, fills me with desire." Here Don Dionisio can no longer keep his temper and seizes the penitent's shoulder violently.

"It's your fault, Father. You would never tell me the name of my mother. I yearn for tenderness, for a woman's tenderness. And you have prevented me from being a brother to Marta and María. Then you took away the only thing I valued, my bells, with which I could speak. I taught them to talk to me as I would like to hear all the women on earth talk; I was tender with them as I would be tender with a wife, as I would have been with Marta if you had not separated us. Now, save me from Micaela, who will bring me nothing but evil. If you do not save me, I will go to her. I will make her the victim of my rage. Micaela and I will be the shame of the village. Micaela draws me to her and I shall succumb, in this dark, this cursed night . . ."

Father Martínez is sweating blood. Even in his dream he cannot be sure whether he is dreaming. Is he the victim of an infernal nightmare? No, this is the table and that the chair in his bedroom. He touches his eyes and finds them open. On the right, his groping fingers encountered his bookcase. He touches his cassock and can count the buttons, finds the broken one there had been no time to replace. He lifts his foot and hears the squeak of his shoe. He feels the head of the penitent and touches his rough hair, dishevelled and sweaty. Who is it? Gabriel? Damián? The Devil? A sudden flash of illumination reveals the truth. "It is the Devil! Get thee behind me, Satan; it is written, *thou shalt have no part in me, nor hast thou any power to disturb me.*" The Priest makes the sign of the cross and utters an exorcising prayer.

At that moment there are sounds never before heard in the precincts of the Presbytery. At first, like those of a cat in heat. But they are the cries of a woman in her hour of travail. She drags herself to Don Dionisio's feet and he suddenly finds himself wearing an alb and a red cassock, as though he were going to celebrate mass on the anniversary of a martyr. Who has brought the woman into this sacred place? But now, it is no longer the walls of the Presbytery but the vaults of the temple that echo with her cries. The red light on the altar flickers but the face of the woman is visible. Don Dionisio looks at her as Christ looked at the money-changers in the Temple. At his look she manages to say, "I loved him! I still love him! It was my fault. I wanted him!" Don Dionisio loses control of himself, and, scarcely knowing what he is doing, begins to kick her. "Our Lord did not treat Mary Magdalene like this, nor even the woman taken in adultery." Father Martínez cannot stop. He is beside himself with rage.

"Don't you know me? I'm your niece, Mary Magdalene."

"I have no nieces."

"I'm Marta. Have pity on me."

"Get away from me!"

"I wasn't to blame. Damián took me by force. Please don't tell anyone, Father. Don't you know me? I'm Micaela, and I am damned."

Indeed, he recognizes the dress Micaela had worn on Maundy Thursday, one of the indecent dresses she had brought back from Mexico City. He cannot see her face or recognize her voice, which is hoarse from sobbing. He prays for a miracle, he prays that the woman may be removed from the sacred precincts. The miracle comes to pass. They are now in Marta's room, before the picture of the Virgin Mother.

"It's your fault. You were so absorbed in your work and preoccupations, you neglected us. You forgot we were women, and frail, disposed to sin, confined in the darkness, anxious for light, tormented by desire. I wanted to have a child!"

"And the Devil has granted your wish."

"No, it wasn't the Devil . . ."

"Who, then?"

"My desire."

"It was the Devil, I tell you it was the Devil."

"But it was your fault."

Again Don Dionisio utters a furious "No!" and hurls himself upon —Marta? María?

"I'm Micaela and I shall be damned and bring condemnation upon you, upon the village, upon the whole world. The child I am bearing is a demon."

Father Martínez loses consciousness but he can still hear the cries continuing endlessly. The woman cannot bring forth her child. Her cries are not the cries of a woman in travail but of a woman condemned to endless torment.

"We shall be damned!"

"Damned for all eternity."

Don Dionisio—*Dies irae, dies illa*—finally awoke—*solvet saeclum in favilla*—but he could not be sure whether he was awake, or asleep, or dead, or if all that he had dreamed was stern reality.

Still uncertain, he jumped from his bed and began to scourge himself pitilessly. Cold sweat changed to warm trickles of blood, but he could find no relief. Dead. He seemed to be present at his own funeral, weeping and singing,

Huic ergo parce, Deus:
Pie Jesu Domine,
Dona eis requiem. Amen.

V

Gabriel had no idea what time it was when he awoke. It was too cloudy to see the sun. He lay there, enjoying a sensation of complete well-being, all his muscles relaxed. Sleep had calmed him. "I am renewed," he quoted.

He wanted to enjoy his feeling of freedom, and began to run at random over the hills; it was a pleasure to climb the slopes with no purpose but the enjoyment of physical well-being, like a young animal. He reached the Mission Cross, intending to go back. Suddenly, he was filled with the desire to see the village from the top of the hill. He moved forward cautiously, like a wary stag. "There won't be anyone there now. Surely they'll all have gone back by this time."

There lay the village below him, its streets empty and silent, as though seen from a celestial tower. He would like to view it from still higher. He climbed up and up, into the dark clouds, on the satiny sky, a prison wall! Higher still, he flew, with arms outstretched, like wings.

"Gabriel!"

The sound brought him down from the heights, back to the prison he thought he had escaped from.

It was as though he were talking to himself and his voice sounded strange in his own ears. Or as if he heard the bells rung by his hands speaking in the tones he had never succeeded in drawing from them.

"What a surprise!"

It took time for the words to reach the bottom of his cell.

"How sorry I am!"

Bells ringing in eternity.

"I can't go on like this any longer."

He waited for the next sound.

"And what about you? I can imagine how you must be feeling!"

Melodious monologue, broken by pauses. No, this was not her voice, this harsh voice, which brought out its words with difficulty, nor was it the harmony of the bells.

"Why didn't you come this morning?"

Question which neither expected nor received an answer.

"I thought I would see you."

Why did it take so long for the words to reach him?

"I wanted to see you."

The words dropped into the well, leaving no echo.

"What do you intend to do?" And, immediately, "If I could—"

What was she talking about? Yes, of course, about his bells.

"I didn't expect to see you here."

Another desperate pause.

"I have often thought of coming here one evening."

Was it because of him that her words dragged?

"I thought I'd hear you ring the bells from here."

Yes, it was Gabriel who was making her words come slowly, it was Gabriel who engraved them forever in his heart.

"And I could see the bell tower and the village filled with sunshine at this hour."

As when he rang the bells slowly.

"That's a pleasure I haven't had yet."

A very short pause. "Will you grant me this pleasure?"

Gabriel felt words welling up, deep inside him, words to interrupt the monologue.

"It's time to go back now."

The statue began to move forward. The fatal words were uttered, "Will you come with me?"

Gabriel felt as though his prison door had been opened. If he had been unable to withdraw at the beginning, now he could not refuse. They went down the hill in silence. The descent was steep, and the goddess found the going hard. Here—he felt the whole world turned topsy turvy—she leaned on his arm. The marble hand and arm were flesh-warm. Darkness and silence. Sinister shadows spread over the rocks. Again she leaned on his arm, and again, and again.

"Why don't you say something?"

The silence continued until they reached the bottom of the hill. Two questions were troubling Gabriel: "Will she want us to go into the village together?" and "If it has rained in the hills and the river is up, how can we cross the river in the dark?"

"What's the matter? Why are you trembling? You are ill."

The river was dry.

"I'll go the rest of the way alone. Thank you very much, Gabriel."

Why can't he say something?

"Good-bye, Gabriel."

Why can't he utter a simple word?

"Give me your hand. Good-bye."

"Seño——" No, that was not the word he wanted to say.

"My name is Victoria."

*

VI

What a row the cats made last night. Nobody could get any sleep.

THE CHAPLAIN

I

UR Chaplain—so the Daughters of Mary call him, half fearful, half ecstatic. There are many who laugh at this form of address and at the man as well; he inspires widespread hostility, yet some would lay down their lives for him.

The Chaplain is Father José María Islas, assistant priest in the parish and Chaplain of the Association of the Daughters of Mary Immaculate; in this post he exerts an influence that makes him respected and feared by even his enemies. Each and every one of the Daughters of Mary understands and obeys his most fleeting glance or gesture. With a single word he can transport souls to heights of bliss or plunge them into an abyss of misery.

Father Islas' power is not immediately obvious to the beholder. One's first impression is unfortunate. He looks ill, as though suffering from constant pain in the nerves and about to faint at any moment; his lips and eyelids quiver and the quivering is always more pronounced just before and after he speaks, an act requiring great effort; his brows are drawn into a frown, a vein throbs in his forehead, his delicate nostrils and large ears twitch. Even when he is silent he still moves the muscles of his jaws. His features and his gestures are sharp, nervous, lacking in cordiality. His voice is high and thin, but devout women find it charming.

To the Daughters of Mary, Father Islas' sanctity is beyond question; the least sign of doubt of it provokes them to anger. Stories abound of the miracles he has worked, articles of faith to many and a matter of local pride to even the incredulous: amazing cases of prophecy and healing and surprising advice; ubiquity, penetration, levitation, and trances; the multiplication of food and help for the needy; settlements of disputes where there seemed to be no solution; finding lost property; reading men's inner thoughts.

At the risk of provoking indignation and being thought envious, Father Martínez condemns facile credulity; he does this prudently but firmly, pointing out the principles of the Church, and the caution with which it officially sanctions Saints or recognizes "miracles," which are often the product of over-excited popular imagination. Privately, Don Dionisio considers Father Islas a virtuous but over-conscientious priest, and tries to restrain him, though with little success. After all, thinks Don Dionisio, excessive scrupulousness purifies the life of the parish and sounds a perpetual warning note which has been very useful to us, provided it does not dry up the virtue of hope. So Father Martínez has chosen Father Islas as his confessor, which adds to the padre's reputation for saintliness.

In his heart of hearts, Don Dionisio would like to see a little charity in his colleague's soul; he often feels responsible for the excessive severity of Father Chemita, as he calls him familiarly, and worries about his spiritual misanthropy.

Father Islas is reserved even with his own Parish Priest and friend. There are days during which he remains absolutely silent and seems to be at the mercy of a mute rage; his jaws work more rapidly, he shuts himself up in his house and refuses to see anyone.

From year to year, Don Dionisio has put off asking the advice of his superiors concerning his assistant. "As long as he doesn't get any worse," he concludes. And ten years have gone by.

In Father Reyes' opinion, Father Martínez and Father Islas are somewhat similar in character and inclinations. It is obvious to him why the Parish Priest chose Father Islas as his confessor: he wanted to stimulate his own conscientiousness and the sense of the restrictions imposed on him by his office and to fortify himself against broad-mindedness.

Ever since his arrival in the village Father Reyes has used the Confessional to get at some measure of Father Islas' influence. He was opposed to the extremes which Father Islas imposed, but with customary discretion refrained from making any comment. When he felt that he had secured the confidence of the Parish Priest, he set to work indirectly to counteract an influence that had turned even grown men a prey to fears. He made friends first with the children and afterwards with the young people by forming a parish choir; he planned to brighten the lives of the women. It was slow and cautious work because of the affinities between his superior and his colleague. What wouldn't he give to dissolve the sadness of the village in laughter, break down the isolation, and introduce some gaiety into religion! Yet he, too, has been influenced by the excessive scrupulousness and he frequently wonders whether Father Islas isn't right, after all: stern watchfulness over the conscience does protect the purity of life. The thought has tempered the ardor with which he carries out his remedial tasks and has even led him to assume some inquisitorial duties in the effort to balk the forces of evil.

The case of Luis Gonzaga Pérez, however, where Father Islas' influence was undoubtedly harmful, brought him into active opposition. He felt it his bounden duty to make the serious charge before Father Martínez that the ex-Seminarist's excesses, manias, and phobias were the fruit of Father Islas' spiritual guidance.

But how could he reconcile the over-conscientious priest's influence with the strong suspicion that Luis Gonzaga actually did attend a Spiritist séance? (This was no suspicion but a certainty in the mind of Father Martínez.) And how could he attribute to Father Islas' influence Luis Gonzaga's dislike of the Parish Priest and his criticism of him? Doubts assailed Father Reyes.

Still, there was no contradiction. Many troubled girls, for instance, have fallen from a moment of desperation into even worse sins. He answered his own question.

In the days after Luis' seizure, Father Reyes visited him and saw in the spasms of mystic rapture and desperation a confirmation of what he believed to be the cause. An unwise zeal had contributed to the madness, if it had not caused it.

No, thought Father Reyes, severity is not the best method of spiritual guidance, certainly not for weak natures like this young man or for the many girls in whom Father Islas has inculcated a gloomy view of existence. To what end? That they may fail in their first contact with reality? For the ties that unite them to God to be ties of fear? A false and precarious piety, with roots in marshy ground! In an anguish-laden swamp, propitious to the growth of disease, lust, and hypocrisy!

The Parish Priest's illness and his strange avoidance of confidences when he recovered, prevented Father Reyes from consulting him about the problem. Then came the dreadful affair of Damián and Micaela, which strengthened Father Islas' authority.

II

How could it help strengthening that authority when the whole village regarded it as a clear case of prophecy fulfilled? Not once but many times, not privately but in public, the Chaplain had declared that Damián was a village disgrace through whom evil would come, tears of blood would be shed, and divine wrath would be provoked. As for Micaela, how he had labored to bring her onto the right road, and how bitterly he deplored the failure of his efforts! His advice, his kindly suggestions, his stern reproaches, warnings, and threats, all failed to have effect. "You are forging not only your own ruin," he told her many times, "but that of your family, and the loss of many souls. Woe unto him through whom scandal comes . . . You can expect no less than a violent death, which will fill the people with terror."

The Chaplain's warnings were fulfilled to the syllable.

III

Other occasions were remembered when it had proved fatal to ignore his warnings. There were the many lives he had guided into the right path. There was the Association of the Daughters of Mary, which had made history under the rule of their "saint," the "wise and virtuous Padre." General anguish found an outlet in a flood of nostalgic memories and comments.

In the chronicle that might be written of this—and many had suggested time and again that it should indeed be written—the first chapter would contain the now legendary story of Teo Parga. Teo was the zealous founder and first president of the Association. A

young woman of lukewarm devotion, living in comfort and security and about to marry a rich man from Juchipila, she paid little attention to Father Islas' admonitions. He had just arrived and was eager to found the Association. "Those who wait for God to call them personally do not realize how harsh His summons may be. You will be sternly called unless you willingly take the path Our Lord has prepared for you . . . Teófila, why do you forswear your name, which means 'Lover of God' and prefer the vain and passing love of a mortal . . . ?"

Days passed, the wedding presents arrived from the bridegroom, the bridegroom started on his journey, accompanied by relatives, friends, and musicians. But man proposes and God disposes. A sudden storm descended upon the travellers, and a bolt of lightning struck Teófila Parga's betrothed. Shaken, Teófila turned from lukewarmness to fervor and renounced her wealth to live a life of strict simplicity. She kept only enough to maintain a home for orphan girls, among whom she was thenceforth to live, and gave away the rest of her fortune. In her devotion to the Association she led a life of strictest piety, for which she was rewarded with a gift that inspired the community with awe: she could foretell the time when people would die; this was revealed to her, usually, in a dream. One morning she awoke announcing, "This morning, early, between two and three o'clock, so-and-so died." The man she named lived a long distance away, in the United States, but the news of his death eventually arrived and the time coincided with the hour Teo had named. "Pray for so-and-so," she would say, on occasion, "because he won't live through the night." And sometimes the person she was referring to had gone to bed in perfect health.

Creaking wood—in a closet, a small chest, a corner cupboard—could also serve as an omen. It was not unusual for her to read the signs of approaching death in someone's face. "So-and-so will die this year." Of another, she would say, "That man ought to prepare for death, he hasn't long to live; he may not see the month out." Teo was not strong enough to bear this exalted existence, and as might be expected the hour of her own death was revealed to her. "I shall not reach the end of the year. Pray to the Holy Virgin for me, sisters," she would say at their meetings. "December is coming."

"But you're in better health than any of us," they would answer.

"Please do as I ask. Of your charity, entreat Our Lady Mother for me."

On the fourth day of the Novena of the Immaculate Conception she went home with a cold, but got up and attended mass next morning. Father Islas ordered her back to bed.

"Ask the sisters to pray that the date of my death may not be changed; it's the Feast of the Immaculate Conception."

"Nonsense, child; it's a cold; you'll get over it if you take care of yourself."

She was in no danger, but to avoid upsetting her, they administered the last sacraments on the sixth of December. The seventh, she awoke without a temperature. Unbelievers began to scoff. But in the afternoon, she sickened again and when she died at one in the morning, the scent of lilies filled the village.

A contrasting case, though none the less edifying, was that of Maclovia Ledesma. One of the first to become a member of the Association, she was noted for her zeal, but she forsook the blue ribbon and silver medal to marry. Misfortune overtook her. Her husband lost three crops in succession, an epidemic of influenza killed off his livestock. She herself had two miscarriages and, to crown her misfortunes, finally went mad.

After her wedding, she fell subject to fits of depression that nothing could cure. With her first miscarriage she began to think she was being persecuted, by her in-laws, then by her husband, finally by the Devil himself, whom she identified with Father Islas. It was rumored that she was possessed by the Devil, who put the sacrilegious idea into her head. When she found out she was pregnant for the second time, she grew delirious and refused to touch food. Then there occurred a scene which people still shudder to remember. One Sunday at market time, she rushed out into the street, half-dressed, uttering horrible cries: "Woe unto you who have abandoned God for a man! You are accursed! Look upon me, consider my state. See what Father Islas—the Devil in disguise—has done to me. Why don't you kill the wretched creature, this devil disguised as a priest? . . . Cowards, cowards all, like my good-for-nothing husband." The angry people threw stones at her, and Maclovia uttered inarticulate cries, shaken by such violent convulsions that three strong men could not restrain her; her face turned purple, she bit her tongue and foamed at the mouth; bystanders, convinced that she was possessed, were undecided whether to stone her to death or to run away from the scene; they would have killed her if the Parish Priest had not taken a firm hand. Before they could carry her home she had her second miscarriage, there in the street, and though they managed to save her life, she lost her reason completely. She lived on for a year and a half, grunted when she wanted food, had no more control of her bodily functions than an animal, and gave no sign of recognizing anyone round her. One morning they found her dead, in indescribable filth.

This story is too sinister an example to be included in the euchology of the Association, seed-bed of such fragrant flowers as Elvira Domínguez, who spent her life tending the sick in the Hospital; Maximina Vallejo, who heroically endured public derision, going around the district to beg for rooms and gifts in order to establish chapels and shrines in the smallest and most remote villages in the parish; Jovita Soto, a legendary beauty, who, to escape the young men who sought her, deliberately exposed herself to smallpox in the Hospital and was horribly disfigured but could thenceforth live as a Daughter of Mary without molestation; Filomena Manzo, who talked with the dead to fulfill the obligations that kept them in Purgatory; Clara Galaviz, who was picked up so often for dead where she had fallen into a trance contemplating God in church; and Crucita Mora, who for many years endured the secret pain of a miraculous stigma on her breast and only revealed it on her death-bed at the orders of her confessor and for the edification of the Daughters of Mary.

A glorious history, which brings an echo of the past to the present; it may be forgotten in the daily round of duties, but the tradition is silently maintained by many of these black-robed women whose blue ribbon and silver medal not even death can tear from their breasts. Bulwarks against the cunning of men, divine hostages in the face of threatened corruption, lightning conductors which protect the village against the wrath of heaven. What would have become of the village without them? It would have sunk into the mire many times. Although they never boast of it, many have been helped by miraculous visions, others have heard supernatural voices, and some will one day be revered at the Altar. (These ideas are taken from Father Islas' sermons.) The villagers know it. They know too that Father Islas is the director of the "Sublime Pleiades," he prunes the "heavenly rose trees" whose perfume "fills the region and rises to heaven as a burnt offering."

IV

The Chaplain's private life is an impenetrable mystery. No one sets foot inside his house; no one can tell what it is like; no one has managed to get a glimpse of the interior through a half-open door or window. There are no signs of life about. Father Islas dislikes anyone to come to his door, but in cases of emergency, when the Parish Priest has to send him an urgent message, or he is needed for a confession, people knock at the window by the door and the message is given and the answer received through the closed door. He avoids people in the street; he doesn't like them to stop him or walk home with him. If someone does go as far as his door, he will wait until the intruder has walked on before he opens it. In the street he walks along quickly with furtive steps, his eyes on the ground and his arms at his sides. Only when it is absolutely necessary does he traverse even the three blocks from his house to the church: once, in the morning, to say mass; again, to return home for breakfast two or three hours later. Then, at three or four in the afternoon he returns to the church and remains there until eight or nine; if he must stay even longer, on some unusual occasion, chiefly in the morning to assist at a ceremonial mass, he has his food brought to him there. He always enters through the door of the church, never through the Presbytery. He never accepts an invitation to a meal with the Parish Priest. Usually he stays in the small sacristy of the Chapel of the Daughters of Mary, which he has made into an office. Like Father Martínez, and even more strictly, he goes to homes to administer the Sacraments in exceptional circumstances only, and then only if it is for one of the Daughters of Mary. He never speaks with a woman alone; in treating of confidential matters, he either sends a woman to the Confession Box (and he hears women's confessions by daylight only) or he stations a witness at a prudent distance. All who wish to speak with him, whatever their sex, age, or position, must sit on the opposite side of the table from him. He is rarely alone, no matter how long he stays in his office.

What does he do during the hours he spends shut up within the four walls of his house? Some say he prays, meditates, goes into a trance in which he talks familiarly with God and the Saints; maybe the souls in Purgatory bring him their entreaties; perhaps he writes mystical books that will surprise posterity; perhaps he lies in his coffin (someone saw a coffin go into the house, but no one has seen it come out) and prays, meditates and sleeps in it; others say he works in his orchard, chops wood, prepares his food, sews and mends his clothes. These are rumors sprung from popular fantasy. The only thing certain is that he never eats meat, and as far as possible ignores bodily comforts; he hates using artificial light or having animals about the house; cats set his nerves on edge and one of the things that irritate him most is to hear them miauling on neighboring roofs.

Two old aunts, both stone deaf, keep house for him; they are, if possible, even more reserved than the priest. They go to the first mass. They do their shopping early. Nobody lays eyes on them for the rest of the day.

Father Islas makes his confession to none of the priests attached to the parish; once a fortnight, or once a month, he makes a trip to the Franciscan Monastery at Clamores, some thirty-five miles away, where the Warden is his confessor.

With the exception of the Parish Priest, Father Islas has few dealings with his colleagues and keeps as far as possible away from the "modernist" and tolerant Father Reyes and from Father Rosas, who is more interested in business affairs than in saving souls.

No one in the Post Office remembers Father Islas' posting a letter, and he rarely receives one. Whenever anyone writes to him—and it is generally one of the Daughters of Mary, away from home and seeking spiritual guidance—he asks the president or the treasurer to answer.

He accepts no gifts. In the first months of his stay in the village, he was showered with gifts of food, which he invariably returned by the bearers. On St. Joseph's day and on Maundy Thursday, for the first two years, the people tried to give him gifts, according to their traditional custom; the Daughters of Mary embroidered handkerchiefs, napkins, hand towels, a surplice with beautiful shirring. The men bought a fine Breviary in leather binding, with gold letters at the beginning of each chant. The exquisite food, typical of Maundy Thursday, knocked at hermetically sealed doors. The money had been spent but he could not be persuaded to accept the gift. Only his evident saintliness could allay their anger. In spite of the lesson, every year the women continued their embroidery, in the hope that he might finally accept their offerings, but he never did. At harvest time, too, there were offerings of corn and beans, a jar of butter or honey, a loaf of sugar, but these never got past the threshold.

The purchases made by his aunts could not have been more meager: for a week, about a pound of rice, beans, white sugar, a small loaf of brown sugar, and lard; everyday, a few cents' worth of bread, five pints of milk, a few pounds of sweet potatoes, and an egg; every other day, five cents' worth of salt. About once a month Father Islas buys sixty quarts of corn, two pounds of *sago,* and a load of wood as well as a few pounds of beans. The sacristan brings him a bag of fruit every day, for which he pays in advance.

His breakfast, which he sometimes has in the sacristy, consists of tea, made from dried orange leaves, a cup of *sago* or *atole,* a glass of milk, and three pieces of white bread.

This way of living has greatly contributed to his reputation for holiness, but what impresses the villagers most is his constant preoccupation with sex and his hostility toward anything that has to do with it; he even looks askance on marriage. This has given new life to the old prejudices, the careful guarding of maidens, and has won him the enthusiastic support of those responsible for the "honor" of the family.

V

How many betrothals he has prevented! In how many others has he sown seeds of doubt and remorse! No one will ever convince him that virginity is not the perfect state. He invariably speaks of "the Most Holy Virgin," or the "Ever Immaculate One, without spot or stain"; never does he refer to "Our Lady" or "Holy Mother." If he had his way, she would always be pictured with hands clasped and downcast eyes, treading the vile serpent underfoot. Whether it is true or he is speaking out of malice, Father Rosas, who always makes jokes at his colleague's expense, says that St. Chemita, virgin and martyr, has even proposed that the statues of Our Lady and St. Joseph should be separated. It is quite true that Father Islas has never celebrated mass in the chapel of the Holy Family; his lack of devotion to St. Joseph is obvious, he never mentions him in sermons and has let fall expressions of disdain for the prayers offered on the seven Sundays to St. Joseph to ask his aid in choosing a suitable husband; he despises the Posadas, too, especially the Procession of the Pilgrims. "This smacks of worldliness," he is quoted as saying at meetings of the Association. He shows his displeasure openly when someone dares to invite him to see a Crib, around Christmas time, a custom which is gradually being dropped in the village, largely owing to his influence. He dislikes St. Anthony, too, and as a result of this, the number of the faithful who keep Tuesdays dedicated to St. Anthony has steadily fallen off, and his novena and feast day are neglected.

With the growing influence of the Chaplain, the private nature of wedding ceremonies has become more marked, and except on the farms there are no wedding feasts or parties. Father Rosas seizes every chance to tease Father Islas on this subject; when he gets him within hearing distance, he calls out: "What a fine pair those two make; I'm going to pray to the chaste patriarch St. Joseph and the wonder-working St. Anthony to help them. I'll do my best to get the knot tied. I'll give them the nuptial benediction myself. I'll get a band of musicians from Teocaltiche or Guadalajara. The girl will have a proper white dress, the wedding will be at ten or eleven o'clock in the morning. They will play wind instruments in front of the church and there'll be a big dinner and a real wedding feast lasting eight days." The brides-to-be are, of course, chosen by the jester from among the most distinguished Daughters of Mary; and he shouts, "Women must be women, and bear sons, many sons, for God and their Country."

Father Islas' obsession has spread through the village. Many women, and some men, are upset and angry if they see an impertinent wind blow men's and women's clothing together as these hang on a line to dry. The least indication of sex or anything that might symbolize it provokes absurd scruples and tragic worrying. The ears of the confessors are filled every day with excessive scruples originating in trifling causes. One woman wondered whether she was guilty of impure thoughts when she put the key in the lock or threaded a needle. Another was afraid it was a sin to take a bath; another couldn't go to sleep for having overheard outside a window a conversation she didn't understand but imagined to be impure.

Doña Simona Cervantes stopped going to her farm so she

wouldn't have to be an involuntary witness to the animals satisfying their instincts. Other women have insisted on their husbands' selling their livestock. Very few stables still have bulls and some have even stopped having cocks.

In season or out of season, in every sermon, in every talk, Father Islas preaches zealously against the sins of impurity; even his voice is affected as he touches on the theme, as if, embarking upon a dangerous topic, he feared to say too much or too little; his movements become spasmodic, his stuttering communicates a painful current to the audience and doubles the efficacy of his preaching.

Children grow up in this dark climate of inhibitions. The silence around them checks their laughter and their games. All life seems to be a mystery. They often hear people say it would have been better for them not to have been born. There's a widespread belief in the atmosphere that they've come into the world along paths of sorrow. They sense that the slightest effort would enable them to discover behind the faces of their parents, underneath the surface of life, something terrible, so terrible that their elders try to hide even its name from them. So the root of fear and curiosity germinates in their hearts; it germinates with long pauses; but it grows.

VI

There was a time when Micaela showed signs of listening to the voice of Providence; she was not moved, however, by the dictates of her heart, but by the fear that Damián's violence had produced and the feeling that she was going to succumb to a morbid passion which would defeat her plans of vengeance. This precipitated her downfall.

With calculated coldness she told Damián that all was over between them, as she intended to enter the Society of the Daughters of Mary; she wanted to serve God and renounce the world. Damián could not believe she was serious. Micaela insisted that she had made up her mind, and immediately made her decision public, telling her aunt, her parents, her friends, and among these María first of all, so that the Parish Priest would know it. She put on a black dress, and went about seeking an interview with Father Islas, making every effort to see that the news was spread and carried to Damián, who certainly had not contrived to see her since the night when she told him of her intention to have no more to do with him.

Father Islas appeared pleased, but advised her to consider soberly, to seek out the origin of her inspiration and demonstrate the firmness of her resolution. "The Association is a carriage which bears souls straight to heaven, but the price is a hard life, austere and full of self-denial; she who joins out of frivolous curiosity, vanity, or for any other worldly reason, is on the brink of a dangerous precipice and it would be better for her never to aspire to the glorious title of Daughter of Mary."

Micaela had dreamed of being declared an aspirant that very day amid solemn rejoicing and of being received some weeks later as an exemplary member, welcomed with one of the Chaplain's finest sermons, in which he would prophesy "heroic saintliness," "edifying virtue," the "sublime prize for the renunciation of the vanities of the world," and the "triumph of the highest purity."

VII

As with a cancerous tumor taking root and growing in his soul from his Seminary days, ever since his youth, Father Islas has lived in fear that he would one day succumb to sins of impurity; his self-distrust has led him to the belief that one day he would be guilty and condemned, impenitent. This fear has goaded him on to over-scrupulousness. This is the shadow that darkens his face. This is why he seeks solitude.

He is like the lonely children who grow up among the black-robed women, fearful of all around them, fearing yet anxiously watching gestures and listening to words of their elders that may reveal the mystery of their own sadness. A lonely priest, constantly struggling, never ceasing his warnings against the Devil, who threatened him at every step and was perhaps already present in his heart.

VIII

Damián decided to speak with the Parish Priest, or Father Rosas, or Father Reyes, or even with Father Islas. Which would be best? His hesitation made him realize he was in love, in spite of himself. Love was stronger than his desire for freedom, capable of sending him forth to move mountains. It was no longer pride; he recognized this in the need to beseech, a new and imperious necessity which brought him to the verge of tears, a ridiculous, uncontrollable impulse.

He would be resolute. He made up his mind to talk with Father Islas himself.

"I have come to talk with you as man to man."

"I can speak only as a priest. I am God's minister, unworthy as I am." (Father Islas' face was like a graven image.)

"I know, but you can try to understand me, listen to the man that I am."

"Do you wish to make confession?"

"No, not now. I have come—I came to ask a favor of you."

"A favor? To ask a favor of me?"

"You're the only one who can do this for me. Only you, dear Padre."

"Don't call me that. Just Padre."

"Very well. Padre. You know what I've come about . . ."

"No. Tell me."

"I think you must know. It's about Micaela, Micaela Rodríguez. She has been to see you."

"What has she to do with you?"

"We, Micaela and I, are—well, we were—we were engaged. I— Well, I . . ."

"What do you want me to do for you?"

"They say she wants to become a Daughter of Mary, and I don't think . . ."

"Do you realize how serious a sin it is to interfere in matters of conscience without being authorized to do so?"

"I have no wish to interfere with the Church. I only tell you plainly, Micaela has said she loves me. I say no more, as a man, and because it's not important at the moment. But she owes it to me to keep her promise."

"The Devil is speaking through your lips. Silence, in the name of Heaven!"

"Please hear me out, dear Padre—Padre. I've never asked a favor of anyone before, and I'm not ungrateful, believe me. Please, let's discuss this calmly. I admit that I was trifling with Micaela in the beginning, but then I began to feel differently, and now I am serious. I know you find it hard to believe because of what people say about me, but my intentions are honorable and I intend to settle down. I swear it." He made the sign of the cross in front of his lips.

"Beware of breaking the second commandment. I can listen to you only in confession. Otherwise, I have nothing to say to you."

"Only let me finish. Look, I am pleading with you, and . . . No, no. Just this. They say you are a saint, and you can see . . ." Father Islas rose abruptly and turned his back on Damián.

"Forgive me if I speak plainly. I am a simple working man. I beg you not to let Micaela become a member of the Daughters—"

"Silence! In the name of Almighty God!"

"Very well, Padre, if that's the way you take it. But it's your duty to keep her out of the Association and advise her to come back to me." Father Islas covered his ears, trembling and muttering unintelligible words. He collapsed on a chair, murmuring prayers to exorcise the evil spirit.

That was the end of June.

ASCENSION

I

ESPONDENCY IS IN the tolling of the bells. Many weep as at news of a public disaster, or as if it were the Day of Judgment. Then alone, surely, will all the bells of the world pour forth such mournful sounds as these, then crack and break.

"Gabriel!"

"It must be Gabriel!"

"It can be only Gabriel!"

"Gabriel's ringing the bells again!"

All over the village, on all lips, as the bells ring, the same word: "Gabriel!" "Gabriel!"

Gabriel is back. Unexpectedly, boldly, he has returned.

"Who's dead?"

No one was seriously ill, that the people knew of.

"Who're the bells tolling for?"

At the first sound some thought they had forgotten it was Ascension Day and that they were ringing for twelve o'clock High Mass.

"Yes, it's exactly half-past eleven."

This thought was still in their minds when they realized that the bells were tolling.

"Gabriel's up to his old tricks again."

"Gabriel's mad! Tolling the bells for the service on Ascension Day, tolling them for the solemn Te Deum! Whoever heard the like! Heaven help us!"

It wasn't Ascension Day. It was two weeks before Ascension Day. It was Thursday, the sixth of May. Father Martínez was seeing to repairs in Retreat House, and the ringing of the bells took him by surprise. He was still more surprised to recognize Gabriel's touch, since he had forbidden him to go up into the bell tower. He sent to learn what was happening, but as the messenger was a long time returning and the bells continued their mournful concert, he went to see for himself. On the way he met Pascual, the sacristan.

"Gabriel has got up in the bell tower and barricaded himself in and no one can get him out, unless you order us to break down the door. I don't know who told him to toll the bells like this—as though the Pope were dead. I don't think anybody told him."

Anxious faces appeared in doorways and windows; shopkeepers came out of their shops, men were standing on street corners. As the Parish Priest went by, he was assailed by questions:

"What's the matter?"

"Who died so suddenly?"

"What's happening, Father?"

"Is it some disaster?"

"Is there a fire?"

"Has there been an earthquake?"

"Has the Revolution begun?"

"Have they discovered the Spiritists?"

The people fired questions at Pascual, too, but he shrugged his shoulders and left the answers to Father Martínez, who muttered an indistinct, "I don't know," or "It must be some nonsense of Gabriel's. He'll pay for this."

II

That morning as he was walking along, at a snail's pace, carrying a load of spring water to the Presbytery, Gabriel had seen, three blocks away, some horses saddled, and preparations being made for a journey. Servants were loading luggage

onto a mule; one of them was opening a sunshade; there was a
horse with a side saddle, and Don Alfredo himself, all dressed up,
was superintending the preparations.

Gabriel's heart sank. The horse with a woman's saddle on it could
belong to only one person. Chalk white, he put down the water jars
on the sidewalk and stood transfixed. His eyes said Yes, but his
heart cried No.

"No! No!"

"It is! It is!"

"No! No!"

Doña Carmen appeared, in her everyday clothes, bareheaded.
And then Gabriel saw Victoria come out, dressed in travelling
clothes, wearing a white coat and a wide-brimmed hat.

His heart cried out that she must be going to some place nearby,
to come back that same day or the next. But his eyes found no
support for such a hope. He picked up his water jars and ran to the
Presbytery, up into the tower, from where he could see the street
along which the little caravan began to move off towards the Guadalajara road, Victoria in front, two servants behind.

The hoof beats of the horses on the cobbled street pounded in
his head. A great wave seized him and bore him up. He would never
know what impulse drove him to seize the bells in a frantic attempt
to find the voice he needed and express the flood of emotion that
was engulfing him. What he was saying not even he could tell; the
words passed unspoken along his sinews, moving the clappers
. . . tongues of fire and eternity. He had found the means to express
his grief in harmonies both new and archaic at the same time, harmonies transcending the human, as though in this concert he were
pouring out all the grief of the world and the ages, all the past,
present, and future agony and hope of mankind. All the forces of
earth combined could not stem the torrent set in motion by the
power of love and death.

On the slope leading to the river, Gabriel could see—it was like a
dagger piercing his heart—how the traveller checked her horse, sat
erect, raised her head, and looked back towards the tower. The
leading bell rang a solemn, measured, unaccustomed melody, followed by a peal of trebles like those for the Hail, Holy Queen, on
Saturday afternoons; then came the tones of the big bass, drowning
the trebles when Victoria raised one hand and, as though borne off
against her will, turned away and continued her journey, lost to

sight in the depression of the river . . . the bells sounded alarm
. . . she appeared on the other side . . . they rang out triumphantly.
But discordant clamor followed as if tower and village, threatened
with destruction, were making a final entreaty.

Dropping farther and farther behind the servants, moving more
and more slowly, as though struggling against contrary winds, the
traveller climbed the hill by the tanneries, her head down, her figure growing smaller and smaller, her features becoming indistinct.
The servants could no longer be seen and Victoria's white horse was
reaching the top of the hill, where the road is lost to sight. Desperately the bells tolled in faster tempo; but their anguish sounded an
appeal . . . an utterance of final hope . . . an eloquent message of
tenderness which Victoria heard. She pulled in her horse, stopped,
raised her right hand and waved a green scarf. Tenderly the bells
replied, in a confused mixture of tears and laughter, chant and
response, pause and burst of sound. For five, for ten minutes they
went on, for centuries it seemed. When the traveller was altogether
out of sight, the mournfulness of the tone grew more pronounced.
The Day of Judgment was here. In reaching beyond earthly expression the bells must crack.

Abruptly the ringing ended. As he brought his eyes from the
empty horizon, Gabriel saw the amazement on the faces of people
in the streets, at windows, on the roofs. There was a loud knock on
the door of the bell chamber. He came back to earth and could
picture how the village must have listened: Lucas Macías' smiling
face; Marta's clenched hands and frown; Father Martínez looking
black as a thundercloud; Father Islas' face twitching; Luis Gonzaga
giggling nervously; Don Timoteo Limón nodding his head; Father
Reyes making firm gestures; the staring acolytes; the President of
the Daughters of Mary with tears running down her cheeks;
the Northerners on street corners; the torrent of words on Doña
Carmen Esparza's tongue . . . He could see the faces and gestures
of the neighbors with extraordinary vividness. He remained motionless, hypnotized. The knocking continued, and he thought they
would break the door down. Pascual, Father Martínez, the notary,
were calling to him. Like a sleepwalker, he went and opened the
door.

Father Martínez checked Pascual's first rush with a gesture, and
stared at the creator of the unexampled commotion.

"Why did you do it?" There was no anger in his voice, only compassion. Gabriel said not a word, and kept his eyes closed.

"Go to your room; I'll come and talk to you later."

In the hall, Marta and María were crying. Marta could not take her hands down from her face. María did, and looked at Gabriel through tears, with an expression that moved him profoundly; he glimpsed a new world, which at first appeared absurd, and then, completely natural—María's love. He thought he would go mad . . .

Mad they all thought him, Father Martínez and the whole village, and in María this thought was what had awakened the feeling in her glance.

III

In vain had Don Dionisio tried to banish the doubts tormenting him since his dream of four nights earlier. He considered the dream a snare of the Devil, so he had resisted looking for meaning in it, but questions kept returning: Why were Marta, María, and Micaela all mixed up together in one person? What was the meaning of defiance in Gabriel, Gabriel usually so distant, so detached from reality? Strangest of all, how came Gabriel to be confused with Don Timoteo's Damián? And that horrible image of maternity and general condemnation? *Lead us not into temptation, but deliver us from evil.*

If these questions have kept him awake for four nights, how will it be tonight when he goes to bed even more worried, disturbed by Gabriel's attitude and sharing the depression which has filled the village since the crazy ringing of the bells? What connection is there between his nightmare and the inexplicable occurrence of the morning? *Deliver us from evil.*

Lying in bed, he went over the events of the day, particularly his conversation with Gabriel. First there was his uneasiness at the thought of something abnormal in his own house. He was furious at the idea of Gabriel playing this trick, but his anger was stilled by the music. Perhaps it wasn't Gabriel. Surely no human hands could ring the bells like that! Spirits! Angels! An apocalyptic miracle! On his way through the streets from Retreat House, he had been infected by the general alarm. Someone told him that the widow staying with the Pérez family had unexpectedly departed, but he gave no sign of being interested in this or even of having heard. The phrase "Gabriel has gone mad," repeated on all lips, absorbed his attention. Yes, only a madman could ring like that. It was the result of taking the bells away from him; he had feared it. And the dream, the language of the dream, the rebellion in the dream? Was the present moment a part of the dream? The commotion, the expressions on the faces of the villagers? The extraordinary music coming from the bells? If Gabriel was mad, Don Dionisio considered himself to blame. He remembered the majestic beauty of the music. His eyes fixed on the steeple, he expected to see winged black horses emerging, or bulls with wings of fire, snow-white angels, lions, archangels. The power, the mystery, the beauty of the music he had heard prevailed over all other feelings. If Gabriel was the author of such a wonder, Don Dionisio would kneel and kiss his hands.

This thought and the sight of strangers forming groups in the Square and crowding round the door of the Presbytery renewed his irritation. They had hurled questions, theories, threats at him: "Men from Nochistlán have come to play a trick and seized the bell tower" . . . "An earthquake has destroyed Guadalajara" . . . "The Revolution has begun in Mexico" . . . "The Spiritists are ringing the bells, throw them out and you'll see." Some of the by-standers had stones in their hands. Don Dionisio restored calm and offered apologies. . . . *as we forgive those who trespass against us.*

What an expression—was it angelic or demonic?—on Gabriel's face! *Lead us not into temptation.*

Father Reyes arrived. "Well, thank God, that disturbing element has gone." An idea began to form in Father Martínez' mind, but it went again. No one could eat. His nieces' tears irritated him. Why make such a fuss over something that might not be serious? If Gabriel was mad, he would recover.

Father Islas arrived. "Praise God, who has removed from our midst the source of so many impure thoughts and desires. In my opinion Heaven set the bells to ringing in lamentation over the infinite evils that woman has left behind her, and in rejoicing at her departure!"

"That might be so," thought Father Martínez, delighted to find an answer to his questions. He would see Gabriel. *Deliver us from evil.*

Gabriel was sitting on the edge of his bed, his head in his hands, his elbows resting on his knees. He sat there, without a word. Don Dionisio began to question him with gentleness, but the memory of the dream was disturbing, and feeling his anger rising in the face of stubborn silence, he turned away. Gabriel ran after him, and fell to his knees in entreaty.

"Let me go away! I must go away!"

Don Dionisio took a few minutes to recover from surprise, then he began to question again. Like an automaton, Gabriel replied, "I want to go away! I can't stay here another day!"

"Did losing the bells mean so much to you?"

"Not that. Not that."

"I know we haven't treated you as we should have."

"You've done more than I deserved. But, it's not that."

"What is it, then?"

"Don't ask me. I must go. Please, let me go."

"Where do you want to go? What do you want to do?"

"Far away, to work."

"To Guadalajara?"

"No, no, no! To the ends of the earth, where you'll never hear of me again." *Lead us not into temptation.*

The dream! As in the dream!

"Gabriel, what have you done?"

And Gabriel, frightened, "I haven't done anything! I won't take a thing with me if you don't want me to, not even the clothes I'm wearing." He seemed out of his mind. He was mad.

"Do one thing. As a favor to me. For your own good. I shall not command you to stay. But first, I beg you, spend a few days in Retreat. Go up to Retreat House now. I'll hold a Retreat just for you; or if you'd rather, another priest will take it. God will show you what you should do."

He agreed. *Thy kingdom come.*

Father Martínez spent the afternoon in hearing confessions, until he was worn out. Before going to bed he spent twice his usual time in flagellation. He tried to sleep. The happenings of the day kept spinning around and around in his head—the ringing of the bells, the dreadful figures of his dream, the different explanations. One event that had seemed of little interest now caught his attention, the sudden departure of Don Alfredo's guest. Ah! That was the elusive thought that had been haunting him all day. He sat up. But then, why did Gabriel want to go in another direction? Still, he felt better; it was that woman and not one of his nieces. It was the boy's innocence in revolt; he was innocent. How, even in a dream, could he have confused him with Damián Limón? *Deliver us from evil.*

Don Dionisio fell asleep.

IV

Gabriel could not sleep. Two ghosts competed for his attention. At first the unaccustomed image of María took precedence, only to be driven out all the more violently by recurring thoughts of Victoria. "Where is she now? Is she crossing the Río Colorado? Is she past El Llano Grande? Will she have a siesta in San Ignacio?" And then, "Did she stay in Cuquío or will she spend the night in Ixtlahuacán?" And, all the time, "What is she thinking? What is she doing? What is she thinking about?"

Victoria. María. The thought of María burned like the memory of a heinous crime. "I'll go away first. I didn't realize . . . Far away. Not to Guadalajara, no, no! I'd die! Not one day, not one night longer in the Presbytery. But I won't go to Guadalajara! I'm going mad. I'll never ring the bells again. If I stayed here another night, I'd deserve to have people spit in my face. She's like a sister. No wonder Father Martínez kept talking about a traitor in Holy Week! Let them cast me out, although it's not my fault. I didn't know. Better to be crushed under a train, far away."

In a cell in Retreat House, throughout the whole endless night, Gabriel tossed sleeplessly, watching two knife-edged wheels constantly turning. Not a sound, not even the shadow of a ghost disturbed him in the great empty place. All through the dark hours. Until morning coming in through the skylight deciphered a verse written on the wall:

> God doth keep you in his sight,
> You are always in his care;
> When your time comes you will die,
> You know not when or where.

But Gabriel's thoughts were far away; in his mind's eye he followed Victoria along her journey. "Maybe she got up early and is now going down the ravine. If she stayed in Cuquío then she'll be near the dam or she may even be climbing the hill . . ."

Mechanically he looked at the wall again,

> You know not when or where.

V

On the third day, contrary to the custom of keeping the retreatant isolated and giving him no news, Father Reyes began to talk to Gabriel after mass and—who knows with what intention—said abruptly, "Luis Gonzaga has run off after the visitor who was staying with them. Everyone thought he was ill, but when he realized that the woman (I think her name is Victoria) had gone, he was frantic to leave, too. He hired horses and set out in a hurry that very Thursday afternoon. Don Alfredo managed to learn which direction he took and followed him that night. Nobody can imagine Luis going off so suddenly like that without telling anyone; it was the last thing in the world Don Alfredo and Doña Carmen would have expected, for they thought her sudden decision to return to Guadalajara was because he was so rude to her and acted so stupidly. They say he acted as if he couldn't stand her."

Father Reyes paused frequently, with sharp eyes on Gabriel. The boy was unable to hide his feelings but he set his lips and stubbornly kept his eyes fixed on the ground.

"Now, let's go to the Chapel. I'll give you some ideas to meditate upon. About Death," Father Reyes added, after a silence.

In the afternoon Father Martínez found Gabriel in a high fever.

"We'll go home."

"No, please!"

"If your temperature is down, you can come back tomorrow."

"If I must go anywhere, send me to the Hospital."

He declared he would not return to the Presbytery, not if he were dying.

He began to vomit, alarmingly. They took him to the Hospital. Marta and María went to see him, and heard him rave of his love for Victoria. Don Dionisio hustled the two girls out of the room. Then Gabriel wept and begged Father Martínez to return. He would tell him the truth, the whole truth.

VI

On Ascension Thursday, at half-past eleven in the morning, as the bells began to ring for mass, some of the pack-drivers who bring fruit from Aguascalientes left the inn leading a donkey with an empty saddle. Instead of taking the Teocaltiche Road they went up towards Retreat House, where Father Martínez was waiting for them with Gabriel. Gabriel knelt to receive his blessing. Then they embraced. Don Dionisio returned to the village, Gabriel followed the pack-drivers, the sound of the bells in his ears.

"How monotonous it is, it doesn't seem like Ascension Day," thought the people on their way to church.

"They say they're taking Gabriel to an asylum."

"I heard just the opposite. He only had a bilious cold, and now that he's better Father Martínez is sending him to León or Mexico City to study under the Salesians."

"Well, in the Presbytery they act as if he were dead. No one mentions his name."

"Worse than that, it's as if they'd never known him."

Gabriel was climbing the hill. What did the bells matter to him? He felt as though he had never loved them. What did it matter that he was going away without finding out more about Luis and Victoria! How strange the name sounded, as if he had known it in a bad dream only!

He yielded to the impulse to turn and take a last look at the village. He could hear, very close and clear, a message from the leading bell; he shivered and stopped, it seemed to be María's voice speaking. It was María. He was drawn back. He started to return. María! María's voice!

How often she had spoken to him in those tones! But he had not known then what a single glance was to reveal to him fifteen days ago.

The pealing drowned the echoes of the small bell. Fifteen days ago. Without wishing or intending it, Gabriel found himself watching the spot where, two weeks ago, he had seen a green scarf and a thin figure in the distance. His pleasure turned to bitterness. Because of his farewell to this woman, María had suffered, so much that jealousy had brought her hidden feelings to her eyes. ("But Victoria's beauty. And Luis? See? You are jealous! María! Is this the way you return hospitality?")

It was the incessant, implacable treadmill. Victoria. María. Neither. Both lost.

When Gabriel turned away, the village could no longer be seen. But he could still make out the road to Guadalajara.

He shut his eyes and mounted the donkey that was to carry him far away.

All this while, María, her face swollen with weeping, refused to leave her room, where she could hear the music for Nones. The sermon would be next. (Father Islas will preach on the appointed text taken from the Acts of the Apostles: "A cloud received Him out of their sight. And while they looked steadfastly towards heaven, as He went up, behold, two men stood by them in white apparel; which also said, '. . . why stand ye gazing up into heaven? This same Jesus, which is taken up from you into heaven, shall so come in like manner as ye have seen Him go into heaven.'" María was still weeping when they sang the solemn Te Deum and the bells began to ring again. How long will María go on weeping?

That afternoon a few drops of rain fell, but without bringing life. Thursday, the twentieth of May, Ascension Day.

THE DOWNFALL OF
DAMIÁN LIMÓN

I

BOUT THE MIDDLE OF JULY, month dedicated to
the Most Precious Blood, it began to be rumored
that Don Timoteo Limón and Micaela Rodríguez were going to be married. Those who found
it hardest to believe were most active in spreading the rumor.

"It's all very well, but they've been marrying
off Don Timoteo ever since Doña Tacha died."

"They say he's really going to do it this time, before the end of
August."

"But why Micaela?"

"That's the way it is. It could be worse."

"That Micaela can give him plenty of trouble."

"I'd like to see Don Timoteo put her in her place."

"And I'd like to see her put another member of his family in his
place!"

"Sh! For Heaven's sake! I know what you're thinking of."

As August drew nearer, the rumor grew.

"Can there be any truth in it?"

"I can't believe it."

"No, it doesn't seem possible."

"Seeing will be believing in this case."

"Still, I tell you, these old men are capable of anything; nothing can stop them once they take it into their heads to marry again."

"But what about her? Not even she could be so rash."

"These girls, these girls! No respect for anybody or anything."

"That's the truth. They're just looking for trouble."

"All fashion and no morals."

The month of August was drawing near.

II

August is the month of death and misfortune. The sword of the Dog Star swings right and left. Don Gregorio, the coffinmaker, makes his preparations ahead of time; in May, in June, he buys the materials he is likely to need and makes two or three extra coffins. This way he won't be caught unprepared at the last minute. Alas for the chronic invalids! Woe to the children! The moon is ill-omened. And the herds are ravaged. Month of drought, of disease-bearing heat waves. Even the clouds are still, with the stillness of sterility. Invalids, pregnant women, farmers, spend the month dreading St. Bartholomew's day. With what reluctance does Don Refugio see the approach of August. He must go here and there, to this farm, to that one; So-and-so is at death's door, the medicine he sent this one hasn't done him any good, it's his fault that someone else has died! And as if there weren't enough deaths from natural causes, what dread mystery surrounds the beautiful August moon? What is there about the sun and the fiery sky and the dry air that causes violent deaths in mysterious accidents or sudden quarrels?

August is the month of tragedy.

III

Some of the traders and villagers who like hustle and bustle are getting ready for the Fair at Jalos on the fifteenth. They are the same ones who went to the Fair at Aguascalientes and they will go on to one after another: to the Fair of San Nicolás in Mexticacán, to that of San Miguel at Yahualica, to Toyahua and Nochistlán in October, to Teocaltiche in November.

They spend their time gambling and betting at cock fights. A bad lot, parasites, without any particular job or responsibility. Fortunately they are few, thank God. What a blessing if they would stay away and not come back to infect others with their ideas! Some of them are trying to persuade Damián Limón to go with them. Damián can't quite make up his mind whether to leave this deadly dull village, go away and try his fortune elsewhere, or to stake everything on staying.

"You didn't get to go to Aguascalientes, so let's go to Jalos; it's a grand chance to buy cattle, and we can make good terms for this year's rice," Don Anselmo Toledo suggested to Don Timoteo Limón.

"It's the next world I'm going to," replied Don Timoteo.

"You've got to put that silly notion out of your head. Besides, it's a sin to think you know better than the just God."

"San Pascual never makes a mistake," Don Timoteo shook his head sadly, "never makes a mistake."

"You need to go to buck up; you'll see, the trip will do you good. It'll stop your worrying. You've had too much trouble. Come on and go."

"Why should we tempt God? I don't want to be buried away from my own bit of land," Don Timoteo looked towards the sky calmly. "Let death find me prepared."

"If I thought it wouldn't make you mad, I'd laugh at your fears."

"I won't see the end of August. San Pascual is never wrong, and if that weren't enough, Orión's howling every night is a sure sign."

"Then," Don Anselmo wondered, "where could this rumor about his marrying Micaela have come from?"

It had come from Micaela. Giving up the idea of an impressive entrance into the Association, and recovering from the fear that Damián's outburst had produced, she returned to her first plan. She would lead Don Timoteo on, infatuate him, and avenge herself on the whole Limón family. She began to be discreetly nice to the old man. She ventured a few sympathetic remarks about the way his children neglected him.

She failed to reckon with San Pascual's warning.

She failed to reckon with fate.

IV

This is when Lucas Macías likes to recall the deaths and misfortunes that have occurred in August. His own memory goes back to 1848 and 1850, and his memory of others' tales takes him still farther back. He says, for instance: "My father used to say that the great flood that destroyed the tannery district was on the very night of the August full moon in 1825. That same year there was a dreadful epidemic of measles, and my father thanked God that I hadn't been born at the time, since every family lost a child. They all say it was the fault of the Governor, Don Prisciliano Sánchez, who was one of the first to admit that he was a freethinker. Masonry was introduced in his time and they made war on Holy Mother Church. But this wasn't as bad as in 1833 when Don Valentín tried to steal Church property, and cholera broke out. In August alone more than two thousand people died, some days as many as two hundred or two hundred and fifty. The village was a cemetery; there wasn't anyone to bury the dead. Neither the parish priest nor his assistants were spared, and by August 12 they were all in the next world. The day the parish priest died, the fourth of August, thirty-three people died in the district—and still they say that God doesn't punish in this life. Just calculate the number that died in the whole country that year if in Guadalajara alone there were over four thousand. Even here the toll mounted to no less than five hundred. It was one of the worst areas. I can remember, and I wasn't very small, either, when people almost died at the thought of that year, to say nothing of the month of August in 1833."

"In which August did you go to the most wakes, Lucas?"

"In 1899. Nearly ten years ago now. You remember Celedonio Ramírez, who was killed in a fight with the Legaspis; they say it was because he wanted to marry their sister Patricia. Less than eight days later, Juan Legaspi was killed by Apolonio Ramírez, to avenge his uncle Cele; then the Legaspis' mother died two days after that, some say of a heart attack, others say spleen. On the fifteenth, Jacobo Partida, a good mason, fell off the tower and they picked him up dead; he left a family of nine including his widow, Doña Chole, now living in Cañadas. On St. Bartholomew's day— what a day!—you remember, Don Victoriano Rábago died; that was definitely from an attack of spleen, because he hadn't a single head of cattle left; he died right after hearing that his last two oxen had gone. On that day, too, Doña Celsa Toledo, Don Anselmo's sister, died, quite suddenly, they say, after quarreling with her sister-in-law; the third to die was Mauricio Reyes' son, who was killed by a horse. They still hadn't buried those three when the body of Alberto, nicknamed "The Cartridge-Belt," was brought in; he'd been struck by a bolt of lightning on his way to the Pastores farm.

"That same year, Don Chencho Gutiérrez, Don Pascasio Aguirre, Doña Candidita Soto, and Don Isidro Cortés all died from old age, without being laid up at all, just from light attacks of diarrhea. Children died, too: one of Don Secundino Torres' sons, another infant son of Valente Mercado, and a little daughter of Zacharías El Mocho. The last day of the month, Father Arcadio Prieto died of pneumonia. That was a fine wake; people were so fond of him that some said they were asking for him as parish priest. And you all remember the funeral. I've never seen such a grand one."

"Not even the Medinas' funeral? When was it they were killed?"

"In August, 1877, on a Monday. Don Lino Villegas was made governor at the beginning of the year, then Don Porfirio was elected and he appointed Don Jesús Camarena governor; Don Lino started an uprising and joined the troops of Don Rosendo Márquez near Mexticacán in 1876. Their enemies circulated a false rumor that the Medinas had been spying for General Martínez and General Sánchez Rivera, who defeated the troops of Donato Guerra and Márquez in Tabasco on the fourth of March. From that time on, they were after them, saying they were followers of Lerdo, and looking for an excuse to attack them. The Medinas went about their business as usual. They had nothing to fear. They were popular with the people because of their generosity. They said Don Lino envied and feared them. Then came the elections in which Don Fermín Riestra opposed General Don Pedro Galván. Don Lino took Don Fermín's side, and, one Sunday evening, about eight o'clock, showed up at the Medinas' house with a troop of soldiers. He wanted Don Trinidad and his two sons to give themselves up; Don Trinidad answered that they were men of peace and there was no reason why they should do so. Don Lino said the government knew they had supported General Galván. Don Trinidad said it was a lie, that if Don Lino had anything against them personally, he ought to say so at once, in private, and that all he'd been saying about them for some time was lies, and, in any case, they'd never surrender to a coward like him.

"Don Lino ordered his followers to break down the doors. The shooting began and it lasted until the early hours of the morning, when the Medinas' ammunition gave out. The soldiers shot down Don Trinidad and his two sons, Don Policarpo and Don Justo. They say that Don Lino even fired at them as they lay dead, and then, furious with the people who crowded round weeping, wanting to see the bodies and saying that the Medinas were innocent, tried to drive them away with rifles. It was a dull, cloudy day. It seemed as if the village father were dead. The poor wouldn't leave the bodies, which lay on crosses formed from ashes. Don Trinidad and his sons had been Christian and charitable. Many people went to the funeral in spite of Don Lino's threats. But Father Prieto's funeral was better, because the anger and fear of the people robbed this occasion of its dignity, whereas Father Prieto's funeral procession was a solemn ceremony. Neither one of those two funerals is likely to be forgotten.

"I could go on forever telling you of the disasters which have happened in August. There are families, as you very well know, where someone dies every August, and sometimes more than one."

V

Father Islas left no stone unturned. Seeing that Micaela was again hesitating about entering the Association, he visited her and encouraged her to become a member, smoothing away the difficulties, and affectionately urging the step upon her.

"It's a matter that requires much thought, as you said," the young girl replied mischievously, with a return to her coquettish manner. From that position neither Father Islas nor members of the Association could make her budge.

"Your hardness of heart grieves me, for your sake, for your family, and for the whole village. May God avert the punishment that awaits you. You are fashioning your own destruction and that of others!" Thus Father Islas in one of his last conversations with her.

VI

Since, in spite of everything, Don Timoteo's passions were still strong, he was not insensible to Micaela's charms.

At first, however, he was repelled by her advances, for he thought she was trying to reach Damián through him. Gossip about Micaela came to mind, and he was shocked at the thought of having Don Inocencio's daughter for a daughter-in-law. He would have spoken to Damián about it, if their relations hadn't been so strained and he hadn't feared a definite rupture would follow if there was the slightest clash. The boy was getting more and more touchy.

People said she was shameless. He couldn't get the word out of his head. Shameless! Yet because he grew used to it, or because Micaela's advances came to be more open and frequent, the expression gradually lost its shocking character and began to suggest a world of obscure attractions. Shameless! The very word filled his mind with pictured intimacies. Like fruit unexpectedly falling from a tree, they were to be stealthily picked up and hoarded. The word could be thrown away, as the peel of the fruit, and the image remained, developed and persistent. Prayers could not expel the images, nor could even the more powerful echoes of the bell of San Pascual Bailón which Don Timoteo had listened to on the seventeenth of May, the day of the Saint who thus announces to his devoted followers their approaching death.

It hadn't been a dream. The bell woke him. He was wide awake when he heard it ringing. It wasn't fear, either. He clearly heard a sound of bells not rung by human hands; the strokes went straight to his heart, piercing, unmistakable. Monday, the seventeenth of May, early in the morning.

It might be that day, that week, that month, or the next, or the one after that. It might be in August, the end of the year, or the beginning of the next; but it would be before the next San Pascual's day. Sometimes the Saint gave exactly a year's notice. It might be that day. It might be in August. *All they that take the sword shall perish with the sword.* More dead than alive, he rose and almost ran to the church. From that morning he prepared for death, meditating on his coming end, and the gravity of his sins. (On the seventh of August it would be twenty-five years since Anacleto had died by Don Timoteo's hand, and with every return, the dead man's expression was more vivid and threatening.) He spent nearly all his time in church. He went to confession every day. He started to make his will, to forgive his debtors, to settle his accounts and give away his worldly goods.

But, oh, the indomitable power of the flesh! A few glances from a woman, a few words and gestures could set his blood on fire, silence the echoes of the mysterious bell, and fill his thoughts, especially in those hours when daily cares and preoccupations keep men awake. His imagination fed on details of his meetings with Micaela, on the meaning behind her words and the tone of her voice.

The first time he was seriously troubled was in the middle of July, one night as he was coming from the Rosary. He was walking along the sidewalk in front of the church when he slipped and fell full length on the pavement, the force of his fall knocking the breath out of him and leaving him dizzy. Hands, warm young arms, smelling of perfume (never had he felt such pleasant sensations) helped him up; he could feel Micaela's young body touching him, straining with the effort. Her handkerchief passed over his face, wiping away the dust. He had never imagined that anything could be so soft. How gentle and moving her voice was: "I'm so sorry, Don Timoteo. Shall I help you home? You aren't hurt?" Then, "Why isn't there someone with you?" Finally, "*Wouldn't* you like me to take you home? I'd be happy to care for you. How cold and selfish your children are! You need affection."

In all the years of obsession with images of women he had never imagined a woman like this. A tiny flame of hope flickered in his mind. Why shouldn't he marry a young girl of good family? Why not?

The next day she came towards him with hands outstretched, and, simply and naturally, asked how he was, if he had suffered from the fall, if they had looked after him. "I was thinking about you all night, wondering whether you'd been left alone, if someone had brought you a cup of hot tea and seen to covering you up well."

It wouldn't be the first marriage like this. No. It wouldn't.

During the celebration of the Carmelite Jubilee, they met several times, and the old man managed to brush against her dress; she sent him a flattering smile; on one of these occasions she said to him, "I'm not forgetting that you need help. Remember."

Many marriages like this are happy. What's the good of money if one isn't happy? And he had never been happy! He thought again of the public gossip about Micaela, but this time he felt neither his first repulsion nor the desire that followed it, but only indignation at malice directed against an angel. But what would her father, what would Don Inocencio, think of the matter, if he were to approach him formally? What would he say?

Don Timoteo's daughters began to look at him with disapproval and to make malicious remarks. But the way they escorted him to church and saw to it that he never went out alone only made the "crazy old man," as they called him among themselves, the more agitated.

Alas! His hopes were short-lived! The first of August, San Pascual repeated the warning more clearly, more insistently, the mournful sound of his bells filling the air strangely. As if that weren't enough, Orión added his howls, beginning at dusk. ("This month! I shan't see the end of August!") Orión's howling all night long and in the early morning of the seventh was so insufferable that Damián shot the dog.

It was twenty-five years since the expression on the face of the dead Anacleto had first begun to haunt Don Timoteo. Now the death of Orión, son of the faithful dog that was with him on that day, widened the gulf between Damián and his father.

Coming out of the service on the night of the thirteenth, Micaela clasped the old man's hands warmly, but his blood no longer responded. "Leave me in peace," he said, in a hollow voice, and hurried away, as cold as death.

Micaela recognized the note of madness in his voice and couldn't help laughing. "Crazy old man! He's no saint, to be warned of his forthcoming death."

VII

Having made up his mind to go back to the United States, Damián, they say, was only waiting for his father to make his will, and to receive his share of the estate. His passion for Micaela seemed to have cooled, and, if she hadn't publicly insulted him, the tragedy would never have occurred.

Micaela's last words, "Don't do anything to him. Let him go! It isn't his fault. I wanted to go, because I love him more than anyone else. Let him go!" gave rise to the most contradictory comments, ranging from outrage at her shamelessness to ingenuous theories intended to excuse her. There were other confusing factors. Don Inocencio let it be known of his own accord that his daughter's one idea had been to get away from the village, that not a day passed but she kept at him about it. She plagued him angrily. She refused to eat. She moped. She wept. On the night of the fifteenth she was again on the subject, vehemently, and had said things which Don Inocencio had then paid little attention to, "If we don't go away, or if you won't send me away alone, you'll be to blame for what happens." But how many times had she tried to gain her way with similar threats! "The night before this," he said, "I found her packing her clothes, and before I could ask her any questions, she said, 'There must be someone who will take me out of this inferno even if you won't!' We had such an argument that, I confess, I was beside myself and struck her." Why, then, asked the curious, did Micaela refuse, at the risk of her life, to go with Damián? And why, after he did what he did, did she admit publicly that she had loved no one as she had loved him?

Don Timoteo's relatives declared loudly and repeatedly that Micaela had stirred up Damián against his father and Ruperto Ledesma against Damián, that these two had been on the point of coming to blows several times and villagers had had to separate them.

At any rate, Micaela had, in public, directed cutting jokes at Damián in the presence of Ruperto Ledesma, on the fifteenth, while leaving mass. They were sarcastic enough to have made the Northerner furious if he'd had water in his veins. Damián was in the gateway opening from the atrium upon the Calle Derecha, and Ruperto was standing on the corner by the Flor de Mayo with friends when Micaela came out with the López girls (dreaded for their sharp tongues). Seeing Damián there, she burst out laughing and said something which he couldn't hear. The others laughed, too, the girls who were with her and the people standing near. (Later, it was learned that she had said, "How do you like Pugnose's fancy breeches and yellow shoes? I'll take you up close to him and see if you swoon the way they say other girls do, from merely hearing an English word and smelling cheap hairdresser's oil." She made other silly remarks of the same kind.) Without returning Damián's greeting, she walked up to Ruperto Ledesma, smiled at him, and deliberately let fall some flowers she was wearing. Ruperto picked them up and waited for Damián, who passed him with the words, "I'll leave the second- or third-hand pickings to you." Ruperto's friends had to keep him from rushing after

Damián. Some say that that afternoon or the next day he sent word to Ledesma that two men shouldn't quarrel over a wretch like her.

What did he mean by second- or third-hand goods?

On Monday, the sixteenth, Damián declared in Pancho Pérez' shop that he was going away. He wouldn't dirty his hands. That week no one saw him anymore; they thought he was at the farm.

Now they wondered if he wasn't the horseman heard passing along the street by the Rodríguezes' very late at night or in the early hours of the morning on the days between the seventeenth and the twenty-fourth of August.

Doña Rita, the seamstress, said that one morning—yes, it was Wednesday, the eighteenth—she found a crumpled envelope, like a love letter, at the corner outside the Rodríguezes' house. What a pity she threw it in the fire!

And in the Flor de Mayo they say that on Tuesday one of Don Inocencio's servants came to buy a sheet of paper and an envelope, and they teased him, asking whether it wasn't for Damián or Ruperto or, maybe, Don Timoteo. The boy, Crescencio, admitted that Micaela had sent him secretly to buy paper and an envelope, but that was all he knew, and he certainly hadn't taken a letter to anyone.

The eve of fateful St. Bartholomew's day, Prudencia received a message from Damián, asking whether his father had decided on the division of his property. He was leaving for California that very week, he said, and wanted to get the matter settled before going.

So the twenty-fourth of August arrived.

VIII

Rescued from the wrath of the people, safe in prison, Damián took refuge in silence, almost unbroken.

"Kill me, can't you?" he kept saying, like a sleepwalker. Blood dripped down his face, from the blows of the crowd.

"Why did you do it?"

"Why don't you kill me?"

"You'd better tell the whole truth, and right now!"

"Kill me!"

Sometimes he added, mechanically, without conviction, "You're cowards. Let me have a gun and I'll end it all now." He seemed not at all drunk, as the Deputy had thought at first.

"Put me to death. That's all I deserve."

The fury of the crowd could be heard outside: "Father killer! Kill him! They'll let him go free because he's a Mason!"

Father Martínez kept them from storming the jail, but some of the villagers, zealous for justice and distrustful of government intrigue, kept watch that night and the nights following.

Who could sleep, that night? All, to a greater or lesser degree, were affected by the tragedy. Even those who hadn't yet reached the age of reason could feel the abnormal pulse of the village: knocks at the doors, heated conversations, candles lighted, rapid comings and goings in the streets, and from house to house. Many of the children heard the shots, the running, the cries, the lamentations, the tolling of the bells; others had seen the culprit, led away dripping blood, surrounded by guns, amidst clenched fists, in a shower of stones, with curses and sobs, in the growing darkness of the evening; and certain phrases echoed mysteriously in their innocent ears: "He's a monster!" "He killed his father!" "He killed a woman!" "He nearly killed the village saint!" "He's a monster!" And the phrase, "He killed a woman, he killed a woman . . . woman . . . woman," echoed in the frightened young minds.

"He killed a woman! He killed his father! He nearly killed Father Islas! Father Islas, the saint!"

Many voices asked the question, "How did Father Islas come into it? How did it concern our Chaplain?" The story of Pascual, the sacristan, who was with Father Chemita, as he calls him, was as follows, leaving out the comments and interjections:

"When I heard the shots, I couldn't help going out in front of the church, to see what had happened, and I saw Juanita Rodríguez come running like a madwoman, calling out, 'They killed her! They killed her! A priest! A priest!' I knew Father Martínez wasn't there, or Father Vidriales, so, catching Juanita's anxiety, I ran to the Chapel to tell Father Chemita, without waiting to find out exactly what was the matter. I'd barely told him he was the only one in the church when he heard the cries inside the building, and got up at once. 'Oh, Padre, what an awful thing! They've killed Micaela. Come see if we can get there in time. Come! Run!' said Juanita, forgetting where she was.

"The three of us rushed off through the crowd of milling people.

We saw Damián on horseback, galloping out of the lane by the Naranjos', followed by a lot of men shouting, 'Seize him!' When he recognized Father Islas, he spurred his horse, at full speed, raised his gun, and shot twice, point-blank. He was foaming at the mouth. He said, 'You're the one I was looking for, Padre—you're to blame for everything, you and the Parish Priest . . .' By the mercy of Providence, the two shots just grazed our hats. When he shot again, his horse slipped and fell. It threw him, and the bullet went wild. Then all of us—Crescencio, Juan Lomas, the Champurrado, Uncle Cejas, and I don't remember who else—threw ourselves on him and held him down. That was when we learned he'd killed his father, too. I dropped him as if he'd been a scorpion, or I'd been struck by lightning. I think I must have given him a kick in the ribs. He choked and had trouble getting out his words, 'You cowards!' he said. He was having a hard time breathing. I remembered Father Chemita and got over to Don Inocencio's house as fast as I could and made my way to the door of the bedroom where they'd taken the dying girl. I stayed there till Father Islas came out, tears running down his cheeks. I'd never seen him cry before.

" 'Could you confess her?' I asked him—we all asked him. He didn't answer. He paid no attention to anyone, but went out into the street, motioned to me to return to the church, and went home. They say that they knocked at his door time after time, but got no answer. Sometime in the early hours of the morning he sent a message to the Parish Priest that he was going to Clamores and would be gone a week, in Retreat."

"It was a job to capture Damián," old Cejas was saying to the crowd in the Flor de Mayo. "We had to chase him half through the village, and at one time we thought he was going to get away down the Teocaltiche Road. To start with, none of us had weapons or horses; we'd have to wait till he rounded a corner and then follow him. All we could do was follow and shout. I was one of the first ones. On my way from Las Trojes, after work, I heard Crescencio shouting 'Stop him!' Somebody came out of Doña Celsa's shop. Damián saw us and drew back. Crescencio and I followed him, ducking when he fired at us, and others joined in. Luckily, Juan Lomas and some men on horseback were coming along the Teocaltiche Road. They raised their guns and Damián jumped over the ditch and we closed in on him at Don Matías' wall. Don

Matías fired the first shot, but his old rifle doesn't carry much farther than its own muzzle. He fired point-blank and missed. Someone, I don't know who, shouted, 'Don't shoot him, take him alive!' and we brought him back through Naranjos Street. All this time there was no sign of the Deputy; he turned up with the soldiers after we'd disarmed Damián and tied him up, as meek as a lamb. All the Deputy did was to save his life; but if he hadn't been there, they'd have lynched Damián."

Wearing an expression no one had ever seen before, Father Martínez came into the Flor de Mayo, and urged, in an exhausted voice, "Go home and pray in this affliction. Go on home. It won't do any good to make more trouble."

The villagers hadn't turned out like this for a long time. The Parish Priest broke up crowds in the streets and got people to shut up the windows, doors, and shops, where the curious were congregating.

Poor Father Martínez! He had been supervising work in Retreat House when he heard the shots, rushed down, and heard the sorrowful news. He wanted to be everywhere at once. He sent word to his curates to go to Don Inocencio's house and to wherever they had taken Damián. Finding himself near Don Timoteo's, he went there. He met with utter confusion at the gates, inside the yard, in the doorway. It was useless to ask the people to go home. Hundreds of voices shouted out accounts of what had happened. He ordered them to shut the gate, and made his way, as through a crowded church, into the bedroom of the dead man. Father Reyes had anointed the body, after administering conditional absolution.

"All you can do now is be silent and pray," the Parish Priest said firmly, above the sound of murmurs and tears, quelling his audience with a look. He sent everybody out except the relatives; finally, he took Prudencia aside. She had clung to him from the moment he arrived. More to calm her than from a desire to know details, he asked her gently what had happened.

Disjointed phrases, interrupted by sobs, sighs, maledictions, answered him. Don Dionisio learned that Damián had arrived about mid-afternoon, apparently calm, and said he wanted to talk to his father. "Whatever you do," Prudencia had warned, "don't mention the will or anything likely to upset him." "Don't worry," Damián replied, his voice for the first time without a trace of his usual brusqueness. "The change in Father's feelings must have worked a change in his, too," thought Prudencia. She could hear their quiet voices. "I don't know where you got this idea from of going away again, when there's enough work to do right here, on your own land, and you can make as much money as you like," she heard Don Timoteo say, in a fatherly tone. She felt easier in her mind, and went back to her work. There was no one else in the house. Don Timoteo came out into the patio. "Prudencia, go ask Zenón Placencia to send me his accounts for the corn bought at harvest time. I'll wait for you to bring them back yourself, I need them." Prudencia wasn't gone long. Don Zenón was in the orchard, but anyhow, in less than a quarter of an hour she was back. The gate was open. Damián's horse was gone from the patio. There was money scattered on the ground. Prudencia's heart turned over, she called out to her father, to Damián. There was no answer. She ran into her father's room, and there he was, dead!

Father Martínez exerted himself to get her to accept the blow with Christian fortitude and resignation. He assured her that her father was well prepared for death. She must forgive, and of course it was her task to keep the household going and to see that the body was properly prepared for burial.

As soon as possible, Don Dionisio went to the Rodríguezes'. The Deputy and Don Refugio, who had come to examine the wounds, were leaving as he arrived.

"A bullet through her lungs. A common crime, one of those 'crimes of passion,' as they call them," the Deputy hastened to say, adding, "You see how disorder is spreading; you should make up your mind to help us form a party on the side of law and order."

A crime of this magnitude, a "common" crime! Parricide a "common" crime, when the annals of the whole region within a radius of a hundred and fifty miles have never recorded such a case! To treat it so airily and try to make political capital of it! Father Martínez' blood was boiling, but he held his tongue, bade the Deputy good-bye, and entered the house, to share his parishioners' distress.

In this crime the details were much more distasteful than in the case of Don Timoteo; but he learned from the versions of many— all so eager to tell him that they kept interrupting each other— how Micaela had been coming back from the López place, where she used to go nearly every afternoon, when Damián caught up with her. Rita, the seamstress, heard him say, "If you want to come, you'll have to come right now, and hurry, for I'm in trouble." Rita didn't open her window because the man's tone frightened her. (Later, as she kept repeating them, she kept adding to the words she had heard from behind the window where she was sewing.) Crescencio said he saw that as Micaela was about to go around the corner towards the house, Damián tried to carry her off by force. He ran to help her, just as she managed to break away, and Damián fired at her, still trying to force her into the saddle. When he saw Crescencio, he made off. Micaela took a few steps before she fell, and it was when Don Jacinto Buenrostro, his wife, and children picked her up that she said, "Don't do anything to him. Let him go! It isn't his fault. I wanted to go, because I love him more than anyone else. Let him go!" Then Doña Lola and Juanita arrived. (Don Inocencio was in the village and heard the news without warning in the shop of Don Hermenegildo Quezada.) Even then, Micaela managed to say, with great effort, "I won't be bothering you anymore." They say these were her last words, but she still showed signs of life when Father Islas arrived.

At the sight of Father Martínez, Doña Lola's cries became heart-rending, "Is she damned? For God's sake, tell me she's not damned!" Father Martínez tried to calm her and console her. As though she hadn't heard him, Doña Lola began to cry out again, like a mad-woman, "What have we done to God that He should treat us so? It's not fair!" As blasphemies kept pouring from her lips, those who had begun by covering their ears began to leave the house. Don Dionisio remained to see her through her hysterical seizure. There was no help from Don Inocencio; he had shut himself up in his room and refused to see anyone.

Father Martínez went on to the prison. A common crime . . . a common crime!—when there hasn't been a murder in the village for almost ten years! Satan is testing the work of many years. Perhaps, he thought, his sins of commission and omission have combined to undo it. Poor shepherd, full of weaknesses, poor flock! He had ordered the bells to be tolled as a collective penitential hymn, in prayer for the dead and the living, and to plead for the repentance of the evil-doer, who wrung his hands and muttered:

"You needn't suppose I'm going to make my confession! Let me alone!"

"I've come to see what I can do for you, for no other reason," replied Don Dionisio, gently, but his words were met by a silence into which the tolling of the bells fell like an accusation.

"Why can't you stop those bells?"

"How can we silence God?"

"They drive me mad!"

"That is because you refuse to hear their message."

"Stop them!"

"How shall we stop the dogs that fill the night with their barking?"

"Yes. Even the bells are better than the barking of the dogs." Another long silence in the cell, with its sinister light from a pine torch.

"Would you really do something for me?"

"I have told you, that is why I am here."

"Ask them not to leave me in the dark."

"I'll send you an oil lamp."

"You'll tell them I'm afraid."

"You *ought* to be afraid—of God."

"I don't believe in God."

"Then why do you flinch at the barking of the dogs or at being left in the dark? Are you afraid they'll kill you?"

"I'm ready to die, and if I thought you capable of it, I'd ask you to kill me. As a favor, Father."

"It was you who wanted to kill me."

"Why should I deny it? . . . Well, why don't you go?"

"I haven't come to burden you with reproaches. You had your reasons for what you did. I have mine for wanting to keep you company and comfort you."

"I ask you to leave me. And, as for why I did what I did . . ."

"I haven't asked to know that."

"Leave me. I blame you for fostering an atmosphere that makes it impossible to breathe in the village. I blame you, but chiefly it's that Father Islas."

"An atmosphere in which offenses against God's laws cannot thrive."

"I'm not going to argue."

"I have no wish to argue, either. Rest. And when you feel like thinking, listen to the voices in the darkness, to the dogs, to the bells. Are you hungry? thirsty?"

"No."

"I'll send you a jar of water. I hope you rest. I'll leave instructions for them to let me know if you want anything. Now I'm going to ask you to do just one thing, something easy. Now, tomorrow, or later, whenever you remember some prayer, say it. Don't reject it. Say it with your lips at least, even if you cannot mean it. I know—you must believe me—it will make you feel better. If the barking of the dogs bothers you, pray, and little by little you'll forget it."

"There are things we cannot forget."

"These are the things of the soul."

Father Martínez walked towards the door. The bells had stopped ringing. The barking of the dogs sounded louder.

"Listen." Damián's voice was a groan. "How can I believe in the soul?"

"Don't fear your doubts. Don't reject the thoughts that come to you. Listen to them."

"I'm not afraid, but it's terrible to be alone."

"Let yourself believe, and you'll find you are not alone."

"Aren't you glad that this has happened to me?"

"How can you think so? I'd like to be a father to you; I wanted to, against your will, because it was part of God's plan, and if it were possible, I would undo what has happened."

"That's impossible. Impossible. But sometimes I think it's all a bad dream."

"What is possible, believe me, is the salvation of your soul."

"Leave me. It's no use to hope I'm going to make my confession."

"Confession is free, and no prison in the world can take it from you. Good-bye, Damián, and may the Lord open your eyes."

In the doorway, he turned back, "We are both sinners, you and I, but God's mercy makes us all equal in his sight."

When he reached the street, the moon was bright, the calm August moon that brought so much ill, that brought blindness in its train.

His soliloquy continued, "Poor shepherd, full of weaknesses, the sheep entrusted to your care have gone astray; the wolves are howling all around. How will you account to God for one of the lambs lost, and how many you have lost already? Micaela . . ."

His thoughts capriciously turned to his niece, María. "Wouldn't it have been better if she'd died as a child in some epidemic? Then, today or tomorrow, she couldn't be the victim of an epidemic of the soul." Selfish concern for his own flesh and blood, human rebellion, filled him, and he controlled himself only by a great effort. "You ought to feel the same concern, even stronger, for all your parishioners; you ought to be above having favorites and family ties." His feelings drowned his thoughts: "María! María! What's to become of you?" Another thought pricked like a thorn, "Gabriel!"

When he reached the Presbytery, Marta begged him to eat his dinner, but he couldn't eat so much as a mouthful, nor, when he returned from the wakes, could he sleep.

Contrary to custom, the bells tolled all night long, in general invitation to repentance; they tolled through the tragic night and through the hours of the next morning; every hour they tolled.

"How different they sound from when Gabriel was ringing them!" the people whispered in frightened tones, in the privacy of their bedrooms, those who could not sleep, huddling in patios and hallways.

"As though the bells had died, too, that day when Gabriel rang them for the last time."

IX

It was neither surprise, nor grief, nor withdrawal, nor simple regret, nor even plain dislike that Bartolo read in the eyes of his wife. Torn between panic and satisfaction, he came to tell her of what had happened, and he ventured to look into her eyes, curious to see what they would reflect. Better he hadn't. What he saw was hatred, held in check for years and now suddenly blazing forth as at an enemy, at a thief who has possessed stolen goods, at an executioner, the man responsible for Damián's misfortune. Worse than if Damián had left seven bullet holes in his heart. Not a word passed between husband and wife; nevertheless, both knew that from that moment life had changed for them. Bartolo, stricken to the depths of his being, decided, then and there, to go North, the sooner the better.

X

The bodies were buried as soon as possible, lest a doctor be sent from Teocaltiche to perform autopsies. "Cut them up like cattle," was the opinion of the people, "on the pretext of needing evidence for the trial. Anything but that. What good would it do? They're dead, and no amount of facts would bring them to life again." The haste which cut short the ceremonies was one of the most painful details of the tragedy.

The village meted out its own justice by going to Don Timoteo's funeral mass and burial but staying away from Micaela's. Only Father Martínez, the close friends of the family, or those under financial obligation to the Rodríguez family, were present.

Even at the wake for the poor girl the hostility could be felt, in the scanty attendance and coldness. Lucas Macías was present during the first part of the night, but, as there was no one to ask him questions or keep up the conversation, he went off to the Limóns' earlier than he had planned. At the Rodríguezes' he had tried to talk about the "ley fuga" in the days of General Tolentino, round about 1883 and '84.

Settled down at Don Timoteo's wake, with an encouraging audience, he began his stories with one about a circus girl, a juggler who used to juggle with burning coals and knives. "But once, at the Fair in Nochistlán, two red-hot coals collided; one of the knives went right through her heart, and the burning coals fell on top of her, and when they tried to put the fire out, she was just a bleeding coal herself—they didn't even try to save her . . ." This was, of course, Micaela's story transferred to a distant time, place, and situation. By one o'clock in the morning there was no one left at the Rodríguezes' but peasants and sleepy farmhands, nobody with initiative to keep prayers going on for the dead girl. At Don Timoteo's, on the other hand, rosaries followed each other without interruption every half-hour, and the house was full until the time for the funeral.

Father Martínez was criticized for sending dinner to the murderer. There were sarcastic remarks about Micaela's white coffin. The Limón family announced that they would not send their father's body to the church in the hearse that had carried "the cause of it all," and they finally succeeded in having Don Timoteo's funeral precede Micaela's.

"How can they let the body of a —— into the church?" muttered the Limóns' following. "She didn't even make her confession," they added.

When Micaela's scanty procession passed from the house to the church and from there to the Cemetery, not a window or door opened to show any relenting of hostility; even men in the streets avoided the procession.

"Ruperto," they said afterward, "had no more self-respect than to go to the funeral."

"And they had no more than to let him."

"And he went around saying Damián would never leave the village alive—he'd settle accounts with him."

"He'd have already settled accounts with him if he'd been a man."

In the Cemetery, Lucas Macías was pointing out the graves of those who had lost their lives by the ley fuga.

"If Damián were only a follower of Reyes . . . nowadays it's only political prisoners they apply this law to," commented one of his hearers.

XI

"Now we have Prudencia, Clementina, and Juan to deal with," said Don Timoteo's debtors. "The children are worse than the father. They'll skin us alive."

XII

The soldiers sent to take Damián away arrived. They would take him to Guadalajara, not Teocaltiche. Father Martínez went to ask the Deputy for safe conduct for the prisoner.

"I know nothing about it. Orders are orders. The corporal in charge of the troop is the one who knows whether anyone else can go along. Now, if you were supporters of Corral's, I might be able to do something. Besides, the prisoner has refused to make any statement. That goes against him."

Only the Parish Priest took an interest in Damián's fate. He visited him every day. Though the tone of his admonitions became more earnest every day, he made no impression on him. Damián still refused to agree to the company of a priest on his journey to the capital, or to death.

When they brought him out of prison in the early morning of the thirty-first, San Ramón's day, windows and doors were opened out of curiosity.

"So he didn't make his confession after all!"

"He wasn't handcuffed."

"He won't reach La Labor."

"Father Reyes' going with him won't make any difference."

"He wouldn't say anything."

"He wouldn't make his confession, for anything."

"And Ruperto?"

"Fine, thank you."

"Didn't he go out to meet him? Didn't he even have a shot at him?"

There was no sign of Ruperto.

"He must be hiding under the bed."

"In women's clothes."

When the group accompanying the prisoner passed by La Labor of San Ramón, the drum and the pipes were playing, rockets and firecrackers were going off, which started the rumor in the village that Damián had been shot at—Damián, the disgrace of the district.

STUDENTS AND
ABSENT ONES

I

OST OF THE STUDENTS who are away at school begin to come home for the holidays early in September. At first the gloom of the village dampens their high spirits and draws them into the general atmosphere. But little by little the effect is reversed, and student sunshine dispels the gloom of the people.

Most of them are from the Seminary. People are disarmed by its Levitical name. From it ministers of the Lord have come, scattered all over the Archdiocese. It's rare for fewer than twelve students a year to begin their Latin studies there; the number is usually greater. And rare the year when at least one son of the village doesn't say his first Mass.

Holidays are a time of anxiety and danger for the Parish Priest. In these months of liberty, how many young men, already studying philosophy or even theology, and seemingly firm in their vocation, renounce their calling, returning to a former waywardness or yielding to a new one! As it usually goes, the backsliders among the Seminarists will take up with some girl or other, out of vanity, or just to have something to do, and when they return to their studies they find it hard to settle down after their fling. In the course of the year, even if they do not become formally engaged, they flit, like humming birds, from flower to flower in the dazzle of the sun-lit world. Here, they sing the songs of that world and play the guitar; there, they are applauded for reciting romantic poetry, playing cards, and telling off-color stories; and so they scandalize the authorities by their lack of devotion, pay court to more and more girls, and, one fine day, turn their backs on the cloister or, if they stay, become only passable priests.

The vocations come to nothing are not the only harm done; there is also the deep and lasting damage to the conscience of the women, who are taken by surprise, exalted, made restless, lost in illusions and fears. How many—Lina, Magdalena, Gertrudis—have waited for years in hope and despair! How many have grown old in vain waiting! How many will begin their uncertain wait this year with remorse at the thought that they are working against God, defrauding Him of a laborer in His vineyard! Remorse which the year cannot silence, nor many years. Anguish at receiving or not receiving letters from the absent one.

How many of the students will return determined to give up their calling and disappoint the hopes of the Parish Priest or the parents and relatives who had hoped for the glory of a minister of the Most High in the family! How many others, this year, will sow the first seeds of their final downfall! *Many are called, but few are chosen.*

How many young men? How many young women? As if the poor Parish Priest had not enough to keep him sleepless!

II

The bustle of the outside world, darkness disguised as light, all the various issues of the moment, enter the village with the students, whose chatter comes like a long echo of foreign agitation and soils the silence in the souls of the villagers.

Lucas Macías hastens to exchange old stories for the latest news. He cannot believe all they say, but "all is grist that comes to his mill." What is happening in politics? Is Don Porfirio still there? Is there going to be a revolution? What are they saying about the Centenary?

All the gossips of the village pump the students, an easy job, since the newcomers are only too delighted to show off their knowledge, their perspicacity, the accuracy of their judgment and predictions, as though they held in their hands the strings of the universe and the destiny of Man.

They talk about a certain Francisco Madero, who is going around in the northern part of the country making speeches against the re-election of Corral. He must be crazy; some say he wants to be vice-president, next to Don Porfirio, no less; others say he's a Mason and a Spiritist, and that when the time comes he'll have the help of the Yankees; still others say that he won't amount to anything since not even General Reyes could change things. The fellow would certainly lead us into a state of anarchy. But he doesn't matter, he's not a general or even a lawyer, just a landowner from Coahuila. When did a revolution ever come from the northern provinces?

"Well, then," says Pascual Aguilera, a student who is reported not to be going back to the Seminary, "why is Madero making such a stir, and why is he listened to everywhere, and founding the Anti-Re-electionist Party, and why do so many poor people follow him although he is rich? This is the way the Apostles began. Let the political wiseacres take care and remember the story of David and Goliath. Mark my words." But nobody shares Aguilera's opinion. The one thing the students agree on is that Reyes will not fight and that everything will go on as it has done for thirty years.

Lucas Macías fixes the description of Madero in his mind: "A short man, fair-skinned, bearded, wiry, and a good sort." Lucas wouldn't be able to explain why, from the very beginning, he connected the name and figure of Madero with the most sensational news the students brought—the return of Halley's comet—news that for most people put political topics in the shade and sowed the seeds of panic.

"There's no doubt that there will be, if not revolution, wars, famine, and plagues, everywhere," prophesies Lucas, emphatically; adopting Pascual's opinion, he adds, "When apostles appear the world calls them mad, boys throw stones at them, the authorities put them in prison, but nobody can silence them, no one can stop them."

III

"And Luis Gonzaga?"

"Buried in the lunatic asylum of Zapopan," replies the authoritative voice of Fermín García, who has been ordained Friar this year, and bows his head, in season and out, that all may admire his tonsure, which is brand-new, big, and carefully shaven. "It was my duty to visit him just before I came away; I understand that, during the first days of his stay there, they had to put him in a strait jacket; I found him in a period of relative calm; his madness now takes the form of thinking he is an incarnation of the god the pagans called Apollo Musagetes, or, according to the Greek and Latin classics, the god who directs and guides the Muses. Not only the dignity of my office but even the most elementary discretion forbids me to recall the lewd fancies that haunt the mind of our unfortunate comrade; suffice it to report that the women whom Luis in his madness metamorphoses into Muses are well known to all of us." Fermín's affected speech delights his family.

The fate of Luis Gonzaga was certainly no surprise to the village. Lucas Macías had put it into the old tittle-tattle he raked up, and people from Guadalajara made a point of keeping it up-to-date in all the details.

Word of the meeting between Luis Gonzaga and his father was brought back on the following day by the Ruesgas, who had witnessed the encounter. Don Alfredo overtook his son the night of the sixth of May, at the tavern in Contla where he was having dinner, stubbornly intent upon continuing his journey and deaf to the Ruesgas, who were spending the night there and tried to dissuade him. Several travellers had given him information about the lady he was pursuing; he hoped, by going straight on, to catch up with her near Ixtlahuacán. The Ruesgas were not only trying to dissuade him from going on but were urging him to return to the village with them when Don Alfredo appeared in the doorway of the inn. Without giving him time to utter a word, as if expecting him, Luis turned on him, shouting, "Is there nowhere I can escape from you? Is there nowhere you won't come to disturb me? Understand, once for all, no one can stop me now!" His fury increased, with no justification. "Now you know—they must have told you—where I am going: I'm going to marry Victoria, or kill myself if she won't have me! Out of my way!" As he said this, he raised his hand in such a threatening gesture that those present intervened to stop him. Don Alfredo was as though turned to stone. "Let me go!" shouted Luis, struggling to get free. He managed to twist away with a deft movement and fell into a chair, groaning, "It's your fault, you invited her. She got on my nerves, I hated her. But the Devil was with her. I couldn't get her out of my mind. My dreams were full of her. Her perfume was in my nostrils, her voice in my ears and her body always before my eyes, even when I shut them. She possessed my senses, my mouth, my hands, my tongue. It's horrible. I can't live without her. If she won't have me I'll kill myself, and if she does take me, she'll destroy me. But I can't live this way any longer . . ."

His groans grew louder, convulsions followed. Even the hardened pack-drivers began to get alarmed. No, it was no farce, this trembling was nothing to laugh at. The boy writhed and suddenly sat up, saying in a loud voice, "Victoria is my damnation—I cannot escape her!" He muttered a few unintelligible words and fell back on the floor, rigid. When he regained consciousness in the morning he was quite changed. "Where are we, Father? I don't remember leaving the house. . . . Where's Mother? Take me to Victoria—Victoria —Victoria—they told me she'd gone . . . Talk to her . . . I'll go wherever you like, Father." He slept peacefully. A doctor came from Cuquío and advised them to take him to Guadalajara as soon as possible. Don Alfredo sent for Doña Carmen. Luis spent the day in a kind of coma. Next morning the Pérez family set off for the State Capital.

More news reached the village. Afraid of meeting the woman to blame for all this if they went to Guadalajara, the family went to Mexico City. Luis was better, although, from time to time, he had attacks of madness. He said he had been ordered, in a vision, to go back to the Seminary. They were planning to return to the village; now, Luis was determined to become a Jesuit.

In July the news was that Luis had started on his novitiate in the Society of Jesus. In August, maybe on their way back to the village, the family reached Guadalajara. Luis had another attack. Now he is in the asylum in Zapopan.

Each successive item of news seemed more remote. Damián's crime drove them completely into the background.

IV

Only three people knew this, but from the end of May, letters in an envelope of excellent quality, perfumed and addressed in an aristocratic hand to Gabriel Martínez, began to arrive in the village. The first was returned after fifteen days, with "Unknown," "Unclaimed," written on it. The next one was addressed to the Presbytery. It was taken to Don Dionisio; he realized where it came from, hesitated, and decided that his duty was to burn it; the next four met the same fate. Don Dionisio won the co-operation of the Post Office by explaining that the letters could cause great harm. The letter that arrived on August 19 was registered. There was no way to avoid giving the information, "The person to whom this letter is addressed is no longer at this address, and his present whereabouts are unknown." Only the Parish Priest and Father Reyes, whose responsibility it was to check the mail, knew this— and the Post Office official. But the Seminarists have brought back the story of a distinguished lady inquiring which students were from the village, and among the things she asked them was if they knew where Gabriel Martínez, the bell-ringer, had gone, cloaking this question with many others as if it were of no importance. The villagers don't know where Gabriel is. "He went as he came," said Lucas Macías, "mysteriously."

V

Unable to refuse permission, but very much against his wishes, Father Martínez has word from the students that they are going to spend part of their holidays in other places; what bothers him most is their going to the regional Fairs of Mexticacán, Yahualica, Toyahua, and Nochistlán, which are held during September and October. "They come back changed. What's the good of keeping these distractions out of this village, these picnics, suppers, gatherings, parlor games, and still worse, dances, for instance, if the students can have their fling there?"

The worst of it is that they nearly always bring back some fellow student or friend from these places, and in order to show their companions a good time, turn the village upside down, play practical jokes, pretend to be gay dogs, get hold of guitars, sing, and make a commotion, and the villagers not only tolerate but even support them in their escapades. The outsiders give themselves the airs of conquerors; not a single pretty girl is left in peace. Last year, it took all the strong-mindedness the clergy could muster to stop the parties people tried to organize on the initiative of the visitors.

VI

Village chronicle: On the third of September, Father Reyes came back from Teocaltiche, whither he had accompanied Damián Limón. (Some still disapprove of this concern for a parricide and woman-slayer; others approve of the zeal of the priest for the salvation of a soul and accuse the objectors of lacking charity.) On the fifth, Father Islas was back, and there were hopes of learning something. But the silence of the priests disappointed the hopes of the villagers, who only learned that the criminal had not fallen victim to the ley fuga. Disappointment prevailed.

On the ninth, a newspaper clipping from Guadalajara, perhaps brought back by a student, was passed from hand to hand. It had the name of the village in big letters and an account of the sensational crime, with details that the villagers had not known, and which, although they were probably a product of the journalist's imagination, were accepted as incontrovertible truth, since they appeared in print. Some even learned the printed words by heart, for, though the shameful context in which the name of the village appeared caused them some anxiety, it was still a source of pride that the press should take notice of a local happening.

"Did you see what they say in the press?"

The solemn word was pronounced with respectful emphasis. Groups formed in the streets. Even those who couldn't read wanted the clipping, which others could read to them. It was the subject of many heated arguments.

"What do they mean, 'village'? 'Town' is what they should say, and a Christian town, too!" "'A well-to-do farmer,' indeed! They should have said 'Northerner.' When did that loafer ever take a plow in his hands or sow a seed?" and their indignation flared out when they came to the following passage:

"It seems that the splendid rage of the young man roused a sudden frenzy of love in the girl, because her last words were a confession of morbid passion. She who, a few minutes before, had refused

to accompany her enamored suitor, now begged them frantically
not to harm him and declared that it had all been her fault. It is
now up to the criminal as to whether he will plead this in his defense. Some people have no sense of shame! Evidently robbery
was not the reason for the crime, since, after he had committed the
black deed, the offspring of the Devil took only a few coins. It ap-
pears, rather, that rage overcame the unnatural son when his father
refused him permission for the trip he was planning and denied him
his share of the inheritance. There are also some who heatedly maintain that the crime was inspired by jealousy, as it was reported that
the dead man, too, was courting the girl."

And there followed editorial comments: "The cancer which gnaws
at our customs is now invading sacred ground, and it is high time
for society to protect itself by swift, exemplary, and effective justice."
. . . "Public opinion is waiting to see what measures will be taken by
the Magistrate at Teocaltiche, where the prisoner has been taken,
since he comes under that criminal jurisdiction.". . . "May the firing
squad soon bring this drama to its fitting close, punishing the monster as he deserves for deeds that fill with terror the peaceful, smiling region where they took place and will surely fill the rest of the
State and even the Republic with horror."

A legion of unsolicited correspondents made their appearance in
the village, rectifying and amplifying the information; every Tom,
Dick, and Harry became a journalist overnight and sent extensive
communications to *La Chispa, El Regional, El País,* and even to
Mensajero del Sagrado Corazón, publications subscribed to by various villagers, but the contributions never appeared in print nor was
the event even mentioned.

At the end of the month, students who had gone to Teocaltiche
came back with the news that Damián might even be set free: first,
because they hadn't been able to get him to make any damaging
admissions; second, because they said that the results of autopsies
on the two bodies were necessary to determine the guilt of the accused; third, the evidence of the doctor and the authorities who
drew up the accusation and described the wounds was insufficient—
for example, on Timoteo Limón's body they found only bruises
which might have been caused by a fall. Damián persisted in his
declaration that he had not struck his father, and the death might
well have been caused by a heart attack. ("Tricks, tricks, as the

250

press says!") Therefore, the Magistrate had ordered the exhumation of the bodies. Autopsies were to be made in due form.

"Horrors! Let them set him free first, since after all God will punish him; God needs no proofs to administer justice. Rather that than to allow the grave to be profaned."

The hair-raising threat, a collective nightmare, made the people determined; if necessary they would oppose with arms any desecration of the Cemetery and disturbance of the bodies resting there. Bands of children, with stones in their hands, kept watch on the Teocaltiche Road. Wild-eyed men and women stood ready to intervene if the need arose.

An unexpected blow to his own personal feelings distracted the vigilant attention of Father Martínez. He received the following letter:

One of the most moving and inspiring experiences of my life was accorded me in your village, as I listened to the ringing of the bells, which I consider play a great part in maintaining the spirit of devotion that reigns there. I had occasion to meet the humble young man who so skillfully evokes their moving message from the bells, and I have been consumed ever since with the idea of helping him to become a great master, and—why not, by the grace of God?—a great composer of sacred music. With this idea in mind, I have made inquiries here and in Mexico City about the possibilities of his beginning studies that he could afterward continue in Europe. Maestro Don Félix Peredo has offered to give him his first lessons. I will be responsible for his support, and I have written to him several times about the plan, without receiving a reply. I am now informed that he has left the village, and as you must know his present whereabouts, and must be interested in his future, I inform you of my plan. I submit it to your consideration, and ask you to bring it to his notice, so that he may get in touch with me here, and I can place the necessary funds at his disposal.

The letter was signed: Victoria E. Viuda de Cortina, and dated Guadalajara, September 29. Don Dionisio tore it up furiously. "Wiles of Satan!" "Brazen creature!" "Unprincipled effrontery!" He would tell her so. He would not let the letter go unanswered. He would answer it and warn her to desist from disturbing the poor boy. . . . But if her suggestion was made in good faith? Did he have the right to decide Gabriel's future? He decided to ask the advice of—no, not Father Islas—Father Reyes.

VII

Mild golden afternoons. Dusk comes early, and the nights are long; holidays are coming to an end. October falls on yellow fields. This is the time of restlessness and desire. Timid girls, black-robed by day, toss without sleep, suffering because they dare not creep to the keyhole to tremble at words they both long and fear to hear. Hope and fear fill the hearts of boys who have managed to deliver their first letter, and who spend the day trying to guess the meaning of a gesture, a look, who escape from home at night and profane the peace of nine, ten, eleven o'clock, even of midnight! Escape the vigilance, the watchful eyes and ears of the Parish Priest and his assistants, risk being surprised by father, brothers, cousins, and relatives of the girl they seek, waiting until sounds cease and lights no longer filter through the cracks, drawing nearer, nearer, reaching the sidewalk, the wall, the angles of windows and doors, feeling for chinks and keyholes, trying to get a glimpse inside, placing their ears at keyholes, daring to make the slight noises that may bring happiness or disaster. Night after night, in desperation, without success, under the impassive stars.

Some prefer to take advantage of the heavy early-morning sleep of the watchers and leave their beds at three, four o'clock, slip through the streets, feel their way to the house, to the window or door, holding their breath so as not to frighten away the timid rustling that announces the presence of the beloved behind the panels. Desires, driven to desperation, like crazy birds, like birds that have lost their way, beat blindly against crosses, against the framework of doors, against walls, lashed by the Four Horsemen, ubiquitous phantoms, always in the streets, yet always at the four sides of the bed where the girl lies, sleepless with desire and fear. This year, the implacable guardians of the black-robed women all wear the same bloody mask, which reminds them of Micaela.

"Don't you remember me?" says Death.

"Don't you remember me?" says Judgment.

"Don't you remember me?" says Hell.

"Don't you remember me?" asks Paradise.

"Don't you remember me?" Death, Judgment, Hell, and Paradise, all in the guise of Micaela, whose voice cries out from beyond the grave, repeating in chilling tones of agony, "Don't you remember me?"

How can desire overcome this paralyzing terror in the long nights, in the dejection of early-morning hours?

VIII

Don Dionisio addressed a laconic reply to the widow Cortina. The gist of it is as follows:

Before he went away, the young man to whom you refer rejected my suggestion that he should dedicate himself to music, and his horror at the idea seemed to spring from some tragic experience of the moment. In any case I feel it my duty to let him know of the opportunity you offer. For reasons which you will forgive my not revealing, the money that you charitably offer should be set up anonymously as a trust fund with the Archbishop, and administered as though it were a scholarship. The Archbishop will decide whether it is wiser for the recipient to carry on his studies in Guadalajara or elsewhere.

IX

Like nearly all the village girls, especially those in love, Mercedes Toledo regarded Micaela's death as a direct message from God.

On the contrary, Julián, like many other young men, thought it a good time to get married, while his prospective father-in-law and brothers-in-law were chastened by the recent lesson. He managed to suggest this to Mercedes, whose answer was to end their engagement, a decision which only increased their love for each other. Mercedes felt it most and was enveloped in helpless sadness. "I loved him. I loved him. But could I ignore God's message for that reason?" She looked back with melancholy regret to the moment of horror when she read Julián's first love poems to her; she remembered her suffering when she received his first letter; the painful, slow but firm progress of her interest in him, her hopes, her love, nourished after the way of the village in bittersweet secrecy. Marta was her only confidante; Marta encouraged her, opposed the decision to end the engagement, listened to her troubles, and tried to comfort her. But both shared the fear sown by Micaela's death. None of the girls could stop dreaming of the dead girl. Better any sacrifice than such an end.

"And if Julián should lose patience and do the same to you?" The idea came to her one sleepless night.

"*It will be your fault,*" answered the familiar inner voice, "*your fault alone, because you didn't have the courage to reject him as you did the first time.*"

"From the very beginning I loved him." Mercedes hesitated to acknowledge the thought.

"*But you felt guilty, as you do now, now more than ever, much more. Abandoned girl, are you so lost to all virtue that you welcome the idea he may want to carry you off? You do welcome it, you take a perverse pleasure in the thought. You see him shoot you, you feel it voluptuously like her. Like the one who wants to have you in Hell with her!*"

"I can't stop loving Julián; I love him now more than ever," Mercedes would like to cry out. But her lips repeat, mechanically, "No, no, it's all over, whatever happens."

Where could she turn for strength? Who could dispel her fears? If only someone could replace them with happy confidence! Where could she find this? Not under her own roof, or in the inflexible rules of the Chaplain, or even in the charity of the Parish Priest, or in gentle Marta. It never occurred to her to turn to the other priests, the others whom she respected, her other friends. Where could she turn? When she prayed she felt her soul parched, untouched by rain from heaven, impenetrable to divine dew.

X

After the National Holiday—never had it been so lacking in luster—the Deputy went off to Teocaltiche and Guadalajara. He returned in a semi-propitiating, semi-threatening mood, to say that there was now no danger of the bodies' being exhumed; he had arranged it all and the villagers would not be required to go and give evidence at Teocaltiche. This was on condition that they helped him in his Party efforts "in support of the candidacy of the great Don Porfirio Díaz and Señor Corral." Otherwise, he had instructions to take different measures. He would apply the Reform Laws in all their rigor, without closing his eyes to infractions. "The authorities are well aware of what is going on," he added. "I will go on turning a blind eye (which is taking a risk—you know what happened to my predecessor) but you must help me save my neck. Stop making trouble and serve your country. I am risking my job and you must make some return."

XI

Not all desire was frightened into submission. The spectral legions were routed by the eager courage of some of the women, but why should María, niece of the Parish Priest, be among them? It was María who, better than any other, succeeded in shaking off the ghost and the voice of her friend Micaela. Whether through spite or in desperation at Gabriel's behavior, María broke through the hedge of fear. Her sudden feeling of emptiness, when Gabriel was gone and she did not know what had become of him, annoyed her. She could not regard Micaela's tragedy as a lesson. Rather, it drove her frantic, she often felt a desire to run away, or die, like her friend; she believed herself capable of the worst. For one mad moment she wanted to avenge Micaela, not on Damián, but on the village; she wanted to burn it, to grind it to dust, to bury it under the forgetfulness of generations to come. She longed vehemently, and this was no passing whim, to visit the prisoner, and beg him to kill her; she wanted to kiss his murderous hands, or bite them, scratch his face, bless him and curse him; she hated him and admired him, she was filled with scorn and pity. She would gladly have offered to carry the food her uncle sent him from the Presbytery when he was in prison. She was one of those who rose early to watch his departure on the thirty-first. If she had had a gun she would have shot him, only to shout immediately, "Hurrah for the hero!" As he went by, María had a lump in her throat and tears streamed down her cheeks. If only she could have followed him, tormented him, comforted him!

Perhaps most of all, she wanted to leave the village behind forever, risking the probability of a bullet in her back on the way. Her heart and head, her whole body and soul were filled with black thoughts. Each day she was more and more irritable, more insufferable, more bitter. "I deserve to be cast out," she said. And indeed, a breath of wind, the slightest breath of wind, would carry her away.

An insignificant student, perhaps the most insignificant of those home for the holidays, succeeded with no difficulty in getting her to accept him. His companions called him "The Boor." He was the son of Cirilo Ibarra, the baker. His name was Jacobo; "Hermit Crab" was another disparaging nickname often conferred upon him, or "Snotty," in reference to his most striking feature. He was short,

with round black eyes above a flat nose, bushy eyebrows, and high angular cheekbones. He was dull, blind, self-absorbed, capricious, and passionate. No one liked him, not even his own family, and he bothered as little about anyone else. Lucas was the only one to have a good opinion of him: "This baker's son may hide under the banner of a fool, but there's good stuff underneath." Just Lucas' notions! This poor fellow was born to be a stonebreaker or pack-driver! It's ridiculous to see him dressed up in the unsuitable clothes, the cast-offs for which the rich of Guadalajara expect to be considered benefactors of the Seminary students. Jacobo was so insignificant that he went unaware of the pity and the jokes he aroused. If he was absent, no one missed him, if he was present, no one paid any attention to him. In spite of everything, this year he finished and passed his third year. The general impression was that he had not passed and was not likely to.

Jacobo never hesitated about asking for what he wanted; if he thought it over first, he gave no sign of it. So he wasted no time in approaching María, in the shadow of the Presbytery, while the Parish Priest was at supper. "I like you and I'd like you to be my girl." And María answered, quite simply, "I'll think about it; meanwhile, don't start people gossiping." His circumspection during the following days amazed her. "He revolts me," she said to herself. He was the opposite of the romantic heroes of her novels. Cunningly, he would stay in the Sacristy after the Rosary, dusting, sweeping, locking up, putting out the lights, tasks that allowed him to go in and out of the Presbytery. He would wait until the other students had gone; he easily deceived the sacristan, slipped humbly past Don Dionisio, put out all the lights he could. Besides, he was so unimportant that he roused no suspicions. On September 29, four evenings after his first talk with María, he approached her and asked abruptly, "What have you decided?"

"All right," María replied coldly, and to herself, "How common he is! How revolting!" It was an irrational and genuine dislike that irritated her, but the more it grew the greater was her pleasure in not yielding to it, and this pleasure compensated for the lack of other emotions: affection, fear, hope, despair. She was not in love, and she had no hope; Jacobo's presence moved her not at all; she merely found a perverse satisfaction in her irritability and in breaking through the hedge that surrounded the women of the village. "Micaela did it," she would say to herself, without feeling that she was merely imitating. "Micaela and I were like sisters; I mustn't let her rebellion die down. She and Damián are martyrs."

On the other hand, Jacobo was a companion in distress: her own dreams had always been despised, regarded with pity, trampled on. She and Jacobo disdained the hostile circumstances of their lives. He could hardly be more ridiculous. For this she despised him, and herself too, and he would end by despising her. If Jacobo irritated her, she would not show it, and a measured coolness governed their meetings. "The Boor" was falling violently in love; he tried to hide it from her, unsuccessfully, and her irritation made her colder.

"It's time you acted less formal with me," he suggested about the middle of October.

"As you like," answered María indifferently. And the following day, "You don't love me," said Jacobo.

"You say that because I agreed to your proposal so quickly."

"Don't be so formal! Listen! Can I talk to you? A real conversation?"

"What for? There's no point in it."

"I have a lot to say. But I know you don't love me."

"Why shouldn't I?"

María brought no conviction to the words, which, as usual, were interrupted by some inopportune noise. Cheap, fleeting meetings. In her boredom María persisted in keeping them up. It was something that they met secretly in the shadow of the Presbytery, something to stand unmoved beside this dull clod whose mounting passion evoked no response in her. What a far cry he was from the heroes she read about in her novels, and the criminals whose deeds filled the papers! One of these nights she would slap his face, as if he were a servant.

In the endless hours of the morning and in her despondency at twilight, she felt like running through the streets shouting, "Jacobo Ibarra is in love with me!" After the Rosary, she had a crazy impulse to betray him, to tell the Parish Priest and the sacristan about his artful tricks. Yet when the time came, she did her part to facilitate the meeting in the shadows, where it would be completely uninteresting, they would have nothing to say to each other, and she would only grow more irritated and frustrated. No one could serve less than Jacobo to satisfy her great desire to see the world, Jacobo, who knew nothing and cared less about geography, who was ignorant of music and fiction, who had no wish to travel, Jacobo, without money or future, Jacobo, who at best would be a clerk, if he even managed to get a job.

Why, then, had María rebuffed the young man from Teocaltiche who was staying with the Aguirre family? They said he was finishing his work in the medical course. (During his visits to the village he had given magnificent proof of skill and charity, curing the poor for nothing and bringing relief in many old and difficult cases.) Handsome and well-spoken, rich and mannerly, he had been courting María almost from the moment of his arrival in the village round the beginning of October, and this was publicly known, and, rare occurrence, it was whole-heartedly approved of by all factions, who openly supported the foreigner and declared themselves on his side. Busybodies, including Daughters of Mary, whispered encouragement in the girl's ear and even quoted what the Doctor had said here and there. Father Martínez had opened the doors of the Presbytery to him and enjoyed his company; making an exception to his usual custom, he even invited him to dinner several times. María rejected him in public. He persevered, patiently enduring her rudeness and disdain. The trip he was planning to Europe when he finished his studies, his accounts of his travels in the principal cities of the country, his impressions of the books he had read, left María unmoved. She refused to listen to him, returned his letters unopened, and ignored his very presence. How annoyed she pretended to be, and how pleased she actually was, when Jacobo said one night, "I know I can't compete with him and I don't want to stand in your way. You're free, María!"

In her bitterness, it was a relief to savor the trembling that accompanied these words.

"I'm not a piece of merchandise," she replied tonelessly, with an angry gesture.

The night after the Doctor went away, Jacobo came to María with tears in his eyes. "You're the only person I want to say this to, but I'm quite sure I'll be a success, even though nobody believes it, not even you. I have everything arranged to go to school this year, and you can cut my head off if I don't graduate as an engineer in four years. I can support myself this year without help from anyone. Do you believe me?" He took one of her hands firmly, and kissed it. That indeed was a surprise. This time María was moved, and scratched him fiercely, almost lovingly. On the following nights, she avoided meeting him, but he managed to have a secret word with her, in church during mass on the last Sunday in October, without anyone noticing it. (He was so little regarded that everyone thought he was giving her a message from her uncle.) "I'm leaving early tomorrow. I'm not suggesting anything or asking anything of you. You're free. But I shall always remain faithful to you. If you'd rather not, we won't even meet tonight." (They did see each other that night.)

"I thought you were going to give up your studies so we could get married," said María with unfeeling indifference.

"We would, if you loved me, but I wouldn't give up studying."

"You're right, I don't love you and never will."

"Thank you for being frank. I'll always feel bound to you, and faithful, like a dog. You'll see." They had no time for farewells.

XII

"If only they were all like the young man staying with the Aguirres! What in the world was María thinking of to turn him down!"

As in past years, the village students invited friends from other places to spend part of the holidays with them and these profaned and dispelled the atmosphere of mourning in the village with their uproarious behavior, tricks, and love affairs. Outside the doors and the tightly sealed windows, shouts, loud conversations, boasts, nicknames, whistling, could be heard, songs, and even the scraping of guitars which sent a shudder through the crosses and stones of the conventual walls. Profanity leaped the walls and disturbed the sanctity of patios, bedrooms, and the ears of women and children, like a dust storm whirling dust and rubbish into the farthest corners. Their jokes and tricks were retold in the intimacy of the houses with smiles or wrath.

If only all had been like "The Boor," "The Hermit Crab," whose relations with María nobody suspected, whose lips and steps betrayed not the slightest indiscretion!

As in other years, there was boasting which destroyed the reputation of this, that, or the other woman. . . . Conceited Lotharios, headed by the outsiders, stirred up wasps' nests of gossip, murmurs, and open scandal.

As in other years, October was a nightmare for the relatives of young girls; there was fighting in the streets when suspicious prowlers were driven away, although, this year, there was no blood-shed. What father of a young girl could get his full night's sleep? At the slightest sound in the late hours of the night, or in the early morning, he would be out of bed. Parents began to breathe easy again only when the students showed signs of leaving. But the last days were the most dangerous, precautions were redoubled from the twentieth to the thirtieth of October; it was then that desires and regrets made their final assaults. When November came, laden with sadness, those who were about to depart, after waiting for weeks, hovering in vain around dark streets, doors, and walls, by day, by night, and in the pre-dawn hours, spent all their youthful energy trying to obtain a word, a handclasp, perhaps a kiss, and at a distance, on the way to church, followed the figures, the voices, the steps that included those of the girl they would be leaving for long months, perhaps forever, knowing that she perhaps had never even noticed a devotion doomed to go unexpressed.

The day before their departure they make no attempt to see or talk to the object of their devotion; they are content to be heard, to be felt, and their steps and their songs resound outside the houses. But those who have reaped rewards are unwilling to leave without a further proof of affection to carry away on their journey, and the last proof must be no less than the earlier ones. If they have exchanged words through the keyhole, they now want to hold the hand of the beloved; if they have already done that, they want to caress an arm, breathe the perfume of the beloved presence. And the black-robed women who have resisted for weeks and weeks? Their hearts are like clocks, slowly ticking away the days and hours left before the men depart, before the village turns empty, more cloistered and gloomy; when there will be no more singing in the streets, no more nervous steps, imploring whistles, at night and in the small hours of the morning; when they will repent, but in vain, that they resisted the call of the blood. So there were many in these last days of October who broke through the hedge of fears and went out to meet an ephemeral happiness, which would soon, maybe the very next day, turn to unhappiness, turn into the daily bread of affliction and remorse, perhaps eternal punishment. The desires of the pale women overcame the triple barrier of fears: the fear of being forgotten, of being the targets of gossip, and of losing their eternal souls.

For this reason—thanks to the indiscretion of boastful young men and the watchful zeal of the "sisters" and Father Islas—Soledad Sánchez, Margarita González, and Rebeca Saldaña were expelled from the Association in disgrace, and the full session that expelled them warned three other "sisters" as well. ("And how many others were there that the good Chemita didn't catch!" murmured Father Meza and Father Vidriales slyly, while gossip named daring, crazy girls who had listened to the lies of students and with the cunning of Beelzebub had escaped Father Islas' condemnation, but not that of their neighbors.)

The expelled and the warned will carry the burden of their shame for a long time, perhaps for always. The village is hostile, their friends have nothing to do with them, refuse to speak to them in the street, and avoid them like lepers in church.

XIII

It was rumored that Julián was marrying on the rebound—a girl he met in Teocaltiche, where he had gone to get over being jilted by Mercedes.

Back in the village he boasted of his coming marriage and the moral and physical attractions of his bride-to-be.

XIV

The students, both novices and old hands, count the remaining hours and a lump comes into their throats. They try to fix everything in their memory and feeling—the pattern of streets, the outline of walls, the silhouettes of crosses, the taste of homemade food, the country air and light, the fragrance of the smoke, that haunting smell of burning leaves at the end of autumn. On their final rounds they fill eyes, nose, ears, lips, hands, and heart with it all. They visit the houses of relatives and friends, fix the geographical features of the village in the mind's eye, walk again and again through the streets, enjoying even the echoes of their own footsteps on the pavement. They cannot bear to stop talking to those who will remain behind. Tomorrow all this, so deeply rooted in their hearts, will be so far away!

When the time comes, they leave with downcast eyes, clinging to the sight of clustered houses, the tower, the landmarks, as though they were never to come back.

XV

When Mercedes realized that she had lost Julián once and for all, and, with him, all hope of marrying, she rebelled as against an unexpected and fatal diagnosis.

The village was left alone, its bells ringing for All Souls' Day. The students hold it in memory: the rejoicing over the blessed souls in Purgatory; the coming and going at each Station of the Cross for indulgences for the faithful dead, the Requiem Mass sung by Father Reyes' choir, the ringing of the bells.

The ringing bells bring back memories of Gabriel. How different they sound!

Conversations revive the memory of the dead, of those who have lain in the Cemetery for years or those who have just died; those who died in the promise of sanctity, and those who came to a tragic end. Even those are remembered who died far away. Endless, as in other years, are Lucas Macías' reminiscences. On his rounds from grave to grave this shining afternoon of November 2, 1909, he interrupts them, fixes his eyes on the sky, and says:

"I think if Luis Gonzaga could make his incendio this year, he'd put Madero's portrait in it instead of Don Porfirio's," and, as though to himself, he adds, "A short man, fair-skinned, bearded, wiry, and a good sort; they say he's crazy and a Spiritist."

He soons returns to the subject of the dead.

"Well, life plays some strange tricks! Whoever would have said that the famous Espiridión Ramos, Antonio Rojas' friend, who made the earth tremble at the time of the French invasion, would be dug up to make room for Don Timoteo! Don Timoteo, you should know, was the son of Don Arcadio, the man who killed Espiridión and wouldn't let him be buried until the body stank. The neighbors had to offer the wretch two thousand good pesos for permission to bury it. Who can tell, now, which are the bones of the wicked guerrilla? And look, here, side by side, are Micaela and the virtuous Teo Parga, who performs miracles, they say. Life does strange things!"

They interrupt him again, "Tell us something about the comets, Lucas."

"That's a long story. The comets . . ."

PEDRITO

I

NCIRCLED BY SO MANY SUFFERERS—María, Mercedes, Micaela, Soledad, Margarita, Rebeca, and Gertrudis—and breathing the same parching air, Marta had her own trouble, so different from that of the others, which throbbed, like invisible stigmata. They would think her puerile, they would laugh at her if she confided it in her own simple words, for her words could not express the troubling sickness that she did not understand.

On the surface, she was anxious to find a foster mother for Pedrito, worried about her failure to find a candidate to her liking yet really unwilling for the child to be anyone's stepson. To attribute her unhappiness to these preoccupations would be beating round the bush. Marta disliked meddling in other people's affairs; her interest in the orphan is pure affection, this is quite transparent. There is no question here of compassion, zeal, or abstract charity; it is this particular child that has roused her compassion, zeal, and charity, touching a very human chord. Marta would like to be the real mother, or rather the foster mother; she wants a tie to establish her rights and give her authority over the child without the danger of someone coming later to take him away from her. If only they would give him to her, for always, without conditions! If only she could buy him, just as one buys a desired object! The horrible pain that Pedrito's mother suffered before she died, the precocious, invincible sadness that this left in the little child who witnessed it, the way he has been passed around among pitying or duty-bound neighbors, who grew tired of being magnanimous, all these were additional reasons for Marta's selfless and painful concern. A deeper root saps away at her happiness. Marta's trouble, like María's, like Mercedes', like that of nearly all the black-robed women confined in the barren precincts of the village, is a vague pain, of obscure origin, which vanishes when one tries to put one's finger on it; it seems to be an overshadowing fear of sin, despair because of sin, the sin against the Holy Ghost, the absence of the theological virtue of hope. In Marta, the despair is human, not divine. What will become of the orphan in this life? What rough, uncharitable hands will guide him? Whither? Why is it her responsibility? Who has given her jurisdiction over the fate of this human being? Are these the arguments of the Devil? Does her interest spring from a tainted source? If not, why the vehemence, the anxiety, the sadness, the attacks, the grief that shorten her breath and undermine the foundations of her ancient fortress, corroding the source of her happiness?

II

It is not clear why certain busybodies—to call them nothing worse—have started talk because María, the Parish Priest's niece, will have nothing to do with the young man from Teocaltiche, just as if Gabriel were dead, or as if María were like the girls who nowadays lose their heads and throw everything to the winds, just for a pretty speech or out of a need for power. They will learn! The student certainly did his best! The reason for María's coldness must be loyalty to the absent Gabriel. Incidentally, the Parish Priest has sent Gabriel to school in León, not to a seminary. He will probably come back a lawyer, a doctor, or something like that! But why make such a mystery of it? Perhaps Father Martínez, influenced by Father Islas, is opposed to their marrying, as if what happened to Micaela weren't warning enough to let nature take its course.

III

An unexpressed rivalry has grown up during recent years between Father Reyes and Father Islas over celebrating the Festival of the Immaculate Conception and the Festival of Our Lady of Guadalupe. Last year there were unpleasantnesses arising from the zeal of partisans to make their respective ceremonies excel.

"The music was better on the eighth."

"It wasn't! It wasn't a bit better!"

"There's no comparison between the sermon on the Feast of the Immaculate Conception and that preached on Guadalupe Day."

"The fireworks weren't very good."

"How could the Daughters of Mary put on a program like the one Father Reyes had?"

"Your Altar wasn't much to brag about."

"You only had Matins at eleven o 'clock!"

"What taste to decorate a church in!"

"What cheap flowers and candles!"

Next to Holy Week services, the celebrations on December 8 had undoubtedly been the most long-established and splendid. When Father Reyes came, he encouraged devotion to the Virgin of Guadalupe, and saw to it that December 12 was celebrated with great solemnity, making the festival each year more magnificent— "and more worldly," added the conservatives, basing their opinion on the number of decorations in the streets, the numbers of programs printed and given out for the concert, the firecrackers, and procession of children dressed as angels, missionaries, Indians, and conquistadors. There were fireworks last year, and this year they are planning a big procession which will halt at four altars, each with a tableau representing one of the Four Last Appearances.

Celebration of the Feast of the Immaculate Conception begins on November 30, the first joyous peals of the bells mingling with the last mournful tolling of the month of the Faithful Departed. On November 30 begins the famous Novena, in which the literary taste of several generations of villagers has been formed, even if the Devil does cunningly make a misuse of it to arouse sensuality in weak characters inclined that way. Luis Gonzaga Pérez knows it by heart.

Micaela used to love hearing it. It is paraphrased in not a few of the love letters passed round clandestinely, since it takes its savor from the Song of Songs.

To match Father Reyes' choir, whose co-operation they declined, the Daughters of Mary persuaded Father Islas to bring musicians from Guadalajara, both singers and accompanists, to say nothing of Canon Silva, a very famous preacher.

Father Martínez and Father Islas, well aware of the kind of people these musicians often are, made one condition: that the stay of the guests should be limited; they would arrive in the morning of the seventh and leave right after the ceremonial mass on the eighth, without any parties being given for them, and they should be lodged, not in private houses, as was suggested, but in Retreat House.

"What won't Father Reyes do," the people said, "not to be outdistanced!"

"What can we do," his anxious followers asked Father Reyes, "to go them one better?" "Don't let money stop you," said the supporters of Guadalupe.

"We'll see, we'll see. Don't worry," replied Father Reyes with his usual calm.

IV

As she helped Mercedes through the trial of Julián's arrival with his bride in the first days of December, Marta thought she realized the cause of her own depression. She was not resigned to being an old maid. This thought disturbed her, for she had never attached much importance to marriage, nor wanted to be engaged or needed to school herself to accept the absence of something she had never missed.

"They will have children that might have been mine!" This most persistent lament of Mercedes', still in revolt against a fate which she felt inevitable, illumined Marta's hidden thoughts like a flash of gunpowder. A thousand and one pictures passed through her mind, none the less intense for their rapidity; so fast did they follow one another, some trivial, others almost forgotten, that they branded new meanings on her mind, and brought her flashes of categorical evidence. The desire for a child! The coveting of a child! The refusal to accept, without realizing it, the spinsterhood which condemned her to the precarious possession of other people's

children: children of the catechism class, Pedrito; the wish to found
an orphanage, a school for needy children! Was it rebellion, this sadness which she had felt lately while watching and being with children, like coveting someone else's possessions, this sadness, like the
fear of death, or of sin, which had assailed her since Pedrito became
an orphan? Her sorrowful flight from the exalting, wonderful, fearful knowledge of the mystery of motherhood, whose patron is the
Holy Mother with the Child in her arms? Wasn't it also her feeling
against spinsterhood, complicated by a mother's tenderness, that
turned to the hope her sister would marry and have children? Her
affection for Gabriel and the disappointment his behavior towards
María caused her? Her desire that María would marry the young
man from Teocaltiche? From the thousand and one pictures, there
arose a voice which moved her deeply, "Old maid! Forever an old
maid!" It moved her to no rebellion, it moved her to tears.

Other things, too, have become clear to her through Mercedes'
suffering: before the crime, her submissive feeling in Damián Limón's presence; her feeling of pity for him afterward; the compassion she now felt at the memory of his fate, when all were cursing
him or beginning to forget him. For her he had always been, and
always would be, manhood personified. Marta regarded herself,
and Damián too, with horror, seeing things in the light of Mercedes' experience. In that lurid flash she regretted the occasions
when, unconsciously, scarcely realizing it until today, she would fix
her eyes on Damián and on other men, wondering vaguely what her
sons would be like, and whom they would marry.

Mercedes was still chafing under the sentence of perpetual loneliness. "I'll never be able to bear it! Never, never! Knowing that the
village is watching me when I meet them, and she tries to greet me
like any other neighbor, thinking that we can be friends. How can
people bear such suffering, bury it in their hearts? To have them
next door to me, always, to get used to meeting them at any time, in
church, in the street; to see their happiness, their children, watch
the children grow, while everyone forgets that a tormented soul is
consumed with envy, perhaps still in love! Growing older every
year, getting weaker, feeling more alone, and desperate! It's horrible! Father can't have eyes in his head, or a heart, or he'd take me
away from the village, even for a few days. How can I say anything? Even to Mother! They'd say I'm being ridiculous. That
would be worse, I'd hate them. I feel like hating everyone. I'd like

to scratch them, all of them, who stare at me, all my relatives who come to watch me suffer and make malicious remarks. Heartless, unfeeling wretches!"

Marta's nerves were vibrating in such close sympathy with Mercedes' laments that she fainted, and Micaela's ghost appeared to her for the first time, saying, "Don't you remember me?"

V

Pride goes before a fall. The musicians arrived, more dead than alive from sheer weariness. And very late, almost five o'clock. When they got off their horses they could hardly stand on their feet. Scarcely any of them had ridden before, still less for three days, up hill and down dale. Vespers had to be put off till eight o'clock, and then what a disappointment! There were false notes; naturally they were out of tune, came in at the wrong time, played with manifest unwillingness. They were almost yawning. The officers of the Association, who had been so eager to bring the musicians and had been talking of nothing else for days, were at a loss to put a good face on things. Even the farmers were asking, "Is this what all the money was for?" As they came out, they saw Father Reyes' choir doubled up with laughter. Even those who were no judge of harmony could measure the disaster. It was no better at High Mass. In the morning the musicians were furious at their lodgings; they had been unable to sleep; they went to see Father Islas, determined to be gone at once; they had been deceived, the cold in Retreat House was bad enough, but the beds and the kind of food they were given were worse. Father Islas retorted by reminding them how badly they had played the night before. The musicians grew angrier, and, to add to the humiliation, Father Reyes had to intervene, and the musicians, still muttering, without practicing, went up into the choir stalls, determined to go through with it just any old way, amid the rage of some and the mockery of others. Children from the catechism class or a band from any farm would have done a better job. But that was not the end of it. The musicians refused to leave that afternoon, according to the previous arrangement, saying they had to rest. They demanded better lodgings, and, as if they had given a good performance, settled themselves in the Square and did as they pleased, made friends with villagers, ended up by getting drunk, and, aided and abetted by the Deputy, maybe even at his suggestion, had the audacity to organize a "serenade" through the village, in which they played and sang beautifully.

On the morning of the ninth a verse appeared on a door, that of the President of the Daughters of Mary:

> 'Tis good for you, my children,
> Vainglory to eschew,
> God doth reward the humble,
> And adds his blessing, too.

VI

How many wounds were re-opened by the playing and singing of the musicians! Their melodies, never heard before—of love, dreams, tender melancholy, secret joys, emotions long unexpressed—kept people awake and revealed a world, a new language, to adolescents on that night between the eighth and ninth of December, a world and language felt to be very near but inaccessible, full of celestial and, at the same time, human charm; a world and a language of daily desires, hitherto hidden, but now magnificently illumined by harmonies, of instruments and voices, which sent words of love and sadness winging forth, common words but transfigured like the dingy rockets that suddenly burst into color and brilliance and trace briefly, in flight, ineffable thoughts. It was a world and a language of desire loosed so freely for the first time in that village. The vibrant cries, which could suddenly die to trembling murmurs in the surrounding solitude, took old men and adolescents by surprise, held them awake in an enchantment new to their ears, so different from the church music to which they were accustomed. Their wakefulness was pierced by darts of melody that passed through the thickest walls, reached the heart and instilled their sweet poison—metallic darts of the 'cello, brittle darts of the violins striking against the roofs, fragile airy darts of flutes, moving upward towards the crosses to fall on the heart, piercing darts of words sung by tenors, baritones, basses. The village was as if all ears, to miss no single note that sonorous night.

As though lovers gone forever had come back, the students of this and other generations, those who had long ago shocked the village with their loves, those whose presence had troubled generations grown old or growing old and forgotten; as though men and women here and now awaited the coming of those they were fated to love.

In hearts that had longed for them, Victoria and other fair visitors became grievous memories again. Anxiety stirred once more over women unhappily married and those suspected of easy virtue. Old maids felt the pangs of loneliness, and the heartache of those on the verge of spinsterhood was sharper. Wounds inflicted by students reopened. Many a pillow was wet with tears. But no one would have had the music stop, the sounds that brought visions of impossible happiness, or promised good fortune to those still free to hope and wait, without the scars of disillusionment. No one would have had the music stop, neither the old, whose age it dissolved, nor the young, for whom it built castles in the air; nor even those who suffered, for though it renewed their suffering, it offered at the same time solace; nor those who hoped in vain, for it enabled them to dream again; nor those who were happy, for it confirmed their happiness. María wanted it to continue, for in it she heard the living voice of cities, and the village would be narrower, more dreary, when it was silent. Mercedes wanted it to go on, for it promised rewards for the suffering she had endured, and Marta, who forgot her pain and recovered her optimism, and Soledad, Margarita, and Rebeca, their shame vindicated as the music brought them messages from a world whose language they had begun to understand in the follies of the students; and Lina, Magdalena, and Gertrudis, whose lamps of patience were lit again. Lucas Macías had his different reason: never had he heard in such a direct and natural way what they were like, his heroes and the customs of olden days—this was music heard in palaces and hovels, music played and whistled in the streets, music that was even then moving hearts in Guadalajara and Mexico City, in Querétaro, in Puebla, in Guanajuato and in San Luis; the *language* of music, badly uttered in the uproar of the students. No one wanted it to stop, unless, perhaps, the Chaplain and the Parish Priest, fearful of the revolt of the senses and the even worse evils likely to result if they interfered. The virtuous castle walls of the Daughters of Mary were shaken. They had brought these musicians, these disreputable mercenaries, who had to be drunk and play profane music to be inspired: this 'cellist, that violinist, that tenor; the drunker they were, as now, the better they played.

Silence lends its acoustics, in the perfect, clear night, where the music is weaving its web, in the transparent December night, pierced by flame-tipped arrows of melody—and desires, triumphant, clad with light, wing away—into the serene night, which has

silenced even the barking dogs on the outskirts, and sorrows, worries, and remorse; and the Four Horsemen are for the moment caught in the lariat of music, in this unhoped-for diaphanous night of December.

The experience enabled María to formulate, and formulate categorically, the idea that she had earlier developed only vaguely. She was now firmly convinced that no one in the village had ever felt the passion of love—ecstasy and madness, complete surrender, both painful and happy, braving all fears and daring all risks—the heroic love that filled the books she devoured, and by which she was devoured. No, no one, neither Micaela, her friend, a common coquette, nor Luis Gonzaga with his neurasthenic pretenses, nor the girls carried off on dark nights, victims of fatal curiosity, nor those who get married come hell or high water only to fall into the routine of wedded life, nor Mercedes, the victim of self-righteousness, nor Damián with his brute strength breaking down obstacles out of sheer pride, nor the heroines of Lucas Macías' stories, only half-alive; nor Soledad, nor Rebeca, nor Lina, nor Margarita, nor Magdalena, nor Gertrudis, nor Eustolia, eager only for new sensations and instinctively anxious to get married but lacking the unselfish and irresistible love that marks the true passion. No one, no, not even she, sad, bitter, a failure, without hope, incapable of being moved by the lofty passion glimpsed that night in the multitude of common desires let loose in the village. How different the two loves were, how different this ideal of hers from everything sordid, mean, and transitory! Pure desire, free from the flesh, the essential spark! If Gabriel (why had María been thinking of Gabriel all night?) could listen to this music, he would find the answers to all the dark questions he had asked of the bells. Gabriel found only the ladder of Death beside the door of Love, he had been unable to enter into the sweet precincts, or at least unable to direct María in the way to go, except obscurely and bitterly. (María did not know that the ears of a woman, the ears of the fatal foreigner, had heard the voice of love in Gabriel's ringing.) María developed her idea further: love is not an instinct, it is not a routine of living together, it cannot turn into a mere habit, it is not a passing delight of the senses, it is not a capricious game; love is the identity of two souls, and all the rest is superfluous; two spirits which possess each other, and all the rest is only a hindrance; suffering in love comes from collision with the perishable; fear in the face of love is the inheritance of the flesh; heroism in love is the victory over all that hinders union, the spiritual possession frequently frustrated by custom and the daily round of living. Doubtless Gabriel caught a glimpse of this. The beauty of the music brought back to María the memory of Gabriel's bell-ringing. "But why am I thinking so much about Gabriel?" María wondered for the second time.

Next morning, María, the black-robed women, the pale youths, who had strained to hear every note of the serenade, if they plucked up the courage to express their feelings at all, could only say, "How nice . . . last night!"

Their faces when they awoke were changed, some more than others. But their lips were silent. When some of them spoke, it was to complain of the noise, to express their horror of the drunken musicians, to speak of the fiasco of the Association. "A fine mess our excellent Chemita made of it!" was the sly comment of Father Meza and Father Vidriales.

María, moved by her new comprehension, turned to Marta, "How lovely it was, last night!"

Perhaps Gabriel could have said no more. *incorrect*

VII

The harvest was bad. Heaven rained down its punishment upon a region that could give birth to such a criminal as Damián, whose wickedness had found its way even into the newspapers. There was little rain. A severe drought lasted through August into September, an unheard-of thing, which made God's anger manifest, unappeased by petitions, vows, and pleas for pardon. Plague destroyed the livestock. Crop-destroying pests infested the land as they had not done for years.

Leonardo Tovar did not reap so much as the value of the seed he had sown. All his work had gone for nothing. And in addition there were the debts from his wife's illness, and what he owed Don Timoteo.

When the time came to settle accounts, he owed the late Timoteo Limón's heirs alone, three hundred pesos. Besides, he owed Don Eladio García for the use of two yoke of oxen, Don Tereso Robles eighteen pesos for various articles of food and clothing, and small amounts to other neighbors, without counting Pedrito's keep. The little one had been passed from house to house, dependent on fickle public charity.

Don Timoteo's children—eager to disown their brother Damián—were implacable towards their debtors. They took not only the small patch of ground Leonardo had mortgaged to them, valuing it at a hundred and twenty pesos—not a hope of fighting that injustice!—but whatever else he had of any value: some saddles, two plough-shares, a pick, the chest. They all but took the dead Martina's bed, too, and he still owed them a hundred and fifty pesos, for which they wanted him to give them an IOU and work on their farm, with Pedrito serving Prudencia or Juan as errand boy. "Better dead," Leonardo said to himself. The only thing he could do was to go North. But what about Pedrito? He could neither take him nor leave him to the tender mercies of neighbors, as he had done since Martina's death. He would leave him with Father Martínez only. Maybe Señorita Marta would take charge of the boy, she seemed to like him, or perhaps the nuns in the Hospital would look after him. He went to Don Dionisio for a talk, although he did not venture to suggest that Pedrito should live at the Presbytery.

"The boy's big enough now to run errands for the nuns, and he could be an acolyte; he could bring water from the well, and I think he could even cut their wood; he's obedient, he gives no trouble, and he's grateful."

Marta, who knew the demands of the Limón family, dared to intervene:

"Why couldn't he stay here? We need someone to run errands now that Gabriel's gone."

Marta and Leonardo fixed their eyes on Father Martínez, over whose face a shadow passed when his niece mentioned Gabriel.

VIII

The men back from the United States were the most enthusiastic participants in celebrating the Feast of Our Lady of Guadalupe. Father Reyes' appeal to their patriotism succeeded where his attempt to organize a religious co-operative society had failed.

There was no question as to which celebration was the good one. The Mexticacán band, famous for its wind instruments, arrived in the morning of the eleventh and left the same afternoon after an impressive procession. As might be expected, the singers in Father Reyes' choir surpassed themselves, at both Matins and High Mass.

Then came the surprise—the civic-religious procession, composed chiefly of Northerners who, shouting "Long live Mexico! Hurrah for Our Lady of Guadalupe!" and carrying tricolor lanterns, led the march. The village was deeply impressed, and the League of Our Lady of Guadalupe was inaugurated. Officials carried a platform on which there was a scene showing the appearance of the Virgin to Juan Diego in Tepeyac. The seriousness, the stillness throughout the procession, and the good acting of the boy who took the part of Juan Diego amazed everyone. It was Pedrito, dressed by Marta and María. The procession halted at four stations in different parts of the village. Little girls recited appropriate verses; the people sang the hymn to Guadalupe, and the patriotic shouts increased in volume. At the end, the fireworks display by specialists brought from Yahualica was excellent. There were lights in the tower of the Parish Church.

No one was so pleased as Marta.

"This young Reyes is a wizard! How has he managed to win over the Northerners?" wondered Father Vidriales and Father Meza.

IX

For Marta, recognizing the cause of her sadness was like cauterizing a wound healed only on the surface. Once she had put her finger on the trouble, it healed firmly and rapidly. She looked forward to the future again, with a feeling of happiness ahead, which was soon justified by the plea of Leonardo and its favorable reception by Don Dionisio. Pedrito came to live in the Presbytery, on condition that his father should have no claim to him until he was old enough to decide on his future for himself. What more could Marta ask? This young life was hers—almost hers—to mold as she molded the wax for the altar candles. Pleasant burden of a responsibility she had longed for. Whole series of plans, new ones every minute, filled her hours.

María, whose opposition they had feared, shared her joy, and looked after Pedrito like a little girl playing with a doll, finding in him an escape from the bitterness that was poisoning her soul. She helped to dress him as Juan Diego, made him several suits, combed his hair every day, took the lead in entreating Father Martínez to let them have Posadas this year, so that Pedrito could play the part of a shepherd. It was she who had the Nativity Scene ready a week ahead, and if she failed to get Posadas in the Parish Church, she did get permission to have a Nativity Scene in the living room of the Presbytery.

Plotting secretly with Marta, she smuggled toys and clothes into the Presbytery so that, against all local tradition, the Christ Child might come on Christmas Eve and leave his gifts in the shoes of the little orphan. His delighted surprise on Christmas morning made them all three happy.

María made up wonderful stories to set the child's imagination soaring. Marta rejoiced in her sister's childlike happiness, and dreamed of looking after *two* children, whose future depended upon her.

HALLEY'S COMET

I

HE FIRST OF JANUARY, 1910, was like any other day in the village. Christmas and New Year are festivals of minor importance here, even less important than Sundays, for the bustle of the market is missing. Nor is it customary for families and friends to exchange gifts and greetings. Christmas lacks even what they have on All Souls' Day, the special liturgy of the three masses said by the same celebrant. Midnight Mass is not sung every year, and when there is one, it is a simple mass, sung without special pomp or hymns. By Christmas time an aura of sadness, which has been gathering since the celebrations of the eighth and twelfth of December, begins to make itself felt. It deepens as the end of the year draws near, and is clearly evident in the slow ringing of the bells for the services of thanksgiving and repentance on December 31. The bells ring from twilight to midnight, becoming more and more solemn, more

mournful, as they sound the death knell and the tocsin, as if the world and life were inexorably coming to an end, as if the sun were slowly setting, never to rise again. Shadows of memories, of remorse, of lost treasures, of failures, of horizons unreached, now forever unattainable; shadows of impotence; regret for the flight from opportunity which can never be recaptured, in spite of hands contracted in covetous gesture; regret for the passing of ephemeral things which yesterday were alive, and will soon, no one knows when, be buried or thrown to the winds: kinsman or dream, affection, a business affair, perhaps one's own life with its flowers, roots, and leaves; pessimistic sadness because of the uncertain future, routine, work, trouble, tasks renewed; sadness rising from soul searching, from inner condemnation, from plans undertaken with lack of conviction and enthusiasm, problems which time cannot solve; sadness at being unable to find love; sadness for known or unknown death. All faces bear the look of mortal weariness on the morning of the New Year. Like convicts reluctantly confronting a new day, before a task as useless as it is overwhelming. So the greeting "Happy New Year," which foreigners sometimes voice, sounds like a joke in bad taste; it is an empty and repugnant conventional remark, never used between friends and neighbors, a stylized greeting out of keeping with the norms of the village. One hears, instead:

"What calamities will this year bring?"

"For how many of us will it be our last?"

"Who would have thought that so-and-so, so full of life this time last year, would now be underground?"

"If this year's as bad as last, I don't know what I'll do!"

From the pulpit, from the Confessional, warnings are heard: "Will you fail to take advantage of this respite granted you by Providence?"

"Will this be another lost year in your progress towards salvation, the only affair that should interest you?"

"This may be your last year on earth!"

Personal warning and advice. On the surface, as people meet and go about their business, the first day of the year is like any other day; there is no exchange of embraces, nor good wishes, nor meaningful smiles; it is rather a day of sadness, friends avoid meeting friends on this day, the loneliness of the streets is accentuated.

Unaware of this further peculiarity of the village, the Deputy went around greeting and embracing people, shaking hands. The coldness and surprise that met his advances nonplussed him. In a bad humor, he went home and shut himself in, following the common practice.

The first of January brought nothing new.

II

In the first days of the year, Don Alfredo Pérez came to shut up his house and sell the rest of his possessions for what he could get. He arrived the very night they lit the first gas lamp ever seen in the village, at the Flor de Mayo, and it was the wonder of all eyes.

"What a light it gives!"

"It's almost like daylight!"

"But how pale all the faces look, like corpses!"

"And that buzzing sound."

"They say they sometimes explode, and people have been burned and killed."

"We'd better stick to our little old oil lamps and tallow candles."

Many men gathered in the shop, attracted by the novelty of the bright light. Lucas Macías was there, of course. He had just been to see Don Alfredo and the conversation, which was already getting along fine, became more animated with his eloquence.

"They say the first lamp with a wick was lit here at the end of 1857, when Ciriaco Ruelas stopped using tallow candles and installed chandeliers. The neighbors used to meet and gossip every night, to raise their spirits, or depress them, by the rumors they heard or invented. That was just after '52 or '53 or thereabouts, in the time of the famous Amito, who was shot at Lagos—let me think —yes, it was on September 5, four months after the attack on the village. After that, as I was saying, there was peace round here, but the rumors started . . . that there was going to be a fight . . . we'd have to take up arms against the enemies of the Church . . . a man called Juárez was President . . . Miramón was conspiring against him . . . there were uprisings in Nochistlán, and in various parts of the Altos . . . the volunteers from Teocaltiche would soon be here. Well, there was something new to talk about every night, even if nobody came in from outside with trouble. Ciriaco's packdriver brought in a copy of the Constitution that was causing all the commotion. There was a fellow named Don Casimiro Torres, from the lowlands, rumored to be a heretic; well, they nearly killed

him. He disappeared one night, and it was afterward learned that
he was with Don Santos Degollado and wanted to come and burn
down the village for a nest of fanatics. When they heard of Miramón's victory in Salamanca and the uprising of Colonel Landa in
Guadalajara, and it was even rumored that Juárez and his ministers had been killed—that was sometime in March of '58—Ciriaco's
shop was filled with people eager to get into the fight, though they
weren't entirely sure of what it was all about. It was discovered
afterward that some went off with the Liberals and others with the
Conservatives. There was the case of the two brothers nicknamed
"The Acolytes," who went off together to join Osollo. One turned up
in San Juan de los Lagos when Miguel Blanco stole a hundred thousand pesos from Our Lady and carried the money off in willow
baskets, and they said he killed his own brother in the taking of
Santo Domingo. Maybe it was for that, but I think it was on account of the robbery in San Juan that he was paralyzed and had to
beg for his living. I knew him round about '70, when he lived at
the Pastores farm. Even Ciriaco himself went off to fight and they
nearly shot him in Querétaro. But he managed to escape and, by
walking only at night, reached the village. In the Delgadillo's Oratory over there is the ex-voto of the miracle which the Virgin of La
Soledad performed. He certainly spent the rest of his life repenting
that his shop had been the cause of many not coming back from the
war . . ."

"Well, what did Don Alfredo have to say to you?"

"Poor man! In his place, I'd be crazy. To leave the village with no
hope of coming back! To have to take what he could get for the
few things he had left! To be left with so many memories of other
days and to have to give away the poor boy's things! He's got his
troubles. Go and see him, just go. He won't come here, he's too
proud. Every time he meets a friend it re-opens his wounds. He
won't come here, much less with this light—it makes you feel
naked."

"Almost enough to send you to the Revolution, isn't it, Lucas?"

"Just about! Just about! Do you know what Don Alfredo said to
me? That the comet has made people everywhere afraid. It's not
for nothing that I keep saying to you, all day long, that we're going
to have more than war; plagues too, and hunger; I don't think even
I, old as I am, will escape. You'll soon see!"

Fascinated by the new light, more and more men arrived, and

went on talking until after ten o'clock—a new cause for comment in the village—and not even Lucas' prophecies could lessen the pleasure of those present, meeting and talking without noticing how time was passing, nor the bells ringing at sunset or curfew, hardly even remembering that their families were waiting up for them, or feeling their eyelids heavy with the unaccustomed lateness. The pleasure of an old habit, difficult to overcome. They could come back tomorrow, and the next day, and Thursday, and Friday, and Saturday, and Sunday. Why hadn't it occurred to anyone they could meet like this every night and get some relief from their isolation?

When the miraculous lamp was put out, the darkness of the streets seemed more intense, walking along the irregular sidewalks seemed harder, the light of the oil lamps, hung at distant intervals through the town, seemed paler.

Nevertheless, the pleasure of meeting together remained, and the echo of the words repeated or heard.

(How much would a gas lamp cost?)

III

The comet! The comet! People ran out into the streets, up onto the rooftops; filled the squares; the curious crowded up into the tower. They knelt with their faces towards heaven and began to pray aloud; they felt like shouting, moaning, fainting.

Nobody knows who first saw the bright star, at sunset on that third of January, and proclaimed it with a shout; but the news found its way, like lightning, into houses, chapels, and Confessionals, into the hearts of children, old people, and invalids.

The star grew brighter as though it were swiftly moving towards the earth, and people instinctively shut their eyes, expecting a collision. Fifty struggling hands seized the bells and rang them noisily. Men and women ran into the churches, crowded in the doorways, not without bruises. The illusion persisted that the star was getting bigger and coming nearer. People closed their eyes as at the end of the world and the joys and remorse of their whole lives passed before the troubled conscience—important and unimportant memories, commonplace scenes, shameful actions, dreams that never came true, all mingled with feverish prayers.

How weak and powerless was the voice of Father Reyes as he tried to calm them! How long it took to find someone to support his words! "It's the evening star, look. Can't you see it's the evening star? Where's the tail? It isn't a comet, it has no tail, just look. Look, it's the evening star, it's always bright like this at this time of year."

Disappointment at not being witness to a catastrophe that centuries had awaited only increased blind panic. The people were not going to be done out of their full-scale drama.

IV

Don Alfredo Pérez ("What a nice man Don Alfredo always was!") has wound up his affairs and goes back to Guadalajara tomorrow. Tomorrow is the eighteenth of January.

"What a bitter fifteen days, the worst days of my life, I can tell you, my friend. Do you think it's easy to make an end, you might say, of one's life? When I was first married and Carmen couldn't get used to living in the village and tried to persuade me to move to Guanatos, it seemed impossible to me then that the day might come when I'd be selling my land. If I had to go to the Capital on business, the days seemed endless; I couldn't get home fast enough. Even when poor Luis went off, I left everything here, thinking I'd be back in a week. It was mostly because I was in such a hurry to get back that I was so impatient with the doctors. I can't see how people enjoy living in the noise and bustle of a city—I don't even want to visit a city. Hardly a night goes by that I don't dream of being here, and when I wake up, you can't imagine, it's as though I were a prisoner. Every minute I'm thinking about the village, wondering how so-and-so is, thinking, 'This one will be going by at this time and we'll pass the time of day'; 'Now they'll be ringing for the St. Vincent Address'; 'Now they're ringing for this or that.'

"And, getting up or going to bed, I just say, 'Another day, and no hopes of going home yet!' I'll never get used to it, never in this world! Everything is different; the people are strangers, even the people from here, even my relatives. It's all pretense, hypocrisy, and double dealing. The food is bad and expensive; you won't believe me, but the meat, milk, eggs, tortillas, and bread, even the beans, all taste different, not to mention the lard, chocolate, and peas. Everything's all wrong.

"As for Mexico City, don't even talk about it. Lots of people here want to go to the Centenary. I certainly wouldn't give up my peace of mind, my meals the way I like them and when I like them, and my bed, to put up with trouble and discomfort! The Centenary! Don't mention it. Nobody'll convince me that that didn't cause the beginning of the trouble with my poor boy—trying to write a poem to be printed, and wanting to be crowned the best poet in Mexico! And that brazen woman drove him out of his mind!

"Don't let's talk of these unhappy matters. These fifteen days of clearing out my house and selling my things are enough. When I decided to come, and even after I got here, I still hoped things might change and I might be able to bring Carmen back and live in peace. It was like the hope of somebody being led out to be shot, but it was a hope, at any rate. For two days I didn't do a thing. Never had the village looked so good to me, in spite of the bitter memories each step brought back. But there wasn't any way out. I began to arrange for the transfer of the house and the sale of the land, to collect what was owing me, to see this one and the other, having to repeat to each one the whole sad story. Every time I settled anything it was like cutting off a hand, or an arm, or a leg. But I just couldn't bring myself to sell the house, the house my great-great-grandfather built, bringing the stone from Yahualica and stone masons from Guadalajara. That would have been like cutting off my own head. No. My great-grandfather was born there, and my grandfather, and my father. I was born there, too, and my poor son. There—God's will be done! No, for two days now, I've been here, lost in these memories. I've not been outside these walls; I've just been rubbing my hands along them, kissing the doors, lying down in the patio beside the well, staring up at the sky, or pruning Carmen's plants. You can imagine what tonight will be like! My last night in this room where I thought I would surely die!

"No, I've no hope of coming back again. I'm old and the city has me in its clutches. Guadalajara has no heart for poor people who live by their work. Doctors, druggists, hospitals, and travelling around from place to place, have taken all I had. In Mexico City there was a doctor who charged me twenty pesos a visit. I'm up to my ears in debt. I tried to pay my way, and lost everything. I had to get a job in a hardware store, La Palma. I'm not afraid of being a clerk. But to live there, far away from my own bit of land! As soon as I'd finished packing the things I was going to take with me—I did it with tears in my eyes, why shouldn't I admit it, my friend?—I went to the Cemetery to visit the graves of my parents and kinfolks. How lucky they were, not to have to give up their land! I meant to go back this afternoon to say good-bye to them. I don't know if my courage failed me or if I couldn't bear to leave these walls until I had to. It's hard, hard. Here, Carmen and I used to talk, making plans before the boy was born; here, he took his first steps; here we got a fright the first time he fell down; here, Carmen gave him her blessing when he went to the Seminary for the first time; here are his books and papers, his drawings and paintings; there, he used to quote Latin at us—thanks, my friend, thank you. No, I'm resigned, God's will be done, but it's hard."

Shortly after midnight, Don Alfredo left the village to which he would probably never return.

V

It was at the beginning of February that several mysterious strangers passed through the village and left a vague, uneasy dread in their wake. Seven men, of nondescript appearance, carrying suitcases on their shoulders and leading pack horses, arrived at the inn at about seven o'clock at night; one of them went out to buy bread and two cans of sardines at old Ladislao's, as he is the only one who sells "those smelly fish"; they sent the boy to a tavern for beer.

No one knew where they'd come from or where they were going. They left next day, early. Who could say that he really had a good look at them? Afterward, it was learned that many villagers had heard voices and strange steps throughout the night, that the strangers had asked peculiar questions of this one and that one, but the versions of the questions were contradictory: Was it the number of priests or of police in the village that they had wanted to know? How frequently did armed troops come, or qualified doctors? Any discontent because of abuses or the state of religion? The easiest ways of getting to the village, the inaccessible points of the region, or the most pressing needs of the people? Were these strangers Protestants or revolutionaries? Were they going to the North or coming from there?

One thing was certain: their ignorance of the district. They didn't even know the name of the village; they hadn't even known of its existence. They ate sardines and drank beer! They certainly couldn't have been from these parts. There was some evidence to suggest that they were engineers, for they brought transits, but what were they doing on foot? It was supposed that they were adventurers in search of mines or hidden treasure, things some said they asked about.

The Deputy decided to take a hand in the matter, since the state of collective alarm was disturbing and the village kept expecting something dreadful to happen as a result of the visit. The Deputy, on the other hand, had no doubt that they were spies in the service of insurgent forces trying to overthrow the peaceful and progressive regime of the Republic. One thing prevented him from reporting the occurrence immediately to the authorities, the feeling that he should have arrested the suspects; but, to give him his due, he was one of the last to get the news, when it was already too late in the morning. That day and the following days, those who entered the village were closely questioned, wherever they came from. An inquiry was made among the villagers who had farms near roads leading out of the village; there was no result, nobody would admit to having seen the men. This set the village in an uproar.

What connection was there in the minds of ordinary people between the strangers, the fabulous report of a comet, and the rumors of earthquakes, calamities, revolutions, and danger in faraway or nearby places? They provided additional reason for the increasing panic which was now mingled, but not confused, with chronic fear of the end of the world. This was a new fear that something would happen on earth. Fear that they would still have to wait for the end of the world. Fear of man, fear of nature, fear of the anger of God. A definite new panic mingling with the old.

But the coming of Lent brought its own atmosphere. The various Retreats would soon begin and the growing devotion was heightened by this latest sense of danger.

VI

Many people scarcely remembered the incendios of Luis Gonzaga and some had forgotten them completely. Where had the ex-Seminary student left the figures he used on his famous altars? Don Alfredo ingenuously gave Father Martínez "the boy's paraphernalia." Out of pity, Don Dionisio refrained from burning the stuff; he put it with the rubbish in the Presbytery.

The Parish Priest woke that morning with Luis Gonzaga on his mind. Father Martínez was one of the few whom Don Alfredo wanted to talk to about the boy, and he told his story pathetically, making no attempt to omit the obscenities. This was the pattern of the syndrome: His outbursts were followed by periods of depression from which he would gradually recover, but his mind would be less clear than it had been before the attacks of frenzy. He seemed to have forgotten everything, and, though his sense of guilt persisted, it was not quite clear what he was repenting of, nor did he realize what he was saying, or appear to recognize anyone, not even his parents. When people asked him questions or talked to him, he either did not answer or answered nonsense. The Seminary, books, drawing, the village, names of women he knew, which used to rouse his interest before, had lost all meaning for him. All he thought about was eating. His appetite became ravenous. He was exaggeratedly humble and polite. Without distinction, he treated not only Don Alfredo and Doña Carmen but the lowliest servants of the asylum, the Fathers in charge, the doctors, visitors, and other inmates with the greatest ceremony. He bowed to all and sundry, with high-sounding, meaningless phrases; he obeyed all orders docilely; his humility came close to abjectness. The sore points in his past life found vague allusions: prostrating himself before a keeper, he would call him Father Martínez; mistaking a lay brother for the Archbishop, he would ask permission to enter—he didn't say what; once he knelt before a visiting young priest, begging him to go over his verses.

It was soon discovered that women, even his mother, had an extraordinarily disturbing effect upon him. When he saw them he would grow abusive. Everything in his mind seemed to revolve around obscene themes. His caricatures of the forms of courtesy made an odd contrast to his lewd words, gestures, and expressions. The outburst would be devastating; it could not be stopped, but it was not accompanied by attacks of frenzy. He obeyed if told to be silent, only to begin again, going on and on, as if with whooping cough. At first he said that women descended from Heaven, naked, to visit him, then that they lived with him, and he would choose nine to be his wives and slaves; his problem was to penetrate their disguises and to recognize among so many those who were really Muses, destined to be his pupils and, later, rulers of the world because of their beauty. He adopted a pose of ridiculous arrogance, refused to allow anyone to touch him . . . How could they fail to recognize him as Apollo, the son of Jupiter, ruler of Parnassus, master and guide of the Muses? Muses they were, only sometimes Urania was called Victoria, and received harsh words from Apollo and treatment designed to make her cry out with pain.

"Micaela—I mean Terpsicore—dance, dance, like this, look . . ."

and the leader of the Muses would leap about like an abandoned faun; "Marta—that's not your name, you're Euterpe—and you, María, you're tragedy. Don't let Micaela usurp your role. You are Melpomene, Micaela is comedy, mere comedy, Thalia." At other times he would walk angrily through the corridors, "I want Clio, Polymnia, and Calliope." At night the silence of the house would be rent with his cries: "Calliope, Calliope! Why did you leave me? Calliope, I'll excommunicate you!" There were certain days when Apollo Musagetes played the vulgar role of an impresario proposing a new show to the Muses. "I'm taking you to Mexico City for the Centenary; maybe Don Maximilian of Austria will take one of you away from me, or Doña Carlota may fancy some of the others as ladies-in-waiting. You'll be a great success, singing, dancing, acting, all together."

They began to ration his food, and he suffered from attacks of madness. They took away the books with pictures of women in them, finding that he could feed his mad fancy on the pictures. They shut him away in a separate apartment so that nobody would hear his scandalous words or see his outrageous gestures. His obsession with obscenity respected nothing. He took it into his head to caper around naked, as befitted a god in perpetual levitation. One day he refused to open the door of his room, declaring that he was besieged by thousands of women begging a place in the chorus. The third day, when they forced the lock, Apollo hurled himself out with fury against his enemies, and they had to put him back in his strait jacket. The walls were covered with huge drawings of women in poses that filled the good Fathers with consternation. They had never before had a case of such persistent and ungovernable sexual madness. (Even Don Alfredo didn't know the worst of it: Luis, taking advantage of a free moment, had mutilated himself and attempted suicide.)

"Ah, Padre! Pray for him, I beg you. Pray that God will take my poor boy soon, if he cannot be cured. Is it wrong for me to wish him dead? Imagine how things must be for me to be thinking that! For a father to wish such a thing! And we had such high hopes for our only child. Wasn't he intelligent? You know he was. In my opinion, and I'm not blinded by a father's love, he was cleverer than anyone else. Who could talk the way he did? You remember how they praised him to the skies during his first years in the Seminary. They had hopes of his being another St. Augustine, or St. Thomas.

They were proud of him; he had honorable mention in all his subjects. I'd give anything on earth if only he could get better! But, like this, he's better off dead. I say it even at the risk of invoking God's wrath. What greater punishment could I have? Sometimes I think he isn't my son, but the Devil himself. I'm ashamed to say so. But it's frightful. You should see him! Please God you won't see him, nobody will see him like this. Isn't it better for him to be dead? Do you know what it takes to make a father wish for the death of his son, his only son, who might have been a great man? With all his talents! Padre, what can I offer God to cure him for me? My life, and Carmen's? We've all but given our lives. If you could see my poor wife! You wouldn't know her. She's a pitiful old woman. In six months, she seems to have aged a hundred years. My possessions? I've already lost everything. Now I've even had to give up my home. What more can I give?"

And, as he had done dozens of times before, he implied that Luis' madness might be due to the comet, and saw a glimmer of hope that when this passed, its effect might pass too.

Don Dionisio had no heart to interrupt the account of the obscenities, though they sickened him. Don Alfredo's suffering was so great. His tears moved the Parish Priest to compassion, and he could not refuse to hear the disagreeable confidences.

"Would you believe it, Padre, the woman had the impudence to visit us and invite us to stay with her? The shameless creature! Carmen had to speak to her plainly, and still she pretended to be surprised and offended, after doing all she could to harm us, setting everyone against us, causing people to shut their doors on us, even Carmen's people. We had to tell her the truth, to get things straight. You know, of course, that they say the sly creature was going around asking about Gabriel's whereabouts, because, they say, she wanted to help him. It's quite possible that she's cast her evil eye on him, too, to destroy him. It was an unhappy hour when Carmen decided to invite her to spend Holy Week with us in this house, to which she brought nothing but destruction. I don't know how they can think she's so virtuous in Guadalajara; her house is always full of the best people, they say even the Archbishop accepts her invitations. She's President or Treasurer of nearly all the Associations or festival committees. If they knew the kind of woman she is!

"Maybe this is only gossip, but one sees so many things! And, as they say, it's better to be forewarned . . . I've heard it going round among the students up there that one of those giving up the ministry is Jacobo, the baker's son, the one they nicknamed 'The Boor.' It's no surprise that he'd give up his studies, but what I think I ought to tell you—whether I'm doing the right thing or not, I don't know—is that they say—but I don't believe it—that Jacobo got engaged to your niece María during the last holidays, and that's why he's leaving the Seminary to get a job. It wasn't from one person only I heard it, but from many. Frankly, as I said, I don't believe it. How could there be any truth in it? But many things have begun in this way, by gossip, and anyhow, you ought to know about it.

"I heard them say in Guanatos that Damián Limón will get the death penalty in spite of all efforts to save him. I happened to visit the laurel patio in Escobedo Prison, where the executions take place, and I don't know why, but I couldn't help thinking of you. I know what you must have suffered with these terrible happenings in August; it must have been hard for a parish priest. The newspapers made a big scandal of it. But I was thinking of you more than anyone. And then I learned that Don Inocencio's girl, too, was after Luis at one time. We never know all the evils surrounding us at each step, as the prayer says! Don't you think all these calamities might have been caused by the comet?"

Compassion held Don Dionisio back from halting Don Alfredo, or changing the subject, but his curiosity and his scruples paralyzed him, too. It was hard to judge just how far he was to blame for what had happened to Luis Gonzaga, either through excessive zeal or negligence in advising him, or through not knowing how to direct him in the right path. Because he was sure of one thing: it was mistaken spiritual guidance that destroyed the boy's sanity and drove him mad; he considered Father Reyes right in that, and there was no point in determining the responsibility of others. The pathetic account—it was heart-rending to see a strong, kindly man like Don Alfredo cry—brought home to him again the wisdom of tempering severity in guiding souls, of limiting the influence of Father Islas and giving Father Reyes a larger share in the ruling of the parish and letting him put into practice his new ideas. The old Parish Priest had gradually become convinced by evidence that things were changing and his flock could not escape the change; it was a feeling in the air, like the warm wind that announces nearby land, like the smell of smoke at harvest time, like the cold air that, one morning or afternoon, is a harbinger of winter. Whereas, before, he had been indefatigable, now Don Dionisio began to feel weary and to look forward to death. He was dissatisfied with himself, and was amazed to note regrettable changes—for instance, this repugnant curiosity which made him listen to worldly tales and be disturbed by them; the confusion in his reactions as a priest and an uncle; the depression when faced by worldly troubles, and, maybe, a lack of faith, of that serene, blind faith which he had had in Providence. He felt more and more a need to talk with Father Reyes, to open his heart and confide in him.

That day, after Don Alfredo had gone, Father Martínez sought out Father Reyes, and although he withheld some of the details of Luis' state, alluding to them only indirectly, he experienced the ease of unburdening his mind and the comfort of an old man who finds a young one to lean on.

"I want you to take all the Retreats this year."

When the Retreats began, Father Reyes hesitated at first, but he finally felt secure enough to institute a series of reforms, chiefly in behalf of the young men and women. He still proceeded with jesuitical care, but certain lugubrious elements, such as the procession of the bier on the night of the Meditation on Death, the cries and trumpetings on the night devoted to Judgment, the smell of sulphur and the dragging of chains to aid the meditations on Hell, were suppressed; darkness for the collective use of the discipline was done away with, and, instead, this was left to individual devotion, and could be replaced by other means of mortification.

There was much criticism. "At this rate, next year they'll be bringing their beds and good food; they'll be able to chat and eat at all hours, maybe even go out when they want to. That's no kind of Retreat!"

"Less talk and more action," said Father Reyes.

This nearly caused an open breach between Father Reyes and Father Islas, and the matter remained unsettled: Father Islas refused to sanction "this modern softness," or share the responsibility in actions relating to his Association. Long arguments came to the ears of the public, sowing discord. The Chaplain left the village in the middle of Lent, and tongues wagged.

These were cares to trouble the old Parish Priest as the Friday of Dolores came round, these and the knowledge of the evil turn Luis Gonzaga's madness had taken. There was another thing, too, that preyed on his mind: since last year, he had had apprehensions of impending betrayal. The Spiritists? The Northerners? A member of his family? He could find no consolation in the thought that the expected betrayal might be the behavior of Gabriel and Victoria, the crime of Damián, or the growing worldliness of his flock. Harsher blows were in store for him, it was the fear of a deeper dagger thrust that kept him awake, his anxiety redoubled by the thought that his fear was a temptation against Faith, Hope, and Charity.

VII

On Saturday, the ninth of April, the gathering under the aegis of the gas lamp in the Flor de Mayo, which had declined as a result of Lent and Retreats, again increased in size. They were talking about an article which had appeared in the last Sunday issue of *El País*, according to which there was danger of the earth's colliding with the tail of Halley's comet on the nineteenth of May; even if this didn't happen, the earth might still explode, or spring a wide, deep hole at the North Pole; in any case there was a grave danger that it would be driven out of the sun's orbit and converted into a wandering star, according to the prophecies of Flammarion.

"They want us to be gored by the bull's horns, anyhow." But nobody was much amused at Lucas Macías' words.

VIII

María's respite was a short one. She grew tired of her doll. Pedrito's childishness irritated her. It wasn't long before the mirages of the distant world, her secret reading, and the widespread rumors of important events taking place everywhere made an end to her moment of calm.

A few words spoken by Don Alfredo Pérez on the day he came to visit Father Martínez started her off again.

"You won't know Guadalajara the next time you see it. They're filling in San Juan de Dios River from Agua Azul to beyond the Alameda; it's very pretty. And there are streetcars, and lots of new buildings; on San Francisco Street there's a five-story building, American style, they call the Mósler. Then there're lots of cars—lots of noise. You remember where the streetcar station is? Well, right in front of it, in the street, they're finishing a monument to Independence, which, they say, is going to be the best in Guadalajara.

"Talking of Mexico City—there's such a hubbub there you can't hear yourself speak! The monument there is getting high, too, higher than the Cathedral, I think. They say they're going to put an angel six feet tall on top of it, as though it were flying, and you'll be able to go up a circular stairway and see the whole Valley, from Chapultepec all round, and you can see the volcanoes clearly. There're big iron girders everywhere: the National Palace, the Legislative Building—an absolute fever of building. The one I like best is the Post Office. You should see how beautiful it is! Near the Department of Mines, in front of the Alameda, near the National Theatre they're building, all marble, you can't imagine what it's like. I was always getting lost the month we were there and I even came to like getting lost because I got to know the city better. Babylon must have been something like that."

As he was saying good-bye to Father Martínez in the doorway, Don Alfredo saw María.

"Well, look who's here! I thought I wasn't going to see you, since I'm hardly ever outside my door. How are you? I've been thinking of you. Luis thinks of you too . . ." María surprised a furious glance from the Parish Priest, which Don Alfredo, too, must have understood, because he took his leave hurriedly.

"Ah, Don Dionisio, may God keep her always good and pure." His voice trembled and his eyes filled.

IX

NEWS FLASHES: The Anti-Re-electionist Convention, meeting in Tívoli del Eliseo in the Capital, proclaimed the candidacy of Madero–Vázquez Gómez in the forthcoming elections. On May 1, according to Flammarion, when the comet collides with Venus, we mortals will witness wonderful fireworks in the sky, more beautiful than any pyrotechnic display. Don Francisco I. Madero had an interview with Don Porfirio. On May 23, there will be an eclipse of the moon, possibly seen by no one, since the tail of the comet will reach the earth on May 18. Great manifestation in honor of Don Porfirio, glorious President of Peace. Since midnight the comet has been visible in the east through simple apparatus.

X

María's behavior kept Marta awake. She would rouse between two and three in the morning, between one and two, unable to sleep, and lie there, a prey to thought, obsessions, crazy monologues. Unable to stand it, long before four, she'd get up, try to fill her mind with other thoughts, to pray. She'd climb to the bell tower and wait for the dawn, trying to find new hope.

Don Dionisio noticed her early rising and questioned her. "I get up early to look for the comet."

He believed her, or appeared to do so. In the village as in Guadalajara, in Mexico City, in New York, in Madrid, Paris, Rome, Berlin, people were doing this. Vain effort. The comet could not be seen with the naked eye. Marta, though, wasn't looking for the comet. María's words kept echoing in her ears; she kept seeing María's angry, spiteful glances. "Do you think I'm resigned like you to being an old maid and staying in the village? No, I don't know what I'm going to do, but this can't go on, even if I have to do something desperate."

Something desperate! Marta knew her sister was right. . . . Something desperate. Truly it was hard to be resigned. . . . Something desperate. . . . And one was never completely resigned. There was Mercedes, nearly crazy because Julián's wife was pregnant. Something desperate . . . something desperate.

XI

The eighteenth of May. Not even on Maundy Thursday had so many gone to confession. Not even the most notorious sinner failed to make his confession. Parents got the children up early. Nobody worked. Nobody could work. It grew hotter towards mid-morning. In the afternoon it clouded over and began to rain. It was still hot. The sky began to clear and there was a wonderful sunset. Dust had turned to glowing specks of light flying through the air, and the clouds were rimmed by colored spokes. Night came. The children fell asleep. Weariness overtook their elders, weary of waiting in vain for days, and throughout the hours of this day on which the event foretold did not take place, and they neither saw the phenomenon nor felt the emotions predicted. Midnight came and the catastrophe had still not occurred, nor were there visible any signs of the slightest touch of the comet's tail, which some imagined would be like a rain of sharp swords or tiny stars. Some managed to stay awake till dawn.

A few days later, a letter arrived from the Franciscan Friar Fermín García, and was read with reverent respect. From it the following passages are taken:

As the authorities have conferred upon me this year the undeserved distinction of naming me assistant in the Physical and Astronomical Laboratories, the honor and glory of our beloved Seminary, I have been able to follow step by step the progress of Halley's comet in its passes before the astonished eyes of mankind, and I have been aided in this by two men famous not only in our glorious Archdiocese, cradle of wise men and saints, but within and without the Republic: I refer to the famous priests Don José María Arreola and Don Severo Díaz, to whom fell the honor of being the first to discern the heavenly prodigy in the sky above Guadalajara.

I shall never be able to forget it. This was on Wednesday, April 20, and the tail of the comet was not yet visible. We knelt and gave thanks and sang hymns of praise to the Creator, saying with the psalmist, "The Heavens declare the glory of God." But I can find no words to describe the beauty of the phenomenon and my intense emotion on May 12 when the great tail of the comet could also be seen through the telescope in our observatory shortly after 4:30 P.M. It is an inexpressibly beautiful sight, and I can only repeat that text of Holy Scripture, "Eye hath not seen, nor ear heard, neither have entered into the heart of man, the things which God hath prepared for them that love Him." Yesterday, the twentieth, we could still see the comet in the west, a little after sunset; it was surrounded by Sirius, Procyon, Castor and Pollux, forming a beautiful group. When you receive this letter you will probably have been able to see with the naked eye this anticipation of the joy that awaits us for all eternity if . . . By then, the eclipse of the moon, which, God willing, occurs the day after tomorrow, will be over. In my next letter I shall describe my impressions of it as seen through the telescope.

I hope that these happenings have not provoked a superstitious response in the village and given birth to sinful fears, excusable only in the ignorant, as they did among the common people in the Capital, and even among those who might be expected to know better. It was ridiculous to see the general commotion on the eighteenth, when the tail of the comet was visible; people milled about in panic in the churches, squares, and on the rooftops . . .

Fermín García's father went around bursting with pride, showing the letter to everyone, feeling superior to ignorant people who had been filled with mortal terror.

"But you, too, were scared out of your wits on the day of the eclipse," some of his closest friends reminded him.

"Fear is catching, you can't escape being affected by it. But I soon recovered. Didn't I help old Cecilio when his wife fainted?"

"Well, how do you explain the things that happened that night? Julián's boy born dead, Father Islas' seizure, the howling of the dogs, and so many farmers dying, not counting what happened in other places . . ."

On June 2, between nine and ten at night, the comet was visible in the village; and on the eighth the weather cleared up and it could be seen at half-past eight. It was visible for the last time on the sixteenth, at seven o'clock. But by then, another event of overwhelming importance was occupying general attention. Don Francisco I. Madero had been arrested in Monterrey and taken to San Luis Potosí. In the distant peninsula of Yucatán, in the Valladolid district, revolution broke out. The headlines in *El País* excited the villagers; they waited anxiously for the arrival of the mail and quarreled over copies of the paper. Conjectures and prophecies disturbed the peace. On June 25, hundreds of corpses and fragments of human bodies reached Guadalajara, from a train wreck near Sayula. Madero wrote to Don Porfirio: "If civil war breaks out, you alone will be responsible in the eyes of the world and in the pages of history." On July 7, there were grave disorders in Puebla. On July 10, the presidential election took place. Porfirio Díaz and Ramón Corral were re-elected President and Vice-President, respectively. A proposal from Madero's supporters to annul the elections was rejected. Madero was still a prisoner.

Then came the golden interlude of the Centenary. Ambassadors arrived, there were sumptuous banquets, with toasts and speeches; the National Palace was converted into a wonderful ballroom. The police broke up manifestations of the independent clubs organized in honor of the heroes of Independence. The press no longer mentioned Madero.

"A short man, fair-skinned, bearded, wiry, and popular with the common people . . ." Lucas Macías knew by heart what Madero said to the correspondent of *El País* in the famous interview.

XII

When Julián's child was stillborn, the morning after the eclipse, Mercedes was thrown into a fever of remorse. "I killed him with my envious thoughts! But I didn't mean to, I tried to repress them." She could neither eat nor sleep and would see no one. She was ashamed even in Marta's presence, as if Marta, too, like all the rest, had come to blame her. She lay prostrate, sobbing day and night, her temperature rising, her face and her hands like wax, her eyes glazed . . . "I killed him!" Don Refugio advised them to take her to Guadalajara at once. "Envying the good fortune of others!" The long-ago days when Julián was courting her and she rejected him. Bottomless abyss of memories . . . Her envious glances at the belly of Julián's wife, and her bitterness at Julián's air of happiness. "I killed him!" The feeling of being possessed by evil the night she received his first letter. "Envying the good fortune of others!"

Don Anselmo Toledo, losing no time, and against Mercedes' will ("I want to die here! Don't take me away from the village, for God's sake!"), carried her off to Guadalajara in the first days of June. For many hours, for many weeks and months, Mercedes' cries as they carried her from the house, as she disappeared from sight on the other side of the river, echoed in Marta's ears and in the village memory. ("They're taking me away to die! They're taking me away to die!")

But Father Islas' seizure had been even more sensational. Much more. So sensational that many would never escape from the doubt into which the event had cast them. It was a nightmare, taking place under the most frightening circumstances. He had just drunk the consecrated wine from the chalice and had not yet reached out his hand for the basin of water when he suddenly began to shriek, and was seized with convulsions; no one could do anything with him. He bit his tongue, he foamed at the mouth; his face was covered with froth; his body swelled and his groans seemed to come from the other world, while his strong hands shook convulsively and clawed the air. Many of the faithful fled, others came to see but could not bear the sight of the bitten tongue, the agonized eyes, the frothing mouth and the dreadful cries. All forgot where they were and rushed about, sobbing and panic-stricken. Father Martínez arrived, and for the first time looked disturbed, full of a fear he could not hide. He gave orders for Father Islas to be borne into the Presbytery. It took seven men to carry him, for his horrible stertorous breathing and the diabolical contractions of his face, in contrast with the sacred vestments he was wearing, sapped their strength and filled them with panic. How many would ever escape from the doubt the event created?

XIII

The funerals and the August heat, the civic duty of celebrating the Centenary of Independence in the village, and the enjoyment some got out of going to celebrations in the capital of either the State or the Republic, relegated to the background such matters as Don Francisco I. Madero's imprisonment, hopes of seeing the comet again, or the outcome of Damián's trial.

Among the victims of dog days, this year, was Justino Pelayo's oldest daughter, a lively little girl, not quite eleven. She died on the thirteenth, the day of the death of the Virgin, and everyone was saddened. The Parish Priest was at the funeral and, as very rarely happened, the memory of a confession (of Justino's two Lents before) came back to his mind. It was an account of how, one night, he set out towards the river, in search of a woman; hiding from everyone, from his own thoughts, on the point of turning back several times, harassed by desire and shame. He couldn't get the woman out of his mind; she had arrived only that week and was the topic of secret conversations, but the thought of his wife and his children gave him no rest. What would they be doing at the moment? Consuelo, the lively one, would be saying her prayers, or begging her mother to tell her a story about the saints. How far removed his family were from the act he was contemplating, how far from the desire that set his blood on fire, from the longing that drove him out into the night! If something happened to them through his fault! Desire proved the stronger and prevailed over remorse. Exhausted, he knocked at the woman's door. What could his wife and children do now? He was the traitor who bargains for pleasure and receives pain. Worse, he knew that his sin would have tragic consequences. He could not turn back but he wished he had never left the house. He felt far, far away, lost, condemned never to return. It seemed an endless time before he could leave, go out into the street, reach the village again, say good night to a neighbor. His embarrassment was unbearable at home, having supper, listening to innocent remarks. They must know of his treachery. But how could they? They couldn't even suspect, and that made it worse. If he could confess to his wife, and keep away from his children. He had no right to touch his oldest daughter. But that was impossible. His stained hands must rest on innocence.

These details came back to the Parish Priest's mind. It was the first time such a thing had happened; always before, he had had the gift of forgetting whatever was confided in the secret of the Confessional; never did anything, however shocking or unusual, remind him of what he had heard; but now it was as if God had forsaken him, it was torture to feel that he was violating the seal of the Confessional by remembering the subject of a confession once the penitent was absolved. He turned red; he began to sweat; he moved away from Justino, keeping his eyes fixed on the ground, afraid his unwelcome memories would show in his face.

Again, through some inexplicable association of ideas, his dream came back to haunt him, revived his anxiety about Marta and María. What carelessness had made him neglect the obvious symptoms? María's silences, irritability, and touchiness. Had not someone told him, or did he imagine it, that María had been seen on the tower one afternoon, looking towards the quarter of the bad women, or that she was talking with one of those creatures in front of the church? It must be a temptation of the Devil! Nobody could tell him that or even insinuate it! No! . . . or that she often chatted with Lucas González' widow and read forbidden novels, and made bold remarks.

The shovelfuls of earth fell on the child's coffin like blows on his temples. *Better María.* He shuddered and rebelled at the thought. *No! My little girl! My poor little girl!* And he felt a longing to see her, to put his arms round her as he did when she was small; he forgot everything but her happiness; he was terrified at the thought that when she met him she might have no affectionate word or smile for him; he, so cold, so much to blame for the hate his favorite niece was now feeling. *Lucas González' widow was heading for trouble. That, at least, was no secret of the Confessional. But María could not be talking to her. Why did he keep Gabriel away? If they loved each other, it would be better for them to get married . . .*

The old man felt sick; he wanted to vomit. Justino's hoarse voice cut short the thread of his thought:

"What hurts most is to know that it's my fault. And someday nobody will miss her, nobody—not even me. She'll be forgotten."

Then after a burst of sobbing, "The only thing that consoles me is that God took her before she ran into any danger."

Before she ran into any danger. Danger. Danger! Father Martínez left the Cemetery with but one thought in his mind, to seek out María, find her and talk to her like a father. *Perhaps she would smile one of the dear smiles of her childhood.*

But María was not in the Presbytery when he got home.

XIV

The students returned with talk of the comet, infused new life into the languid plans of the Patriotic Committee in charge of the Centenary celebrations, improvised a pseudo-historical procession which was not on the program, made speeches and recited poetry, and renewed or inspired restlessness in the women.

It was never quite certain afterward whether it was during September that the meetings began in which, as was discovered later, certain students played a leading role; the secrecy that the conspirators maintained was remarkable. Some say the meetings had started earlier and those involved had been in contact with the Estradas of Moyahua, and with other people in the Canyons. But others thought the plot took definite shape at the end of October or the beginning of November, basing their opinion on the fact that the students most fully informed had made their preparations to return to school, and some—Chencho Martínez, Patricio Ledesma—went to Guadalajara, enrolled, and disappeared to take part in the movement. It was the general conviction that the organizers of the meetings were Pascual Aguilera, Pedro Cervantes, and Dimas Gómez, abetted by Northerners that Father Reyes could not influence, those who, later, became famous guerrilla leaders.

Certainly nobody suspected anything. No one. Not even Father Martínez, who was most affected by the events.

The people turned their attention to the comet again.

XV

If only someone had been putting two and two together!

After sulking for many days, María got up in a good mood one morning and was playing soldiers with Pedrito when Marta heard her say, "What a pity you're not older!" Marta said nothing, lest she lose her temper.

On another occasion, María said, "Wouldn't you like Pedrito to grow up and make the village famous, and have everyone talking about him? It's time for this village to produce someone who'll chop a lot of heads off their shoulders!" Marta had been thinking somewhat the same thing, but María's phrase shocked her, she didn't know why.

Dimas Gómez was one of the speakers on the night of the fifteenth of September and mentioned democracy many times. The Deputy, wishing to avoid trouble, turned a deaf ear, all the more that nobody seemed to be paying any attention to the seditious nonsense.

Pascual Aguilera left the village twice, and was careful to tell everyone that he was going to the farm.

It was apparently a coincidence that Don Román Capistrán and a group of Northerners travelled to Guadalajara and Mexico City together for the Centenary and came back with some gentlemen from Moyahua and Juchipila, who stayed in the village for a few days on their way home.

But why was nobody surprised at the frequent visits of so-called merchants, from Mexticacán and Nochistlán, from Jalpa and Tlaltenango, on the pretext of buying corn, livestock, wool? A certain Enrique Estrada from Moyahua, a certain Pánfilo Natera.

"Where there's smoke there's fire." That was all Lucas Macías could say, in his sibylline manner, perhaps because he failed to get at the secret behind the ominous reserve. He tried all his tricks to renew a conversation he had had with Aguilera the year before, but Pascual seemed to have forgotten, or was no longer interested.

"What news of Señor Madero?" Lucas fired this suddenly. "Well, never mind. You were in San Luis; you're just back from there now. But so that you may know I can be trusted, I'll not ask you again, nor will you ever hear me making indirect remarks that may arouse suspicions." Pascual persisted in treating this as a joke, but Lucas kept his word, stopped saying that where there's smoke there's fire, and turned his conversation into other channels: students' tricks of other times, famous instances of village girls being carried off, stories of buried treasure.

To no one else did it occur that Pascual had been in San Luis with Madero.

XVI

Don Román Capistrán went to say good-bye to the Parish Priest on the eve of his departure for Mexico City, the second of September, to be exact. As Don Dionisio was busy, María went to the door.

"Well, now, Mariquita, come to Mexico City with me; we'll have a grand time. All you have to do is say you'll come. You won't be sorry, I promise you."

Whatever prompted his words, jest or evil intent, they took María by surprise. The former Deputy was no friend of hers; he had rarely come back to the village since his resignation, and she could hardly remember what people said of his character and morals. (Don Román was no longer a figure of interest to the villagers.) Shocked, embarrassed, confused, she fled, her blood boiling chiefly because she could think of no answer; but she was mortified. "Come on . . . come to Mexico City with me" might have been a childish joke, and this irritated her the more. Was she a child, to be treated like this? Or had someone told the old man of her mad longing to escape? In any case, why should he make such an insulting proposal? What did the village think of her? Was their opinion reflected in his senile insolence? Did they think she was shameless, like poor Micaela?

Her anger rose. "I should have told the old hypocrite what I thought of him. Why did I give him the pleasure of seeing me run away shamefaced?" Plans for vengeance filled her mind, vengeance first on the author of the insult, then on the whole village, on one and all of her hateful, insufferable neighbors, on the walls, the horizon, the confining sky, vengeance on everything that kept her prisoner in this corner of the world.

"Come to Mexico City. Travel. . . . Not be sorry." His words assumed greater importance, took on broader implications, a new meaning: "Come on, let's get away from this hole. . . . Come on, take off those black rags that make an old woman of you. . . . Come on, you're too young to let yourself be buried alive without knowing what it is to have some fun. . . . These black rags. Come on!"

Her whole life spent between Retreat House and the Cemetery! Her head always covered by a shawl! Virgin widow. Long black sleeves reaching to her wrists, her throat invisible, skirts covering tight high black boots, coarse black cotton stockings. Long, clumsy petticoats.

Who would avenge this insult, man to man? She had no one to depend on. Why tell her uncle about it? He would never understand.

In her distress, she reviewed the young men, one by one: Gabriel, Damián, Jacobo, Luis Gonzaga, the student from Teocaltiche . . . Gabriel, no: she didn't even know where he was; nor Damián, he never paid any attention to her and it was only his crime that made her notice him; Jacobo? She hadn't heard from him all year, nor was she looking forward to the thought that he would come during the holidays; she hadn't so much as given him a thought in the course of the year, not even out of curiosity. The student from Teocaltiche? What impudence! There was definitely no one she could count on. Certainly no man had interested her, nor had any man been interested in the sad, black-robed, unhappy, unsatisfied woman, envious and rebellious.

Then came the procession of heroes from her novels and the newspapers that had caught her first fancy, a procession brusquely interrupted by an extraordinary thought: Don Román Capistrán wasn't really an unattractive man, he wasn't at all ridiculous . . . on the contrary, he was attractive, vigorous, confident; his health and strength could be seen in the color and firmness of his skin; his beard was thick, his eyes clear, his nose well-shaped, his eyebrows well-marked, his hair neat, his mouth generous, his teeth gleaming, and his gray hair gave him a patriarchal majesty. A strong man, accustomed to deal with people, easy-mannered, with contagious laughter and ready speech . . .

María dared not go on with the portrait. But the image returned in dreams and became confused with that of Damián, both alike in virile attraction, in brute force. Between them, they drove sleep away, from midnight on. Near her bed, threatening, lay the long black dresses of yesterday and tomorrow.

Marta slept in tranquil resignation.

XVII

Each arrival of the mail with the newspapers describing the splendid celebration of the Centenary and demonstrating the strength of the government afforded the Franciscan Friar Fermín García an opportunity to make a sententious speech, as he went about seeking an admiring audience:

"I very much dislike talking politics, which is out of keeping with my character and my orders, but it will do no harm to repeat what is clearer than daylight, to dissipate groundless fears and alarm. . . . Clearer than daylight: a highly respected government—witness the brilliant representatives from all over the world who have come to attend these celebrations; an Army second to none; national prosperity and wealth, demonstrated in each ceremony of the civic program. . . . The Centenary celebrations have come to be the most effective blow to malcontents. . . . We've seen what happened to the followers of General Reyes, and the outcome of the efforts of Madero, laughingstock of all sensible people. . . ."

The retorts and heckling by Pascual Aguilera and other students were considered only an attempt to irritate the prudish friar.

Generally speaking, the villagers found Fermín's conclusions, drawn from the evidence, incontrovertible. His reasoning was as follows: "Why should there be a revolution? Here, in our district, for example, no one is dying of hunger, all can work freely, with security and guarantees; the fact that some years are bad is the fault of the weather and the pests, not the government. Tell me: who would revolt round here? They're all good people, with nothing to complain of."

There were times, however, when the agreement with such speeches was not so general; names were mentioned of victims of usury, of people whose property had been taken from them; many were remembered who could never get out of debt, however hard they worked; besides, there were the despicable pretexts used by the Deputy, Sunday after Sunday, to arrest people who came in from the farms and force them to work for him; arbitrary administrative decisions in judicial affairs; forced gifts of money or ploughshares made to landowners or the Deputy and permanent or temporary government employees; frauds concealed under the guise of contracts, to the disadvantage of the poorest or the most helpless.

Father Reyes advised the Seminarist to change the subject. But the success with which his ideas were received was flattering.

XVIII

Jacobo Ibarra did not come home for the holidays. It was learned in the village that, since the beginning of the year, he had been studying in high school and working at the same time in the office of a lawyer.

María received a message from "The Boor" without knowing how it reached her. "Unforgettable María, if you are wondering why I do not return, know that I am faithful to my promise and I trust you, although I respect your freedom. J. Ibarra." The Parish Priest's niece was surprised to find herself moved, and kept the letter; but for all that, she saw Don Román Capistrán's face each time she heard the Centenary celebrations mentioned. "He must have been there. He would have heard about that. He has probably seen that." The images invaded her mind against her will, and became hateful to her, but she could not stop them. She certainly thought of Jacobo with more pleasure.

"Gabriel will soon be here," the Parish Priest announced happily, one morning. This sent Marta into transports of delight but left María unmoved.

XIX

The news that Don Francisco Madero had escaped reached the village before it was announced in the newspapers.

A mass of conjectures: he'd run away because he was afraid and wanted to lead a quiet life in the United States; they'd arrest him again and then, he'd get it for playing with fire; he was definitely through with his wild schemes, seeing how impossible it was to overthrow a government as strong as the Centenary celebrations proved this one to be; the naïve Anti-Re-electionists were disappointed again; they were nothing of the sort; Madero was ready to head a revolution, with the help of the United States; wrong, the United States would arrest him if he crossed the border, especially if he tried to violate the neutrality laws.

"And what do you say, Lucas, about all this? It's a long time since you had anything to say about 'that short man with the fair complexion, bearded, wiry, and popular.'"

"Me? I'm closer to the next world than this one." And that was all anyone could get out of him.

It was around about then that Pascual Aguilera left town for the second time.

XX

Don Dionisio had overcome his objections to Gabriel's return. This was the answer he received from the boy:

I won't deny that your decision gave me great pleasure. But in return for all you have done for me, it is only fair to be frank with you; otherwise, I could never look you in the face or continue to accept your kindness. I am quite aware that you are unhappy about me, and about what happened before I left the village; but I will be quite open and tell the whole truth. It is hard to begin, though, without seeming disrespectful. Still, our chaplain has ordered me to tell you everything, so, in spite of my shame and, even more, my fear of offending you, I must say that the longer I am away, the harder it is to put María out of my mind. I keep thinking about her and I can't help knowing that I want to marry her. Forgive me for having to put it bluntly like this, perhaps without proper consideration. I write at the orders of my superior; I have told him everything, and he knows that my intentions are honorable; he tells me to ask you to consider this.

But there is something else, too. My infatuation with the woman who was staying with the Pérez family only helped me to discover what I feel for María. It was a madness which I can't explain, and why be a hypocrite? She has often disturbed me, by day and by night, like a bad dream, but this makes me realize all the more that I need to marry to banish the shadow. Because of her I have not wanted to study music here, or be in the band, although they say I have talent. I chose printing instead, remembering that María loves books. You will see that I am determined to put a troubling memory out of my mind forever, knowing the harm it did me, and replace it with a wholesome attachment. I have spoken frankly, feeling it my duty to do so. I will abide by your decision. Shall I wait awhile? I venture to ask another favor too: if you think it wise, if you think it proper, may I write to María? Forgive me.

Another reason I'd like to come back—here, among the young men, chiefly among those from the North, there is much unrest and talk of uprisings. . . .

XXI

No matter how hard they tried to goad Lucas into talking politics, he'd come out with irrelevancies.

"Since the rebels haven't carried off a single girl, the people—especially the women—say they can't be men, they must be something else. Ha, ha, ha . . .

"In '99, there were certainly enough girls carried off. I think they were afraid the end of the world was coming, and they didn't want to be by themselves. Ha, ha! How many students came home for the holidays and never got away again because they were roped into marriage! Pioquinto Lepe, may his soul rest in peace; Gumersindo Parga, may God keep him in his heavenly kingdom . . . and others, still alive, in addition to those from the farms. There was hardly a night but you heard horses' hoofs, or a morning but you learned of some girl carried off, or placed in the safekeeping of the law. The religious authorities were strict then, and forced the runaways to listen to moral discourses on their knees, with their arms crossed, right at High Mass, where everyone would see them. That was their punishment. Certainly Pioquinto's father-in-law never forgave him. He refused to recognize the grandchildren, an everyday occurrence, perhaps, but the old man, who was rich, was so unrelenting that he let his daughter and grandchildren die in want after Pioquinto drowned without leaving them enough to keep body and soul together.

"And what about all those who have killed their sons-in-law, married and all, refusing to forgive them for carrying their daughters off? The tale of Don Pedro Romo is an old story. You all know it. I tell it every year. But, never mind, I'll tell it again. Don Pedro had five daughters and three sons. Many men came courting the daughters, but Don Pedro and his sons were so jealous they hardly let the girls breathe, let alone see or speak to a man, or go out anywhere. They kept them away from church, unless they were well escorted, and discouraged them from going to Confessional. If they thought that a man was trying to approach the girls, they'd out with a pistol and threaten him; if they saw him again, blood flowed. Two men lost their lives for the sake of the oldest girl—a fellow called Quesada, from Teocaltiche, and another, nicknamed "The Pistol." *They* hadn't cared a hoot for Don Pedro and his sons, and meant to marry the girl whether they liked it or not. Naturally, the two older girls

remained old maids, but there was another man ready to dare anything for the youngest, called María, and he got through the guard
and managed to talk to her and find someone to ask for her hand.
They said the Romos were like men possessed; they were ready to
kill the priest who made the request, they hunted the man up and
down, they beat the girl. But he must have had the Devil on his
side. He got the girl away, but they caught him on the Guadalajara Road. In the shooting, he was killed, and Don Pedro and his
oldest son badly wounded. The girl disappeared a few days afterward; it was rumored that Don Pedro himself had killed her, and
everybody believed it . . .

"I saw the end of the family of the late Praxedis Torres, too. That's
another old story, and a very long one. It began in the time of Santa
Ana. You must have heard it. It was terrible, the worst feud I remember, and it all started with a runaway marriage. The usual
thing happened: a man asked Praxedis for the hand of his only
daughter. He made a great fuss, and tried every means to dissuade
her, but it was useless. Then he allowed them to be engaged for two
years, during which they were neither to see each other nor to write.
At the end of the time, he put the wedding off for another two
years. Naturally the girl ran away with the young man. She was
placed in the Presbytery of Apozol for safekeeping, and they were
finally married. When Praxedis found out where they were, he
went after them, married or not, and, without so much as a by your
leave, killed his son-in-law and left his daughter to fend for herself.
In time a son was born. Praxedis refused to accept it. He denied
that he'd ever had a daughter, and, when driven past endurance,
called her all the vile names he could think of. Years passed, and the
son appeared. They had words, and Praxedis told him his mother
was a tramp, and you know how that ended. The boy killed his
grandfather. So the feud went on. One of Praxedis' sons killed the
boy, and, not content with this, went off to look for his sister. She
defended herself so well that her attacker was soon taken to the
cemetery. His son brought about the death of his aunt in such a
cowardly fashion that her first cousin (they say he was in love with
her), took things into his own hands, and the killings went on. Not
a year passed but somebody killed a blood relation. The feud
lasted till '87, when I saw the corpses of the last Torreses—Don Porfirio and Don Eustaquio, second cousins, who had stabbed each
other to death . . .

"People were very much upset again, when Father Gutiérrez' sister went off with a student, in '93. Father Gutiérrez was the senior curate, and had been in the village for eighteen years, often substituting for the parish priest. He was a sociable man, and everybody loved him for his hospitality and generosity. His sister, she was a strapping girl, often came to stay with him in the village. They said she had had a young man in Guadalajara for eight years, but there were no signs of a wedding. This was the state of affairs when she took up with a certain Tacho Casillas here, who, they said, had several deaths on his conscience. Anyhow, he was a cousin to the late Timoteo Limón. Well, they disappeared one night, causing a great to-do. For weeks, Father Gutiérrez wouldn't go outside his door; he never went out visiting again, and even avoided meeting people in the street. He was so ashamed and worried he began to lose weight rapidly, and within six months, he was a dead man. . . . I don't know how a woman can go off with a murderer. . . ."

XXII

Don Dionisio was puzzled by Gabriel's letter. For a moment he was tempted to show it to María, in the hope that the boy's avowal might cure her peculiar state of feeling, which worried him more and more every day. He delayed answering it, and finally suggested that Gabriel postpone his return, without making any reference to the question raised.

When Don Román returned, the Parish Priest was surprised at the presents he brought his nieces, since they had never been friendly enough to justify them. But, after all, they were religious gifts: rosaries from the Basilica of Guadalupe, with a cross, in Marta's, with the image of the Virgin on it, and, in María's, the outside of the Basilica of Guadalupe. María, secretly, received a bottle of perfume, which she returned at once with the rosary. Don Román began to court her in earnest.

"He's an old scoundrel!" she thought, furiously, the image of the attractive male dwindling.

"When's Gabriel coming back?" The unexpected question astounded her old uncle.

"I thought . . . I want him to finish . . . it seemed best to me . . ."

María felt alone and forsaken.

XXIII

"We're orphans, now! What will become of us without our Padre? The Saint is leaving us!" The most faithful Daughters of Mary accompanied the stretcher on which Father Islas was borne to Guadalajara. After his seizure and paralysis, he had refused to leave the village. The Archbishop had to order him to Guadalajara, offering to pay the cost of treatment there.

"What will become of the village without this righteous man, without its lightning conductor?"

Few villagers went to bid him good-bye. Many Daughters of Mary were missing. The seizure had killed the common belief in the Chaplain's saintliness. There were open expressions of pleasure and looks of satisfaction at the sick man's departure. But the faithful few remained faithful. Thirty mourning, black-robed women accompanied the stretcher on foot, crossed the river, walked for half an hour, flung themselves on the ground to receive his last blessing, and returned in tears.

The public indifference irritated them.

"Our Chaplain has gone! Who will look after us? Who will save us from danger?"

Students, nobody could discover which they were, went through the streets that night, howling: "Here come the wolves, black-robed Little Red Riding Hoods. Woof! . . . Here come the wolves!"

XXIV

Once the problem of the elections was settled, the Deputy set about feathering his own nest; his political zeal waned and he paid no attention to anything outside his own interests. He was amiable towards villagers of good social or economic standing, and towards the turbulent elements that might endanger the tranquility indispensable to carrying out his plans. He made up for this by his harsh treatment of the poor and helpless. Through sharp practice, he got hold of a small farm, which prospered and grew rapidly. Within a year he was the owner of two hundred head of cattle; a house, stables, cow sheds, henhouses, a road, and walls, were all the work of farmers arrested on Sundays when they came to mass and the market, because they weren't wearing trousers, because they left rubbish about, because they left their mules in the street, because they were found with a bottle of wine in their hands, because they relieved themselves in some corner of the village, because the stallholders objected to the ever-increasing tax they had to pay on their stands, even because they shouted or bumped into someone.

At about the time of the National Festival, the Deputy himself confiscated the arms of Rito Becerra, as the man was on his way back to his farm; in vain did he protest that he carried arms for his own personal safety and that he had not taken them into the village. When his explanations got him nowhere, he accused the Deputy of going beyond his rights and resisted; the soldiers hurled themselves on him, beat him, and would have killed him if bystanders hadn't interfered. The Deputy spoke of having him arrested as a revolutionary, but being a laborer and a dependent of Don Anselmo Toledo's, Rito got off with a month of forced labor. (Rito Becerro would never forget, among other gestures of compassion, the kindness of María, the Parish Priest's niece, who happened to be passing by the afternoon the affair took place. She was one of those who shouted out to let him go; she ran up to wipe away the blood and got her uncle and Father Reyes to calm the vengeful Deputy. Grateful, Rito went to thank her when he was released; they spoke of the injustices suffered by the poor, of their hard lives, of how self-respect and a readiness to defend oneself seemed to be dying out. "We deserve all this and more, for being such cowards!" Rito said bitterly. "Someone must put an end to it, and there will be someone!" María said good-bye to him at the door of the Presbytery with a warm handshake, and, returning to Marta, said, "What a pity Pedrito isn't grown up! How I'd like him to throw off this yoke, to put an end to all this injustice!")

The Deputy was blind. How could he fail to notice that Pascual Aguilera went about talking with Rito Becerro and all those who certainly had grudges against the authorities? But Pascual Aguilera had become the inseparable companion of Don Román Capistrán, and the Deputy would not interfere with him in any way.

One thing bothered that functionary and upset his plans: the officiousness of the Parish Priest, and of Father Reyes especially, on behalf of the poor. "I can get along with you easily, but tell Father Reyes not to meddle in government matters," he said to Don Dionisio. The fear of getting the worst of it and setting the people against him made him conceal his real feelings.

"What a pity I'm not a man! There don't seem to be any real men left!" was another of the thoughts that came into María's head.

XXV

Injustice, just as they had expected. Damián Limón was sentenced to six years in prison, that was all, because it could not be proved that he killed his father, they said, and because killing Micaela was a crime of passion. According to the evidence, in the absence of an autopsy, Don Timoteo's body showed only a slight blow, which could have been caused by a fall; Micaela's words, written down in the evidence, had told in the criminal's favor, and Damián continued to maintain that he had been in love with her and couldn't forget her . . . Consensus of popular opinion: "Sheer lies, to cloak injustice!"

Hard on the heels of this, bringing public excitement to its height, came the news of Damián's escape, on the way to the Capital, where they were taking him to serve his sentence.

"Quite a coincidence. He escaped, yet hardly a day passes without our hearing of innocent people falling victims to the ley fuga!"

XXVI

Fear and love grappled in the final moments of desperation, on the eve of farewells and departures. Unfulfilled love, the love of maidens waiting in vain, who had looked forward to the coming of September, remembering or imagining faces that would appear, eyes that would look for them, steps that would seek them. They watched the fields turn yellow, and the time grow shorter, and still no steps followed their shadows, nor were the glances they had dreamed of to be met with anywhere. Village streets, paths from house to church, from church to house, were empty for the sad black-robed women, sad captive women.

The students were still here, there, everywhere, making a commotion. But they passed the eager faces by, the hearts beating with frenzied hope, as if they weren't there. These are the days of complete disillusionment. The students are going away. All Souls' Day will soon come; life will resume its normal routine; the restless nights will return, filled with the sterile rebellion of old maids, with their longing to have been deceived if nothing more, the agonizing conviction of failure even to evoke a charitable lie, or the alms of a passing interest. No one had been able to read their expressions. Now it was too late for anyone to guess their longing for love, their ill-concealed dejection at living in vain hope. Each October night ended an illusion, destroyed afresh a dream. But some kept their lamps lit, remembering unexpected declarations on the very eve or even the morning of departure.

This year the shadow of Father Islas was not there to intervene in the struggle between love and fear. And the relatives of the young girls redoubled their vigilance. They waged war on carelessness, furtive evasions, messages slipped into hands, encouraging smiles. Anxiety increased, glowing hopes were quenched, the girls gave way to desperation, tears, and crazy ideas, as they came into collision with the walls of inveterate restraint.

How many would miss this boon to carry them through the year of stagnation in the daily round of the village! How many girls would not even succeed in stretching out a hand for a parting clasp, or, straining to listen, hear farewell or a promise at the barely opened window or door, or even manage to wave a distant good-bye or watch the departing one!

November would soon be here! The last days of October! Desperate murmurs of grieving women in the secret of the Confessional, salty tears shed in secret under the blows of Death, Judgment, Hell, and Heaven; women shipwrecked by love and fear.

XXVII

There was reason to expect a new travesty of justice if Damián returned to the village and the Deputy did nothing, as he had done in the case of other delinquents and fugitives who procured immunity with money or threats. The thought of such a thing aroused the people, even the normally peaceful among them; they would take matters into their own hands if justice was balked by corruptness this time.

"I give you my word, if that man dares to come here, I'll take him to Guadalajara, dead or alive."

Damián defied the popular anger. He dared to come. Arriving on the Eve of All Souls' Day, he crept cautiously through the streets, unshaven, disguised as a pack-driver. In the distance, he could see the lighted Flor de Mayo, with its gathering; he listened to the voices of the choir directed by Father Reyes, practicing the Requiem Mass; a soprano voice caught his ear, attracted him, and he went into the darkness of the Atrium, and stood in front of the Presbytery windows. It was a young boy's voice, but it sounded like a woman's. What he was looking for was there: memory and voices of death. *Grant them Thine eternal peace, O Lord.* He defied shadows and dangers. He intended to go to the Cemetery, look for Micaela's grave, and spend the night beside it. The bass and soprano voices held him back: *Day of wrath! O day of mourning!* A faint light showed him the hall of the Presbytery beyond the intervening room. He would have liked to go in and talk with the Parish Priest. It was nearly ten. A woman crossed the hall and came to shut the window. Damián recognized María. Wasn't he looking for her, too? He had forgotten. María or Micaela. *Deliver them from the deep pit and the lion's mouth, that hell may not swallow them up, and may they not fall into darkness, but may Thy holy standard-bearer Michael lead them into the holy light . . . deliver them.* Damián had had his hand on his gun ever since, under cover of darkness, he had come into the village. He went to the window and listened to María's footsteps. He wanted to knock. Micaela, María. *May light perpetual shine on them.* He waited awhile. Should he go into the Presbytery? Should he go away? He felt a strong urge to talk with Micaela's closest friend. If he knocked, she would not open the window. He tried whistling softly, a song Micaela used to sing. The footsteps halted. Damián kept silent. He felt that she was near, beside the shutters. Knowing full well the horror he might arouse, he still could not contain himself:

"María, it's me, Damián. Damián Limón. Listen."

Unexpectedly, the window opened.

"Don't you know they want to kill you?"

"I know. I wanted to see you. It's worth the risk. Listen . . . I never knew . . ."

"That I was the woman you would have killed."

María's words disconcerted him.

"Who knows! I can't think of Micaela without thinking of you. Are you afraid?"

"I'm not afraid of death."

"You're like Micaela. You're the same woman. No one can master you."

"Did you come to kill me?"

"You're alike. I *wasn't* wrong. Now I'm sure. Don't you feel sorry for me? You'd better go now. No one must know that you talked to me. You've been waiting for me. You knew what you were going to say to me."

"Perhaps."

"Do you like danger?"

"I don't know what I like. I might like to call out and have you arrested."

"Who would dare?"

"That's the worst of it. Nobody."

"Except you."

"Then go away."

"María! María! Why do things happen the way they do? Let me say good-bye. No. I won't touch you. Call out to them to come and get me. I won't try to escape."

"I want you to go. Go."

"You're braver than I am. Good-bye. I'll come back when you no longer pity me."

"Pity? I don't feel either pity or surprise. You can see that. Go away, though, and don't ever come back."

"Does it make you afraid to think I might come back without having to hide from anyone?"

"It tries my patience to see you still here. Listen to me, Damián. Go."

"All right. I understand. Good-bye, María."

"Go where nobody knows you."

"On condition that . . ."

"Do you hear me? Not another word. Good-bye."

He left reluctantly. María stood at the open window for a long time, listening to the sounds of the night. The bells had rung for ten o'clock as she spoke the last words. The practice was over. The choir came out onto the street noisily. Dogs barked furiously. Gradually stillness reigned. She still waited. Convinced that all was well, she finally closed the shutters cautiously.

XXVIII

Deliver them from the deep pit and from the lion's mouth, that hell may not swallow them up, and may they not fall into darkness, but may Thy holy standard-bearer Michael lead them into the holy light . . .

From before dawn until nearly midday, the bells had tolled in the village of death, as masses succeeded each other in groups of three. The gold flames of the wax tapers and candles, the gold of the ornaments and the sun alternated with the black of the coverings on the biers, with the whiteness of the skulls placed upon them. Black garments and pale hands and faces. Eyes and teeth shining in greeting. The streets were animated with the solemn observance of this day in the village. At eight o'clock, a mass was intoned, celebrated by three priests. Since before dawn, in the parlors of the houses, in all the houses, candles had been burning in front of the statue of Christ, and they would burn until they were burned out, presiding over domestic rosaries said for the dead members of the family. The whole village was a funeral celebration for the Feast of All Souls. It would be the same in the Cemetery, when in the early afternoon, under the open sky, the Brotherhood of Happy Death made the round of all the graves, as they do every year, and held their service there with responses, amid the interminable clamor of bells and the chorus of men and women, old men and children, singing along the way:

> Come out, ye souls, from death's dread pains,
> Holy Rosary break your chains.

Before dawn, as people met on the way to the first mass, it was rumored that a stranger had been seen in the streets in the night, near Don Inocencio Rodríguez' house, and going towards the Cemetery, about eleven o'clock.

"Nothing to it!"

"A ghost?"

By the time they came out of High Mass, it was almost certain that Damián Limón had been in the village. The accounts of the stranger tallied: his face, his walk, the places he visited. People who had seen him couldn't have been mistaken, or victims of hallucinations. The things he did were perfectly understandable: he was haunted by the memory of his victims.

"And he's supposed to be so brave! Why didn't he show himself?"

The Deputy, sure that the fugitive wouldn't come back, boasted, "I can't arrest a shadow. If you'd told me in time, he wouldn't have escaped."

Worn out with an effort she herself would not have believed she was capable of, María could hardly bear the weight of her secret.

At half-past three, the bells began tolling again, for the procession organized by the Brotherhood of Happy Death. Everyone came.

The priests were clad in sumptuous black vestments embroidered with gold, shining in the afternoon sunlight. The tall cross and candlesticks shone in the hands of the acolytes who led the procession. After the Rosary, hundreds of voices sang the mournful words:

> Come out, ye souls, from death's dread pains,
> Holy Rosary break your chains,

while, in María's ears, there echoed an infernal voice, insistent, "Come on, come on with me!"

As they were nearing the Cemetery, there was a disturbance: whispered muttering, increasing in volume. Everybody tried to hear what was going on. The acolytes halted and looked ready to run. Father Reyes, visibly agitated, tried to restore order, and the Parish Priest, too, turned pale. The muttering rose to a shout:

"There he is!"

"There he is!"

"Don't let him jump over the back wall and get away!"

"Seize him!"

The gate of the Cemetery was wide open, less than fifty yards away from the cross and candlesticks. Some villagers stepped back, some of the women; but most of them became galvanized. A horse neighed loudly. Calm now, the Parish Priest walked forward; in vain did Marta and various others try to stop him. But he stood still of his own accord when Damián appeared in the gateway, leading his horse by the reins.

The fugitive respectfully removed his hat at the sight of the procession. Astounded, furious, or admiring, the villagers who had threatened to seize him remained motionless. They watched him prepare to mount, coolly, bravely. (In María, the voice, "Come on, come on, then," was no longer the repugnant voice of the insolent old man, but a familiar command, "Come on!") Francisco Limón, gun in hand, hurled himself at his brother, but María was ahead of him, and jumped quickly in between, knocking the gun out of his hand. Damián, on his horse, without taking out his gun, disappeared up the lane leading to the Canyons. There were shouts of "Murderer!" "Seize him!" "Don't let him get away!" Pointless rushing to and fro. Clementina Limón shouted at her brother, "Kill her!" and flung herself on María, who was immediately defended by Rito Becerra. Opinion was divided.

"She did right. How could she let the brothers kill each other?"

"It was her fault they didn't get him!"

"She was right. There'd have been a fight and a lot of people killed."

"She's his accomplice!"

"She was right to be on his side. He's a brave man."

Then, a question was added to the argument: "Why did she do it?"

And a welter of suppositions, "She admired Damián's bravery."

"To prevent a fight."

"To keep a brother from killing a brother!"

"She's in love with the murderer."

"Because she's a bad lot."

"I've always said she's a bad lot."

But María refused to answer either the Parish Priest, or Marta, or the Deputy, or Father Reyes; she would answer none of their questions. There was consternation, indignation. Tardy plans of action. Mutual recriminations and excuses. The ceremony was postponed, and the gates of the Cemetery were shut.

"They ought to arrest her!"

"She's a bad lot."

"They ought to make an example of her!"

"To let that monster escape! He's a disgrace to the district, a man who'd kill his father and shoot a woman!"

"Coming back to make fun of us all!"

"She ought to be arrested. She's a bad lot."

"And Rito Becerra defending her, too!"

"Yes—a Socialist."

"Justice! Justice!"

Father Reyes then scored his greatest triumph by persuading the people to go home early, and not to meet at the Flor de Mayo that night. There were no bells either at eight o'clock or at ten. Lucas prophesied, flatly,

"This will be the death of the Parish Priest."

And this had been the decisive argument of Father Reyes, "Do you want to kill him outright? We had to carry him to his bed. Poor man!"

XXIX

If it hadn't been for the violent state of her emotions, the pressure on her nerves, and the persistent rebellion she

felt, María could not so easily have overcome her scruples in opening a letter from Gabriel addressed to her uncle.

The woman who had been unafraid to talk with the cruel murderer, or to rouse the anger of the village, the same woman who showed
no signs of repentance, made no excuses, faced insults, threats,
death prophesied for loved ones, now trembled, wept, was overcome, as she pored over these lines:

Your silence concerning my proposals—and I have now had three letters
from you without any mention of the matter, beyond saying that you approve of the postponement of my return—has removed any hope I had
that María might be my salvation. At first I regretted my frankness; but
I could not return without letting you know my intentions, and telling
you how I have lived with the thought of María from the time you sent
me here. My first idea, after your silence, was to go, anyhow, and speak
openly to her to learn what hopes I had. I was stopped by the fear of upsetting you and perhaps endangering your health. It was hard to do but
I decided not to go behind your back, and, although I realize that you will
not approve of what I'm doing, I think it will hurt you less than obtaining
María's consent against your wishes.

I did not tell you how often Señora Victoria has offered to help me
dedicate myself to the study of music, first in Guadalajara or Mexico
City, and afterward in Europe. It seems a pity to neglect my own talent.
I don't know how she found me; she wrote several letters, then she came
twice herself. I concealed this, for I had decided not to accept her offer,
and told her so. I had to thank her, however, for one thing: it was through
her that I learned what I felt for María. This was why I asked you to let
me write. But I have given up hope. I must get all thought of María out
of my head. I will not be disloyal to you. I have yielded to the other temptation which, you know, I struggled against. Señora Victoria has come
back and I have accepted her offer. I have left the Salesians and I set out,
today, for Veracruz to take ship for Spain. It is no good trying to make
me change my mind. The only thing I regret is the sorrow I am causing
you, but this is less than if I succeeded in winning María's affections
against your will. It is wrong, I know. Forgive me! And try to understand.
I cannot forget María, in any case, and so it's better to put land and water
between us. May God reward you for all you've done for a poor orphan,
and even for keeping me from some day making María unhappy . . .

Death blow. Yes, this was to experience death, or love: to discover, in a flash of lightning, that dissatisfaction, bitterness, boldness,
envy, madness, desire, sadness, morbid curiosity, were only this,
which, once revealed, dissolved; a bubble, long beside one, breaking

on sight. Suddenly to taste the sweet flavor, only to lose it forever; the sweet flavor, made bitter by anger; anger, love, and death, their poisons mingled in a deadly narcotic, which turned the last layers of gentleness to stone. *Victoria!* What did she care for her honor? She wanted to be loved. *Gabriel!* What could she hope for now? What did it matter if they arrested her? She decided to give herself up.

"Why, no, no one has thought of arresting you," answered the surprised Deputy. "There's no reason to, even though Doña Clementina Limón comes to ask me to do it every day. But I'll tell you now that I didn't approve of what you did at all, especially when that bandit Rito Becerra came into it. He has some accounts to settle with the law. Go on back home, and don't get yourself talked about anymore."

"Suppose I join the Revolution?"

"Ha, ha! . . . What revolution? Especially in this district. Didn't you hear what Friar Don Fermín had to say? Come, now, don't say things like that, even as a joke; they don't become a woman. You wouldn't want me to tell your uncle about this, would you? Go home now, and don't have anything more to do with that Rito Becerra."

XXX

"It's Halley's comet that's affected her mind," was the happy explanation found by the Deputy, after racking his brains for a long time to find a way to placate those who demanded María's arrest and to check the village gossip.

He reasoned this way: "If I arrest her, I'll have to fine her or send her to Guadalajara. The very people who talk of arresting her would be the first to complain, and the last thing I want is for a scandal to reach the Governor's ears. I don't want any notion of Reform to get about, either; the important thing is to hush the matter up, convince the government that it's an unimportant private affair, and, for all my efforts, I didn't manage to capture the fugitive; besides, I'm pretty sure the government's protecting Limón. But I can use it all to do a little domestic pruning and cultivate my garden. Rito Becerra still has some horses and he builds a good wall. And I may be able to get another rifle as good as the one I got out of him in September. Pascual Aguilera is a coward, and we can incriminate him easy enough. No one will risk coming to his defense, and he hasn't got it in him to carry tales to the authorities. We can get a few head of cattle out of Pancho and Clementina Limón by feeding their hopes that justice will be done. And how many of the poor we can bring into the business! It's easy to get them tangled up and see what we can shake out of them, even if it's only work for the town council and they're now thinking of improving the road leading to my farm." The crafty old plotter chuckled to himself.

And so the despoiling of the poor and the weak went on. But his idea of attributing María's strange behavior to the comet was a great success.

XXXI

Lucas Macías couldn't rest until he got someone to read him the Plan of San Luis Potosí, a few copies of which were secretly circulating in the village. The old man was so worried he couldn't hide it. "The comet must have affected me, too," he'd reply to the curious.

"Why don't you tell us the story of Father Gutiérrez' sister anymore, or how it is some women can fall in love with a murderer?"

"Because I like the story of Judith better, or the legend about the brother who tried to kill Cain without bringing Abel back to life. Shall I tell you those?"

The old man followed the course of events, wrapped in a mute serenity, and collected his evidence; but he let no one know what he was thinking. He listened, he questioned, he was into everything, he gathered crowds together, refusing to comment on the news. Pascual Aguilera was accused of not having reported that he recognized Damián on his way out along Fresno Street and San Antonio; the Deputy said that out of kindness he would pardon him his complicity and not arrest him, in return for fifteen days' service to the town council. Aguilera escaped and no more was heard of him. So, too, Dimas Gómez and Rito Becerra disappeared. When the police searched Rito's house, annoyed at not finding him, they sacked it, brought out the animals and set fire to house and barn. The meetings in the widow González' house had come to an end. And for the celebration of the twelfth of December Father Reyes had managed to collect very little money. In the village many were going around with new weapons. The peddlers from the Canyons had brought ammunition . . .

Lucas had seen many things for himself: the widow of his namesake, González, chatted with María; these last Sundays few people came in from the farms; to get prisoners to go to the Deputy's farm they had had to strike them; certain villagers stubbornly refused to sell him corn, oxen, or land . . .

At first, Don Román Capistrán's attitude had been a mystery to Lucas, like his connection with certain Northerners and the traders who took to coming to the village, and his presence at the gatherings at the widow's and his conversations with Aguilera. Would he risk his property? Would he join the revolt, to avenge himself for the loss of his position? Or was he, scenting revolution, cunningly lighting one candle to the Devil and the other to St. Michael? That was exactly what he was doing.

Wasn't the Deputy doing the same? He couldn't have missed certain details; he must know at least enough to be forewarned.

No, not even the outbreak of the storm roused him. Deadened, as all noise of the outside world was by the time it reached the village, there came the reports in *El País* of discovering a revolutionary plot. The account was cautious. It gave the impression of referring to unimportant matters. To the villagers who read it, it seemed as remote as if they were reading about something happening in China or Turkey.

Lucas could understand the efforts of some to keep down local excitement, turning conversations towards such things as the fire in the Corona Market, for example.

On the twenty-third of November, newspaper accounts of the happenings in Puebla began to arrive, telling of the resistance of the Serdán brothers and the death of Aquiles Serdán.

Then, the revolution in the northern provinces, the revolution headed by Don Francisco I. Madero!

"The government will soon restore order. Of course there's nothing to fear in this region. All will be kept peaceful. What reasons are there to have a revolution here?" The Deputy tried to quiet the alarm of those who were buying up provisions, hiding their possessions, and moving to the city.

Soon there came rumors and news that caused consternation: revolts in the Canyons, this side of Moyahua, guerrillas in the direction of Cuquío, attacks on the road to Nochistlán.

"Rito Becerra has gone with the revolutionaries!"

"Pascual Aguilera went off with the Estradas of Moyahua!"

"Rito Becerra's on his way here!"

"Rito Becerra's got more than two hundred men with him!"

"We're on the edge of the storm!"

"Here come Rito Becerra's men!"

"I'm already nearer the next world than this one; my heart tells me I'm going to die just as the storm begins; but this time, it's going to be a real storm, I tell you."

Lucas was right. One morning he sent for a priest to come and hear his confession; he had a pain in his chest which moved down his left arm. Father Martínez barely got there in time.

"It's just going to begin! Look after yourself, Padre. Whatever happens, don't be troubled, Padre. It'll be a good storm, and you'll be hit by the first hailstones. Be strong!" Then, as though he were dreaming, as though he were delirious: "a short man, fair-skinned, crazy, they say . . . children and madmen tell the truth . . . be strong."

These were Lucas' last words, cut short by a heart attack. With him ended a chapter of local history. That day it was learned that the followers of Madero had entered Moyahua.

XXXII

Faced with the evidence that Rito Becerra's men were approaching with hundreds of farmhands who had joined them from the estates of Cuquío, the Deputy abandoned the village on the pretext of going for instructions and bringing re-enforcements to protect the district. "What have we got to oppose them with, now, if they come? You'll see, while I'm gone, the way they behave!" He hastily gathered together what he could and went.

Rito Becerra and his men, coming to avenge their wrongs, were too late to find him.

"They're coming! Here they are!"

It was shortly after midday. Shop doors were pulled shut with a bang. Panic-stricken people rushed to and fro. There were shots in the distance. Frantic prayers. Silence.

A silence in which convulsive sobbing, men's voices uttering broken phrases, movements in bedrooms, hearts beating, words sticking in dry throats, could be guessed at rather than heard. Desperate questions: "Where can this one or that one be?" referring to relatives missing from the most secure corner of the house which was now serving as a collective refuge. A silence, but in it sounds of money being stowed away, saddles scraping against walls as they were placed out of sight of covetous eyes, horses neighing where their owners were trying to hide them.

"Will Pedro manage to shut the shop?"

"Will they seize Juan on his way to the farm?"

"Did Francisco stay at the Toledos'?"

A few brave men, who had not run away, saw the heights behind the Cemetery and Retreat House crowned with men. Shots and a troop of horses were heard, and loud cries of "Long live Madero!" Unknown voices sounded in the church tower and the bells were rung in a discordant peal, their victorious tones scandalizing the inhabitants and filling them with fear.

They had little fear of Rito Becerra, but they were panic-stricken at the thought that Damián might come back to take vengeance on them.

The panic increased with the banging on doors and the shouts, nearby or far away, of "Open, or we'll break down the door!" The sound of whip handles, horses' hoofs, machetes beating against doors, shouts of exultation and threats, wild songs. Listening ears could hear Father Reyes in the street; the Parish Priest, mediating between the revolutionaries and the rich who refused to give them what they asked for: a forced loan, restoration of ill-gotten goods and usurious interest collected by force, weapons and horses, saddles, and food.

The scarcely credible news reached the people hidden in their houses: "They're holding the Toledos, the Rodríguezes, and the Limóns as hostages, and they won't let them go until the whole loan is collected. . . . They want ten thousand pesos. . . . They're taking the tithe corn. . . . They took every piece of cloth Pedro Torres had in his shop. They're not satisfied with the three thousand pesos the Parish Priest offered to collect for them. . . . He's with them—where wouldn't he go?—Lucas González' widow and other villagers have gone, too. . . . Yes, it's true—Pascual Aguilera's with them. No, Damián's not coming—Damián went straight to Chihuahua, he's with Pascual Orozco—no, he's with the rebels from the Canyons. The farmhands from the big estates near Cuquío are the worst— they want to sack the village. They broke open Pablo Encarnación's shop and cleaned it out—the shelves are covered with sugar, rice, beans, corn. . . . They want to take Don Refugio with them—they want Father Reyes to go with them. They opened Leonides Islas' bakery. They say that if there aren't any women—what happened to all the women? . . ."

It was getting dark. The unmarried girls were losing their courage in their precarious hiding-places.

"Everyone knows they carry off girls!"

Anguish of mothers, helpless agony of fathers who have watched so carefully over their daughters! Furious lying-in-wait of suitors and brothers, in whom the thought of dishonor and the fear of death struggle for mastery.

"If our Chaplain were here, we wouldn't need to be afraid. Death! Better death than dishonor!" Hearts beat feverishly in the goose-pimpled, black-robed young bodies.

"Will they respect the medal of the Virgin? At least they will respect that. St. Michael and his angels will come down from Heaven and make them respect that." Naïve assurance of the Daughters of Mary Immaculate.

Darkness spread over houses and sky. The crosses on the tops of the buildings were enveloped in shadow. The stars shone. Night fell, the terrifying darkness of night, with no abating of the shouts, bursts of laughter, singing; instead, the noise increased.

"They've got out the guitars and dragged out those who can play. . . . They're all drunk—they broke a violin over Gertrudis Sánchez' head—they danced on Patricio Gutiérrez' mandolin. In spite of Rito's forbidding it, they're drunk . . . they've got many of the most important people in the village lighting the lanterns on the corners . . ."

"Have you heard of any girl carried off?" That was the main obsession.

"What's to keep them from dragging them off? Drunk as they are. None of them pay any attention to Rito or Pascual."

"Damián must be with them."

"They say he's not, but who knows?"

"What's to stop them dragging them out of the houses?"

"Damián!"

"Damián Limón."

"They all say he's not with them, that he didn't come, that he went with Pascual Orozco."

"You know, there're a lot of women with Madero's troops, with rifles in their hands and a cartridge belt slung across their shoulders!"

Not a glimmer of light could be seen around any window or door. Not even a match had been lit in the houses. Parlors, passageways, bedrooms, and kitchens in darkness, in absolute darkness. Children crying, their wailing so persistent that it rose, in crescendo, above the rooftops and descended to the street, doubling the terror of the night, already full of the sounds of running feet, shouting, singing, raucous music.

What time was it? Nine o'clock? Midnight? Who could tell? The children hadn't gone to sleep; the dogs were awake, their barking could be heard above all the hellish noise. The children wanted bread, milk, they wanted to go to sleep. The noise of shooting, close at hand or farther away, increased. The howling of the dogs grew louder. At each shot, through the afternoon, through the night, the villagers' hearts sank.

"Have they killed anybody?"

They began to pray with renewed fervor in their stuffy bedrooms.

"Don't pray so loud. They might hear you."

"No, don't light the blessed candles. The thought is enough."

"Shield that taper so the light won't show."

Endless prayers, offered in that endless afternoon, and all through the never-ending night.

"They've taken the trumpet they use in Retreats for Judgment Day . . ."

"They've got the money and are loading up all the mules from the inn with the stuff they're taking with them . . ."

"This is when the girls are in greatest danger . . ."

"They're going—"

"Now they'll carry off the girls—"

Who could stand such a succession of shocks, emotions, and upsets for so long?

A trumpet sounded, out of tune, a makeshift military call, so rarely heard in the village. The shooting stopped. The noise of horses' hoofs and the shouting gradually moved away.

"There they go!"

"They've gone! They went towards Nochistlán."

"It'll be the Day of Judgment there, all right!"

"There? And what about here? Did you think that was nothing?"

"They didn't kill anybody. They didn't carry anybody off."

After some time, the final piece of news came to startle and set them quaking.

"They took María with them!"

"What?"

"She's just not here, not anywhere!"

After the first rumors, when the news was confirmed, there came the ominous explanation and the harsh comments:

"She went of her own free will!"

"She was in league with Madero's followers!"

"She and Widow González went off together!"

"What!"

"Yes, both of them—on horses they stole from Don Anselmo Toledo."

"I always thought this would be the upshot of it."

"I always said she was no good, ever since she took up with Micaela."

"I always said she'd come to a bad end."

"She was always reading forbidden books."

"She was most peculiar."

"She had her own way of talking and looking at things."

"A bad lot."

"Her poor sister!"

"Wonder how she is? Poor girl!"

"And Father Martínez?"

"He'll never get over it."

"So she went off with Widow González! A pair of hussies!"

"She was seen coming out of her house, after those famous meetings."

"I've often seen her talking to the widow."

"I've seen her several times with Rito, Pascual, and some of the other scoundrels from the North."

"She's probably going after Damián."

"Why didn't they put handcuffs on her that day in the Cemetery? That was the time to do something."

"That's what I said! She's a bad lot!"

"What a disgrace!"

"The one I'm sorry for is Father Martínez—this will kill him!"

"What an insult to the whole village!"

"And Marta? What will she do? I feel sorry for her."

"The only thing she can do is leave the village."

"She won't be able to show her face again as long as she lives."

"Nor speak to anyone."

"But it's not her fault!"

"I saw María talking to Aguilera, one night, both of them sitting on a bench in the Square."

"I didn't want to say anything about the meetings."

"I didn't want to say anything about her friendship with the widow."

"What a blow for Father Martínez! It will kill him."

"He won't survive it, not at his age."

"She was a Judas!"

"They say it was on her account that they sent Gabriel away."

"On account of her? She's a bad lot."

"On account of her they drove Gabriel away! The creature!"

"I'd tear her to pieces if I got my hands on her!"

"What will Gabriel do when he finds out?"

"What an insult to the village!"

"A bad lot!"

"She was bound to come to a bad end!"

And the comments continued all night, all day, all the following days, implacable, uttered over and over again, unending, the voracious comments of men and women, nursing their animosity.

Night and day, during the following weeks. Picking to pieces the memory of the runaway. In bedrooms, in doorways, in shops, in the Square, in front of the church, in the streets, on the roads, in the fields as the seeds were sown; stubbornly.

"They say she was affected by the comet!"

"The slut!"

"They say she went around wishing she was a man. So she could put a stop to injustice."

"Excuses!"

"Even Micaela did better than that."

"This one wasn't content to go off with one, she had to have a crowd. Who ever saw the like?"

"It was her fault Gabriel was sent away."

"She was shouting 'Long live Madero!' when she left, and screaming like a drunk that she was going to fight for justice. She was carrying a cartridge belt and a rifle and she'd taken off her black dress."

"She and Widow González had their colored dresses all ready."

"She was always provoking and willful! Too big for the village."

"Nature will out! The whole troop will have had her by now!"

Even the children took up the tale: "The Parish Priest's niece went off with a lot of men."

XXXIII

"As usual."

This was the resolute answer the sacristan received when he summoned enough courage to go and ask the Parish Priest whether he intended to celebrate the first mass, when the tragic night was over. The sacristan, excusing his officiousness on the grounds of concern, begged Father Martínez not to get up early. Partly out of sincere compassion, and partly out of morbid curiosity, he asked if there wasn't something he could do for him.

A look which brooked no interference and an authoritative gesture checked the intruder, who withdrew hastily, forgetting even to say good night.

No, no one would put gloating fingers to his wound. Shamed, he would resist destruction. Abandoning the feverish search, he had finally shut himself up, refusing to allow even Father Reyes to be with him. He felt as if he bore daggers in his body as he entered his room, struggling against dizziness, struggling to silence the protests of his flesh and the rebellion of his heart. Neither fatigue nor the worries of the day had beaten him, or this final blow to his human affections; only when he reached the shelter of his room did his heart and eyes give way and he could not restrain his tears and sobs. For a moment he broke down, during the first few moments he gave way to his feelings, then he threw himself on his knees and began to recite the psalms of desolation.

For an hour, he remained prostrate. The entrance of the sacristan roused him but, immediately, he went back to the agony in the garden ... "Take away this cup ... take away this cup ... nevertheless, not my will ... all things are possible with Thee ... Take away this cup ... but not my will ..." Worldly images intruded upon his prayers; earthly affection, the pain, the shame, the agonizing future;

María as a little girl, María getting her own way, María precocious, impatient, questioning. Memories of her wheedling, her caresses, her coaxing, burned him like fire. Then the uncouth figure of Gabriel, the ringing of the bells, Gabriel running away from school, Gabriel in the hands of that woman. He had been unable to save anyone. He had been unable to save Luis Gonzaga, or Mercedes Toledo, or Micaela Rodríguez, or Rito Becerra, or Father Islas, or Lucas' widow, or Don Timoteo, or Damián. Unhappy shepherd who allowed his sheep to be stolen! Unhappy player who let the marbles roll at random, unable to guide them into the right path. Year after year, more and more young men who should be working in the Lord's Vineyard had lost their sense of vocation. More and more young women had gone to their destruction, with ever-increasing scandal. What had been dearest to his heart, what he had worked for hardest, was the first to be carried off by the fury of the enemy. He had often consoled himself with the belief that he was doing good work. God had brought down his pride in frightful defeat, wounding him in his tenderest spot. He would be the laughingstock of his parishioners, who saw how he could not save even the lamb he carried in his bosom; he had lost it in disgrace.

The lamp had gone out a long time ago, an hour, two hours. Darkness everywhere. His prayers were interrupted by bitter thoughts: his zeal for purity, Retreat House, his long years of vain severity that defeated its own ends, all had gone for nothing. If only he had let his tenderness overflow! His feet were weary, his hands and knees trembled, he should go to bed. No, no! Even though he was covered with a cold sweat, he must punish the uselessness, the failure of his life.

The lamp without light reminded him, in a dream, of Marta, careful to keep the flame lit other nights, other days. Gentle Marta, forgotten in the egoism of martyrdom. She could not be asleep either, nor had she come to seek consolation, to give comfort, to impose the gentle sway of her solicitude. She could not be sleeping, her suffering was as great as his. She had disappeared when the brutal truth became known. In the Garden of Bitterness, she was not sleeping, either. Even more grievously wounded than he was, how could she come to him? It was he who must look for her, cherish her, comfort her.

Pain, sharp cramping pain, victorious over the will, attacked him. He fell senseless to the floor.

The ringing of the bell woke him. What was it he had dreamed once? It was all a nightmare, a brutal nightmare, the horrible truth. His fainting hand reached for the discipline, and, as every day, he began the flagellation.

Justice! Justice against the careless one. The blows on the tired flesh could not keep yesterday's suffering from returning, the pain of the cruel wound that would never heal. Rito Becerra had tried to convince him of the justice of the revolution. The attempts to justify it had seemed only absurd nonsense. How could theft, murder, depredations, ever be justified? But hadn't he himself preached that calamities must be accepted as the scourges of Divine Justice? Might not the Revolution be the instrument used by Providence to bring the ideal justice and purity into existence?

In spite of sleeplessness, terrors, insecurity, the church was full, full as if it had been a Sunday morning. Coughing and muttering reached his ears; it was as if a thousand ravening jaws waited to rend him; it was the noise of a pagan crowd in the circus. His faithful! The mortifying curiosity of his flock! His shame was deep.

With outward calm, he donned his chasuble and maniple. As the last bell started, he grasped the chalice firmly, and advanced; he walked steadily up the Chancel; calmly he placed the corporal in place, went over to the side table and opened the Missal, came down the steps, head high, and, in his ordinary voice, began:

"In the Name of the Father, and of the Son, and of the Holy Ghost. Amen." Calmly, reverently, he clasped his hands in front of him. Just as he did every day.

"I will go unto the Altar of God . . ."

A woman's choking sob sounded in the expectant silence of the nave. Marta. It might be Marta. He controlled his thoughts and repeated mechanically the words the sacristan had just uttered:

"Unto God who giveth joy to my youth."

The joy of his youth! A wave of bitterness engulfed him. He almost fainted. His youth! The pattern broken, there was a brief pause. But he mastered his emotion and picked up the thread of the service, as he had done every day, for thirty-four years, his emaciated hands trembling in front of his breast. Would he be able to drink today's cup? Would he be able to ward off the dizziness threatening to overcome him, escape the fall that all awaited in sadistic silence?

"Give sentence with me, O God, and defend my cause against

the ungodly people; deliver me from the unjust and deceitful man . . ." And again, the overwhelming desire to break the order of the service and speak the words so often heard on Gabriel's lips:

"Unto God, who giveth joy to my youth . . ."